PRAISE FOR THE UNRAVELLING

A powerful and emotive historical novel of authority and compassion, *The Unravelling* is the genre at its very best. A novel that embraces pivotal events from southern Africa's bygone years to give us a novel that's literate and true to life and sure to grab the attention of discerning readers.

A superb read commensurate with novels by Wilbur Smith, Bernard Cornwell, and Colin Falconer, *The Unravelling* is an unreservedly recommended Golden Quill read.

BookViral Review – January 2024

History comes alive in this 'factual' novel by Michael Chalk. Written with a deep knowledge and understanding of the changes during the 1970-1980s,*The Unravelling* gives, through an array of different characters, an unbiased account of those turbulent days.

The descriptions of Rhodesia/Zimbabwe's beauty as the reader is taken on a tour of this rich and spectacular country are superb. One can really see and feel the magnificence of this beautiful and varied landscape.

This book is not only a reminder of the past, but also an exciting, action-packed and hugely entertaining novel.

Africatalks Review – March 2024

the UNRAVELLING

Michael Chalk

First edition published in August 2023
Second edition published in November 2024

by Michael Chalk Author and Publisher
ABN 16 077 772 457
https://www.authormichaelchalk.com

ISBN 978-0-6458464-3-0 (paperback for IngramSpark)

Cover design and execution by Simon Chalk

Disclaimer

This novel is a work of fiction set in a historical time period. Whilst every effort has been made to accurately represent the events, people, and culture of the era, certain elements have been fictionalised or adapted for the purposes of storytelling.

Apart from historical characters, events, and dialogue which are already in the public domain, all other characters, events, and dialogue are products of the author's imagination. Any similarities to actual people, places, or events are coincidental.

Dedications

I would like to dedicate this book to the following people.

Firstly, to my darling wife, Barbara Chalk. Thank you for your love, support, and encouragement during the twelve months I was engrossed in writing *the UNRAVELLING*. Oftentimes, especially when I was struggling with the more difficult parts of the book, I was so absorbed in my work that I was unavailable to you. Yet throughout, you remained loving, supportive, and caring. Your constructive advice and feedback were invaluable, and I am truly grateful.

Secondly, to the Adelaide '**A**' team and to my brother and his wife, Nigel and Liza Chalk, who graciously and diligently assisted me in proofreading and fact-checking the contents of the book.

Thirdly, to my son, Simon Chalk, for his outstanding design and execution of the book cover. Your creative and technical talents never cease to amaze me.

Fourthly, to the many individuals of all races in Zimbabwe who remain captivated by the country's beauty and promise. Despite the many economic, political, and social challenges, you have chosen to stay in Zimbabwe. Your commitment and sacrifice enable casual visitors like me to return to the country, with relative ease, to enjoy its many delights and treasures.

Finally, this book is dedicated to the millions of ordinary Zimbabweans who have been profoundly let down by the country's ruling governments over the last 60 years — first by the Rhodesian Front and later by ZANU-PF. You have been promised much, received little and endured significant suffering. Yet throughout, you have exhibited patience, resilience, and unwavering hope for a better future.

Please know that many people around the globe share your aspirations and are praying that a new dawn of equality, opportunity, and prosperity will soon arise across Zimbabwe and bring an end to your seemingly endless season of hardship and despair.

Michael Chalk

Map of Rhodesia

The town names shown are the colonial names.

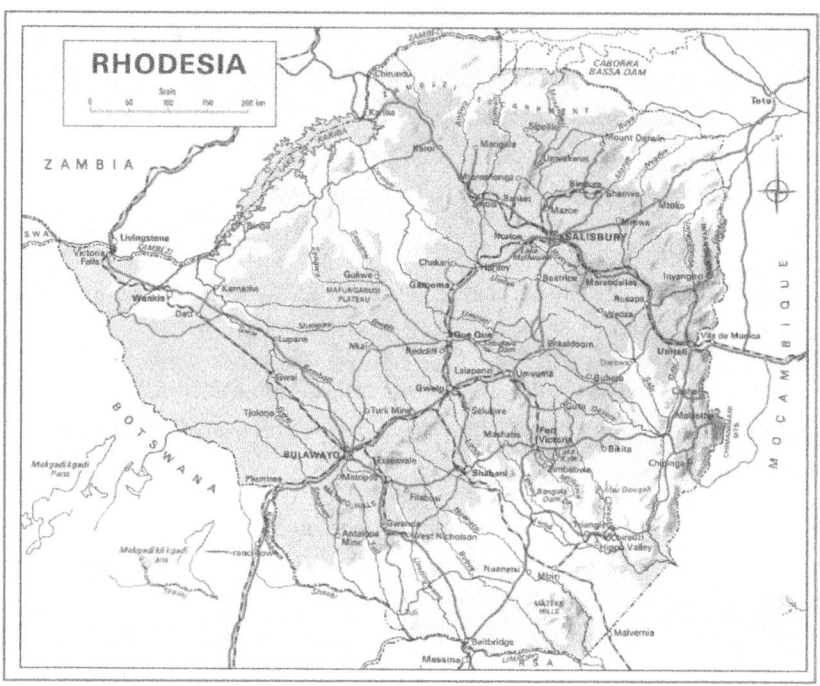

Table of Contents

Chapter 1 – The boy becomes a man 1

Timeline – June 1979 1

Chapter 2 – The birthing of madness 13

Timeline – January 1980 13

Chapter 3 - The change in power 22

Timeline – April 1980 22

Chapter 4 – Hello Mother England 29

Timeline - September 1980 29

Chapter 5 – Meeting the Dixon family 34

Chapter 6 – The consummation 43

Chapter 7 – Hello Scotland 50

Chapter 8 – The early life of Sipho Pukelo 53

Timeline - 1950s to 1970s 53

Chapter 9 – Sipho learns about pre-UDI politics 59

Timeline – 1969 59

Chapter 10 – Sipho learns about UDI 66

Chapter 11 – Sipho learns about ZIPRA 73

Chapter 12 – Sipho shares his desire to join ZIPRA with his parents ... 77

Chapter 13 – Sipho's parents try to dissuade him from joining ZIPRA. 84

Chapter 14 – Sipho enlists with RAR 89

Timeline - 1972 89

Chapter 15 – Johannes du Toit enlists with RLI 95

Timeline - 1967 95

Chapter 16 – Johannes explores poaching as a source of income 101

Timeline - 1977 101

Chapter 17 – Johannes' foray into Mozambique 115

Chapter 18 – Nick's first semester at the University of Edinburgh 127

Timeline – September 1980 to December 1980 127

Chapter 19 – Nick stays in Guildford during the Christmas vacations 132

Timeline – December 1980 132

Chapter 20 – Stuart Dixon's analysis of situation in Zimbabwe 139

Chapter 21 – Nick and Rachel plan to visit Zimbabwe 149

Chapter 22 – Nick's first visit to London city 158

Chapter 23 – Nick's wish for a white Christmas comes true 169

Chapter 24 – Sipho transfers to 1RAR 178

Timeline – April 1980 to July 1980 178

Chapter 25 – Integrating the Rhodesian Army & guerrilla forces 184

Timeline – June 1980 184

Chapter 26 – Sipho's actions with 1RAR in Entumbane 191

Timeline – November 1980 to February 1981 191

Chapter 27 – Sipho resigns from the ZNA 201

Timeline – May 1981 201

Chapter 28 - Sipho joins Mhuka Ranch as its anti-poaching manager 204

Timeline – July 1981 204

Chapter 29 – Johannes plans Operation Nzou 214

Timeline – July 1977 214

Chapter 30 – The execution of Operation Nzou 222

Timeline – late August 1977 222

Chapter 31 – Settling up with Santiago de Costa 234

Timeline – September 1977 234

Chapter 32 – Johannes flees Rhodesia 239

Timeline – September 1978 239

Chapter 33 – Nick and Rachel en route to Zimbabwe 251

Timeline – 31 July 1981 251

Chapter 34 – Nick and Rachel transit through Johannesburg 258

Chapter 35 – Nick and Rachel visit Victoria Falls 263

Chapter 36 – Mosi-oa-Tunya 271

Chapter 37 – Nick and Rachel arrive in Salisbury 282

Chapter 38 – Nick and Rachel's first few days in Salisbury 293

Chapter 39 – Russell Sinclair arrives in Salisbury 308

Chapter 40 – Exploring Imire Game Park & Lake McIlwaine 314

Timeline – 10 August to 14 August 1981 314

Chapter 41 – Nick and Rachel travel to Maleme Dam 328

Timeline – 17 August 1981 328

Chapter 42 – Nick and Rachel explore the Matopos National Park ... 338

Chapter 43 – Nick and Rachel travel to Mhuka Ranch, near Chiredzi 350

Timeline – 21 August 350

Chapter 44 – Nick and Rachel settle into Ukuthula Lodge 358

Chapter 45 – Johannes loiters in South Africa 372

Timeline – October 1978 to May 1981 372

Chapter 46 – Johannes returns to Zimbabwe 381

Timeline - June 1981 381

Chapter 47 – The decision to resume poaching activities 393

Chapter 48 – Groundwork for Operation Chipembere 403

Chapter 49 – Preparing for Operation Chipembere 410

Chapter 50 – Planning Operation Chipembere's counteroffensive ... 418

Timeline – 22 August 418

Chapter 51 – The unravelling of Operation Chipembere 430

Chapter 52 - Farewell to Mhuka Ranch 442

Timeline – 25 August 1981 442

Chapter 53 – Nick and Rachel visit the Vumba 449

Chapter 54 - Nick and Rachel visit Inyanga in the Eastern Highlands 456

Chapter 55 – Nick and Rachel prepare to leave Zimbabwe 470

Timeline – 31 August to 2 September 1981 470

Chapter 56 – Nick and Rachel's farewell dinner............................. 475

Chapter 57 – Nick and Rachel's farewell to Zimbabwe 481

Timeline – 3 September 1981 481

Epilogue 484

Timeline - 1982 to 2022 484

Glossary of Terms 493

Appendix 1.. 506

Appendix 2.. 507

Chapter 1 – The boy becomes a man

Timeline – June 1979

It was June 1979, and the land to the immediate north of South Africa had just changed its name from Rhodesia to Zimbabwe-Rhodesia. Life had become increasingly difficult in the country. It was facing inexorable pressures from the Western world to move from a political system that was dominated by a white minority to one in which all adult citizens, the majority of whom were black, had the right to vote for a political party that represented their hopes and aspirations.

In a desperate attempt to thwart these *winds of change,* the RF[1], the former ruling political party, had cobbled together a complicated set of arrangements which they hoped would result in the country being ruled by a majority black government that would uphold the British Westminster system of government and, most importantly, would not be *anti-white.*

Under these arrangements, in April 1979, Bishop Abel Muzorewa of the UANC[2] had been elected as the country's first black prime minister. Muzorewa had formed a Government of National Unity which included Ian Smith, the former white prime minister, as well as a number of other white ministers who held key portfolios in the government. Muzorewa's Government had taken up office on 1st June 1979.

These changes had been birthed just over a year earlier when, in March 1978, the RF Government led by Ian Smith had successfully

---

[1] Rhodesian Front.
[2] United African National Council.

negotiated an Internal Settlement with the more moderate African nationalist leaders, including Bishop Abel Muzorewa, Ndabaningi Sithole[3] and Chief Jeremiah Chirau[4].

The Internal Settlement was intended to provide a peaceful transition to majority rule on terms that were acceptable to the predominantly white electorate. However, the elections which had brought Muzorewa to power had been boycotted by the two main black nationalist parties of ZANU[5] and ZAPU[6], which were led by Robert Mugabe and Joshua Nkomo respectively. Accordingly, Muzorewa's Government was destined to be short-lived.

Unsurprisingly, the elections which had brought Muzorewa to power did little to stem the harsh and cruel civil war which had been raging since the late 1960s. This civil war was generally regarded by the black population as a war of national liberation, while the white population saw it as a war against extremist black nationalism and communist-inspired terrorism.

In January 1979, Nick Sinclair, who had recently turned 18, had received his call-up papers for national service. At this time, the tentacles of the RF political machinery were still very much intact. Consequently, the majority of the white population was still holding onto the belief that the war was one that could be won. This meant it was the duty of every able-bodied young man to take up arms to defend his country and the way of life that had been crafted over the last 90 years by the hard work and sacrifices of the country's white pioneers.

This propaganda meant that the Rhodesian Security Forces were held in high esteem by the empowered elements of Rhodesian society. Their victories on the battlefield were lauded in the press and on television, and casualties were reported with decorum and solemnity. Little in-depth analysis of the rights or wrongs of the political system

---

[3] Ndabaningi Sithole was the leader of a more moderate faction of ZANU.
[4] Chief Chirau was a notable figure amongst Rhodesia's traditional black chiefs.
[5] Zimbabwe African National Union.
[6] Zimbabwe African People's Union.

that was being defended took place, while the laws of censorship meant that objective analyses undertaken by external commentators were rarely published inside the country.

Consequently, when Nick received his call-up papers for his 12 months of national service, he had a genuine desire to serve his country with gallantry and honour. Nick had finished school in November 1978 and had spent the last two months holidaying in South Africa with a couple of his mates from school. He had learnt of his call-up whilst on the phone to his parents, Matthew and Brenda Sinclair, who lived in Salisbury[7].

Nick's enlistment date was set for 12th February 1979. In discussions with his mates, he had decided that rather than doing his national service as a troopie[8], he would endeavour to get accepted for officer training at the School of Infantry, which was located in the provincial city of Gwelo[9] about 275 kilometres south of Salisbury.

Physically, Nick was reasonably fit and had always enjoyed strong relationships with his friends and colleagues. In addition, he had achieved good results in his A-Level[10] exams at school, so his acceptance into the officers' training program was more or less assured, especially since the exodus of white persons from the country was by then in full swing. This meant that the intake numbers of school leavers for national service was on the decline, and this was causing significant manpower difficulties for the Rhodesian Security Forces.

The two months to Nick's enlistment date quickly passed. Nick returned to Salisbury and began to apply himself to the task of getting as fit and mentally tough as possible. This entailed daily trips to a local gymnasium where he followed a rigorous training program.

---

[7] The capital of Rhodesia. Its name was changed to Harare in April 1982.
[8] Colloquial term meaning a regular member or national serviceman of the Rhodesian Army.
[9] Gwelo was renamed Gweru in 1982.
[10] A-Levels were the Advanced Level of school examinations. It was conferred as a school leaving qualification to senior school pupils as part of the Cambridge International General Certificate of Education.

He was also smart enough to recognise the need to strengthen his mental resilience. A gnawing fear lingered at the back of his mind — that in the event of facing action, he might be found wanting. This fear drove him to focus on building the mental toughness he would need if ever faced with armed combat.

As was expected, Nick easily passed the written and physical aptitude tests that were the necessary pre-cursors for acceptance into the officers' training course. These were followed by an intensive 12-week training course.

Nothing could have fully prepared Nick for the emotional and physical challenges that the course entailed, and he was very pleased that he had used the two months prior to the commencement of his national service wisely.

Three months later, Nick passed out of the School of Infantry as a second lieutenant and was posted to the 3rd Battalion of the Rhodesian African Rifles, which was based just outside Umtali[11] in the Eastern Highlands[12].

The RAR[13] was one of those peculiar regiments that could only ever had existed under British colonial rule. The curious and distinguishing feature about the Regiment was that, until 1977, it consisted entirely of black soldiers and non-commissioned officers, whereas all its commissioned officers were white. While Nick had regarded this phenomenon as somewhat bizarre, he quickly learnt to respect the professionalism of the black soldiers. He also admired the obvious pride with which they spoke about the Regiment, their fellow black soldiers and the white officers who led them.

Nick was, however, somewhat daunted by the fact that he, a fresh-faced schoolboy who had never seen a shot fired in anger, was now

---

[11] Umtali was renamed Mutare in 1982.
[12] The Eastern Highlands is a mountainous area on the border of Zimbabwe and Mozambique. It extends for about 300 kilometres from north to south and includes the Inyangani Mountains, the Vumba Mountains and the Chimanimani Mountains.
[13] Rhodesian African Rifles.

responsible for leading a platoon of battle-hardened soldiers, some of whom had served with the RAR for more than ten years.

In June 1979, some two months after having been posted to 3RAR[14], Nick was leading a small patrol of his beloved soldiers along a narrow mountain path in an area of Zimbabwe-Rhodesia known as the Chimanimani Mountains. This beautiful mountainous area stretched for approximately 50 kilometres along the country's eastern border with Mozambique.

Nick's men had told him that the word 'chimanimani' meant to be squeezed together. Legend had it that long ago, this area had been heavily populated with large apes which, when traversing the mountainous area, had been forced to walk closely together on all fours to avoid falling down the steep slopes on either side of the narrow and treacherous paths that had been made by the herds of wild mountain goats.

During the last few years of the civil war that had been raging in the country, ZANLA[15] forces loyal to Robert Mugabe had been illegally entering the country from their training camps in Mozambique along these same mountainous passes. In an attempt to slow these illegal incursions, the Rhodesian Security Forces had heavily mined these passes with lethal anti-personnel mines.

The day before, a report had been made at the local police station in Melsetter[16] that two of these mines had been detonated by a group of approximately 20 terrorists who had entered Zimbabwe-Rhodesia a few days earlier. The report also stated that the infiltrating terrorists were heavily armed and believed to be heading for the local farming town of Cashel, where it was assumed they would attempt to ambush isolated farming families and abduct, recruit, and train local youth to join their ranks.

---

[14] 3rd Battalion of Rhodesian African Rifles.
[15] Zimbabwe African National Liberation Army. ZANLA was the military wing of ZANU.
[16] Melsetter was renamed Mandididzura in 1982. It was later renamed Chimanimani.

Nick's patrol had been dropped by helicopter into the area where it was thought that the terrorists were located. Their mission was to locate, engage, and destroy the group with air support being provided by a Fire Force response unit, which was based near Umtali.

It was early morning. Being winter, the air was still biting cold, and the morning sun had not yet burnt off the mist that was slowly rising from the soggy ground. The surrounding lush bush was still damp from the rain that had fallen during the night. As the sun caught the droplets of water on the intricate, laced foliage of the abundant tree ferns, the light was refracted and produced the softer colours of the rainbow. The plentiful bird life in the bush was beginning to stir, and Nick's heightened senses marvelled at the varied, yet harmonised, sounds that were all about him.

Nick and his 12-man strong platoon were strung out in single file over a distance of about a 100 metres along a rough path that threaded its way through the surrounding forest. At the front of the file was his platoon sergeant, Gideon.

Gideon was a large man. The camouflaged T-shirt that he was wearing was tightly stretched across his broad shoulders and bulging biceps. He was bald and his ebony-coloured head shimmered in the early morning light.

Nick was second in line and was about ten metres behind Gideon. He turned around to check on the rest of the platoon who were straddled out behind him. As he did so, he caught sight of a flicker of movement to his right and about 70 metres away. His eyes flashed forward to where Gideon was. As if in slow motion, he saw the back of Gideon's skull burst in a shower of red and Gideon dropped to the earth like a felled pine. Instinctively, Nick dived off the path into the knee-high scrub that bordered it, simultaneously yelling a warning to the troops behind him.

The air all around him was immediately filled with the rather tinny sound of AK-47[17] rifle fire from the terrorists, or *terrs*[18] as they were colloquially called.

The *terrs*, who had lain in ambush since before dawn, were a motley and rather ill-disciplined band of men. Consequently, when Gideon had entered the ambush area that they had selected, the *terrs*, who notoriously were known to be trigger-happy, had immediately opened fire rather than waiting for more of the platoon to enter the killing zone, thereby increasing their chances of inflicting heavier casualties.

The slaying of Gideon sparked a frenetic and wild shooting spree by the enemy. On the other hand, the return fire by Nick's troops was far more deliberate and measured. In less than a minute, Nick was able to determine that the enemy was confined to an area about the size of half a football field on slightly rising ground, about 50 metres away in an easterly direction from the path on which he had been. From the tell-tale puffs of cordite fumes that came from their rifles, he reckoned that the enemy numbered about 15 in total.

The enemy held advantageous ground and were well protected by craggy outcrops of rocks. In contrast, Nick's men were still pinned down. While their positions had been somewhat concealed by the knee-high grass into which they had thrown themselves when they first came under fire, the only real protection they had against the fire that was being directed against them was from the rather insubstantial bushes and trees that most of his men had been able to scramble behind. In addition, despite the shot that had taken out Gideon — which Nick surmised must have been a bloody lucky one — the enemy appeared to be living up to its reputation for being very lousy shots.

Nick quickly considered his options. On the one hand, he could call in the Fire Force stick, which was on standby near Umtali. However, he reckoned that it would take the stick about 15 minutes to scramble

---

[17] The AK-47 was developed by the Soviet Union and was the preferred light automatic rifle of the ZANLA and ZIPRA forces.
[18] *Terrs* was the colloquial term for terrorists.

and to reach his position. During this time, his troops would be under sustained fire and could suffer further casualties. Alternatively, and what was for more likely, the enemy would adopt their *shoot and scoot* tactics – i.e., open up fire with an initial salvo of bullets and then scatter into the surrounding bush and forest with the aim of later rendezvousing at a pre-determined site. If they adopted this tactic, it would mean that his company commander would have little alternative other than to initiate a dangerous, costly, and lengthy pursuit operation.

"Fuck the bastards," Nick cursed. Instinctively, he knew that the best option would be to initiate a decisive and bold counterattack. While the enemy held advantageous high ground, the terrain they had chosen was such that, if they were to break cover either to their immediate north or south, they would come under sustained and lethal fire from his troops. He doubted whether the enemy would be bold enough to press home their higher ground advantage by initiating a frontal attack against his troops. This meant that if he was to seize the initiative by ordering a bold counterattack against the enemy, then their most likely response would be to retreat by scattering in an easterly direction back into the surrounding forested areas.

Nick signalled to Phineas, the nearest soldier to him. He quickly outlined to him the plan that he had formulated. The four soldiers who had been at the rear of the patrol were to circle in an easterly direction to form a *stop position* immediately behind and to the east of the enemy. They would have a maximum of five minutes to get into position.

The rest of the men, with the exception of Gideon, whose crumpled and lifeless body lay on the path a short distance away, and Corporal Pukelo, the platoon's MAG[19] gunner, would counterattack the enemy head-on in five minutes time at precisely 06:35 am. The counterattack

---

[19] The Belgian designed Fabrique Nationale (FN) 7.62mm general-purpose machine gun. The MAG was standard issue for the Rhodesian Security Forces.

would be led by Nick, with covering fire provided by Corporal Pukelo who was in charge of the MAG machine gun.

Phineas listened carefully, gave the thumbs-up to indicate that he understood the orders, and then slipped away down the line to pass on these orders to the rest of the platoon.

Nick glanced at his watch. It was now 06:31 am. That gave him no more than four minutes before his counteroffensive move would begin. He knew that his extremely well-trained troops would by now be executing his plans.

In fact, the four troops from the rear of the line were already stealthily moving through the forest to establish a *stop position*. Nick was confident that they would be able to find a suitable location which would provide both a clear field of vision as well as a good line of fire. At the same time, the rest of his troops had already buddied up into pairs and each pair of men had agreed which of the two would lead the first advance with the other providing covering fire.

Nick had been carefully watching the bursts of automatic gunfire coming from the enemy's positions. While most of it was random and poorly directed, Nick noticed that there was one position near the centre of the ground occupied by the enemy, from which disciplined and well-directed gunfire was coming.

"I hope Pukelo has picked that up," he thought. "If not, it will cause problems."

Nick wondered if he should try and alert Corporal Pukelo to this. But it was now nearly 06:35 am and he persuaded himself that if he, an amateur soldier, had noticed this, then Pukelo, a hardened fighting man who had served with the RAR for more than seven years, certainly had.

Nick ejected the magazine from his FN[20] rifle, placed the half empty magazine into his webbing and inserted a new magazine, fully loaded with 20 rounds of ammunition, into the rifle's magazine well.

His watch clicked over to 06:35 am. He, along with four of his men, rose in unison from their positions and dashed forward in a zigzagging manner. Covering fire from Corporal Pukelo and the other buddied troops rang out across the bush. The enemy was slow to react to this initial charge and, when they did, the well-directed covering fire from his troops ensured that the enemy fire was ineffectual.

Nick covered a distance of about ten metres and then dived headlong into a small depression, which he had pinpointed prior to beginning his dash. He glanced around. From what he could tell, it seemed as though he and the other four men had safely navigated the first charge.

"Let's hope this keeps up," he thought.

The initial charge from Nick's troops had caught the enemy unaware. They were still riding high from having seen the large man at the front of the RAR platoon brought down in the initial salvo of fire. Their field commander, a vicious man whose brutality had earned him the fighting name of *Satani*, was still deliberating his next move when Nick's troops suddenly burst from their positions.

"Shit," he swore. "That will not happen again." From the basic training he had received in Tanzania, he knew that this initial charge would be followed by another from those troops who had provided the initial covering fire. He trained the sights of his AK-47 rifle on the area from where he expected the next charge to come from.

A few seconds later, the RAR troops who had provided covering fire, rose from their positions and charged forward. *Satani* had slightly miscalculated this position and had to raise his head a further six

---

[20] This was a light automatic rifle designed in Belgium and manufactured by FN Herstal. The FN was the standard issue rifle for the Rhodesian Security Forces.

inches to get a bead on the leading RAR soldier, who was sprinting forward in a half-crouched manner.

From his prone position on the ground, Corporal Pukelo's eagle eyes discerned this movement, which had come from the same area which had concerned him earlier due to the accurate fire that had been coming from there. Consequently, his MAG was already trained in that general direction. With an expert and deft adjustment, Pukelo moved the bead of the MAG's sights to the rock behind which *Satani* had been concealed and opened fire.

The first round from the MAG shattered the rock edge immediately to the right of *Satani's* face. The second and third rounds, respectively, struck him just below and just above his jaw. His body was thrown backwards and ended up in a peculiar bent position at the base of the rock, with thick dark blood pouring from the gaping wounds that a few moments earlier had been his mouth and nose.

Satani's mutilated figure lay at the base of the rock behind which he had been positioned, fully visible to most of his men. The man nearest to *Satani* looked over his shoulder to the safety of the forested area behind him, panicked, and fled towards those trees. This sparked a general rout amongst the enemy, most of whom rushed madly for the safety and cover afforded by the forest.

Lance-Corporal Ncube was the most senior of the four men who had been sent by Phineas to establish the *stop position*. His expert training and years of counter-insurgency operations had enabled him to accurately predict the enemy's likely path of retreat, as well as pinpointing the perfect position from which the four men comprising the *stop group* would be able to initiate rifle fire without endangering the lives of their fellow troops who were to their west.

They were in position just before 06:35 am and had heard the sounds of the initial counterattack.

A few minutes later, the first *terr* appeared in the killing zone. He was running wildly towards the safety of the thickly forested area, which was some 50 metres away.

"Not yet," hissed Ncube to the other three men. "Wait for the rest of these scared women to appear."

Within a few seconds, five other terrified *terrs* were in the killing zone. Ncube calmly trained his FN's sights on the leading *terr* and pulled the trigger. The other three men did likewise, and within 30 seconds, all six *terrs* plus four others who were hot on their heels, lay dead or wounded.

One of the wounded *terrs* had been critically injured and was beyond hope. Ncube ordered his execution by a bullet to the head. Rudimentary first aid was given to the other wounded men, and arrangements were made for them to be transferred back to base where they were handed over to intelligence officers for interrogation.

Six of *Satani's* more disciplined men had not fled their positions and had attempted to engage Nick's troops. However, they proved to be no match for the superior fire power and tactics that were now brought to bear upon them. Within five minutes, the entire firefight was over. In all, 17 *terrs* had been killed. Against this, Nick's platoon had sustained the one fatality. In addition, one soldier had sustained a relatively minor shrapnel wound to his right leg.

Years later, when Nick reflected on this event, he was still surprised by the calm and decisive manner in which he had acted. This was even more remarkable when he remembered how, prior to undertaking national service, he had been deeply troubled by the fear that he might be found to be lacking when under pressure.

In later years, when he sometimes doubted himself, he would remove, from its black velvet pouch the Bronze Cross of Rhodesia that had been awarded to him for his gallant deeds on that fateful day, and hold it firmly in his hand. As he did so, his mind would clearly recall every moment of that day, filling his body with strength and quelling his doubting mind.

Chapter 2 – The birthing of madness

Timeline – January 1980

It was Christmas Eve, 1979. Nick was lying on his bed in his quarters at 3RAR's[21] barracks. These were located on the outskirts of Umtali[22], a pretty little provincial town in the province of Manicaland. Umtali was only a few kilometres from the border of Mozambique and about 80 kilometres north of the area in the Chimanimani Mountains where Nick had acted with such decisiveness only six months earlier.

However, today Nick was disillusioned and disgruntled. He was also tense, as was evidenced by the unconscious clenching and unclenching of his fists.

"Shit," he muttered. "Bloody Christmas Eve and here I am cooped up in my room like a damn caged dog."

His frustration and anxiety had been growing ever since he had attended a briefing session held by his Commanding Officer, Lt. Col. Terry Lever, a few days earlier. Here, he and his fellow officers had learnt that a ceasefire between the Rhodesian Security Forces and the ZANLA[23] and ZIPRA[24] guerrilla forces had come into effect on 21st December. This ceasefire, assuming it held, was the pre-cursor to general elections that would be held in the country in two-months' time, at the end of February 1980.

---

[21] 3rd Battalion of Rhodesian African Rifles.
[22] Umtali was renamed Mutare in 1982.
[23] Zimbabwe African National Liberation Army. ZANLA was the military wing of ZANU.
[24] Zimbabwe People's Revolutionary Army. ZIPRA was the military wing of ZAPU.

Nick had been stunned at this news. While he had been vaguely aware of the political manoeuvrings that had taken place, both within the country and overseas over the last six months, he had no idea of the significance and rapidity of the changes that were about to envelop the nation.

Given the state of uncertainty and flux in the country at this time, Nick had recently agreed for his period of national service to be extended from 12 months to 18 months. When he heard Colonel Lever's solemn announcement about the ceasefire, rather selfishly his immediate reaction was concern that he might be asked to further extend his period of national service from 18 months to 24 months.

The ceasefire was the topic of animated discussion that night around the bar in the Officers' Mess. The older and more senior officers were extremely pessimistic. They still believed that the war against ZANLA and ZIPRA could be won, especially now that the country had its first black Prime Minister, Bishop Abel Muzorewa.

However, on a more personal and emotional level, the ceasefire with the two black nationalist armies felt like a betrayal of the sacrifices made by all those, both black and white, who had served in the Rhodesian Security Forces over the past decade.

Their views were perhaps best expressed by Major Forsyth, a mountain of a man, who smashed his fist into the gleaming mahogany bar top and exclaimed, "Shit!! You had better believe me. Now that this country is being ruled by the goddamn blacks, it is going to go to rack and ruin. Bloody Muzorewa is as weak as piss. Smith would never have agreed to a ceasefire with Mugabe and Nkomo and all their bloody *gook*[25] stragglers."

Nick, like the other junior officers present that night, was easily persuaded by the views of his senior officers. However, at that time, he had no appreciation of the extraordinary events that had been unfolding in the country over the previous six months. More tragically,

---

[25] A defamatory word for a terrorist.

neither he nor any of the others in the Officers' Mess that night had any idea how prophetic Major Forsyth's words would prove to be. For, while the country would soon hold *one-man-one-vote* general elections, fulfilling the long-held dream of true independence for the black population, these elections would also mark the beginning of a turbulent period in the nation's history, during which political intimidation, the breakdown of the rule of law, hyperinflation, economic collapse, unemployment, and starvation would become the norm for the majority of its eight million citizens.

The momentous events, which had been taking place over the last six months, had been stirred into life when the Conservative Party in the United Kingdom, under the leadership of Margaret Thatcher, had won the British general elections in May 1979.

Margaret Thatcher was an impressive woman. She was proudly British and longed to see some of Britain's waning glory restored. To her, it was infuriating that Rhodesia, a self-governing British colony and part of the United Kingdom's Commonwealth of Nations, had unilaterally declared independence from the United Kingdom in November 1965.

Since then, Rhodesia had been a thorn in the side of various British administrations. Under Ian Smith's leadership, the country had withstood all efforts to suppress its *'act of treason'* and had economically survived despite the international sanctions that had been imposed on it. As a result, when Margaret Thatcher became Prime Minister, one of her foreign policy priorities was to resolve the vexed question of Rhodesia.

In June 1979, spurious general elections had been held, resulting in Bishop Abel Muzorewa becoming Prime Minister and the country changing its name to Zimbabwe-Rhodesia. However, the elections were boycotted by ZANU[26] and ZAPU[27], the two main black nationalist parties, which refused to recognise the legitimacy of Muzorewa's government. They viewed him as a puppet of former Prime Minister

---

[26] Zimbabwe African National Union.
[27] Zimbabwe African People's Union.

Ian Smith and vowed to aggressively continue the guerrilla war they had been waging before the elections, albeit with the enemy now comprising the dual heads of both Smith and Muzorewa.

The British Government, along with the international community, did not recognise the legitimacy of Muzorewa's Government either. Intense international pressure was now being put on Muzorewa to enter into negotiations with ZANU, ZAPU and other Zimbabwean political parties to form a new government of national unity.

Surprisingly, Muzorewa was not opposed to these suggestions. However, both ZANU and ZAPU were violently opposed to any such approaches. They did not trust Muzorewa and, more importantly, correctly gauged that his support amongst the Zimbabwean people was modest compared to the popular support they believed they had.

The British Government was also becoming alarmed at the increasing influence that both China and Russia were beginning to have in Zimbabwe-Rhodesia. The Chinese were backers of Robert Mugabe's ZANU party, while the Russians were backers of Joshua Nkomo's ZAPU party. The British Government was concerned that if the armed conflict continued and either of these two black nationalist parties prevailed, then any semblance of a Western-styled government in Zimbabwe-Rhodesia would quickly dissipate and be replaced by a centralist communist-styled government.

Faced with this predicament, Margaret Thatcher had implemented a bold and daring strategy. Her government let it be known that if the warring parties in the new Zimbabwe-Rhodesia did not come to a quick and meaningful political settlement, then the British Government would recognise Bishop Muzorewa's Government and lift economic sanctions on the country.

This daring strategy had the desired effect. Both Mugabe and Nkomo were fearful of being outmanoeuvred. If Muzorewa's Government was recognised by Britain and other countries, then it would be impossible for either ZANU or ZAPU to claim that they were fighting a war against an illegitimate minority government. Moreover, once international sanctions were lifted, they were fearful that much-needed military arms would be acquired by the Zimbabwe-Rhodesian Security Forces. At that time, these troops were still highly-disciplined and well-trained. If sanctions were lifted, the Security Forces would once again have access to much-needed arms and weapons. This would enable them to inflict significant casualties on the military wings of both ZANU and ZAPU, both of which were poorly disciplined and trained in comparison to the Zimbabwe-Rhodesian Security Forces.

In August 1979, Bishop Muzorewa had attended the 5th CHOGM[28], which was held in Lusaka, Zambia. At that meeting, the British Government, with the support of the OAU[29], cajoled Muzorewa, Mugabe and Nkomo to participate in a Constitutional Conference to be held in Britain at Lancaster House. The purpose of the Constitutional Conference was to discuss and reach agreement on the terms of a new independence constitution for Zimbabwe.

The Constitutional Conference was subsequently held at Lancaster House in London during the period from 10th September to 15th December 1979. It was chaired by Lord Carrington, a distinguished British parliamentarian, and an experienced negotiator. The Constitutional Conference resulted in the signing of the Lancaster Agreement on 21st December 1979.

Under the Agreement, the Muzorewa Government agreed to dissolve itself and to restore governmental power back to the UK, under a caretaker British governor. The warring parties in the country agreed to a ceasefire, while the UK, in its caretaker role, would organise fresh one-man-one-vote general elections, in which all political parties, including ZANU and ZAPU, would participate.

The parties to the Lancaster Agreement also agreed to abide by the new draft independence constitution, which provided for a 100-seat House of Assembly. 80 of these seats would be elected by persons on a common roll, comprising all adult citizens. The remaining 20 seats

---

[28] Commonwealth Heads of Government Meeting.
[29] The Organisation of African Unity (1963 to 2002). It was superseded by the African Union in 2002.

would be reserved for a period of ten years for the white electorate, after which time these seats would return to the common roll.

The three-month long conference was fraught with difficulties, and the fact that a final accord was signed was a significant achievement. One of the most difficult problems had been the question of land reform. Mugabe and Nkomo were adamant that a significant part of the rich agricultural farming areas of the country, which at that time were almost exclusively owned by white farmers, be returned to the local black people. On the other hand, Smith argued that these lands had been legally acquired and developed by their current owners and were the lifeblood of the country's thriving economy.

In the end, Mugabe and Nkomo were persuaded to accept a compromise position whereby farms would only be acquired by the Zimbabwean Government on a *Willing Buyer Willing Seller* basis, using funds which would be provided by the British and American Governments for a period of ten years.

However, Mugabe was never really happy with this compromise, and 20 years later, as President of Zimbabwe, he would unleash a violent and pernicious policy whereby local militia were encouraged by his government to illegally and brutally force white farmers off their lands without compensation.

On 12th December 1979, Lord Soames, son-in-law of Sir Winston Churchill, had arrived in Salisbury[30] as Britain's caretaker governor to restore temporary rule over its former British colony.

Following his arrival, events in the country moved extremely quickly.

A ceasefire agreement was signed on 21st December, and immediately thereafter the Zimbabwe-Rhodesian Security Forces ceased all combative operations. The guerrilla forces of Mugabe and Nkomo did likewise and began to assemble in 16 assembly point camps scattered throughout the country. These camps were supervised by members of the Commonwealth Cease Fire Monitoring Force, which began arriving

---

[30] The capital of Rhodesia. Its name was changed to Harare in April 1982.

in the country just before Christmas. By the time elections were held in late February 1980, it was estimated that approximately 22,000 guerrillas and gathered in the assembly points.

*****

During his national service with 3RAR, Nick had quickly come to respect both the professional soldiering skills and pragmatic logic of its NCO[31]s. He was, therefore, keen to hear their views on the recent events in the country, realising their perspective might differ from his as a white officer.

Accordingly, he decided to have a beer with Corporal Pukelo in the NCO's mess. Both Nick and Corporal Pukelo had been involved in the firefight six months earlier, during which Nick's platoon had *'taken out'* 17 guerrillas for the loss of only 1 of their men. During the firefight, Corporal Pukelo had killed the terrorists' stick commander with a burst of fire from his MAG[32]. The slaying of the stick commander in such spectacular manner had catapulted Corporal Pukelo's reputation amongst the other troops to unheralded heights.

Corporal Pukelo was from the Ndebele tribe, which was an offshoot of the famous Zulu imperial tribe. Their modern history had begun in the early 19th century when their chief, a man called Mzilikazi, had split from the main Zulu tribe in South Africa and moved northwards to settle in the present-day Matabeleland province.

The Ndebele are a handsome-looking people who are proud of their warrior heritage. Historically, they have regarded the more populous Zimbabwean tribe, the Shona, with disdain due to their more benign subsistence farming heritage. However, when the boundaries of Rhodesia were drawn up in the late 19th century by the world's then colonial powers, both the Ndebele and Shona peoples were placed in

---

[31] Non-commissioned officer.
[32] The Belgian designed Fabrique Nationale 7.62mm general-purpose machine gun. The MAG was standard issue for the Rhodesian Security Forces.

the same newly created land, which was to become the country which had recently changed its name to Zimbabwe-Rhodesia.

This accident of history would come to haunt the Ndebele nation at the end of February 1980, during the country's first ever *one-man-one-vote* general elections. At these general elections, the Western democratic principle of *one-man-one-vote* would be applied for the first time ever, and the Ndebele nation would find itself grossly outnumbered, in an electoral sense, by the more populous Shona nation.

Corporal Pukelo had never had any tertiary education. However, his innate sense of history, coupled with a strong dose of common sense, led him to tell Nick that Robert Mugabe's ZANU party would win the forthcoming general election by a landslide.

Nick argued with him vociferously. He said that Mugabe was an unknown entity and that his party had no prior experience of governing anything, let alone a country. However, Corporal Pukelo countered these arguments by saying, "*Ishe*[33], you are thinking from a white man's point of view. Mugabe comes from the Shona nation. Both the Shona nation and my nation, the Ndebele nation, will vote on tribal grounds, so the Shona will win because their tribe is much larger than the Ndebele tribe.

"Mugabe is very clever. He has already mobilised hundreds of thousands of Shona people who have been living in exile in Zambia and Mozambique. They are returning to Zimbabwe on foot so they can vote. And if Mugabe doesn't win the general election, he will fight whoever does. His soldiers have hidden many of their weapons in the bush. If Nkomo or Muzorewa win the election, Mugabe's soldiers will abandon the assembly points, retrieve their arms caches from their hiding places in the bush, and start fighting again. The future is bad, very bad. Mugabe will want to slaughter the Ndebele people because he distrusts us, and there will be no one to stop him."

---

[33] *Ishe* is a term of respect used by RAR soldiers when referring to their officers.

These dire predictions by Corporal Pukelo left Nick with a deep sense of unease. However, later that same day, while watching the evening news bulletin, he learned that despite some breaches of the ceasefire agreement, the truce appeared to be holding and preparations for the forthcoming general elections were on track. In addition, the acting governor of the country, Lord Soames, and the leaders of the four major parties who were contesting the elections, were assuring the country that following the elections, a stable government would be formed, which would promote national unity and reconciliation. These words of comfort did something to ease Nick's strong sense of foreboding doom.

Chapter 3 - The change in power

Timeline – April 1980

Despite the fact that the ceasefire appeared to be generally holding, the situation in the country during the months of January and February was extremely tense.

The commanders of the Zimbabwe-Rhodesian Security Forces had issued orders directing their troops to observe the terms of the ceasefire and to cease all active military operations. However, rumours abounded. One of the strongest and most consistent ones was that the overall commander of the Zimbabwe-Rhodesian Security Forces, General Peter Walls, had drawn up contingency plans which would be implemented if Bishop Muzorewa did not win the forthcoming elections. Under these plans, the elections would be declared as null and void on account of alleged political intimidation by ZANU[34] and ZAPU[35]. The Zimbabwe-Rhodesian Security Forces would seize control of the country and martial law would be imposed until such time as new *free and fair* elections could be organised.

The Zimbabwe-Rhodesian Security Forces' officers, under orders to refrain from combative activities, saw the massing of their sworn enemy in relatively unprotected camps as an opportunity waiting to be grasped. There were many occasions when they were sorely tempted to disobey their orders, and to launch a decisive and lethal attack on

---

[34] Zimbabwe African National Union.
[35] Zimbabwe African People's Union.

the camps, thereby delivering a fatal blow to both ZANLA[36] and ZIPRA[37]. The fact that this never eventuated underscored the extraordinary discipline that existed within the country's Security Forces at that time.

In February, just prior to the elections, there were two failed assassination attempts on Robert Mugabe. Mugabe accused General Walls of organising these attempts on his life. In response to such accusations, General Walls reportedly replied, *'If these assassination attempts had been performed by my men, you would be dead!'*

In later months, suspicion for these attempted assassinations fell on forces loyal to Joshua Nkomo. Although such suspicions were never proven, Mugabe never forgot the incidents. His deep distrust of Joshua Nkomo and the Ndebele nation might help explain why, three years after independence, and amid bogus claims that Joshua Nkomo was plotting a military coup against him, Mugabe imposed a curfew in large parts of Matabeleland. He then ordered his North Korean-trained 5th Brigade to unleash a campaign of intimidation, violence, and mass murder on the Ndebele population in the southern part of the country, resulting in the deaths of nearly 20,000 Zimbabwean citizens.

The situation in the 16 assembly points was also extremely tense and difficult. Their tented accommodation was uncomfortable, and the guerrillas were bored. Communication lines between the men in the camps and their political leaders were poor. This often resulted in confused and misleading instructions being received by the guerrillas. Moreover, the guerrillas did not respect the authority of the Commonwealth Ceasefire Monitoring Force, and this was exacerbated by the fact that they knew that these forces were under orders to withdraw if hostilities broke out between the guerrillas and the Zimbabwe-Rhodesian Security Forces. They were naturally deeply suspicious of the Security Forces themselves. This suspicion was only heightened by the decision of the British Governor, Lord Soames, to use the Security Forces to deal with any breaches of the ceasefire,

---

[36] Zimbabwe African National Liberation Army. ZANLA was the military wing of ZANU.
[37] Zimbabwe People's Revolutionary Army. ZIPRA was the military wing of ZAPU.

notwithstanding that the Lancaster Agreement stated that such breaches were to be dealt with by commanders from both sides.

The fact that things remained relatively peaceful in the assembly points was, in a large part, attributable to the fact that the local authorities did a splendid job in ensuring that the camps were supplied with plenty of locally brewed beer, prostitutes, and marijuana[38]!

Notwithstanding these tensions, the fragile ceasefire held, thereby enabling the country's extremely efficient public service to organise and hold general elections within ten weeks of Lord Soames' arrival in the country. Once again, this was no small feat, especially since prior to Lord Soames' arrival, the common voters' roll did not even exist.

The election was held in two stages. The first stage occurred in mid-February and related to the 20 seats which had been reserved for the white electorate. The second, and more important stage, related to the 80 seats that were to be elected by persons on the common voters' roll. This stage of the elections was held over the three-day leap year period, from 27th February to 29th February 1980.

Tensions remained extremely high throughout the country, both in the lead-up to and during the voting period. To ensure that the election was as free and fair as possible, the Security Forces, together with the Commonwealth Peacekeeping Forces, were mobilised to provide security at all voting booths and protect key assets across the country. For its part, Nick's platoon was deployed to guard the impressive Birchenough Bridge, which spans the Sabi[39] River and lies about 130 kilometres south of Umtali[40] on the main road between Umtali and Fort Victoria[41].

The voter turnout at the elections, at approximately 93% of the electorate, was impressive. Many people stood in the voting queues

---

[38] Marijuana is an alternative name for the psychoactive drug cannabis.
[39] The Sabi River was renamed the Save River in 1982.
[40] Umtali was renamed Mutare in 1982.
[41] Fort Victoria was renamed Masvingo in 1982.

for over 24 hours, just to ensure that they could be part of this momentous day in their nation's history.

Actual voting procedures at the election booths were both novel and ingenious. As no black electoral roll had ever before been compiled, black voters were required to dip their hands into an indelible ink that stained their hands, thereby preventing people from voting multiple times.

Despite some political intimidation which occurred in several provincial areas, the elections were surprisingly free and fair by African standards. This was vouched by the Commonwealth Observer Group when, on 2nd March 1980, it declared that the elections had been sufficiently free and fair as to constitute a genuine expression of the electorates' wishes.

On the 4th March 1980, the results of the elections were announced. As had been predicted by Corporal Pukelo a few months earlier, Robert Mugabe's ZANU party, which had contested the elections under the name ZANU-PF[42], had a runaway victory, winning 57 seats of the 80 common roll seats. Joshua Nkomo's ZAPU party, which had contested the elections under the name Patriotic Front – ZAPU, won 20 seats, with Bishop Muzorewa's UANC[43] party winning the remaining 3 seats. Ian Smith's RF[44] party, won all 20 of the seats reserved for the white electorate.

When news of Mugabe's election victory was announced over the radio and on television, thousands of his supporters took to the streets, waving his party's symbol — the cockerel or *'jongwe.'*

That night, in his stirring victory speech, Robert Mugabe took on the mantle of a true African statesman when he stated that, *'I urge you, whether you are black or white, to join me in a new pledge to forget our grim past, forgive and forget, join hands in a new amity, and*

---

[42] Zimbabwe African National Union – Patriotic Front. ZANU-PF is a political organisation that has been the ruling party of Zimbabwe since independence in 1980.
[43] United African National Council.
[44] Rhodesian Front.

together as Zimbabweans, trample upon racialism, tribalism, and regionalism, and work to reconstruct and rehabilitate our society as we reinvigorate our economic machinery.'

Whether these words were prompted by a genuine desire to foster racial reconciliation in the country, or whether they were driven by the pragmatic realisation that, at that time, most of the country's economic power and intellectual know-how was in the hands of the white sections of the population, is debatable.

In any event, Mugabe was very keen to avoid the situation which had occurred five years earlier when Zimbabwe's eastern neighbour, Mozambique, had achieved independence from Portugal, following which there had been a mass exodus of the Portuguese section of the country's population and this had left the Mozambican economy in disarray.

The pace of change in the country did not slow down after the election results were announced. Shortly after their announcement, the country began preparations for its official Independence Day celebrations, which were to take place on 18th April 1980.

Nick was fortunate to have a weekend pass over that weekend and so he took the opportunity to attend the lavish official celebrations, which took place at the Rufaro soccer stadium in Salisbury[45]. Nick, along with tens of thousands of other spectators, watched as Prince Charles, amid much British colonial pomp and ceremony, gave a farewell salute and the Zimbabwe-Rhodesian Signal Corps played *'God save the Queen.'*

The Independence Day celebrations were attended by many important foreign dignitaries, including Prime Minister Gandhi of India, President Shagari of Nigeria, President Kaunda of Zambia, and Prime Minister Fraser of Australia. The events were widely reported around the world, and for the first time in almost 25 years, the country was once again accepted back into the international community.

---

[45] The capital of Zimbabwe. Its name was changed to Harare in April 1982.

It was with much relief, that in early July 1980, Nick received notification that his period of national service would conclude on Friday, 15th August 1980, when he would be demobilised.

These orders were accompanied by a letter, personally signed by General Peter Walls, informing Nick that he had been awarded the Bronze Cross of Rhodesia, for the courage and leadership he had shown in June 1979, when his platoon had been ambushed whilst on patrol in the Chimanimani Mountains.

This news came as a complete surprise to Nick. He was humbled by the honour, especially since he felt that the success his platoon had enjoyed that day was due more to their excellent soldiering skills than to his own abilities as a relatively inexperienced 2nd lieutenant.

The events of the last 18 months had been so turbulent and dramatic that Nick had not even considered what he might do once his period of national service was over. With no real idea of what he wanted to do but driven by a strong desire to leave Africa and to further his education in Europe, in early June he had started to discuss his options with his parents.

Nick's father, Matthew Sinclair, was a prominent local businessman who had made his fortune in the tobacco industry. Matthew was very keen for Nick to go to university, and was delighted when Nick told him that, if at all possible, he would like to go to the University of Edinburgh to study business and economics.

Matthew had plenty of influential business contacts in Britain. These contacts had been nurtured by Matthew during the 1970s, when Rhodesia had successfully evaded the international sanctions that had been imposed upon it. Using such contacts, Matthew was able to secure a place at the University of Edinburgh for Nick, and so it was, that on Sunday, 31st August 1980, Nick boarded an SAA[46] flight to London.

---

[46] South African Airways.

Nick was filled with both excitement and trepidation. He had never travelled outside Africa before, and the thought of starting his studies in a few weeks in a new and foreign country filled him with a fair degree of anxiety.

Unconsciously, he slipped his hand into his trouser pocket to check that the treasure he had stowed there before boarding the flight was still safely in place. His fingers quickly found the metal object at the bottom of his pocket and gently stroked the velvet pouch containing his Bronze Cross of Rhodesia.

He was immediately filled with a deep sense of peace and calm, which enabled him to enjoy several hours of deep sleep as he flew north towards Britain.

Chapter 4 – Hello Mother England

Timeline - September 1980

Nick's flight to London passed quickly and uneventfully. Although he was travelling in the cramped conditions of economy class, he did manage to get some sleep. His sleep however was fitful, and he slipped in and out of a dream of which he remembered very little, other than a persistent and recurring image of being in an alien land and feeling very desolate and alone.

As morning broke, Nick was awakened by an air hostess who offered him a freshly steamed face cloth, which he used to wipe away the dregs of the night before. He stretched his arms and legs, unwound himself from his cramped seat and went off to find the toilet. That too, was very small. Having relieved his bladder, he returned to his seat to idle away the last hour of his journey.

Nick had never travelled outside of Africa before, and he wondered what England would be like. At junior school, his teachers had always spoken of England in favourable terms. History lessons were usually sprinkled with romantic tales of England during the height of her Imperial days when she dominated the globe. However, by the time Nick started high school, the grip of international sanctions had begun to harm the Rhodesian economy, and the country's political leaders were vehement in their condemnation of how Rhodesia had been betrayed by England.

This political propaganda had begun to influence the curricula in government schools, and gradually the history of England was being recast to focus more on her inglorious moments. This included rumours that Cecil John Rhodes, the great English entrepreneur, and coloniser of Africa, was also a homosexual[47].

Whilst he was at senior school, Nick had become friendly with a boy called Philip McIntosh. Philip's father had been transferred to Rhodesia from the UK when Philip was about 15 years old. When he had commenced school in Rhodesia, Philip's parents sent him to one of the country's pre-eminent government schools for boys. This was Prince Edward School in Salisbury[48], which both Nick and his brother, Russell, also attended.

When Nick met Philip, he and Philip struck up an immediate friendship. Nick loved Philip's apparent disregard for all forms of authority and his willingness to always push the boundaries. Philip was also full of exciting stories from England, and over the two or three years that he and Nick knew one another, Philip had painted a picture of England as being a country full of vibrancy, with a life-pulse like nothing that existed in Rhodesia. According to him, it was full of beautiful women who were sexually liberated and more than willing to take young men, often a lot younger than themselves, to bed.

So, with all these mixed images of England in his mind, Nick disembarked from his flight and followed the exit signs at London's Heathrow Airport. The throng of people inside Heathrow's Terminal 3 was bewildering, but Nick followed the crowd and soon found himself lining up to complete immigration formalities

The immigration officer waved him forward and asked for his travel documents. Nick handed over his green coloured Rhodesian passport, which had the country's national coat of arms emblazoned on its cover.

Ever since international trade sanctions had been imposed on Rhodesia in the mid-1960s, Rhodesian passports had been blacklisted

---

[47] This rumour was based primarily on the fact that Cecil John Rhodes never married and did not have any known long-term romantic relationships with women.
[48] The capital of Rhodesia (now Zimbabwe). Its name was changed to Harare in April 1982.

by most countries in the world. Consequently, holders of Rhodesian passports had been prevented from travelling to nearly all countries other than to South Africa and Israel, both of which had remained friendly to Rhodesia throughout the many years of international sanctions. However, Rhodesia was now known as Zimbabwe, and international sanctions against the country had been lifted over six months earlier, following Robert Mugabe's electoral victory in the country's first ever *one-man-one-vote* democratic elections, held in February 1980.

Nonetheless, the immigration officer viewed Nick's Rhodesian passport with suspicion. "Excuse me, sir," he said. "Are you aware that you are travelling on a Rhodesian passport, and that this passport is not recognised by Her Majesty's Government?"

Nick was shocked. He couldn't believe that after all the publicity surrounding the recent elections in Zimbabwe, that this immigration official was making such an ill-informed statement. He took a deep breath and instinctively reached into his pocket, feeling the familiar velvet pouch which housed his Bronze Cross of Gallantry.

Then, in a steady and calm voice, he said "Yes, sir. I do understand that the British Government has not recognised Rhodesian passports for many years now." For an instant he was tempted to add the thought that such non-recognition had occurred despite the fact that many Rhodesians had both fought and died for His Majesty's Government during both world wars. But he thought better of it!

Instead, he calmly added, "However, I am sure you realise that democratic elections were recently held in my country, as a result of which Robert Mugabe was voted into power. Sanctions have now been lifted and Rhodesia, which is now known as Zimbabwe, has been welcomed back into the international community."

The immigration official looked a bit taken aback by Nick's confident reply.

"Would you mind waiting here, sir, while I check with my superiors?" he said.

With that, he picked up the phone on his desk, pushed a few buttons and then had a brief conversation with someone on the other end. Nick strained his ears to try and catch what was being said, but apart from a few mutters and grunts from the immigration officer, he heard nothing that he could make any sense of.

After a few minutes the immigration officer put down his phone.

He turned to Nick and said, "Welcome to England, Mr Sinclair. I do apologise for the confusion. I hope you have a pleasant trip."

With that he stamped Nick's passport and waved him through.

Nick followed the signs to the baggage carousels and quickly found his bags. He then located the green customs route and cleared customs without any issues.

He walked through the international arrival doors and scanned the mass of persons who were waiting there to meet and greet arriving passengers. His father, Matthew Sinclair, had arranged for a business colleague of his, Stuart Dixon, to pick him up at the airport. Nick's father had told him that Stuart would probably send a driver from his company to meet him, so Nick scanned the placards held by some in the waiting crowd, searching for one with is name.

After a minute or two, he saw his name in dark black letters on an A4 piece of card which, to his surprise, was being held by a pretty woman with long blonde hair. Nick guessed she would be about his age. She had sparkling bright blue eyes and was wearing the ubiquitous, blue-faded Levi denim jeans and a tight-fitting black polo-necked jumper. Her snug clothes enhanced her obvious good figure, and her sparkling eyes and blonde hair made her stand out from the crowd.

"What a bit of luck," Nick murmured under his breath. He walked confidently over to her, held out his hand and said, "Hi, my name is Nick Sinclair. I see from your placard that you are looking for me."

The blonde-headed girl took his hand and gave him a warm handshake.

"Hi Nick. I am very pleased to meet you. My name is Rachel. My father has unfortunately been held up at a meeting in London. He was going to pick you up himself, but apparently there is some sort of drama going on at work, and so he has asked me to help out."

"That's a bit of luck for me," quipped Nick. "You lead the way, and I will follow."

Chapter 5 – Meeting the Dixon family

Rachel exited Terminal 3's arrivals hall and followed the signs to the nearby multi-storey car park. Nick followed a few paces behind. His senses were in overdrive as they tried to assimilate all the new sights, sounds, and smells that abounded everywhere. He also appreciated being behind Rachel as this allowed him to admire her fantastic figure without appearing to stare!

They took the lift to level two of the car park, which was a reserved level. Nick was impressed by the number of high-end luxury cars parked there. Rachel stopped beside a white Jaguar XJ6 and opened the boot.

"Dump your bags in there and jump in," she said.

Nick heaved his rather heavy suitcase into the boot and then slid into the comfy leather front passenger seat. He admired the interior of the car. The polished oak dashboard was stylish and the instrument panel was well organised. The car still had that new car smell.

"Nice car," remarked Nick.

"Thanks," said Rachel. "It was a present from my parents for my eighteenth birthday. It's a new Series III Jaguar XJ6, and I've had it for about six months now. It's got lots of cool gadgets, including a combo radio-tape deck and a sunroof. It even has cruise control. I love it."

"You're kidding," said Nick. "This is your car?"

"Yes, that's right," said Rachel. "My parents spoil me. But my Dad is loaded, so it's OK. But please could you stop talking for a minute? I need to concentrate to get us out of this airport. The roads are so damned confusing."

"Sure thing," said Nick.

For the next few minutes nothing much was said between them as Rachel followed the exit signs. Nick eventually broke the silence by asking Rachel where she lived.

"We live in Guildford, which is in a county called Surrey," replied Rachel. "It's about 45 minutes away, that is if the traffic behaves and there are no roadworks. I need to head for the M25 and then exit at the A3 turnoff. The street directory is in the glove box. Would you mind grabbing it for me? I may need you to help me navigate."

Nick grabbed the street directory. Rachel had marked the relevant pages with pieces of paper, and pretty quickly Nick was able to orientate the map to his surroundings. Occasionally, he made a few observations about where they were, but, in truth, Rachel seemed to be managing quite well without his help. He marvelled at how well she handled the car. The traffic and confusing maze of roads did not seem to phase her at all.

"Geez, the traffic is unbelievable. I've never seen anything like it before," said Nick.

"This is London," said Rachel. "You'll get used to it."

As they drove to her parents' house, Rachel chatted away quite happily. She told Nick that she was a second-year student at Oxford University, where she was doing a four-year Bachelor of Arts degree in Classics. Her semester had started a few weeks earlier, but she had returned home this weekend because one of her close school friends, Claire, was celebrating her nineteenth birthday, and she had invited Rachel to her party.

"The party is this weekend," said Rachel. "Would you like to come? I'm sure Claire wouldn't mind. If you would like to come, I'll give her a call when we get home and clear it with her."

"That sounds great," said Nick. "My first date in England. I am looking forward to it."

As he said this, he gave a quick sideways glance at Rachel. He thought he saw a slight smile flicker across her face. Then it disappeared. He wondered if he had imagined this, but he doubted it. The thought of accompanying Rachel to the party gave him a warm feeling. He was sure she would be good company.

Nick quickly gathered from his conversation with Rachel that she came from a respectable family. Her father was evidently well-off, though her explanation of his work was somewhat muddled. It seemed he was involved in the import and export business, dealing in rather unusual products.

"He trades in anything and everything that's hard to get," Rachel said. "This includes arms, antiques, rare paintings, uranium, rare earth minerals, and of course tobacco from Rhodesia. My dad believes that the more restrictions that are placed on goods people want, the higher their market value. I don't know much about his dealings with your father, but I've occasionally heard him thank the British government for imposing sanctions on Rhodesia. Apparently, they only served to inflate the prices his customers were willing to pay for exports from Rhodesia, and Dad always had plenty of customers who were willing to do business with Rhodesia, even though many of those dealings were probably illegal."

Rachel seemed to be at ease with the fact that her family was very well off and that much of that wealth had been generated from her father's rather dubious international business dealings. However, at the same time, she did not flaunt the very comfortable lifestyle that she obviously enjoyed.

Rachel was an only child, and both her mother and father doted on her. She was well aware of this and ready to use it to her advantage when it mattered. But rather than use it to bring financial benefits to herself, it seemed that she had used her obvious charms to persuade her father to become quite a philanthropist. Apparently, he made significant charitable donations to various wildlife organisations that were operating in Africa, as well as to humanitarian organisations in both Africa and in some of the poorer Asian countries.

She told Nick that before starting university, she had spent three months doing volunteer work at some orphanage in Sri Lanka. The experience had deeply affected her. As she spoke about some of the things she had seen and experienced there, especially the abject poverty, Nick could sense the empathy and emotion behind her voice. He found this tenderness in her quite enchanting.

"Don't you think it is a bit odd that your Dad seems to make a lot of money doing dodgy business deals and then uses that money to make donations to charities he chooses?" queried Nick. "Maybe he is just trying to appease his conscience?"

"I suppose there may be some truth in that," replied Rachel. "But if my dad didn't get involved in those kinds of business transactions, someone else surely would. What's more, I'm fairly certain that the profits they made wouldn't be spent as generously as my father chooses to spend much of his."

About an hour after they had left Heathrow, they arrived at her parents' house. Guildford is an affluent town, and the Dixons' house was situated in a road called Chantry View Road, which is one of the town's prime residential streets. The approach to the house was along an oak tree-lined driveway that passed through about two acres of beautifully manicured gardens.

The house itself was an attractive Edwardian home that had been extensively renovated when the Dixons moved into it, two years earlier. The renovations had been done in a way that brought all the modern conveniences to the home, without detracting from its original charm and character. Many of the period-style features had been retained, including leaded windows, fireplaces in several rooms, moulded picture rails, attractive detailed cornices, and intricate, ornate tin-pressed ceilings in the two main formal reception rooms. The house was a two-storey building with a large heavy timber front door, which opened into a spacious reception hall, from which a wide and attractive staircase rose to the galleried landing above.

"Your room is up the stairs and is the first on the left," Rachel said. "I am sure you must be dying for a coffee after your long trip. Why don't you go and unpack and freshen up? Then I will take you into Guildford for breakfast."

"That sounds great," replied Nick. "I will see you down here in about half an hour."

With that, Nick strode upstairs and found his bedroom. The room was large and bright with double windows that overlooked the front garden. He was pleasantly surprised to find it also had an ensuite bathroom with a large shower. He unpacked his suitcase and jumped into the shower. The hot water and soap suds washed away the dross from the night before, and pretty soon he was feeling fresh and invigorated again. He slipped on a pair of denim jeans, a T-shirt, and a casual sweater and went downstairs to find Rachel.

Rachel was waiting for him in the reception hall. She ushered him outside and into her car, and the two of them sped off to her favourite café.

The café was quiet when they arrived, and they found a corner table bathed in sunlight streaming through a nearby window.

Rachel ordered a glass of freshly squeezed orange juice, scrambled eggs, and bacon, while Nick opted for coffee, fried eggs, and bacon. They then spent well over an hour chatting together.

Nick told Rachel a little about life in Zimbabwe but spent more time quizzing her on what life was like at Oxford University, and what she wanted to do once she finished her degree.

For her part, Rachel spent time asking Nick why he was going to Scotland to study business and economics, and how he thought he would adapt to life as a university student in Scotland, compared to what he had been doing over the last 18 months in Zimbabwe as a soldier.

Rachel was also keen to find out from Nick what it had been like serving in the army, but she was sensitive enough to notice that this was a subject that he did not particularly want to talk about, and so she did not press the matter.

Time passed quickly as they were both genuinely interested in each other. It was clear that, with enough time, they could easily become very good friends. Nick was captivated by Rachel's good humour, easy manner, and striking looks. Rachel was drawn to Nick's handsome features, adventurous spirit, youthful mannerisms, and a perspective on life that was very different from those of her friends and colleagues.

She was also surprised that instead of expressing contempt for what was happening in Zimbabwe, he was not at all astonished that the country had taken the path it had.

"Look at this way," he said. "Think of the Scots in the 14th century when they were being exploited by the English barons. When Robert the Bruce called them to arms, they eagerly followed him, and in fact, as I understand it, they give the British a good bashing at Bannockburn. It's no different in Zimbabwe. The blacks have been exploited for years by a white minority group. Why should anyone be surprised that they have followed people like Mugabe and Nkomo? Both of these guys promised them freedom from a pretty miserable lifestyle and made promises of prosperity and power.

"I am sure that if I had been a black peasant tribesman, I would have sided with the likes of Mugabe or Nkomo. However, it's unfortunate that neither Mugabe nor Nkomo seem to share the same love and respect for their nation that figures like Robert the Bruce had for their people. While it's quite possible that things may go horribly wrong in Zimbabwe, that doesn't make Mugabe's election as Prime Minister inherently wrong.

"Black Zimbabweans need to find their rightful place in the world, they need to choose their own leaders, and develop their own systems of government. If they stuff up, they will learn from their mistakes. Eventually all nations do. That is the history of the world. Bad rulers and unjust systems of government never survive in the long term. I just fear that there may be much unhappiness and suffering during the transitionary years. But that's the natural order of things."

Little did Nick know at the time that these musings, shared with a beautiful young woman in a quaint coffee shop in Surrey, England, would prove to be prophetically true over time.

Nick and Rachel eventually got home just before lunch. Nick excused himself for a bit of catch-up sleep, while Rachel said she would contact her friend Claire to check if it would be OK for Nick to accompany her to Claire's birthday party that weekend.

That evening, around the family dining table, Nick met Rachel's father, Stuart Dixon.

Nick guessed that Stuart was in his early fifties. He was a distinguished-looking man. His full head of hair was silvering around his temples and sideburns, and this gave him an air of sophistication. His skin was slightly tanned, and his body was still trim and firm. These features set him apart from the vast majority of his fellow middle-aged Englishmen, who were generally overweight, balding, and pasty skin-coloured.

Stuart had poured himself and Nick a tall glass of gin and tonic, while Rachel and her mother, Lynne, enjoyed a glass of sparkling wine from the Champagne region of France.

Stuart then recounted how he had first met Nick's father, Matthew. Stuart's story revealed things about his father that Nick had neither known nor appreciated before.

Apparently, Stuart had met Matthew at the Grande Hotel in the Mozambican seaside city of Beira[49] in the mid-1970s. Matthew happened to be staying at the Grande Hotel at the same time as Stuart was.

Following Mozambique's independence from Portugal in 1975, many white ethnic Portuguese left the city, which quickly began to decay. Matthew was in Beira on a mission to assess how the rapidly deteriorating port facilities would affect Rhodesia's sanction-busting

---

[49] Beira is on the east coast of Mozambique and is the capital and largest city in the Mozambican province of Sofala.

efforts. Meanwhile, Stuart represented a South African company selling arms to the newly emerging Mozambican resistance movement known as RENAMO[50], which fiercely opposed the communist leanings of Frelimo, the party that had recently assumed power. RENAMO was secretly supported by both the Rhodesian and South African governments, who feared that Frelimo would be sympathetic to the military wings of Mugabe and Nkomo, potentially aiding terrorist incursions into Rhodesia and South Africa

"Your father was a fine man," said Stuart. "He was smart and had an uncanny knack for correctly reading the tea leaves of southern African politics. I learnt a lot from him. And we did some great tobacco deals. These efforts allowed me to meet the needs of my British and American cigarette manufacturing customers while simultaneously providing Rhodesia with desperately needed foreign currency. I genuinely enjoyed my business trips to Mozambique, Rhodesia, and South Africa, and I came to admire and respect the Rhodesian businesspeople I encountered. They were a tough but fair lot, and I appreciated their tenacity and optimism. The sanctions imposed by our British Government on Ian Smith's administration were entirely unjustified, and I was more than happy to contribute to helping Rhodesia circumvent them."

The banter at the dinner table was lively and animated throughout the night. Nick was drawn to both Stuart and Lynne — they were delightful people, and he could easily see where Rachel had inherited her fine character traits. For their part, Stuart and Lynne took an instant liking to Nick.

During the evening, Lynne told Nick that she had never met his father, but that Stuart had often spoken fondly of him. "Having met you," she said "I can see why Stuart likes your father so much. When you head off to Scotland, please make sure you stay in touch. You will always be welcome back here."

---

[50] The Mozambican National Resistance Movement. It was opposed to Frelimo. The name RENAMO is from the Portuguese phrase - *Resistência Nacional Moçambicana*.

Later that night, Lynne excused herself and headed off to bed. All the sparkling wine she had drunk left her feeling a little light-headed.

She also had the strange feeling that she and Stuart would be seeing Nick again.

That possibility gave her a warm and comfortable feeling.

Chapter 6 – The consummation

It was early morning on Saturday, 6th September. Despite having watched television with Rachel the night before until nearly midnight, Nick still had awakened at dawn, much to his annoyance.

"I guess it must have something to do with the early morning rises in the army," he muttered to himself as he let the hot shower water slowly wash away the slightly foggy feeling in his head.

The house was still very quiet. Not wanting to disturb anyone, Nick decided to take a jog around the neighbourhood. He had been inactive for the last week, and he knew a bit of physical exertion would make him feel better.

The morning air was crisp and chilly, a sure sign that autumnal weather was on its way. The sky was beginning to turn blue, and the sun, though still low in the sky, felt satisfying on his back as he walked down the long tree-lined driveway back towards Chantry View Road.

The lawns had been mown the day before. They had that manicured striped appearance that Nick associated with the fairways at the Royal Harare Golf Club[51] back home. The leaves on the oak trees were turning wonderful shades of rust-orange and ochre. Whenever a slight breeze blew, the more ripened ones would gently fall from the branches above and lie on the pristine lawn below like discarded confetti.

---

[51] The Club had changed its name to Royal Harare Golf Club at independence in 1980. Prior to that, it was called the Royal Salisbury Golf Club.

The birdlife in the garden was just beginning to stir. Nick tried to identify some of the sounds he heard, but they were strange and unrecognisable to his ear. Nonetheless, the chorus of birds, coupled with the majestic stature of the line of oak trees, lifted his spirits, as always happened whenever he was close to nature.

Nick reached the end of the driveway and broke into a gentle, rhythmic jog as he entered Chantry View Road. The road sloped gently upwards, and his body gradually warmed, dispelling the cold morning chill that had enveloped him when he first left the house.

He was one of those lucky people who could simply switch off his mind and allow his body to do its work. He lengthened his stride and let his breathing gradually deepen. He felt good as the bitumen passed beneath his strides, and a thin sheen of perspiration began to gather on his brow.

His mind wandered, and for a while, he was transported back to the beauty of the Chimanimani Mountains, where he had so often run for miles and miles with his platoon of RAR[52] soldiers. Spontaneously, he began to hum the RAR's haunting regimental song, 'Sweet Banana.' As he did so, he lost all awareness of the toil his body was doing. He ran strong and hard, but his breathing remained controlled, and his mind was back with his men in the mystic Chimanimani Mountains.

Nick had a good sense of direction, and not once did he need to stop to check where he was. An hour later, he arrived back where he had started. The sheen of perspiration was now heavy on his forehead and had slightly dampened the back of his T-shirt. However, the exercise, coupled with his African reveries, made him feel fulfilled and complete.

That afternoon, Rachel took Nick to watch a rugby union match between two local sides — Old Ruts Rugby Club and Reeds Weybridge Rugby Club. Nick had always enjoyed rugby union, and today was no exception. The weather was still fine, even though very cold. As the two forward packs came together for one of the many scrums, steam

---

[52] Rhodesian African Rifles.

rose from the panting chests of the two front rows, and hung above the mound of heaving human flesh and muscle.

The large crowd gave enthusiastic support to their local heroes. Rachel, in particular, was very animated. Every now and then, she would spontaneously reach out and grab Nick's arm, squeezing it in excitement. This gave him an extraordinarily pleasing sensation.

Having gone to an all-boys' school, Nick had not spent a lot of time in the company of the opposite sex. Sitting close to Rachel, and having her snuggle up to him to keep warm felt both natural and exhilarating. He instinctively knew that he could grow to be very fond of her, and he was sure she felt the same way. This was very unexpected as they had only known each other for a few days. However, he was convinced that the universe had conspired to bring them together in this beautiful and quintessential part of the English countryside.

After the game, Nick and Rachel enjoyed a beer in the clubhouse. Rachel knew many people there, and it quickly became obvious to Nick that she was a popular and well-liked member of the local community. She introduced him to a number of her friends, who were instantly drawn to him because of his distinctive clipped African accent and because his background was so very different to most of the other people there.

Rachel couldn't help but notice how comfortable he seemed to be with all these new people and how they took an instant liking to him. Her keen female instincts also alerted her to how his presence seemed to titillate the various young women to whom he spoke and interacted with.

Given Nick's handsome looks, this was hardly surprising. Standing just over six feet tall, with an athletic build, dark wavy hair, and piercing chestnut brown eyes, he exuded a dashing and commanding presence.

"I am looking forward to getting to know Nick a bit better," she mused. "He really is very hunky."

That night, Rachel and Nick went to Claire's nineteenth birthday party. The party was being held at her family's stately home, which was close to Rachel's home. A large marquee had been erected in the front garden and it was lit up by a pretty array of fairy lights. The driveway to the house was long and straight, with a multitude of luxury vehicles parked along both sides, including several chauffeured cars.

The party itself was a lavish affair. Guests were seated in a large marquee, and Nick estimated there were about 120 people present. Fifteen tables, each with eight seats, were arranged around a dance floor in the centre of the marquee. In one corner of the dance floor, a band played a selection of favourite hits, both current and classic, throughout the night. The song choices must have been perfect, as the dance floor remained packed with couples joyfully dancing together all night long.

Dinner was served at around 9:00 pm. The food was delicious. Nick had no idea where it had been prepared, but he was certain that it could easily have graced the tables of any leading restaurant.

After dinner, Rachel suggested that she and Nick should go outside to get some fresh air. She led Nick out of the marquee and into the garden. The night air was cold, but it was a welcome relief from the warm temperatures in the marquee. Rachel led him to a gazebo in the garden, which also twinkled with attractive fairy lights.

They sat down on the steps leading up into the gazebo. Rachel snuggled close to Nick. He instinctively put his arms around her shoulders, both to keep her warm and as a sign of the fondness he felt for her.

"You really are a lovely lady," he said. "I am glad I met you so soon after my arrival in the UK."

"Why, thank you Nick," Rachel replied, and, with that, she moved even closer to him. He let his leg press against hers and for the next few moments they said nothing much, but just enjoyed the solitude of the moment and being in each other's company.

Nick gazed up at the night sky.

"That's strange," he said. "There are so few stars in the sky compared to back home. England is a pretty place, but somehow it lacks the natural beauty of Zimbabwe. One day, I would love to take you there and show you some its treasures."

"I would love that," whispered Rachel. "From what you have told me, I am sure it must be a very special place."

The sound of the band drifted across the garden towards the gazebo.

"We had better get back," said Rachel. "I don't want my friends thinking I have abducted you."

"Now that's an appealing thought," chuckled Nick. "But I agree, let's get back. My butt is beginning to freeze."

For the rest of the evening, Nick and Rachel spent very little further time together. However, every now and then, their eyes would lock together across the throng of people, and a smile of pleasure would flicker across both their faces.

They arrived back at Stuart and Lynne's house around 1:00 am. Rachel suggested that she should drive as she had drunk very little, and Nick gladly accepted her offer. He knew that drink driving was strictly forbidden in the UK and that any violation of the relevant laws would result in significant penalties. This was a stark contrast to the situation in Zimbabwe, where the laws were far less strict and rarely enforced.

The drive home was a pleasurable one. Nick and Rachel conversed together easily and naturally. Their conversation was liberally scattered with flirtatious comments and they both enjoyed the sexual inuendoes that underlay much of the banter between them.

When they arrived home, Rachel unlocked the front door. There was an awkward moment between them as they stood in the reception hall. Nick's natural instinct was to give Rachel a long, passionate kiss good night. However, he was still a little unsure of himself in this new environment, where so much was different to what he knew from back home.

Rachel ended his dilemma when she pecked him on the cheek and said goodnight.

"Good night, Nick. What a lovely evening. Thank you so much. I'll see you later." With that, she floated upstairs to her bedroom.

Nick climbed the stairs to his bedroom. He got undressed and, as was his habit, put on his sleeping shorts and vest and climbed beneath the duvet. The night was cold, and it took Nick several minutes until he was warm.

He was pondering what Rachel had meant when she had said '*I will see you later.*' His imagination was running hot, but even so, he was tired and quickly dropped off to sleep. But his sleep was shallow, and his dreams were punctuated by sweet thoughts of Rachel's tender touches and her flirtatious comments.

Some hours later, Nick became aware of a rustling noise in his bedroom. As his sleep had only been shallow, it only took him a moment to open his eyes and to realise that Rachel was in the room. He had not fully drawn the curtains when he had got back to his room after the party. The moon was full that night, and its soft-muted light meant that his room was not shrouded in darkness. In the dim light, the white lace of Rachel's nightie was unmistakeable, as was the silhouette of her sensual figure beneath the nightie.

Nick's breath caught in his chest as he realised what was happening.

He drew back the corner of his duvet, and in a soft voice said, "You are gorgeous. Please climb in."

Rachel snuggled in with him and Nick took her into his arms. She gave herself to him completely and their first kiss was a long passionate one. As they explored each other's bodies, their desire for one another grew. Rachel could feel Nick's hardness against her thigh, and she tilted her pelvis invitingly towards him.

Nick was a considerate lover, taking his time to explore her body and allowing them to both enjoy the tantalising foreplay.

Then they began to move together in a slow, sensual rhythm, which gradually increased in intensity.

Rachel felt herself getting closer and closer to the edge. She wanted Nick to take her there, to push her over, but he held back. The anticipation was almost too much to bear, but she savoured the sensation of him moving deep inside her.

Finally, Rachel's body couldn't take it any longer, and she climaxed in Nick's arms. He held her tightly, as she rode the wave of pleasure, and then he released himself inside her.

Then it was over. They were both spent, and they fell back on the bed exhausted.

"That was wonderful," said Nick.

"Yes," whispered Rachel. She took Nick's hand in hers, and they lay like that in silence for a few moments. "I think I just may fall for you Mr Sinclair," she said. And she meant it.

"Well, that goes for me as well, Miss Dixon," Nick chuckled. "You certainly are one in a million. I cannot believe my luck in having met someone as wonderful as you, and so soon."

They lay quietly in each other's arms, fully gratified and content. There was no need for either of them to say anything — they understood that words were unnecessary. Their closeness enveloped them completely, and that was all they needed.

Nick could have remained like that for the rest of the night. However, Rachel knew that by coming to Nick so soon in their relationship, and while in her parents' house, she had broken a few unwritten family rules.

She whispered, "Nick, thank you for coming into my life. But I better get back to my room. My dad is an early riser, and I wouldn't want him to find us together in your bed. Sleep tight."

With that she gave him a tight hug, slipped on her nightie, and left his room.

Chapter 7 – Hello Scotland

It was four days later, and Nick had just said goodbye to Rachel and boarded his train to Edinburgh. The days since they had consummated their relationship had flown by in a blur. They were both in a state of euphoria, completely captivated by each other. However, since their relationship remained undeclared to anyone else, they hadn't been able to openly express their feelings in public.

In some ways, this secrecy heightened the thrill of their rapidly developing feelings for each other. Whenever possible, they would sit together, and when their legs, feet, or hands touched, a tingle of anticipation flickered between them. On the rare occasions they were alone, they embraced in tender, ardent hugs, filled with expectation. Even their brief kisses were charged with desire.

As much as Nick and Rachel tried to keep their emotions in check around others, Rachel's mother, Linda, quickly sensed the sparks flying between them. She shared her suspicions with her husband, Stuart, the day before at breakfast. To her surprise, he had noticed the same. Agreeing, he remarked, "Let's hope their relationship develops into something more solid. But with Nick going to Scotland, it's going to be difficult."

Rachel had driven Nick to King's Cross Station in London, from where he would catch the express train to Waverley Station in Edinburgh. During the drive, Rachel was quiet, and Nick sensed her apprehension about what the future held for them. He reached out and placed his hand on her thigh.

"Rachel, darling, I know me leaving for university so soon after we met is going to be tough for you. It's tough for me, too. I've fallen for you in a big way, and I sense you feel the same way."

Rachel placed her hand on top of his, giving it a gentle squeeze.

Nick continued, "I promise I'll keep in regular touch. The phone will be easiest, but I'll try to get back to London every couple of months. Hopefully, you can come to Edinburgh, too. I know long-distance relationships are hard, but I still can't believe how lucky I am to have met someone as wonderful as you. I'm not going to let you slip away. I hope you believe me."

Rachel took her eyes off the road for a second, leaned over, and kissed him gently on the cheek.

"Thank you," she said. "You know what they say, absence makes the heart grow fonder. It won't be easy, but you're definitely worth it."

At the station, they said their farewells. Tears streamed down Rachel's cheeks, and even Nick's eyes glistened.

Nick pulled Rachel close, whispering in her ear, "The time will fly by, and we'll talk often. Every time we meet, the pain of us being apart will be swept away by the joy of us being together again."

They clung tightly for a moment before Nick gently let her go. He hauled his suitcase onto the train and found his seat, his heart heavy as a few more tears ran down his cheeks.

He reached into his trouser pocket and felt the velvet pouch containing his Bronze Cross of Rhodesia.

"Everything's going to be just fine," he murmured to himself.

His breathing steadied, and his eyes dried. He still couldn't believe his luck at meeting someone like Rachel so soon after arriving in the UK.

As the train began its journey, his thoughts turned to what lay ahead. The trip to Edinburgh would take about five hours. Once there, he would take a taxi to the Pollock Halls of Residence, his home for the first year. The taxi ride would take about fifteen minutes, and Nick had calculated that, if the train ran on time, he'd be settled into his room by 6:30 pm.

In his research, he had learned that the halls of residence were about a 20-minute walk from George Square, where the business school was located. He figured the daily walk would be good for him and help him stay fit.

Nick closed his eyes and imagined what life as a *'uni student'* would be like over the next four years. But his reflections were frequently interrupted by sweet thoughts of Rachel. These memories softened his features and brought a smile to his lips.

Soon, he was peacefully dozing.

Chapter 8 – The early life of Sipho Pukelo

Timeline - 1950s to 1970s

You will remember that Corporal Pukelo was the MAG[53] gunner who had been involved with Nick in the firefight with a gang of guerrillas in the Chimanimani Mountains in June 1979. During the firefight, Corporal Pukelo had killed the terrorists' stick commander with a burst of fire from his machine gun. The slaying of the stick commander in such a dramatic manner had catapulted Corporal Pukelo's reputation amongst the other 3RAR[54] troops to unheralded heights.

Corporal Pukelo was from the Ndebele tribe. This tribe was an offshoot of the famous Zulu imperial tribe. The Ndebele tribe had been founded by a man called Mzilikazi Khumalo in the early 19th century when he, together with his followers, had split from the main Zulu tribe in South Africa and moved northwards to settle in the present-day Matabeleland province of Zimbabwe.

After King Mzilikazi's death in 1868, a bitter and bloody dispute had erupted as to which of his many sons should be the successor to the throne. The crown had initially been offered to one of King Mzilikazi's sons from an inferior wife. This son's name was Lobengula Khumalo.

However, one of King Mzilikazi's favoured chiefs, Mbiko Masuku, had disputed Lobengula Khumalo's ascension to the throne. Masuku had preferred Lobengula's half and elder brother, Nkulumana Khumalo, as

---

[53] The Belgian designed Fabrique Nationale 7.62mm general-purpose machine gun. The MAG was standard issue for the Rhodesian Security Forces.
[54] 3rd Battalion of Rhodesian African Rifles.

the successor. However, Nkulumana Khumalo had been banished back to Zululand by King Mzilikazi and could not be found at the time of Mzilikazi's death.

After two years of bloody conflict, Lobengula's claim to the throne prevailed and he was crowned the second king of the Ndebele nation in 1870.

The Ndebele are a proud and striking people, deeply rooted in their warrior heritage. Historically, they have viewed the larger Shona tribe with disdain, owing to the Shona's more peaceful, subsistence farming traditions. However, both tribes were brought together within the same newly formed borders when the colonial powers redrew the map of central and southern Africa during the Scramble for Africa in the late 19th century. This artificial amalgamation of tribes would backfire on the Ndebele nation during the country's first universal franchise elections in February 1980, as they found themselves significantly outnumbered in an electoral sense by the Shona under *the one-man-one-vote* system.

Corporal Pukelo had been born at the Inyathi Mission on 23rd January 1954. The day of his birth was seen as being especially auspicious by his parents, Mandla[55] and Nandi[56] Pukelo, as it occurred 60 years to the day after the death of King Lobengula[57].

Mandla and Nandi had been so thrilled at the timing of their son's birth that they gave him the name Sipho which means *Gift*.

The Inyathi Mission, where Sipho[58] was born, is situated approximately 100 kilometres north-east of Bulawayo, the capital of Matabeleland and the country's second-largest city.

The Mission had been established by Reverend Robert Moffat in 1859. Robert Moffat was a member of the London Missionary Society, which

---

[55] Mandla is a Ndebele boy's name meaning Power and Strength.
[56] Nandi is a Ndebele girl's name meaning Sweetness.
[57] King Lobengula Khumalo was the second king of the Ndebele nation. His assumed date of death is 23rd January 1894 near Bulawayo.
[58] Sipho is a Ndebele boy's name meaning Gift.

had been established in England at the end of the 18th century, with the aim of spreading the knowledge of Christ among heathen and unenlightened nations.

In terms of spreading the Christian message, Inyati Mission was an abject failure. However, in terms of its contribution to other aspects of local life at the Mission, it was a resounding success.

This was especially so in the field of education. In 1920 the Mission had established a school for boys. Initially, the school only offered basic primary school education, but in the 1950s, a secondary school was added.

Mandla was initially employed at the school as a garden labourer. However, he was a diligent and honest worker who quickly endeared himself to the Mission's administrators. By the time Sipho was born, Mandla was in charge of all grounds maintenance work as well as looking after much of the Mission's non-technical maintenance work. His young wife, Nandi, was also employed at the Mission where she worked in the kitchen as a kitchen hand.

Mandla and Nandi initially lived in the Mission compound in a traditional African round hut made from mud with a thatched peaked conical roof. However, after Sipho's birth and as result of the higher income that Mandla and Nandi were by then earning, Mandla had been able to finance the building of a modest two-roomed concrete block house with a corrugated iron roof and concrete floor.

The house did not have electricity or plumbed water, but it was located close to the village borehole, which had never run dry, and which included a well-maintained hand-operated water pump. So, by the standards of black rural communities at that time, their house would have been regarded as quite grand by the local community.

As a young boy, Sipho attended the Mission's primary school where he mixed with the white children of local miners and farmers as well as with the local black children. In those days, while school attendance was compulsory for white children, this was not the case for black children. In addition, while the Rhodesian Government provided ample funds for white education, this was not the case for black education, which was poorly funded. Consequently, considerable responsibility for black education fell on the altruistic efforts of missions and other charitable organisations.

Government oversight of the mission and charitable educational sectors was however scant and inadequate. On the one hand, this was a problem for these sectors when it came to funding and allocation of resources but, on the other hand, it did mean that the sectors had significant latitude in terms of the subjects they taught and the curricula that they implemented.

So, while the Rhodesian Government had stipulated that the education to be offered to black schoolboys was to be practical in nature so as to prepare pupils for work as labourers in the agriculture, mining or construction sectors, this mandate was often ignored by the administrators of mission schools.

This was certainly the case at the Inyathi Mission School, where black and white pupils were largely taught the same subjects and classes were not segregated on racial grounds.

Sipho was a bright and likeable child. His mother and father were both well-respected at the Mission, and so it was not surprising that Sipho's teachers paid special attention to him, and this helped him to excel at school.

After successfully completing primary school, Sipho was granted a place at the Mission's secondary school. In those days, such an achievement was quite rare for black children, making his commencement at secondary school a proud occasion for his parents.

Head or senior teachers at mission schools were often expatriates from England or other developed countries. Driven by a mission-oriented mindset, they aimed not only to spread the Christian message but also to improve the lives and prospects of their students. Concepts of racial separation and subjugation were generally frowned upon by such teachers. As a result, the culture at these mission schools was often conducive to fostering black revolutionary consciousness.

Consequently, the secondary school at Inyathi Mission became a formidable foundation for nurturing black African nationalism in the 1960s. Moreover, this vulnerability remained largely unnoticed by the distant Rhodesian Government until the mid-1970s.

Sipho was about 15 when he first encountered the concept of black nationalism and the idea of resisting the prevailing status quo, which was so blatantly tilted in favour of the white-ruling class.

The defining incident had occurred in the first term of 1969 after a soccer match against another mission school, which was located in the Matopos area south of Bulawayo.

Sipho had scored the winning goal and was celebrating the win with his teammates outside the Mission's village store. Close to the village store, there was a group of five or six boys who were listening earnestly to a couple of young men who were not from the local area. These young men were talking excitedly about a bright new future for the country, which they said was going to be renamed Zimbabwe. This new country would be ruled and governed by black people. Black people would own the farms and businesses and live in the fancy houses in Salisbury[59] and Bulawayo. Good schooling and medical facilities would exist throughout the country, and these would provide services to both black and white people.

The young men stated that they had travelled from Bulawayo to the Mission and would return in about four weeks to inform the schoolboys about what they needed to do to be part of the country's exciting new future.

That night, during the family's evening meal, Sipho recounted the whole episode to Mandla and Nandi. Both parents listened carefully to Sipho's story without interrupting him or questioning him.

---

[59] The capital of Rhodesia. Its name was changed to Harare in April 1982.

This was not the first time Mandla had heard such a story as this. Indeed, over the last year or so, stories or reports such as these were being heard by Mandala quite often.

Following Sipho's narration of the incident, Mandla said, "So Sipho, what do you make of the things that these men have told you? Do you think they are telling the truth?"

Sipho replied, "Ubaba[60], I don't know what to make of them. Obviously, what they are saying sounds attractive. I would love to be able to go to university, to be able to buy a car, and to own a farm. But that is not the life I know. If it was so easy, why has it not happened before now?"

Mandla paused for a few seconds. The pause was long enough to ensure he had the full attention of both Sipho and Nandi.

"Sipho, my only son, thank you for telling me these things. A father cannot know of such things if his children do not share them with him. Indeed, I have heard similar stories in other places. But I want you to know that what these young men are telling you is all lies.

"These men are working for skellums[61] who live in the big cities. They are as dangerous as inyokas[62]. Do not listen to the lies that their messengers are telling you. You are a bright boy who has done so well in school. Your mother and I are both so proud of you. If you continue to study hard, you will get a good job, marry well, and have children of your own. You will be able to care for Nandi and myself when we grow old, as is your duty as our eldest and only son."

No more on this subject was spoken that night. However, it was a matter on which Sipho pondered much in the following days.

---

[60] Ubaba is the Ndebele word for father.
[61] Skellum is a local word meaning rogue or troublemaker.
[62] Inyoka is the Ndebele word for snake or serpent.

Chapter 9 – Sipho learns about pre-UDI politics

Timeline – 1969

Sipho's[63] meeting with the two men from Bulawayo and his subsequent discussion about the incident with his father made a deep impression on him. Although he was unsure why, he felt that this chance encounter was significant and would lead him to make decisions that would have a lasting impact on his life.

Over the next couple of weeks, he began discussing the meeting with other boys from the Mission School. To his surprise, many of the black boys, particularly those older than him, were quite well-informed about the concepts the two strangers had mentioned. In contrast, almost none of the white boys he spoke to had any understanding of what he was talking about.

Sipho had learnt about Rhodesia's UDI[64] at school. He had also heard about the rise in African nationalism since then. However, he had little in-depth knowledge of why these events had occurred and was keen to learn more.

Fortunately for him, he had a good relationship with most of his teachers at school and especially with Mr Godfrey Miller, his history teacher for the last two years. Mr Miller's teaching had focused primarily on the First and Second World Wars. His lessons on these two global conflicts had always been thought-provoking and sprinkled

---

[63] Sipho is a Ndebele boy's name meaning Gift.

[64] Unilateral Declaration of Independence. The Government of Rhodesia declared UDI from Britain on 11th November 1965.

with many interesting stories and illustrations. Sipho was therefore sure that Mr Miller would be able to help him better understand the events that had led to Rhodesia's UDI, and the subsequent rise in African nationalism.

One day, after their weekly history class, Sipho asked Mr Miller if he had some time to discuss some matters that were troubling him.

"Of course," said Mr Miller. "In fact, I have some time now. So, what is it that you want to know?"

"Well, Sir," said Sipho, "I am trying to understand why Rhodesia declared independence from the UK in 1965. Can you explain it to me?"

"Hmm," said Mr Miller. "That's quite a complex question, but I'll do my best. You may remember from your school lessons that Rhodesia used to be known as Southern Rhodesia. At that time, it was a self-governing colony, meaning it could make most decisions without consulting the UK, except for constitutional changes.

"The country had been granted this status in 1923. Before then, the country was administered by the British South Africa Company, which was founded by Cecil John Rhodes. While Rhodes is often regarded as the founder of Southern Rhodesia, it's important to remember that the land was inhabited by the Shona, Ndebele, and other tribes long before British colonisation."

Mr Miller continued, "In August 1953, Southern Rhodesia joined Northern Rhodesia, now Zambia, and Nyasaland, now Malawi, to form the Federation of Rhodesia and Nyasaland, or simply the Federation[65]. The aim of the Federation was to promote economic development and create a multi-racial society, thereby distinguishing itself from South

---

[65] The Federation of Rhodesia and Nyasaland was a colonial federation that consisted of three southern African territories, namely the self-governing British colony of Southern Rhodesia and the British protectorates of Northern Rhodesia and Nyasaland. It existed between 1953 and 1963.

Africa that had adopted its apartheid[66] policies shortly after the Second World War. However, the Federation dissolved by the end of 1963."

"I knew about the Federation but didn't realise it only lasted ten years. Why did it end?" asked Sipho.

"Good question," replied Mr Miller. "While the Federation was economically successful, many local people, particularly the black populations in Northern Rhodesia and Nyasaland, were suspicious of it. They believed it was a mechanism to strengthen white minority control in Southern Rhodesia.

"By 1963, many European colonial powers had already granted full independence to their African colonies, and the British government itself had become increasingly supportive of decolonisation. Consequently, once the Federation dissolved, its member countries were eager for their own freedom from British rule. In fact, within a year of the Federation ending, both Northern Rhodesia[67] and Nyasaland[68] gained independence from Britain."

"What about Southern Rhodesia then?" asked Sipho.

"After the Federation dissolved, Southern Rhodesia was renamed Rhodesia. The Rhodesian government believed it would quickly be granted full independence, a belief based on undertakings made by the UK during the Federation's dissolution talks and the fact that the country had been a self-governing colony for 40 years. The Rhodesian Government considered the country the most prosperous and developed region in southern Africa after South Africa, reasoning that

---

[66] Apartheid is the Afrikaans word for apartness. It was a system of institutionalised racial segregation that existed in South Africa and South West Africa (now Namibia) from 1948 to the early 1990s.
[67] Northern Rhodesia became independent from the United Kingdom on 24th October 1964 and renamed itself Zambia.
[68] Nyasaland became independent from British rule on 6th July 1964 and renamed itself Malawi.

if any country was capable of self-governance, it was Rhodesia, having effectively done so for the past 40 years."

Mr Miller paused. "However, after the Federation ended, the white voting public in Rhodesia became increasingly extreme in their political views. They feared that the UK would link independence to the principle of *one-man-one-vote*, which had been applied in other newly independent African countries during the 1950s and 60s, often with disastrous consequences. A recent example was Kenya, which gained independence in 1963. The ten years leading up to Kenya's independence had been particularly violent, largely due to the Mau Mau Rebellion[69]. Many white Kenyans left during that time and resettled in Rhodesia, and they reinforced the belief that independence based on *one-man-one-vote* would lead to instability, as had happened in Kenya."

"I see," said Sipho. "But why do you think the UK was so keen on granting independence to its former African colonies and requiring them to adopt the principle of *one-man-one-vote*?"

"That's a complex topic," Mr Miller replied. "I think the main reason was probably because during the Second World War global opinions had shifted away from colonialism. During the war, many Africans were exposed to new ideas of self-governance, making it harder for the colonial powers to maintain control of their colonies afterward. Additionally, the war left European powers financially strained, with significant manpower shortages due to heavy fatalities and casualties during the war. Moreover, the United States generally supported national self-determination and pressured the UK and other colonial powers to expedite their decolonisation processes. All these factors empowered African nationalists to push for quicker decolonisation."

---

[69] The Mau Mau Rebellion was a war in Kenya between the British authorities and some of the local Kenyan tribes who opposed the white colonial settlers. The Rebellion officially lasted from 1952 to 1960 but in reality, continued until Kenya became independent on 12th December 1963.

Sipho frowned. "So, if that happened in many other African countries, why didn't it happen here, in Rhodesia?"

"Another good question," Mr Miller said. "General elections were held in December 1962, and these were won by the Rhodesian Front, which replaced the ruling United Federal Party. The RF[70] was initially led by Winston Field, but less than 16 months later, the RF lost confidence[71] in him and replaced him with Ian Smith. Smith strongly opposed the principle of *one-man-one-vote*, preferring instead to keep the existing voting system that granted voting rights based on a person's financial and educational qualifications."

"But that seems fair to me," commented Sipho.

"On the surface, it might appear so," Mr Miller replied. "However, the 1961 Constitution, which outlined the voting system, was problematic. While the financial and educational requirements were lowered, thereby increasing the number of eligible black voters, it would take decades before blacks could challenge white dominance. This meant that blacks would remain subordinate for a long time."

Mr Miller continued, "The other thing to remember is that, at the time of the referendum, there were about 84,000 registered voters, most of whom were white. Approximately 75% of registered voters participated in the referendum, and of those, only about 65% voted in favour of the new Constitution. This represented less than half of the registered voters. Therefore, it can be argued that only about half of the existing voters, most of whom were white, supported keeping the existing qualified voting system. More importantly, almost all black people were opposed to retaining the current voting system. As black individuals were generally ineligible to vote, it is difficult to determine the strength of their opposition to the proposed changes. However, the main black political party at that time, the NDP[72], claimed to

---

[70] Rhodesian Front.
[71] No confidence vote was held on 2nd April 1964.
[72] National Democratic Party.

represent about 500,000 black adults and alleged that less than 0.2% of its supporters were in favour of retaining the current system."

Sipho remarked, "If the UK was involved in negotiating the proposed new Constitution, I'm surprised it didn't accept the vote of the people, even though most of them were white."

"Good point," Mr Miller said. "However, Britain insisted that the proposed Constitution had to be accepted by the whole country, not just those eligible to vote. They didn't consider the 1961 referendum to be representative of the country's overall opinion, a view reinforced by the black nationalist parties' rejection of it, which complicated matters for the Rhodesian Government.

"To try and secure Britain's acceptance of the Constitution, Ian Smith proposed a new referendum in 1964 to gauge public opinion. He suggested that white and urban black opinion could be gauged through a general referendum of registered voters, while rural black views could be obtained through a national indaba[73] of chiefs and headmen.

"The British Prime Minister at the time, Sir Alec Douglas-Home of the Conservative Party, told Smith that while this proposal satisfied him personally, he couldn't accept it until after the UK's general elections, which were due in October 1964. Assuming his Conservative Party won, Sir Alec assured Ian Smith that his government would accept the indaba process. Moreover, if the indaba process was successful, Britain would grant Rhodesia independence within a year."

Mr Miller puffed on his cigarette and continued, "In October and November, Ian Smith held several indabas with the tribal chiefs and headmen to gauge their views on the 1961 Constitution. Although the chiefs and headmen voted in favour of the Constitution, the black nationalist parties dismissed the indabas as an accurate representation of the black community's views.

---

[73] An indaba was the name given by the local tribespeople to collective meetings of chiefs and headmen.

"In Britain's general election, Harold Wilson's Labour Party defeated Sir Alec Douglas-Home's Conservative Party, resulting in Wilson becoming Prime Minister. He adopted a much tougher stance on Rhodesia than Sir Alec and refused to be bound by any verbal promises made by his predecessor."

Mr Miller continued, "Ian Smith argued that the instability in newly independent African nations showed that black leaders weren't ready to govern. He also highlighted Rhodesia's contributions in both world wars and suggested that Rhodesia, together with the Portuguese administration in Mozambique and South Africa, could form an anti-communist alliance in southern Africa that which would benefit Britain and its allies. He was furious when these arguments were dismissed out of hand by Harold Wilson."

Sipho chuckled. "I understand now why some of the white boys at school have '*I hate Wilson*' stickers on their school cases."

They both laughed.

Mr Miller glanced at his watch. "Goodness, nearly an hour has passed. I've enjoyed our conversation, but we'll have to continue another day. I have a staff meeting."

"Thank you, Sir," said Sipho. "Perhaps next time you can tell me more about what happened in November 1965 and about Joshua Nkomo and the other black nationalist leaders."

Chapter 10 – Sipho learns about UDI

Sipho's[74] quest to find out more about the events leading up to UDI[75] and immediately thereafter continued in earnest following his meeting with Mr Miller.

On the day after the meeting, Sipho visited the school library to see what more he could learn there. To his surprise, there was very little information in the library about these events. However, fortunately for him, the school did have quite an extensive collection of back editions from the two leading newspapers in the country at that time - *The Chronicle*[76] and *The Rhodesia Herald*[77].

The school prefect who was in charge of the library gave him access to copies of the editions from Friday, 12th November 1965 of both newspapers. This was the day immediately after UDI.

The headlines in *The Chronicle* read '**Independence is Proclaimed**,' and the opening paragraph of the lead article read as follows: -

'Rhodesia has become independent. The Prime Minister, Mr Ian Smith, made the announcement in a 20-minute radio broadcast to the nation at 1:15 pm. Britain has stated that Rhodesia's independence has been declared illegally and economic sanctions have been imposed. Several

---

[74] Sipho is a Ndebele boy's name meaning Gift.

[75] Unilateral Declaration of Independence. The Government of Rhodesia declared UDI from Britain on 11th November 1965.

[76] *The Chronicle* was published in Bulawayo and mostly reported on news affecting the Matabeleland area in the south of the country. It was first published in 1894.

[77] *The Rhodesia Herald* is the country's foremost national paper. Its origins date back to 1891.

countries have said that they will not recognise the Rhodesian Government.'

The article then went on to discuss Britain banning future purchases of tobacco from the country, the Rhodesian Government implementing tougher controls on cash and trade and introducing press censorship, and Zambia declaring a state of emergency.

The headlines and lead article in *The Rhodesia Herald* were very similar.

Sipho still had vivid memories of listening to the declaration of independence on the radio as a young boy, a little over three and a half years ago. However, as he re-read the articles in both newspapers, he now had a much better appreciation of how significant this event was, as well as a greater understanding of the political events leading up to UDI. He realised that this was due to the insight and information that Mr Miller had given him the day before.

He was very much looking forward to their follow-up meeting.

Sipho did not have long to wait, as a few days later Mr Miller asked him if he would like to continue the discussions they had started the week before.

"Yes, please Sir," replied Sipho. "Since we last met, I have managed to get copies of the 12th November 1965 copies of both *The Chronicle* and *The Rhodesia Herald*. I have read them both with much interest. You have taught me so much and I am looking forward to learning more."

Mr Miller smiled to himself. He was amazed at how keen Sipho was, and at how proactive he had been, in finding out more information himself. "The boy is bright," he thought. "He is going to go a long way."

"Well, take a seat boy," said Mr Miller. "So, as you will have read in the newspapers, Ian Smith declared independence from the UK on Thursday, 11th November 1965. When he addressed the nation over the radio, he stated that independence had been declared because it had become clear to him that the British Government was stringing Rhodesia along, with no real intention of arriving at a solution that

Smith's Government could accept. He stated that it would be wrong to allow Rhodesia to continue drifting in its present state of paralysis, which was causing a lot of anxiety and problems for all Rhodesians.

"Mr. Smith stressed that the declaration of independence would not diminish opportunities for black people in the country to advance themselves. He assured them that his government would continue to strive for racial harmony and provide every chance for black citizens to succeed. While he commented on the potential effects of sanctions on the country's economy, he expressed confidence that the nation would adapt and innovate to overcome any short-term difficulties they might cause.

"I remember him asking the country to recall its pioneering spirit, which had always held it in good stead and would continue to do so. He ended his address by declaring that now was the time for the country to stand up for what it believed to be right, whatever the consequences, and that the country needed to make a stand for the preservation of justice, civilisation, and Christianity."

"So, Sir, did you agree with him?" asked Sipho.

Mr Miller paused as he thought about his answer. Then he said, "I certainly can understand why Smith declared independence. The British Government, especially under the prime ministership of Harold Wilson, had made it abundantly clear that independence under the provisions of the 1961 Constitution was not acceptable. At the same time, the electorate in Rhodesia, which remember, was predominantly white, had made it clear that they were not yet ready to accept the principle of *one-man-one-vote*. I think Harold Wilson had wrongly assumed that Ian Smith would not press ahead with his threat of declaring independence. At the same time, I think Ian Smith had wrongly assumed that significantly greater concessions would be forthcoming from the British Government, especially after the successful outcomes from the indabas[78] that Smith had held in late

---

[78] An indaba was the name given by the local tribespeople to collective meetings of chiefs and headmen

1964. I also believe that Ian Smith had no idea about how much influence the leaders of the black nationalist parties had already gained by 1965.

"However, while I understand the reasons why the Rhodesian Government declared independence, that does not necessarily mean that I agreed with the decision at the time it was made. Certainly, I do not agree with it now. Reflecting on how I felt at that time, I think I probably was more in favour of the decision than against it. I guess I believed Ian Smith when he said that he and his government were committed to seeing the black people make real progress in the country. However, events since November 1965 have not demonstrated this, have they? And now I am really concerned that the country is on a trajectory which will ultimately lead to civil war — both white against black and tribe against tribe. I am also fearful of how countries like Russia and China might use the current situation in the country to their advantage."

Sipho frowned and looked confused. "I am not sure I understand," he said.

"Well," said Mr Miller, "if the black people of the country are really going to advance and eventually govern the country, they not only need to be given educational and economic opportunities, but they also must be allowed to have a political voice. And that voice needs to be their voice, and not a voice which will only be allowed if it is acceptable to the white people.

"Ever since the late 1950s, the history of the Rhodesian Government has been to ban any black party[79] that was opposed to the white ruling party. It is obvious that any black party is going to be opposed to the white ruling party because, generally, black political parties will be

---

[79] The Southern Rhodesia African National Congress ('SRANC') was banned in 1959. At the time of its banning, Joshua Nkomo was its chairman. The National Democratic Party ('NDP') was formed in January 1960 by Joshua Nkomo and others from the banned SRANC. It was subsequently banned in December 1961. Following the banning of NDP, Joshua Nkomo immediately formed the Zimbabwe African Peoples Union ('ZAPU'). ZAPU was subsequently banned in September 1962.

wanting black people to advance as quickly as possible, while white political parties will want any such advancement to be as slow as possible, so as not to weaken their hold on power.

"History, however, has shown us that whenever political parties like these are banned, their leaders become more radical. And more worrying, the black party members themselves start to feel that the only way to make progress is to move away from peaceful dialogue. They then move towards more militant and violent ways of protesting.

"All this leads to a build up of unrest in the country. This unrest is first directed against the government, which is clearly identified as being white. But ultimately, I fear that the unrest will be directed against all white people, regardless of what they may think, as it is they who are directly benefitting from the government's policies. And of course, there are plenty of mischievous countries in the world that are more than willing to use the build up of unrest to their own advantage — and by this, I mean countries like Russia, China, North Korea, and Cuba."

"I understand that," said Sipho. "I can also understand how this might lead to civil war between the black and white people. But I don't understand why you are fearful that it might also lead to civil war between different tribes in the country. Can you explain that?"

"Well," said Mr. Miller, "I suppose that statement is more speculation on my part, but it's based on my understanding of African history and the nature of power struggles on the continent. Currently, there is undoubtedly a power struggle in this country. Most people view it as a conflict between black and white, but I believe it goes deeper than that. Examining the recent history of many African nations, you'll see that post-independence problems often stem from tribal differences rather than solely from racial tensions.

"As you know, the two major tribes in the country are the Ndebele and the Shona. Historically these two tribes have had very different histories. That history shows us that the two tribes do not really get on and have often been at war with one another.

"The history of your tribe, the northern Ndebele, can be traced back to the central Nguni tribe, who are Zulu-speaking. The growth and strength of the Zulu nation were founded on its military organisation and skills, particularly during the reigns of King Shaka and his successors, King Mzilikazi and King Lobengula. The northern Ndebele nation has a long history of military conquests, often subjugating other tribes and bringing them under its rule."

Sipho smiled and said, "I have often heard my father and other elders talk with pride of their military history. I think one day I would like to be a soldier. That would bring much honour to my father."

"Well, that is another matter," said Mr Miller. "But now let's look at the Shona tribe. The Shona people are a Bantu ethnic group. They were not organised on military grounds like the Zulu or Ndebele nations. For them, trading, mining, pottery, dancing, subsistence farming, and herding goats and cattle were important activities. In addition, because of their gentler nature, they were relatively easy targets for warring nations like the Ndebele, who quite often took Shona people into slavery."

"So, are you saying that the Ndebele and Shona nations will not be able to live together?" asked Sipho.

"No, I am not necessarily saying that," Mr Miller replied. "However, we should remember that the Ndebele and Shona nations were only brought together geographically in 1891 during the Scramble for Africa. Over the last 80 years, their relations have been significantly influenced by the moderating control of the white government. Additionally, both tribes have had to focus more on how to interact with their colonial masters rather than on their inter-tribal relations. When the country's voting system becomes more democratic, as I am certain it will, I'm unsure how these two tribes will work together in governance, especially given their recent history."

He thought for a couple of moments, and then, in a solemn and grave voice, said, "We should also remember that most of the country's black political leaders, including Joshua Nkomo, Robert Mugabe, Ndabaningi Sithole, Edgar Tekere, and Leopald Takawira, have all been imprisoned or detained by the Smith government under its anti-terrorism laws. The Smith government believes that incarcerating them will eliminate their influence.

"But I don't think that is the case. I think that imprisoning these leaders has forced the black parties that they represent, that is ZAPU[80] and ZANU[81], to simply go underground. Now that these parties have gone underground, it will make it very difficult for the government to monitor their influence.

"So, Sipho, I think the next 10 to 20 years in the country are going to be extremely interesting. At the end of that period, I doubt whether white people will have much influence at all. It is far more difficult to predict how much influence the Ndebele nation will have compared to the Shona nation. It would be nice to think that their tribal differences will not matter. But somehow, I do not think that will be the case."

Sipho nodded his head in agreement. "Thank you so much Sir," he said. "You have taught me a great deal and given me much to think about."

---

[80] Zimbabwe African Peoples Union ('ZAPU') was formed by Joshua Nkomo in late 1961 and was subsequently banned in September 1962

[81] Zimbabwe African National Union ('ZANU') was formed on 8 August 1963 when Ndabaningi Sithole, Henry Hamadziripi, Mukudzei Midzi, Herbert Chitepo, Edgar Tekere, and Leopold Takawira decided to split from ZAPU. ZANU itself was subsequently banned in August 1964.

Chapter 11 – Sipho learns about ZIPRA

There was a palpable sense of excitement and anticipation at Inyati Mission[82]. Rumour had it that the strangers who visited about four weeks earlier would be returning the next afternoon with exciting news. It was said that all young men interested in playing a significant role in the country's future should be at the village store at 2:30 pm.

The rumour mill in the black rural areas, colloquially known as the *bush telegraph*, was a fascinating phenomenon. Its uncanny accuracy and ability to reach only those who needed to know were remarkable. With no telephones and infrequent postal deliveries in the bush, it was hard to comprehend how it operated with such speed and precision. Yet, as expected, by 2:30 pm the next afternoon, the strangers from Bulawayo returned to the village store. They were surrounded by a crowd of eager young black teenagers, keen to hear what they had to say.

Amongst their number, was Sipho[83].

The young men from Bulawayo advised that the banned political party known as ZAPU[84] was flourishing, albeit that it was now operating underground. They said that ZAPU's leader, Joshua Nkomo, who had

---

[82] The Mission had been established by the Reverend Robert Moffat in 1859. It is situated some 75 kilometres north-north-east of Bulawayo. Moffat was a member of the London Missionary Society, which had been established in England with the aim of spreading the knowledge of Christ among heathen and unenlightened nations.
[83] Sipho is a Ndebele boy's name meaning Gift.
[84] Zimbabwe African Peoples Union ('ZAPU') was formed by Joshua Nkomo in late 1961 and was subsequently banned in September 1962.

been in detention at the Gonakudzingwa[85] Restriction Camp since 1964, was still directing operations through a complicated secret network of runners and message smugglers. Sipho learnt that the Restriction Camp was located in a remote south-eastern part of the country close to the Mozambican border, approximately 500 kilometres away and adjacent to the Gonarezhou[86] Game Reserve.

The Restriction Camp was reserved mainly for Ndebele political detainees. These detainees were not strictly prisoners, as generally they had not been found guilty of any crime. But they had been detained on the grounds of their potential to endanger public safety or public order. The nature of their detention meant that, compared to usual prison conditions, the detainees enjoyed more freedom of movement. In addition, formal supervision or oversight by government officials was scant with the only supervision coming from a little frontier police post called Vila Salazar[87] on the country's border with Mozambique.

This lack of supervision did not, however, mean that escape from the Restriction Camp was easy. The limited perimeter fencing did not present any major difficulties from a flight perspective. However, the camp's location in a particularly remote, hot, and dry part of the country, and in close proximity to the expansive Gonarezhou Game Reserve, presented escape challenges which few were prepared to risk. The game reserve was home to an abundance of large and dangerous animals such as elephants, buffalos, lions, and rhinos. And even if an escapee managed to avoid these dangers, the likelihood of dying from heat, thirst or malaria was very real.

At any one time, the number of detainees held at the camp could range from a few dozen to many hundreds. These numbers began

---

[85] This is a Shona word meaning where the banished ones sleep.
[86] Gonarezhou is a Shona word meaning *place of elephants*.
[87] The town is now named Sango.

rapidly increasing after the Rhodesian Government declared UDI[88] in November 1965.

Despite the large number of political detainees at the camp, its facilities and accommodation were basic and limited. However, the absence of formal supervision allowed the detained black nationalist leaders to meet regularly without much hindrance. During these gatherings, they discussed the political situation in the country. To help alleviate the pervasive boredom among the detainees, senior leaders like Joshua Nkomo held regular teachings on the principles of Marxism and Leninism.

The young men who were addressing the youth at the Mission were especially excited that ZAPU's leadership had recently decided on a change in tactics. They explained that the party had grown tired of its old political strategies, such as peaceful protests and labour strikes that had largely been ineffectual. So, the party was now moving towards a strategy of armed force and insurrection. They said that a military wing of ZAPU was in the process of being formed. The military wing would be called the Zimbabwe People's Revolutionary Army, or ZIPRA for short.

The young men explained that the leadership of ZIPRA[89] was now in the process of recruiting talented, young men who would be sent to Moscow for one year, where they would be trained in conventional and guerrilla warfare, intelligence gathering, and strategies on how to educate the Rhodesian public on the evils of the Rhodesian Government. When this announcement was made, there was a general ululation and clapping among the gathered throng.

The men from Bulawayo then invited anyone interested in joining ZIPRA to come forward with their names. This would allow for further discussions and arrangements to be made for the selected individuals to be transported, either by truck or bus, out of Rhodesia into Zambia,

---

[88] Unilateral Declaration of Independence. The Government of Rhodesia declared UDI from Britain on 11th November 1965.

[89] Zimbabwe People's Revolutionary Army. ZIPRA was the military wing of ZAPU.

before being flown to Moscow for training. Around a dozen young men stepped forward with their names.

Sipho, however, was not one of these. He knew that this was an important matter and potentially dangerous and that he should first discuss it with his parents.

Chapter 12 – Sipho shares his desire to join ZIPRA with his parents

Sipho[90] was troubled. He knew that he needed to talk to his parents about the visits by the men from Bulawayo and their attempts to recruit boys from the Mission to join ZIPRA[91]. He was also aware that even thinking about enlisting in ZIPRA was a serious criminal offence that could result in his imprisonment if his intentions were discovered.

Sipho also understood that his parents were not political people. Consequently, they did not concern themselves much with the current political developments in the country. They both enjoyed life on the Mission and were happy in their respective jobs. He was sure that they would not want to risk their current lives being disrupted.

A couple of days later, Sipho finally gathered the courage to bring up the matter with his parents during their evening meal of sadza[92], kale, pumpkin, relish, and goat meat. His father, Mandla[93], was in an especially good mood that night. The school had recently been gifted a tractor to help maintain the sports fields, and the Mission manager had informed Mandla that they would teach him to drive it and assist him in obtaining his driving licence.

---

[90] Sipho is a Ndebele boy's name meaning Gift.
[91] Zimbabwe People's Revolutionary Army. ZIPRA was the military wing of ZAPU.
[92] Sadza is a thickened porridge made with white maize meal. It is one of the staple foods in Zimbabwe.
[93] Mandla is a Ndebele boy's name meaning Power and Strength.

"The tractor is going to make such a big difference to the school and to my work," he explained to Nandi[94], his wife, and to Sipho. "I feel blessed that the Mission's bosses have sufficient confidence in me to teach me how to drive it and to help me get my driving licence. I am very fortunate."

Sipho decided that he would use his father's enthusiasm to test the waters regarding what he was thinking of doing. He clapped his hands together and said, "Ubaba[95], that is such good news. You have always worked hard for the Mission. I am sure you will be the best tractor driver in the whole of Matabeleland."

He paused for a few moments and then said, "Ubaba and Umama[96], as you know I am now 15 years old. I am no longer a child and I think it is time for me to start thinking about what I want to do when I leave school. Quite a lot of the boys in my class have also been asking themselves similar questions."

Mandla interrupted him and said, "Umfana[97], I am glad to hear of it. As you know, in the old Ndebele culture, it was customary for Ndebele boys to undergo circumcision in their teens, and that, only once a boy had been circumcised, was he allowed to join the King's army and to fully participate in tribal affairs. So, I am pleased that you are now thinking of adult things. Have you any idea of what you want to do when you finish school?"

Sipho hesitated for a moment. He was horrified at the thought of being circumcised as a young teenager and was glad that Ndebele customs had changed.

Once he had composed himself, he replied, "Well, Ubaba, you might remember that I told you and Umama some weeks ago about the men who had come to the Mission from Bulawayo and were telling some of

---

[94] Nandi is a Ndebele girl's name meaning Sweetness.
[95] Ubaba is the Ndebele word for father.
[96] Umama in the Ndebele word for mother.
[97] Umfana is the Ndebele word for son.

the boys at school about a new Rhodesia that would be governed and ruled by black people."

"Yes, I remember," said Mandla. "I also remember telling you that they were skellums[98] and that you should not believe anything they told you."

"Yes, that is right father," said Sipho. "However, after they visited, I did a lot of research to learn more about the country's government, why it declared independence from the British, and about black political parties like ZAPU[99]."

"That's a good thing my son," said Mandla. "It is wise to learn more about things that you don't understand. But has your research helped you decide what you want to do when you finish school?"

"Not yet," Sipho said. "But the men from Bulawayo have come back to the school and told us more about what's happening in the country. They said the leaders of ZAPU have been jailed by the government, and that ZAPU has been banned. But the work of ZAPU is still going on in secret. They said their leader, Joshua Nkomo, is getting ready for the party to take over the country. To do this, they're building an army called ZIPRA. It's going to be big and strong, and many soldiers are already training in Zambia. The Russians are helping with the training, and some men are even being sent to Moscow for further training. The men from Bulawayo were looking for people to join ZIPRA, to go to Zambia and Russia for training, and to then come back to fight and defeat the Rhodesian Army. Once that happens, they said there will be new elections where all black adults can vote, and a new black government will be in charge."

Mandla raised his hand to stop him. "Hold on a minute Sipho. I want you to think very carefully about what you have told those men from Bulawayo. Can you remember what you said to them?" asked Mandla.

---

[98] Skellum is a local word meaning rogue or troublemaker.
[99] Zimbabwe African People's Union.

"Nothing," replied Sipho. "I only listened. I didn't want to say anything until I had spoken with you and Umama. The men did ask for the names of any boys who were interested and some of the boys gave their names. But I did not."

"Well, that is a good thing," said Mandla. "I have heard that the police have got spies in ZAPU. If these spies hear the names of boys who are planning to join ZAPU or ZIPRA, they will give these names to the police. The police will then arrest the boys and their families who will be imprisoned for a long time."

Sipho was shocked. He hadn't thought about it like that before. After a few moments, he said, "Ubaba, you're right. You're very wise. But I've told you before that I want to be a *masodja*[100]. Joining ZIPRA would be hard, but I think it's something I want to do."

Nandi shrieked. "No," she cried. "You are still a young boy. You know nothing about being a *masodja*. It is too dangerous. The Rhodesian Army is too powerful. You will be killed, my son. That will leave your father and I broken-hearted. And if you join ZIPRA you will bring much shame and dishonour to your family."

"Is that what you think Ubaba?" asked Sipho.

There was a long pause whilst Mandla carefully considered Sipho's question. He was proud that Sipho was wanting to play a meaningful role in the future of the country, but he was also concerned that Sipho may be making wrong choices.

Eventually he replied, "My son, your mother is right. What you are thinking of doing is very dangerous, and I don't think you have thought things through well enough. The Russians are white – just like the British. What makes you think they will be more sympathetic to black people in Rhodesia than the British? Hardly any Russians speak English, and none of them speak Ndebele. How will they be able to teach you anything if they can't speak the languages you understand? They know very little about Africa and absolutely nothing about Rhodesia. I know

---

[100] *Masodja* is the Africanised word for soldier.

that there are some white Rhodesians who dislike black people and so treat them very badly. But most white people I've met seem to get on well with black people, and they are quite fair. Some of them speak Ndebele very well. And many of them have lived in the country for a long time now, so they understand quite a lot about our beliefs and customs."

Mandla paused to give Sipho time to think about what he had just said.

Then he continued, "Have you even thought about how you will get to Zambia. It is going to be very difficult for you to be smuggled out of the country by truck or bus into Zambia. There are roadblocks on all the main roads, and if you are found hiding in a truck you will be arrested. Even if you go by bus, how will you explain the reason you are travelling to Zambia? And it is too far to go there by foot. That would take many weeks. What would you eat and drink? Where would you sleep? I am sure you would be discovered by the authorities and arrested."

Sipho said nothing.

Mandla continued. "Even if you did make it to Zambia and received some training there, and maybe even some in Moscow, have you thought about what would happen when you returned? You would have to come back into the country as a terrorist. You will be hunted by the Rhodesian Security Forces. They are very powerful, and they receive a lot of help from South Africa and from the Portuguese in Mozambique. ZIPRA will be no match for them. And even if ZIPRA eventually became strong enough to force the white government to give power to the blacks, I am not sure how well the black people will be able to govern this country. As you know we are from the Ndebele tribe. But most black Rhodesians are from the Shona tribe. I don't think it will be easy for the Ndebele and Shona people to govern the country together."

Sipho sill remained silent.

Mandla waited for a few seconds and then continued. "If you really want to be become a *masodja*, then why don't you join a real army?

One that will give you a proper training. And one that people respect, unlike the skellums that make up ZIPRA."

"There is no such thing," retorted Sipho.

"Yes, there is," said Mandla. "If you really want to become a *masodja* then I think you should consider joining the RAR[101]. RAR soldiers are fine and brave men. They are well-trained and are respected by many black persons, and of course by all the white people. If you do some more research into the RAR, you will then be able to make a better decision rather than just listening to the rubbish that these skellums from Bulawayo have told you. In fact, I must insist that you do this first."

Sipho was silent for a long time. Indeed, Mandla thought he was not going to reply. However, he eventually said in a soft but firm voice, "Ubaba, I have heard what you have said. As always, you have shared many wise things. I will do as you wish. But if I do, then you and Umama must promise me that if I still decide to join ZIPRA, you will support me in my decision."

Mandla paused. Then he said, "It is too soon for me to make a promise like that my son. But we will definitely talk again once you have done your research into the RAR. And I think I can help you with that. I am quite friendly with Mr Jacob Mpofu, who is a teacher at the Mission School. He has a cousin who is a *masodja* with 1RAR[102] in Bulawayo. I am sure he would be able to help you learn about the RAR. I will speak to him about this. But, in the meantime, I want you to promise me and your mother that you will make no further mention of your meetings with these men from Bulawayo, or of your thoughts of joining ZIPRA, with anyone else. It is too dangerous to do so. There are lots of spies everywhere."

---

[101] Rhodesian African Rifles.
[102] 1st Battalion of Rhodesian African Rifles.

Mandla put his hand on Sipho's slumped shoulders. "Do you promise me?" he said.

"I promise Ubaba," said Sipho. "Thank you for listening to me and for your words of caution."

Michael Chalk

Chapter 13 – Sipho's parents try to dissuade him from joining ZIPRA

The night after Sipho's[103] unexpected announcement that he was considering joining Joshua Nkomo's army was incredibly difficult for Nandi[104]. Sleep was elusive, and when it finally came, her dreams were vivid and disturbing. She dreamt that Sipho had decided to walk to Zambia with two other would-be ZIPRA[105] recruits. They had become hopelessly lost in the Rhodesian bush for weeks, with barely any water and no food. Their situation grew desperate, and, in their struggle, they stumbled upon a remote African village. While the women of the village sympathised with their plight, the chief was not so kind. He reported their presence to the DA[106] of the TTL[107] where the village was located. Sipho and the other two men were arrested by the police and sent to the remand section of Khami Prison in Bulawayo. There, they languished for months without being charged, denied access to a lawyer or visitors, while the police investigated their case, preparing to charge them with terrorism offences under the Law and Order Maintenance Act.

---

[103] Sipho is a Ndebele boy's name meaning Gift.
[104] Nandi is a Ndebele girl's name meaning Sweetness.
[105] Zimbabwe People's Revolutionary Army. ZIPRA was the military wing of ZAPU.
[106] District Assistants were junior staff members in the Ministry of Internal Affairs ('INTAF'). INTAF was responsible for the welfare of rural black Africans living on Tribal Trust Lands.
[107] Tribal Trust Lands. These were large tracts of land, usually sub-optimal, which were set aside for settlement by black Africans.

When Nandi woke early in the morning, her head throbbed with a vicious ache, brought on by the clenching of her jaws during her troubled sleep. Mandla[108] had also risen early. Nandi heard him in the kitchen, boiling water on their small kerosene burner. Once the water was boiled, he made two mugs of tea and brought them into their bedroom, where Nandi was still lying in bed.

"Thank you, Umyeni[109]," she mumbled. "I did not sleep well. I am so worried about what our son wants to do. I feel we have failed as parents."

"Sssh my love," said Mandla. "Do not be so hard on yourself. Sipho is still a boy and so thinks as a boy does. We just need to give him guidance and direction. He is not a fool. Once he understands how dangerous his plans are, he will change his mind. And I am sure Mr Mpofu from the school will be able to help him learn more about the RAR[110]. I will speak to him in the next few days. I also want to speak to the headmaster, Mr Sykes. Now don't fret anymore. Everything will be all right."

Nandi nodded her head. "I hope you are right."

As soon as Mandla got to school that morning, he went to the headmaster's office, Mr Peter Sykes. Mr Sykes was an early starter and, fortunately for Mandla, he was able to see him straight away.

"Good morning, Mandla," Mr Sykes greeted him warmly. "I'm delighted you've been selected to learn how to drive the new tractor. It's going to make a big difference in maintaining our sports fields. Congratulations! Now, what would you like to discuss with me?"

Mandla skipped the usual pleasantries and went straight to the point. "Sir, as you know, in my job at the school, I often talk with the boys. Lately, I've heard some things that are troubling me," he said.

---

[108] Mandla is a Ndebele boy's name meaning Power and Strength.
[109] Umyeni is the Ndebele word for my husband.
[110] Rhodesia African Rifles.

"I am sorry to hear that," said Mr Sykes. "What is it that you have heard?"

"Well," said Mandla, "apparently, over the last few months, some young men from Bulawayo have visited the Mission and spoken to some of the boys about recent events in the country. That, of course, is not a problem. However, I have heard that these men are encouraging some of the boys to join ZIPRA and to then travel to Zambia, and even to Russia, to receive military training. Once trained, they will return to the country to fight against the Rhodesian Army."

Mandla was careful not to mention that one of these boys was his son, Sipho.

"Hmm, I agree that is troubling," said Mr Sykes. "As you know, since the country declared UDI[111], there has been an increase in political awareness and activity amongst some sectors of the African population. I guess that is understandable. But talk of military action against the government is worrying. Have you spoken to any other staff members about these developments?"

"No," said Mandla.

"Well, that is good," said Mr Sykes. "What you have heard is probably harmless fantasising by some of the boys. There is no need to cause needless anxiety amongst the staff. Leave this problem with me. I will take care of it."

"Thank you, Sir," Mandla said. "As you mentioned, it's likely just daydreaming by some of the boys. But I felt I should let you know, in case you've heard similar things from others. I'm sorry for interrupting your day. I'll leave you to get back to your work."

With that, Mandla left Mr Sykes' office and made his way to his workshop to start his working day. He was glad he had mentioned the matter to Mr Sykes and was confident that he would investigate the

---

[111] Unilateral Declaration of Independence. The Government of Rhodesia declared UDI from Britain on 11th November 1965.

matter further and, if necessary, implement measures that would ensure that these types of visits to the Mission by strangers were stopped.

Mandla's confidence in Mr Sykes was, however, misplaced. This was because, unbeknownst to Mandla, Mr Sykes had, in fact, received two similar reports over the last six months from two teachers. He had dismissed the first report as an isolated incident. However, now that he had received two other similar reports, he knew that he should no longer keep this information to himself and should report it to the authorities.

However, he had decided not to do so. This was because he knew that any such report was likely to cause considerable trouble for the school, as the police would want to question many of the boys and staff. Depending on what they might discover, he was certain that some staff, and even some of the boys, might be detained for further interrogation. In addition, Mr Sykes was not a supporter of the current government. He had been dismayed when the government had declared UDI and was enraged by the arrest and detention of those who were outspoken critics of the government's policies. Secretly, he hoped that political pressure against the government would mount to such an extent that it would be forced to amend its current racially discriminatory policies.

That day, Mandla made it a priority to catch up with Jacob Mpofu, a mathematics teacher at the school. Jacob was one of the few black African teachers in the country qualified to teach senior school students. He had completed his A-Levels[112] at Fletcher High School in Gwelo[113] and then earned a teaching degree from the University of Fort Hare in the Eastern Cape, South Africa.

Being a graduated black teacher in Rhodesia in the 1960s was exceptionally rare. Jacob and Mandla had developed a close friendship

---

[112] A-Levels were the Advanced Level of school examinations. It was conferred as a school leaving qualification to senior school pupils as part of the Cambridge International General Certificate of Education.
[113] Gwelo was renamed Gweru in 1982

and often met for social chats. During one such conversation, Jacob had mentioned that one of his cousins lived in Bulawayo and was a sergeant with 1RAR[114].

Mandla confided in Jacob about Sipho's interest in joining the army and shared that he had suggested Sipho consider enlisting in the RAR. Naturally, he made no mention of Sipho's interest in joining ZIPRA.

Mandla asked Jacob whether he would be able to arrange for Sipho to meet his cousin, sometime during the forthcoming school holidays, to enable Sipho to learn a bit more about the RAR.

As Mandla had hoped, Jacob was most obliging and agreed to make relevant arrangements with his cousin.

That night, Mandla was able to share with Nandi and Sipho the progress he had made with Mr Mpofu. He was, however, careful not to mention anything about his discussions with Mr Sykes.

Nandi's sleep that night was far less troubled.

Sipho, on the other hand, went to bed with a mind confused by thoughts of the RAR and ZIPRA. As a result, he had a restless night and woke in the morning feeling jaded and tired.

---

[114] 1st Battalion of Rhodesian African Rifles.

Chapter 14 – Sipho enlists with RAR

Timeline - 1972

As Mandla[115] had hoped, Jacob Mpofu, the mathematics teacher at the Mission School, kept his promise to speak to his cousin about helping Sipho[116] find out more about the RAR[117].

It was particularly surprising that this undertaking crystallised at all, considering Jacob Mpofu was one of the more nationalistically inclined black teachers at the Mission School. When Mandla first asked Jacob if he would be willing to speak to his cousin, Emanuel Wushe, Jacob's initial inclination was to decline.

However, Jacob was fond of Mandla. He also had a lot of respect for his cousin, Emanuel Wushe, in spite of their differing political views. Whereas Jacob related well to the politics of the black nationalist parties, Emanuel did not. Instead, Emanuel had a strong affinity for the law and order that the white colonial settlers had established in the country. He was therefore proud to be part of the Rhodesian Government's armed forces, which helped ensure that such law and order was preserved. As such, he had enjoyed a distinguished career with 1RAR[118] having progressed to the NCO[119] rank of sergeant, following his enlistment, five years prior.

---

[115] Mandla is a Ndebele boy's name meaning Power and Strength.
[116] Sipho is a Ndebele boy's name meaning Gift.
[117] Rhodesian African Rifles.
[118] 1st Battalion of Rhodesian African Rifles
[119] Non-commissioned officer.

Jacob's fondness for both Mandla and Emanuel made it easier for him to set aside his concerns about Emanuel's political views. This enabled him to persuade Emanuel to agree to show Sipho around 1RAR's Methuen Barracks[120] just outside Bulawayo during the upcoming Easter school holidays.

If the occurrence of the visit by Sipho to 1RAR's Methuen Barracks was surprising, the success of that visit was even more remarkable. Sipho and Emanuel connected like long lost brothers. So much so, that Sipho, after having been initially somewhat reluctant to travel to Bulawayo to learn about the RAR, became so enthralled about what he learnt from Emanuel and at what he saw at the barracks, that over the next 18 months, he voluntarily returned there on two more occasions.

In addition to these visits, Sipho also did a lot of his own research into the history and culture of the RAR by reading many books and articles about the Regiment.

By the time Sipho finished his senior schooling at the end of 1971, all thoughts of him enlisting with ZIPRA[121] had vanished. Instead, his driving motivation was to successfully complete the selection process for enlistment into the RAR.

At the end of 1971, Sipho wrote an application letter to the RAR recruitment officer, expressing his strong desire to join the Regiment. He accompanied his application with a supporting letter from his new friend, Sergeant Emanuel Wushe. Emanuel had informed Sipho that RAR's selection process relied heavily on personal recommendations, as experience showed that familial or collegiate pride in the RAR contributed significantly to recruitment efforts. Consequently, new recruits were often selected from applicants with strong connections to serving RAR soldiers, especially those who had performed well in their service.

---

[120] These were previously named the Heany Barracks.
[121] Zimbabwe People's Revolutionary Army. ZIPRA was the military wing of ZAPU.

Accordingly, Emanuel's record of service with 1RAR put Sipho's application in a strong position.

Fortuitously, Sipho's application letter was accepted, and in February 1972, he was asked to report to Methuen Barracks to participate in the initial selection, which lasted five days.

The popularity of the RAR as an employer of young black men was clearly demonstrated by the fact that approximately 1,000 letters of application had been received for the February training intake of 120 recruits. Of these applicants, only 300 had been invited to attend the selection exercise and, of these, only about 40% were expected to be successful.

During the five-day selection process, candidates were tested primarily for physical and mental toughness, and Sipho excelled in both.

One particular feat of Sipho's made a significant positive impact on the members of the selection panel. Sipho could not swim, which was known to the instructors overseeing the selection process. One of the instructors ordered a group of ten candidates, including Sipho, to climb the high diving board at the barracks' swimming pool and jump into the deep end.

To the astonishment of the instructor, Sipho completed this task without hesitation. Of course, Sipho could not swim, so one of the other candidates had dived into the pool to rescue him and to help him, coughing and spluttering, to get to the side of pool.

When the instructor asked Sipho why he had carried out this task even though he could not swim, Sipho had unhesitatingly answered, "Because you had ordered me to do so, Sir. And I knew that if I started to drown, you would send someone to help me."

After successfully completing the five-day selection process, Sipho also excelled in his six-month initial training course. The training was rigorous, professional, and comprehensive. Once again, Sipho distinguished himself, ranking at the top of his squad in marksmanship, weaponry, and drill.

Sipho's success in training was not only due to his physical and mental toughness but also to the extensive research he had conducted into the RAR in the two years prior to his application. This research enabled him to both impress and surprise the course instructors with the answers he gave to various questions that were put to him during his six-month training period.

So, if one was to read through the official record of Sipho's training log, one would find these kinds of entries.

'Recruit Pukelo demonstrated a clear understanding of the history of the RAR. He accurately described the Regiment's formation in 1940 and was aware that its history dated back to the Rhodesian Native Regiment's service during WW1. He was aware that during WW2 the RAR had seen active service against the Japanese in Burma, and of its subsequent post-WW2 deployments in Egypt[122] and Malaya[123]. He was also cognisant of the RAR's role in civil duties during the time of the Federation[124] and of the Regiment's return to the sole command of the Rhodesian Army after the Federation's dissolution.'

'When asked about his motivation to join the RAR, Recruit Pukelo shared that spending time with his friend, Sgt. Emanuel Wushe, at 1RAR over the last two years had greatly influenced his decision. He admired the RAR's dedication to duty and country, with RAR soldiers prioritising this above their loyalty to tribe, politics, or family. Pukelo also expressed appreciation for the competitive pay and other benefits, such as housing, medical care, and uniforms.'

'During our discussions on ZIPRA and/or ZANLA insurgents, Recruit Pukelo expressed strong disapproval of their gratuitous violent actions, citing accounts of tribesmen who had been beaten to death by

---

[122] The RAR was deployed to Egypt during the period 1951 to 1952 in response to the Suez crisis.

[123] The RAR was deployed to Malaya during the period 1955 to 1958 in response to the Malayan Emergency.

[124] The Federation of Rhodesia and Nyasaland was a colonial federation that consisted of three southern African territories, namely the self-governing British colony of Southern Rhodesia and the British protectorates of Northern Rhodesia and Nyasaland. It existed between 1953 and 1963.

insurgents and of a Ndebele woman whose face had been horrifically disfigured when a ZANLA insurgent used a pair of pliers to tear off her top lip. He found it difficult to comprehend how such cruel acts could be perpetrated by an insurgent against his own people, notwithstanding that their victim came from a different tribe.'

'Regarding the ethnic makeup of RAR soldiers, Pukelo demonstrated awareness that approximately 85% of recruits were of Shona ethnicity, while about 12% were from of Ndebele ethnicity. As a Ndebele recruit, he was unconcerned about the low representation of the Ndebele tribe, highlighting the RAR's principle of prioritising duty to the Regiment over tribal affiliations. In any event, he pointed out that the ethnic make-up of the RAR broadly mirrored that of the country. He also stated that he believed increased Ndebele recruitment might aid better integration between the two tribes in the country.'

'When asked about recent RAR activities, Pukelo mentioned Operation Cauldron from December 1967 to May 1968, and the significant role the RAR had played during this Operation in eliminating numerous ZIPRA terrorists who had infiltrated the country from Zambia. He advised that he obtained this knowledge from his friend, Sgt. Emanuel Wushe, a current serving member of 1RAR.'

*****

Following successful completion of his six-month training period, Sipho was posted to D Company of 1RAR where he saw significant action and served with distinction. By early 1979 he had risen to the rank of Corporal.

Shortly thereafter, he was posted to the newly formed 3ʳᵈ Battalion of RAR which was based in Umtali[125] under the overall command of Lieutenant Colonel Terry Lever.

---

[125] Umtali was renamed Mutare in 1982.

It was here that Corporal Pukelo found himself in a platoon under the command of 2nd Lieutenant Nick Sinclair, and where his reputation as a first class *masodja*[126] had been propelled to new heights as a result of a firefight in the Chimanimani Mountains.

---

[126] *Masodja* is the Africanised word for soldier.

Chapter 15 – Johannes du Toit enlists with RLI

Timeline - 1967

Very occasionally the universe conspires with itself to produce an individual who has absolutely no redeeming qualities.

Johannes du Toit was one such person.

Johannes was a South African national who had been born in Pretoria, South Africa, in 1950. His parents migrated to Rhodesia in 1957, when Johannes was only seven. Even at that young age, and despite being particularly bright, Johannes displayed personality traits that would have troubled most parents; however, these were barely noticed by his own parents, Dirk and Skylar du Toit.

Dirk and Skylar, together with their only child, Johannes, lived in a modest house in the suburb of Lochinvar about 12 kilometres south-west of Salisbury[127]. Dirk worked as a fitter and turner with Rhodesia Railways, which was the state-owned national rail operator. Skylar had trained as a hairdresser and ran a makeshift salon from the garage at their home, from where she serviced a small circle of regular female clients.

If one was wanting to find a single word to describe Johannes' character, the word psychopathic would be the most obvious and fitting. He was absolutely callous, unemotional, and morally depraved.

---

[127] The capital of Rhodesia. Its name was changed to Harare in April 1982.

His callousness started to exhibit itself from a very early age. When his parents arrived in Salisbury, they enrolled Johannes in the local primary school. At that time in the country, one of the *'crazes'* amongst junior school kids was collecting and playing marbles. Johannes' parents were not well off and, consequently, Johannes' marble collection was modest in comparison to those of the other children in his class. To make up for this, he habitually stole marbles from the bags of marbles that the youngsters used to keep in their school desks. On one occasion, when Johannes was no older than eight, a boy named George caught him stealing his marbles and reported the incident to the teacher. As punishment, the teacher made Johannes write the sentence, "*It is wrong to steal things,*" twenty times on a piece of paper.

In retaliation for this humiliation, a couple of weeks later, Johannes took a hammer to school, secretly removed the bag of marbles from George's desk, and smashed up the entire bag of marbles with the hammer. He put the shattered marble fragments back into the bag and returned it to George's desk, after hiding the hammer in some bushes near the school tuck shop.

When George later discovered the smashed-up marbles, he had burst into tears, at which point Johannes taunted him with the words from the popular nursery rhyme, *Cry Baby Bunting*.

Of course, suspicion had immediately fallen onto Johannes. However, he adamantly denied any involvement in the incident whatsoever. The class teacher was not convinced of his innocence and had required Johannes to swear an oath on the Bible that he had not been involved. Johannes did this without batting an eyelid, notwithstanding the teacher's dire warnings of eternal damnation if Johannes should lie while swearing an oath to God on the Bible.

As it was impossible to prove that Johannes was indeed the perpetrator of the act, no further punishment was handed out to Johannes. However, Johannes continued to taunt George for months afterward, calling him a *cry baby*.

Johannes prematurely completed his senior schooling at Ellis Robins High School[128] at the age of 16, after having successfully completed his O level examinations. He left school under a cloud, as just prior to departing, he was accused of being in a sexual relationship with a 14-year-old Italian girl named Rita, who attended the nearby Mabelreign Girls' High School. The allegation was that Johannes and Rita had been regularly meeting in a seldom-used storage shed on the grounds of Ellis Robins School, where they would read Playboy magazines and engage in sexual intercourse.

Rita had shared details of this salacious love tryst with one of her friends, who then reported the matter to a teacher at her school. When the teachers started asking awkward questions, Johannes threatened to burn down Rita's parents' house and poison her dog unless she stated that what she had told her friend was mere fantasy, and that, in reality, she and Johannes had a purely platonic relationship.

Rita succumbed to Johannes' threats, and shortly thereafter Johannes left the school, so the matter died.

After leaving school in 1966, Johannes drifted for a while from one casual job to another. These ranged from legitimate jobs like working as a labourer with the Rhodesia Railways, to illegal ones like breaking into cars and stealing items left in the vehicle.

However, in early 1967, he decided to enlist in the RLI[129] as a regular soldier. It had been a little over 12 months since the country had unilaterally declared itself independent of Britain. Most black nationalist parties in the country had been banned. Some of their leaders had gone into exile outside the country, while those who had remained, had either been imprisoned or detained. Consequently, black political activism had essentially been forced underground. Strategies being pursued by the underground or exiled leadership had

---

[128] Ellis Robins School is a boys' high school that was founded in Salisbury in 1953. It is located in the suburb of Mabelreign.
[129] Rhodesian Light Infantry. This was an infantry regiment and was one of the country's main counter-insurgency units during the Rhodesian Bush War.

now shifted decidedly away from peaceful protest and the withdrawal of labour, towards military confrontation and civilian insurgency.

The Rhodesian security apparatus had also changed the way it needed to operate to counter these new threats. It was in this environment that the RLI was now operating. In many ways, Johannes was the ideal *foot soldier* for the RLI. He was smart, street savvy, cunning, knew no fear, and was ruthless. His instructors quickly recognised his innate fighting abilities. What they now needed to do to transform him into their ideal fighting machine was to instil in him, without any shadow of doubt, the belief that the cause for which he was fighting was a noble and justified one, and that victory could only be achieved if the enemy was totally defeated.

In these endeavours, the instructors did a commendable job. However, given Johannes' psychopathic personality traits, one danger they overlooked was the high risk that, under the right circumstances, his sociopathic tendencies could override his training regarding the absolute necessity of obeying orders.

A particular incident occurred shortly after Johannes had completed his initial training, which ought to have raised alarms. The first major action that Johannes had experienced was during *Operation Cauldron*[130] as a member of 1 Commando RLI. At one point in this operation, the troop that Johannes was part of, was required to sweep through a village which was suspected of harbouring ZIPRA[131] guerrillas.

Johannes was part of the sweep group and was under orders to eliminate any *gooks*[132] who were discovered. As the troops were advancing through the village, a number of guerrillas who were hiding in the village huts had lost their nerve and had decided to flee rather

---

[130] *Operation Cauldron* was launched by the Rhodesian Security Forces in response to an incursion by ZIPRA insurgents on 28 December 1967. *Operation Cauldron* continued until 31 May 1968.
[131] Zimbabwe People's Revolutionary Army. ZIPRA was the military wing of ZAPU.
[132] *Gook* was a defamatory word for a terrorist.

than run the risk of being discovered by the advancing RLI troops. As they fled, they were joined by a number of panic-stricken villagers.

The fleeing villagers included a large woman with a young infant strapped to her back. Johannes knew the fleeing individual was a woman with a baby strapped to her back. Yet, he deliberately took aim with his FN[133] rifle at the infant on her back with the objective of killing both the infant and the fleeing woman with a single shot.

During his subsequent debrief of this *kill*, Johannes showed no remorse for deliberately shooting two civilians, nor did he hesitate to describe his intention to kill both the fleeing woman and her child with a single shot. Rather than feeling any regret, he felt a surprising sense of pride in his actions.

Shortly after this incident, Johannes was involved in another dubious incident in which his callousness was again demonstrated. On this occasion, Johannes' cruelty was directed at a domesticated animal. He was on deployment with 1 Commando RLI when the camp pet, an adopted cat, had annoyed him. He grabbed the cat by the scruff of its neck and proceeded to strangle the poor creature with his bare hands. He was oblivious to the pitiful animal's yowls and desperate clawing and scratching. When all life had ebbed out of the cat's body, he tossed its lifeless corpse onto the campfire and let it burn to a cinder without offering any word of explanation to the stunned onlookers from his troop.

Given Johannes' personality traits, it is perhaps not surprising that he was unable to recognise the depravity of his actions. However, what was more worrying was that none of his superior officers ever spoke negatively to him about his behaviour in either of these incidents.

Whether his superiors' silence indicated a darker culture within the RLI is debatable. The truth was likely that the regiment itself didn't have an endemic darker culture, but rather that several high-ranking

---

[133] This was a light automatic rifle designed in Belgium and manufactured by FN Herstal. The FN was the standard issue rifle for the Rhodesian Security Forces.

individuals had become hardened and calloused by their experiences during the Rhodesian Bush War.

Regrettably, and as subsequent events were to later show, Johannes' narcissistic nature would lead him to blatantly disobey the RLI's code of conduct and command structure, thereby bringing the Regiment's otherwise good name into disrepute.

Chapter 16 – Johannes explores poaching as a source of income

Timeline - 1977

It was early 1977, and Johannes du Toit was now serving with the RLI[134] in the south-eastern part of the country close to the Mozambique border and adjacent to the Gonarezhou[135] National Park.

This area of the country fell within a military operational area called *Operation Repulse,* which had been established in May 1976 in response to a rapid build-up of terrorist activity in many parts of Rhodesia.

Despite his psychopathic tendencies, Johannes was now an NCO[136] with the rank of sergeant. His advancement within the RLI was more a testament to his innate fighting abilities, rather than in recognition of any leadership qualities that he possessed.

The country was now facing a sudden and dramatic increase in terrorist incursions, and Johannes' fighting abilities were, more than ever before, desperately needed.

The sudden escalation in terrorist activity since the mid-1970s had occurred primarily because of two significant geo-political events.

---

[134] Rhodesian Light Infantry. This was an infantry regiment and was one of the country's main counter-insurgency units during the Rhodesian Bush War.

[135] Gonarezhou is a Shona word meaning *place of elephants.*

[136] Non-commissioned officer.

The **first** of these had occurred in the Portuguese colony of Mozambique, which was Rhodesia's eastern neighbour. A military coup had taken place in Portugal in April 1974. The coup resulted in the replacement of the former authoritarian right-wing Portuguese Government with a new left-leaning interim military junta[137].

The military junta wanted to put an end to the guerrilla wars that had been waging for more than a decade in many of Portugal's African and Indonesian colonies, including Mozambique.

Following the coup, Portuguese political, military, and economic leaders were hurriedly withdrawn from Mozambique, and that country was earmarked for an immediate handover to Mozambican nationals.

Frelimo[138] had been founded in 1962 as a nationalist movement fighting for the self-determination and independence of Mozambique from Portuguese colonial rule. Following frenetic negotiations with the Frelimo guerrilla force, Mozambique was granted independence on 25th June 1975, and Frelimo assumed power under the presidency of Samora Machel.

Frelimo was sympathetic to the goals and methods of ZANLA[139] and supported their struggle for independence. As a result, ZANLA now had permission to establish guerrilla bases in Mozambique with the full backing of both President Samora Machel and Frelimo.

On the other hand, the Rhodesian Security Forces now faced the challenge of defending an additional 1,100 kilometres of border. Moreover, Rhodesia no longer had unrestricted access to the

---

[137] This military junta was subsequently replaced in 1976 by a centre-left socialist government.
[138] The Front for the Liberation of Mozambique.
[139] Zimbabwe African National Liberation Army. ZANLA was the military wing of ZANU.

Mozambican ports of Beira[140] and Maputo[141], both of which had been crucial to its sanction-busting operations.

The **second** event occurred around the same time. The Government of South Africa, which had historically supported the Rhodesian Government since UDI[142], altered its stance in late 1974. The South African Prime Minister, John Vorster[143], had come to the painful conclusion that Rhodesia's position had become untenable. In his view, it was impossible to try and maintain white minority rule in a country where blacks outnumbered whites by more than 20 to 1.

He also believed that South Africa's interests would be better served by collaborating with other black African governments on a Rhodesian settlement. Naively, he hoped that such cooperation might win South Africa some international legitimacy and allow it to preserve its policy of apartheid[144].

Accordingly, Vorster pressured Ian Smith to accept a détente initiative involving the African Frontline States[145]. This required Smith to order the Rhodesian Security Forces to implement a ceasefire and release ZANU[146] and ZAPU[147] nationalist leaders from detention, allowing them to attend a conference[148] at Victoria Falls under the UANC[149] banner, led by Bishop Abel Muzorewa.

---

[140] Beira is on the east coast of Mozambique and is the capital and largest city in the Mozambican province of Sofala.

[141] The capital and largest city in Mozambique. Prior to July 1975, Maputo's name had been Lourenço Marques.

[142] Unilateral Declaration of Independence. The Government of Rhodesia declared UDI from Britain on 11th November 1965.

[143] John Vorster served as the Prime Minister of South Africa from 1966 to 1978.

[144] Apartheid is the Afrikaans word for apartness. It was a system of institutionalised racial segregation that existed in South Africa and South West Africa (now Namibia) from 1948 to the early 1990s.

[145] These were a loose coalition of African countries from the 1960s to the 1980s committed to ending white minority rule in Rhodesia. They included Angola, Botswana, Mozambique, Tanzania, and Zambia.

[146] Zimbabwe African National Union.

[147] Zimbabwe African People's Union.

[148] The conference was held on 26th August 1975.

[149] United African National Council.

However, the détente initiative, along with the related ceasefire and the release of the black nationalist leaders, was poorly conceived. Not only did the ceasefire provide the military wings of the black nationalist parties with the opportunity to regroup and reassess their operational strategies, but it also gave the rural population the impression that the Rhodesian Security Forces could be defeated, and that the guerrillas might soon replicate Frelimo's victory in Mozambique.

Predictably, the Victoria Falls conference itself was a dismal failure, having collapsed after nine and a half hours of fruitless talks, with each side blaming the other for the breakdown.

With all sides no longer observing the ceasefire, the Rhodesian Government halted the further release of black nationalist prisoners. Surprisingly, rather than now supporting the Rhodesian Government, John Vorster pressured Ian Smith to return to negotiations by beginning the withdrawal of the South African Police. This withdrawal placed a huge additional burden on the Rhodesian Security Forces, as the South African Police had been assisting in patrolling the vast Rhodesian countryside.

Guerrilla incursions immediately ramped up, and in the first few months of 1976, there were three large and significant incursions of terrorist crossings from Mozambique.

Intelligence reports now indicated that around 1,000 guerrillas were already active within Rhodesia, with a further 15,000 encamped in various states of readiness in Mozambique.

In February 1976, Ian Smith addressed the nation, warning that a new terrorist offensive had begun, and that to defeat it, Rhodesians would have to face heavier military commitments.

Shortly thereafter, on 3rd March 1976, Mozambique formally declared a state of war with Rhodesia.

The rapid increase in guerrilla incursions into the country from 1976 saw the Rhodesian Security Forces react by significantly modifying their counter-insurgency tactics.

Three more Rhodesian military operational areas were defined, including *Operation Repulse* which was announced in May 1976.

In addition, and in order to maximise their modest air assets and sparse manpower reserves, the Rhodesian Security Forces developed what became known as Fire Force tactics.

Fire Force tactics were designed to enable the Rhodesian Security Forces to rapidly react to guerrilla sightings and farm attacks. In addition, Fire Force assistance could be called upon by members of the Security Forces as reinforcements or to counter ambushes.

The preparatory deployment of Fire Forces was highly flexible and quick — all that was required to establish a forward base was an airstrip. There would usually be three main Fire Force combat groups in operation at any time, each of which would be handled by a company-sized body of men, usually one of the RLI commandos or a company of the RAR[150]. The combat group in question would be posted at a forward airfield for six weeks and given responsibility for thousands of square kilometres of Rhodesian countryside.

Using conventional reconnaissance techniques, patrols of five or six men drawn from national servicemen or reservists who knew their operational area intimately, or from the RAR, would be used to locate guerrilla groups.

Heliborne sticks[151] of RLI troops would then be dropped off to provide both assault troops and *stop groups*. The *stop groups* would be deployed along possible lines of escape.

The helicopters[152] would then orbit the area and, together with the assault troops, seek to acquire and engage individual targets or sweep the guerrillas towards the *stop group* positions of the previously deployed ground troops.

---

[150] Rhodesian African Rifles.
[151] Usually a four man half-section.
[152] Helicopters were the French manufactured Allouette III helicopters which were configured either as K-Cars (command choppers) or as G-Cars (gun choppers).

The objective of Fire Force was to trap and eliminate guerrilla groups before they could escape, making the element of surprise crucial. The need for surprise was greatly aided by the Selous Scouts' concealed forward observation posts (OPs), which enabled rapid responses by Fire Force to enemy guerrilla sightings.

These changed operational tactics proved very effective, and the Rhodesian Security Forces gradually began to gain the upper hand. At the same time, the doubling of the length of national service from six months to twelve months, helped ease some of the manpower shortages that the Security Forces were facing.

It was while serving with the RLI in *Operation Repulse* that Johannes du Toit discovered, quite by accident, a lucrative illegal activity which was relatively low risk and provided substantial financial rewards.

Three unlinked factors provided the setting, which enabled Johannes to identify and then exploit this lucrative illegal activity.

Firstly, the operational methods of the Selous Scouts and the RLI; *secondly*, the abundance of big game in Gonarezhou[153] National Park, which lay within the operational area of *Operation Repulse*; and *thirdly*, the park's proximity to Mozambique and the relative ease of arranging vehicular transport from the Rhodesian-Mozambican border to the port of Beira on Mozambique's eastern coastline.

The Selous Scouts were a special forces unit of the Rhodesian Army that operated from 1973. The unit was named after legendary African bush hunter, Frederick Courtney Selous, and it specialised in so-called pseudo-operations. Operating under official cover as a military tracking unit, the Selous Scouts were, in fact, involved in far more perilous activities. These would often involve white scouts being paired up with black scouts, or, more often than not, being paired up with former

---

[153] Gonarezhou is a Shona word meaning *place of elephants*.

ZANLA[154] or ZIPRA[155] guerrillas who had been captured and then turned to fight against their former comrades.

A small team of scouts, both black and white, would move into covert OPs[156]. The white scouts would remain hidden at the OP, while their black counterparts would infiltrate into nearby villages reported to have been occupied by terrorists.

This could continue for days on end until either the terrorists revealed themselves, or until a slight change in the pattern of the village life was observed, which indicated the presence of terrorists. Once terrorists were sighted, or believed to be present, the leader of the OP stick would radio the relevant details back to the Fire Force base. The relevant Fire Force unit would then be quickly deployed to attack the village and eliminate the nest of terrorists.

Successful OP deployments required patience and care. The biggest threat to a successful deployment was boredom. The boredom stemmed from spending days in stillness and silence, which was not easy for fit young men. The ever-present mopane flies and mosquitoes could also make the deployments tremendously uncomfortable.

Despite these difficulties, the Selous Scouts became so adept at masquerading as ZANLA or ZIPRA fighters that there was a significant risk of RLI or RAR troops mistaking them for genuine guerrillas and engaging them in a firefight.

To minimise this risk, whenever the Selous Scouts were operational in a given area, that area would be *frozen*. This would mean that other members of the Rhodesian Security Forces would be prohibited from carrying out military operations in the *frozen* area unless prior authority was first obtained.

These tactics considerably reduced the risk of Selous Scouts being mistakenly attacked by RLI or RAR troops. However, to miscreants like

---

[154] Zimbabwe African National Liberation Army. ZANLA was the military wing of ZANU.
[155] Zimbabwe People's Revolutionary Army. ZIPRA was the military wing of ZAPU.
[156] Observation Posts.

Johannes, these tactics also presented opportunities for the perpetration of nefarious criminal activities with minimal risk of encountering members of the Rhodesian Security Forces.

During one particular deployment in a *'frozen'* area, Johannes was part of a small team comprising four RLI infantrymen and two Selous Scouts. They had been tasked with setting up and manning an OP overlooking a small rural village near the Gonarezhou National Park.

The village was suspected of harbouring terrorists. A covert OP had been established on a hill about 1,200 metres away. Two Selous Scouts, both black soldiers, infiltrated the village to gather intelligence, while one of the four white RLI infantrymen took hourly turns scanning the area through high-powered binoculars. The other three troopies[157] rested in their well-concealed *lay-up* position, hidden from view.

However, and notwithstanding these unpleasantries, the deployment had proven to be particularly exciting for Johannes. This was because the hours of boredom were occasionally interrupted by the sighting of herds of elephants or crashes of rhino. And it was not the magnificence of these animals which caused Johannes' heart to race. Instead, it was the size of the elephant tusks and rhino horns that caught his attention.

Johannes was street-smart and had a knack for spotting opportunities when they arose. Legalities and other such formalities didn't concern him. This was a chance to make easy money and have some fun along the way.

He had already concluded that the reason why there was such an abundance of big game, not only in this part of the country but indeed in most parts of Rhodesia, was due to the intensity of the war that had been waging against the *gooks*[158] during the previous decade.

---

[157] Colloquial term meaning a regular member or national serviceman of the Rhodesian Army.
[158] A defamatory word for terrorist.

This meant that poaching, while widespread in many other parts of Africa, was relatively rare in Rhodesia due to the number of Rhodesian troops on active duty throughout the country. If members of the Rhodesian Security Forces happened to come across poachers, their most likely response would be to open fire on them. To Johannes' mind, and indeed to many others, a dead poacher was just about as good as a dead *gook*!

Johannes started to make some discreet enquiries into the trade of rhino horn and ivory. He quickly learnt that, on a kilogram for kilogram basis, rhino horn was substantially more valuable than gold.

He discovered that rhino horn was crushed into powder and used in traditional Chinese medicine to treat ailments such as hangovers, fevers, and even cancer. He also learned that its main markets were in China and various south-east Asian countries, including Vietnam and Thailand.

As far as ivory was concerned, it was worth about a tenth of the price of rhino horn on a kilogram-for-kilogram basis. However, the weight of a pair of elephant tusks far exceeded that of a pair of rhino horns.

Another factor which made ivory attractive was the fact that the supply of elephants far exceeded the supply of rhinos. And, on the demand side, the demand for carved ivory products[159] was particularly strong amongst the upper classes of Chinese and Hong Kong societies. Moreover, very often these products, particularly ivory jewellery like bracelets, were inlaid with gold and silver, which further increased their market appeal.

Johannes did not believe that finding and killing rhinos and elephants would present many difficulties. Hunting big game had been considered an honourable pastime by many of the country's early white pioneers in the late 19th century. Although such activities became illegal early in the 20th century, unsanctioned big game hunting continued, especially among wealthy white landowners.

---

[159] Ivory products include ornaments, figurines, carvings, jewellery, chess sets and piano keys.

Consequently, there was a plentiful supply of young RLI troopies and Selous Scouts with an unquenchable thirst for shooting elephants, rhinos, large cats, and antelope.

Johannes had no doubt that he would easily be able to recruit about half a dozen of such individuals who would comprise his elephant and rhino spotters and shooters.

However, the challenge lay in how to tap into the rhino horn and elephant ivory markets and organise the transport of the horn and tusks to those markets. Johannes knew that these two aspects of his planned criminal activity would need to be handled by others, so he began searching for solutions.

It did not take long for Johannes' antennae to sniff out an answer to his problem.

During a briefing session in May 1977 at 1 Commando's field camp near Buffalo Range, the officer in charge of 1 Commando RLI, Major Ferguson, had advised that Battalion HQ had become concerned about the number of high-profile political detainees who were still incarcerated at the Gonakudzingwa[160] Restriction Camp.

Since the Restriction Camp was situated in a remote, arid region of the country with numerous dangerous wildlife, including lions and elephants, security was never a major concern. Most detainees understood that while escaping might be easy, survival was nearly impossible. This was because escapees risked being eaten by lions, trampled by elephants, dying of thirst, or, if fortunate, being shot by a member of the Rhodesian Security Forces!

However, the top brass at Battalion HQ had become concerned that, due to the camp's scant security, a brazen group of terrorists might attempt to mount an assault and liberate the camp's political detainees. If this occurred, it would be extremely embarrassing for the Rhodesian Government and a significant propaganda victory for the enemy. Accordingly, 1 Commando RLI was tasked with visiting the

---

[160] Gonakudzingwa is a Shona word meaning *where the banished ones sleep.*

camp to review its existing security arrangements and ensure they were fit for purpose — if not, they would make recommendations for necessary improvements.

This task was far from appealing. The drive to the camp would be long and arduous. Then, after completing the review of the current security arrangements, a detailed report with relevant recommendations would need to be prepared and submitted to Battalion HQ. In all likelihood, the report would sit on someone's desk for months, with no action taken, as more pressing issues were prioritised."

However, Johannes' instincts told him that this was an opportunity to solve a problem he had been contemplating for several weeks. This issue, of course, had nothing to do with the terrorist war the country was fighting — it was far more important than that!. The challenge was figuring out how, after killing an elephant or rhino and removing its tusks or horn, he could transport the spoils to Beira for shipment to the lucrative markets in China and south-east Asia.

So, without being asked, Johannes said, "Sir, I would be happy to take on that task. I know the area quite well having been on an OP there recently. Let me take a couple of troopies and I will check it out for you. I reckon we will need two or three days."

Major Ferguson was somewhat surprised by Johannes' offer. He knew that all his men would prefer to be doing real soldiering rather than pussyfooting around the country looking at security arrangements at some hell hole for detainees. But the offer was there, and it meant he would not have to order one of his other NCOs[161] to take on the task.

"Good on you, Sergeant," he said. "Pick out a couple of men, organise a vehicle, and make arrangements to leave tomorrow."

Johannes got to work straight away. There were two troopies whom he knew would be ideal for this task — Henrik van der Merwe and Keith Oosthuizen. Both were national servicemen who had recently completed their initial training and had been posted to the RLI. Their

---

[161] Non-commissioned officers.

lack of experience and naivety made them easy targets for Johannes to manipulate.

Johannes radioed the JOC[162] at Buffalo Range to request a Land Rover as soon as possible. He specified that it needed to be fitted with anti-mine blast plates and roll bars. He was advised that such a vehicle was available and that it would be driven to his current location, approximately 100 kilometres south of Buffalo Range, that afternoon.

Sure enough, the mine-proofed Land Rover arrived at the base camp that afternoon. Upon its arrival, Sergeant du Toit ensured that appropriate rat-packs[163] and other provisions were requisitioned from stores and loaded into the vehicle. These provisions included fencing materials and tools that he thought might be needed to repair or modify the existing perimeter fencing that delineated the camp.

At first light on the following day, Sergeant du Toit accompanied by troopies van der Merwe and Oosthuizen, set off for the Gonakudzingwa Restriction Camp.

The camp was approximately 125 kilometres away, but progress was slow due to the state of the dirt roads that the three men had to travel over. In addition, several stops were required as inspections of suspect sections of the dirt road were made to ensure that these had not been land-mined by the enemy. The men eventually arrived at the camp around noon and without incident.

Sergeant du Toit, together with the two troopies, carried out a cursory inspection of the perimeter fencing surrounding the camp. Having found that it was satisfactory, Sergeant du Toit advised the two troopies that he thought the three of them should now travel a further 60 kilometres south to the town of Vila Salazar[164], which was on the country's border with Mozambique. There was a small frontier police post in the town that was nominally in charge of security at the camp.

---

[162] Joint Operation Centre.
[163] Army ration packs.
[164] The town is now named Sango.

Vila Salazar was a typical African *one-horse town.* However, troop activity in the town had increased substantially since Mozambique had achieved independence from Portugal in June 1975, and Mozambique's subsequent declaration of war against Rhodesia.

Upon their arrival in Vila Salazar, the men made their way to the local police station, which was a smart, white-plastered brick building with a tin roof. Sergeant du Toit ordered the two troopies to remain with the Land Rover while he made his way into the police station to meet with the inspector in charge.

Sergeant du Toit introduced himself to the BSAP[165] inspector and advised him the purpose of his visit. The inspector assured him that security arrangements at the camp were adequate. When Sergeant du Toit quizzed him about the possibility of a terrorist-led attack on the camp, the inspector assured him that this was most unlikely, especially since many of the high-profile political detainees, including Robert Mugabe and Joshua Nkomo, had now been removed from the camp.

The inspector's assurance appeared to satisfy Sergeant du Toit, who then started seemingly idle chatter with the inspector.

"Tell me, Inspector," said Sergeant du Toit, "have things changed much in Vila Salazar since Frelimo assumed power in Mozambique?"

"Well," said the inspector, "one would have thought that policing would have become a whole lot harder. But surprisingly, things have not changed that much, really. Which just goes to show what a useless bunch the Portuguese administrators were."

"Really," said Sergeant du Toit. "I don't think I understand. What do you mean?"

The inspector replied, "Well, the Portuguese always seemed to turn a blind eye to fraud and corruption. Frelimo is just as bad. So, crooks in Mozambique continue to thrive. It makes my blood boil. For example, there's this Portuguese fellow named Santiago de Costa who lives just

---

[165] British South Africa Police.

across the border in Malvernia. He pretends to be a businessman, but he's a real lowlife. We've known about his illegal activities for years — poaching, prostitution, bootlegging, drugs, illegal arms deals, extortion, racketeering. He's done it all.

"When the Porks[166] were in charge, we reported this to them, but they did nothing to try and stop him. In fact, we believed that he had the Portuguese authorities from the Gaza province in his pocket. And things are just as bad under Frelimo."

Sergeant du Toit's heart rate quickened. However, his breathing and voice remained steady. "Did you say that he still lives in Malvernia?" he asked.

"Sure does," said the inspector. "I actually have a map which shows where he lives. In fact, it is quite a decent house. It was probably funded by his illegal activities."

The inspector smiled and then added, "Maybe you RLI guys could pay him a visit sometime and shake him up a bit. He's a real bastard."

The inspector pulled open his desk drawer. From it, he took a map of the local area, which included the Mozambican town of Malvernia. A cross marked the house occupied by Santiago de Costa.

"Now there is a thought," said Sergeant du Toit. "Do you mind if I take down some details from this map?"

"Be my guest," said the inspector.

Ten minutes later, Sergeant du Toit exited from the police station and went to his Land Rover, where troopies van der Merwe and Oosthuizen were enjoying a smoke.

"Come on boys," said du Toit. "We have further work to do."

---

[166] Colloquial Rhodesian term for the Portuguese people living in Mozambique.

Chapter 17 – Johannes' foray into Mozambique

Johannes' mind was working rapidly as he walked back to the Land Rover with the two RLI[167] national servicemen, Henrik van der Merwe and Keith Oosthuizen. He knew without question that he needed to illegally cross into Mozambique to pay a visit to Mr Santiago de Costa in Malvernia[168].

From the details of the map that the BSAP[169] inspector had shared with him, he reckoned that de Costa's house was no more than four or five kilometres away, albeit in Mozambique. But to enable him to visit de Costa he first needed to get the two young troopies[170] out of the way.

In his mind's eye, he remembered that the map the BSAP inspector had shown him also showed a small village called Malipati, which was not far away, and which was close to a river called the Nuanetsi[171]. This gave him an idea.

The three men climbed back into the Land Rover. It was now just after 5:30 pm. Johannes knew that within an hour or so, the rapidly disappearing sun would have sunk beneath the horizon, and the

---

[167] Rhodesian Light Infantry. This was an infantry regiment and was one of the country's main counter-insurgency units during the Rhodesian Bush War.
[168] The town's name was changed to Chicualacuala in 1975 shortly after Mozambique's independence from Portugal.
[169] British South Africa Police.
[170] Colloquial term meaning a regular member or national serviceman of the Rhodesian Army.
[171] This river is now known as the Mwenezi River (or Manisi River).

current blood red of the sky would be transformed into the colour of black onyx.

"Well boys," said Johannes, "that was an interesting chat with the BSAP inspector. I have some further business that I need to attend to tomorrow, as do you. Tonight, we will find a spot nearby where we can bivouac. Tomorrow morning, I need to go back into Vila Salazar[172] to interrogate a Frelimo[173] sympathiser. I am looking forward to that!

"While I am sorting him out, I need you two blokes to investigate some intel[174] that the inspector has given me. According to him, the SB[175] boys have recently received some information which suggests that the gooks[176] are planning to blow-up a bridge which crosses the Nuanetsi River. The bridge is on the road to Malipati. It's not far from here. Tomorrow, I would like you to take the Land Rover and do a recce of the road and bridge, to see if there is any truth to this intel. To be quite frank, I highly doubt whether the information is correct. SB's intel seems to be getting worse and worse these days."

"We can do that Sergeant." said Oosthuizen. "You can show us the bridge on the map when we stop."

Sergeant du Toit smiled smugly to himself. Inwardly he was pleased with how plausible this bullshit would have sounded to the two troopies. The fact that he was sending the two men on a wild goose chase, and one which could easily end in grief given how much known terrorist activity there was in the area, did not trouble him in the least.

Johannes just needed to meet with de Costa. Everything else was secondary!

---

[172] The town is now named Sango.
[173] The Front for the Liberation of Mozambique.
[174] Intelligence information (often military in nature).
[175] Special Branch. This was the unit within the BSAP which was responsible for matters of national security and intelligence. During the Rhodesian Bush War, most of their work related to counter-insurgency activities.
[176] A defamatory word for a terrorist.

A short time later, the men found a quiet spot off the road to bivouac for the night. Sergeant du Toit unfolded his 1:500 map and showed the two troopies where the suspect bridge over the Nuanetsi River was located. They would need to drive north back along the road to the Gonakudzingwa[177] Restriction Camp for 15 kilometres and then turn left onto the road to Malipati. The bridge was located approximately 29 kilometres along that road. They reckoned the round trip plus recce would take at least three hours.

Sergeant du Toit advised that he planned to return to Vila Salazar on foot in the morning. He said he thought he would need three to four hours to complete his interrogation of the Frelimo sympathiser. So as to give ample time for contingencies, it was agreed that the three of them would rendezvous back at their bivouac site at 3:00 pm the following day.

All three men woke early the following morning. They brewed a cup of tea on their gas camp stove and had breakfast using items from their rat-packs[178]. The two troopies then headed off to Malipati in the Land Rover, while Sergeant du Toit headed back on foot towards Vila Salazar, which was about a kilometre distant.

During the previous night, Johannes had already planned his course of action for today. To cross undetected into Mozambique was going to be problematical as the border was protected by a substantial border fence topped with razor wire. So, he would need a pair of wire cutters to cut a hole through the fencing. Once through the fence, it was about a five kilometre walk to get to Santiago's house in Malvernia. Fortunately, the house was located within the small town itself. He had memorised the layout of the town and was confident he could find the house without any difficulty. However, he was a *murungu*[179] and was wearing his RLI uniform. While he could easily discard the uniform, his

---

[177] This is a Shona word meaning where the banished ones sleep.
[178] Army ration packs.
[179] *Murungu* is the Shona word for a white person.

pale-coloured skin was not so easy to disguise. So, he had decided that he would need to try and remain concealed.

In a worst-case scenario, and if challenged, he was hopeful that his innate cunning and guile would enable him to make out he was a Portuguese businessman visiting Mozambique and not a Rhodesian soldier!

Once he reached Santiago's house, he would conduct a recce, and only approach the house if he was certain Santiago was both home and alone. If not, he would abort the mission and return to Rhodesia by the same route he had taken.

Assuming Santiago was home by himself, he planned to put his proposal to him directly, appealing to Santiago's disregard for authority and his love of money.

If Santiago was not willing to participate in the proposal, Johannes would simply abort the mission and return to Rhodesia. If, on the other hand, Santiago was not only uninterested in the proposal but also threatened to disclose Johannes' presence to the Frelimo authorities, he would shoot Santiago in the head, abort his mission, and cross back into Rhodesia. In this scenario, Johannes figured it would take several hours for Santiago's dead body to be discovered, by which time he would be safely back in Rhodesia. Moreover, there would be no reason for anyone to suspect that Santiago's killer was anyone from Rhodesia. The Frelimo authorities obviously knew enough about Santiago to know that he was involved in all kinds of illegal activities, and would simply assume that this was a revenge-killing by one of his disgruntled underworld associates.

As soon as the Land Rover was out of sight, Johannes ducked behind some bushes off the road. He removed his webbing and RLI uniform, and changed into civilian khaki shorts and an open-necked shirt that he had brought with him when he left base camp a few days earlier.

He hid his webbing, RLI uniform, and FN[180] rifle within the bushes but retained his Browning semi-automatic handgun, which he had especially drawn from the armoury before leaving base camp. He placed the handgun in the underarm holster beneath his open-necked shirt, and put the wire cutters in the side pocket of his shorts. He did not have any alternative footwear so had no option but to continue wearing his RLI-issued ankle boots.

Having changed clothes, Johannes headed away from the road and went across the scrub in the general direction of the border. Within 20 minutes, he intersected the border's perimeter fence. His crossing was some distance from the official border crossing and, as he had hoped, there were no other persons in sight. In fact, the only sign of life was a couple of vultures that were circling overhead.

Johannes used his wire cutters to cut a hole through the fence and then crawled through the hole. He knew that Malvernia lay to the south. He used his compass to correctly orientate the direction of his travel and then headed off making sure to remain within the scrub.

It wasn't long before his path again intersected the road into Malvernia. The road was deserted, yet he was careful to remain hidden. This delayed his progress somewhat as he needed to make several detours to ensure he was hidden by the low-lying scrub and trees.

Within an hour, he was within the small township of Malvernia. By now it was about 9:30 am. Fortunately, there were very few individuals about, and those Johannes observed were black people. Once again, his progress was slow as he needed to ensure that he remained concealed. He achieved this by skirting along fence lines or behind buildings. The scarcity of people and traffic once again worked to his advantage.

After another half hour or so, Johannes found himself at the rear of the house which he deemed must belong to Santiago de Costa. The house

---

[180] This was a light automatic rifle designed in Belgium and manufactured by FN Herstal. The FN was the standard issue rifle for the Rhodesian Security Forces.

was a large rambling one, but both the house and the garden appeared to be reasonably well-maintained. Johannes had approached the house from the rear as there was a small pick-up van parked in the front driveway. He had concealed himself behind a tin shed in the back garden from where he carried out a visual recce of the house.

He observed that on the house's roof there was a high mast with radio antenna.

Luck was again on Johannes' side. Firstly, Santiago did not own any pets, so Johannes' presence had not resulted in any barking from a disturbed dog. Secondly, Santiago was home alone on that particular day as, on the previous day, his girlfriend had travelled to Mozambique's capital city, Maputo[181], for a few days to visit her unwell mother.

Johannes continued with his visual recce for a full 40 minutes. Having satisfied himself that the only occupant in the house appeared to be a male adult, whom he assumed must be Santiago de Costa, Johannes stealthily made his way to the front of the house. He made sure his Browning pistol remained concealed in his underarm holster beneath his shirt, and then knocked boldly on the front door.

Johannes heard some footsteps from within. The door opened to reveal a middle-aged bearded man with closely cropped dark hair. Surprisingly, for Johannes at least, the man was reasonably well-dressed and had a trim figure.

The man looked at Johannes in surprise. "Who are you?" he said. "What do you want?" His English was good despite a strong Portuguese accent.

Johannes replied, "Sorry to bother you. But I am looking for Santiago de Costa. Is that you by any chance?"

---

[181] Maputo is located approximately 530 kms to the south of Malvernia. It is the capital and largest city in Mozambique. Prior to July 1975, Maputo's name had been Lourenço Marques.

"Yes, it is," the man retorted gruffly. "And who are you?"

"I am glad to have found you at home Mr de Costa. I have travelled a long way to find you. I would like to discuss a business proposal with you," replied Johannes.

The man was stunned and said nothing for a few seconds. Then he said, "Merda[182]! You must be joking. No one comes to Malvernia unless they actually live here."

"I can understand your surprise," said Johannes. "But I can assure you that I have come to Malvernia specifically to find you, as I have a business proposition which I am sure you will find attractive. Do you think we can sit down and have a chat so I can tell you more?"

The man hesitated. He looked steadily at Johannes who held his gaze and gave him a slight smile. "Yes, I suppose so," he said. "But this is one hell of a surprise."

Santiago offered Johannes a cup of coffee, and then the two men sat down at the kitchen table. Johannes then proceeded to tell Santiago his well-rehearsed story which, while containing some factually correct information, was generally a total fabrication.

"Mr de Costa, my name is Johannes du Toit. I am a big game hunter operating in northern South Africa and, until recently, in the lowveld[183] near Gonarezhou[184] National Park. Most of my clients are wealthy American and European hunters seeking elephants, rhinos, lions, and other big game. My operations have always been above board, but my hunting trips in Rhodesia have recently ceased due to the ongoing Bush War.

---

[182] Merda is the Portuguese word for shit.
[183] The term lowveld refers to low-lying, generally semi-arid region characterised by savanna or bushveld vegetation.
[184] Gonarezhou is a Shona word meaning place of elephants.

"On top of that, an internation convention known as the CITES[185] convention, came into force in 1975, restricting the trade of endangered species. Rhodesia hasn't signed it yet, but South Africa has, and many other countries will likely follow. This will seriously impact my business, as hunting elephants and rhinos legally will no longer be possible. I'm not prepared to see my business suffer because of the convention."

"Well, that's interesting, Mr du Toit," said Santiago. "But what does this have to do with me?"

"I'm getting to that," Johannes continued. "Before CITES, my clients paid handsomely to hunt big game. I'd handle everything — licenses, rifle permits, transport, guides — and after the kill, the meat was sold cheaply to the locals while scavengers picked clean the remains. Some clients wanted trophies, and I'd arrange that too. It was a good business model — the clients got their hunt, the villagers got cheap meat, my team had jobs, and I made a good profit. Everyone benefitted!"

"Except for the animals," Santiago interjected.

"True," Johannes agreed, "but the elephant herds in this part of the world are unsustainably large. Culling them helps maintain the environment. And unlike poachers, my clients ensure a quick, humane kill. Poachers use traps, poison, or low-calibre guns, leading to far more suffering. But CITES will push the trade in ivory and rhino horn underground. The black market is already growing, driven by demand from Asia, and as poaching increases, corrupt African governments won't be able to stop it."

"If you're right, that sounds like quite a problem for you," said Santiago. "But why involve me?"

---

[185] Convention on International Trade in Endangered Species of Wild Fauna and Flora. It is a multilateral treaty designed to protect endangered plants and animals. It came into force on 1st July 1975.

Johannes sensed Santiago's interest. "I'm a professional hunter, but I'm also a pragmatist. Many Western countries, including the South African government, believe the CITES convention is beneficial as it aims to protect endangered species like elephants and rhinos. However, they are completely mistaken. In reality, the convention will be disastrous for endangered African wildlife because the trade in ivory, rhino horn, and hides will become illegal. But that doesn't mean the trade will stop — it will simply go underground. As a result, the black market for these items will explode, causing their value to skyrocket.

"I can't stop CITES, and I know corrupt officials will continue to profit from poaching. My clients still want to hunt, so I'm adapting. Hunts for restricted animals will move underground. We'll use codenames for certain species, and all promotion will be strictly by word of mouth. My new business model will also include selling ivory, rhino horns, and hides — and this is where you come in, as I need a way to move these items from southern Africa to the lucrative markets in Asia. My guides will handle distributing the meat, but the valuable ivory, horns, and hides must be smuggled out of Rhodesia and South Africa. I can get them into Mozambique, but I need someone to transport them from Gaza Province to Maputo or Beira for export. That's where you fit in."

Santiago raised an eyebrow. "Why me?"

"I've done my homework. I know about your dealings with the Portuguese, Frelimo, and even ZANLA[186]. I also know you have contacts at the ports in Maputo and Beira[187]."

He paused for a moment. His last sentence was a complete try on, and he wanted to see if it drew any reaction from Santiago. Santiago said nothing. But he did shift his weight from his right leg onto his left leg and rub his earlobe between his thumb and forefinger.

---

[186] Zimbabwe African National Liberation Army. ZANLA was the military wing of ZANU.
[187] Beira is on the east coast of Mozambique and is the capital and largest city in the Mozambican province of Sofala.

"I'd be willing to split the net proceeds 50:50. We'd deduct shipping, freight, and any necessary bribes from the sale price. I'll handle the costs of getting the items into Gaza province; you'll be responsible for getting them to Maputo or Beira. With black-market prices rising, it's a highly profitable venture."

Santiago remained non-committal. After a pause, he asked, "Wouldn't it be easier to use the South African ports, like Durban or the new port facilities at Richards Bay?"

Johannes smiled. Santiago had taken the bait.

"I thought about that. But the South African ports are too well-run, with little corruption. Mozambique is different. Bribery has been rampant ever since Rhodesia started evading sanctions, and Frelimo's arrival has only made it worse. At the same time, under Frelimo, shipping and export systems have broken down, making smuggling far easier. So, using Mozambican ports is the best option."

Santiago was silent for a second. Then he broke into a loud and deep laugh. He held out his hand to Johannes. "Mr Johannes du Toit, I think you and I are going to do very good business together. Let me make us another coffee while we continue to chat."

The atmosphere in the room immediately lifted. Santiago brewed a cup of coffee and the two men continued chatting earnestly to work out further details in relation to their proposed business arrangements.

Johannes had been worried about how the two parties would communicate if the deal went ahead. He hoped however that the high mast with radio antenna on Santiago's rooftop meant that Santiago was in possession of a VHF[188] two-way radio. Santiago confirmed that this was the case. During the ensuing discussions, Johannes established that Santiago had a robust knowledge of radio signal procedures and some knowledge of radio equipment. Based on the equipment that Santiago said he possessed, Johannes was confident that Santiago's

---

[188] Very High Frequency

gear was compatible with the VHF radio systems used by the RLI. The two men even reached firm agreement on the call signs and frequency signals they would be using.

They also discussed financial arrangements. They agreed that all financial transactions would be carried out in either South African rand or in American dollars. It was also agreed that, wherever possible, transactions would be carried out in cash rather than by cheque or wire transfer. It was agreed that Johannes would arrange to open up a South African bank account, which would be used solely for their new business. Johannes would retain total operating control over the account but would send monthly copies of bank statements to Santiago.

Santiago was keen to know when the first consignment of ivory and/or rhino horn might be made available to him in the Gaza province. Johannes assured him that this would happen before long, but that first of all he had to organise various logistic and other business matters.

The two men genuinely seemed to be at ease with one another and their chatter continued unabated. Within an hour or so, most logistical questions had been agreed.

At around noon, Johannes looked at his watch and said he needed to get back to the post office in Malvernia, where he was going to be picked up by one his guides. Santiago offered to drive him the short distance back into town. Johannes politely refused, saying he needed the exercise.

The two men said their goodbyes. Johannes said he would be in contact again within two weeks using the call sign and radio frequency they had agreed upon. With that, they shook hands, and Johannes made his way back towards the town centre.

As soon as he was out of sight of Santiago's house, Johannes moved behind a fence line. From there he tried to remain concealed from casual pedestrians as he proceeded to make his way back into

Rhodesia via the same route he had left. Fortunately, this occurred without incident.

Once back in Rhodesia, he retrieved his hidden rifle from the bushes and redonned his RLI uniform and webbing. He then made his way back to the spot just outside Vila Salazar where he had bivouacked the night before.

He arrived there just after 2:00 pm. Unsurprisingly, the two troopies, Henrik van der Merwe and Keith Oosthuizen, had arrived an hour or so earlier.

The three men conducted a debrief. The troopies told Johannes that he was right in assuming that the intel which SB had provided to the BSAP inspector was lousy. They assured him that there was nothing in or around the bridge over the Nuanetsi River nor on the Malipati road which indicated any sign of *gooks*. Upon questioning, they assured Johannes that they had checked for tracks for at least 200 metres on either side of the bridge.

For his part, Johannes told the two troopies that he had been able to obtain some very useful intel from the Frelimo sympathiser whom he had interrogated and beaten the crap out of.

By now it was too late to start the long drive back to their RLI base camp, so they decided to bivouac for another night at their current location and to head back to their base camp early the following morning.

All three men were tired after their pursuits during the day, and they all retired early.

As Johannes lay beneath his bivvy, he began to mentally itemise the things he now needed to put into place to get his new business up and running.

That night he slept extremely well.

Chapter 18 – Nick's first semester at the University of Edinburgh

Timeline – September 1980 to December 1980

The first few months of Nick's time at the University of Edinburgh flew by. As a child, he had always found it relatively easy to make new friends and adjust to new surroundings, a skill that persisted into adulthood. Consequently, he quickly adapted to his new role as a university student in Scotland, despite the fact that his fellow students and surroundings were unlike anything he had ever known before.

Nick's sharp intellect and general interest in the world meant he had no difficulty grasping the new concepts and ideas he was exposed to during the first semester of his business and economics degree. He possessed an innate ability to manage people and resources, so subjects related to organisational and personnel management came naturally to him. He was also pleasantly surprised at how quickly he adapted to accounting and finance concepts, which were entirely new to him. He suspected his ease with these subjects stemmed from his strong numeracy skills and his knack for recognising patterns and order in the natural world around him.

His preference for order and neatness also allowed him to fully appreciate the Georgian architecture of Edinburgh. One of Nick's delights was to walk down Edinburgh's famous Royal Mile, which covered the area between the Edinburgh Castle and the Holyrood Palace. He would allow his eyes and mind to fully soak up the broadness of the paved pedestrian malls, the imposing townhouses, and moody sandstone churches. He loved exploring the many cobblestoned lanes and side streets, which formed an intricate maze of enticing coffee houses and eateries, craft shops, art galleries, fashion stores, and quintessential low-beamed and soft-carpeted pubs.

He quickly made friends with some of his fellow students who hailed from all parts of Scotland and England. His ear took some time to adjust to the many different accents he heard on a daily basis. These were very different from the clipped vowel accents which he had been brought up with in Rhodesia. The accents which he now found hardest to understand were the broad and harsh accents from Glasgow and other Scottish west coast areas. Fortunately, he had befriended a chap called Brian McKenzie from Edinburgh, who taught him a phrase which he memorised, and which often got him out of trouble. The phrase was, 'Ah'm sorry. Ah cannae ken whit yer saying. Please kin ye speak slower[189]!'

Brian, on the other hand, spoke with a refined Edinburgensian accent. He articulated his words much slower and softer than was the case in the other Scottish accents Nick had encountered. His speech had a silky, caramel-smooth quality to it. Later, Brian informed him that his accent was colloquially referred to as a George Street[190] accent.

The one thing however that Nick had not yet got used to, was the weather. This would remain the case for Nick's entire time at university. There is a Scottish slang word that Nick thought superbly described the weather and that word was shite.

Nick had arrived in Edinburgh in September, and already the days were growing short. It was dark when he woke up at 7:00 am. He would walk to his lectures, which usually started at 8:30 am. The walk from the Pollock Halls of Residence took about 20 to 25 minutes, so he needed to leave by 8:00 am. Even then, it was still not fully light. He typically finished lectures by 4:30 pm, by which time it was already dark, so he often found himself trudging home in the cold and dark.

---

[189] I am sorry but I cannot understand what you are saying. Please can you speak slower.
[190] George Street is one of Edinburgh's main high-end shopping streets.

Daylight hours were limited, and there seemed to be an overabundance of grey, wet conditions, with a complete absence of blue skies and dry weather. Nick often wondered how Scottish folk could survive with so little sunlight, and assumed they must suffer from significant vitamin D deficiency, leading to muscle fatigue and depression.

The shortness of days and freezing weather had also put pay to Nick's hope of continuing to play a bit of rugby whilst at university. He had joined the rugby club at the start of the semester and had played for the 2nd XV for its first two matches. However, he could not hack the freezing cold weather and icy wind, which was further compounded by having to play on concrete-hard frozen pitches. So, he had reluctantly said farewell to his rugby-playing days.

Brian McKenzie, his newly made friend, was a keen squash player. When Nick gave up rugby, Brian suggested he might want to take up squash. Nick quickly discovered that squash was an ideal sport given his current circumstances. As it was played indoors, it could not be adversely affected by the lousy Scottish weather. Moreover, a good game of squash only took about an hour, during which time it provided an excellent cardiovascular workout. To make things even better, he found he had a natural talent for the game.

Brian was quick to spot Nick's instinctive ability for the sport and kindly spent many hours teaching him some of the finer points of the game, and this helped him to improve his overall playing ability. Before the first semester had ended, Nick was a regular member of the university's squash team, albeit at the lower-seeded levels. But more importantly, his and Brian's mutual enjoyment of the game meant they spent a lot of time practising together, and this helped cement their friendship in a short space of time.

The inclemency of the Scottish weather was, however, more than offset by the thrill he felt each time he and Rachel spoke on the phone, which was usually three or four times a week. Both he and Rachel looked forward to these calls with eager anticipation. And each call usually lasted at least half an hour. During their calls, they learnt a great deal about each other. This deepened and strengthened their new relationship despite its long-distance nature.

The relationship was further enhanced by regular letters that they sent to each other. While Nick did not keep these, Rachel certainly did. Soon she had quite a thick file containing all his letters. She often would page back through the file and quiver with emotion at Nick's heart-felt words of tenderness and care.

When Nick had said goodbye to Rachel on the platform of King's Cross station in London back on Wednesday, 10th September, he promised that they would see each other often. However, and despite their best efforts, it was now a week before Christmas, and they had only managed to see each other once since he left London. This had occurred in late October when Rachel had been able to take off a few days from her busy schedule at Oxford University. She had caught a train from Oxford to Edinburgh via Birmingham in the Midlands.

She and Nick had enjoyed a busy and passion-filled long weekend together in Nick's new home city of Edinburgh. Rachel had never been to Edinburgh before, so Nick enjoyed showing her his new home even though many parts of the city were still unknown to him.

However, today was Thursday, 18th December 1980, and Nick was on the express train from Edinburgh to King's Cross Railway Station in London. The train was due to arrive at King's Cross in just under five hours, at 3:15 pm.

The first semester at Oxford University had already ended, and Rachel had returned to her parents' house in Guildford. Later that day, she would be driving from Guildford to King's Cross Railway Station from where she would be picking Nick up. The two of them would then return to her parents' house where they would be spending Christmas together.

Nick was not due to travel back to Edinburgh until Friday, 9th January which would mean that they had a full three weeks together.

Neither of them could wait.

Nick placed his hand into the back pocket of his jeans to ensure that his talisman, the Bronze Cross of Rhodesia, was still safely nestled there.

Chapter 19 – Nick stays in Guildford during the Christmas vacations

Timeline – December 1980

It was just before 3:15 pm on Thursday, 18th December when the train from Edinburgh pulled into platform number six at King's Cross Railway Station. Nick had already retrieved his case from the luggage rack and was waiting at the carriage door as the train pulled to a halt. He stepped down from the train and looked eagerly up and down the busy platform for Rachel.

He spotted her immediately. As always, she was strikingly beautiful. Her long blond hair, slim tall figure and stylish but understated clothes made her stand out. Her sparkling blue eyes caught Nick's searching gaze and she hurried towards him. Nick left his case on the platform and strode quickly towards her. Rachel flung herself into his outstretched arms and they embraced each other tightly, oblivious for a few moments to anything else that was happening around them.

"My gosh, it is so good to see you again," rasped Nick. "I have missed you terribly."

"Me as well," whispered Rachel. "You have no idea."

Nick took her hand, retrieved his case from the platform and the two of them headed towards the exit signs.

"I couldn't face the traffic," said Rachel. "So I've left my car at the railway station at Guildford. We'll have to get the Tube[191] to Waterloo Station, and from there, catch the train to Guildford. We should be home within 90 minutes," she said.

They followed the signs to the Tube station and caught the Victoria Line to Oxford Circus and from there the Bakerloo Line to Waterloo. Nick had never been on the Tube before and was amazed at the throng of persons, both in the carriages and at all the underground stations their train whistled through. He was also surprised at how many people on the train seemed unaware of what was going on around them, as they pored over the contents of the various London evening newspapers. He commented on the crowds of people to Rachel, who reminded him it was just a week before Christmas and coming up to the rush-hour commute.

At Waterloo, they disembarked from the Tube and walked the short distance to the British Rail overground service to Guildford. Once aboard their train, things were a little less hectic. They both talked together excitedly, catching up on what had happened over the last few days since they had last spoken on the phone.

The half-hour trip from Waterloo to the rail station at Guildford raced by. They were extremely comfortable in each other's presence, holding hands throughout most of the journey and enjoying the feel of each other's hips and shoulders against their own. Rachel was also very demonstrative in her body language, often touching Nick on the arm or hand when speaking to him — gestures that filled Nick with a warm glow of happiness.

At Guildford Station, they alighted from the train, and Rachel led the way to the car park. Her route took them past a charming flower stall, adorned with lovely white and green Christmas lights outlining its entrance, while the sound of traditional Christmas carols drifted from within.

---

[191] The Tube is London's underground railway system that services the London metropolitan area.

Nick put his hand on Rachel's shoulder and said, "Just hang on a minute Rach, I would like to buy your Mum some flowers."

They both stepped off the pavement into the fragrant-smelling shop, where Nick picked out an attractive bouquet of white roses mixed with seasonal greenery of holly, ivy, and winterberries.

"I am sure your Mum will like these," said Nick. "I am hoping to see my first white Christmas. So, let's hope the white roses are a sign of things to come."

"Mum will love those," Rachel said. "But I am not so sure you are wise to be wishing for a white Christmas. More often than not, snow just means cold and slush."

The car park was just around the corner. Rachel stopped next to her white XJ6 Jaguar, rummaged in her handbag for her car keys, and unlocked the doors. Nick tossed his suitcase onto the back seat and placed the flowers next to it. Then he climbed into the comfortable passenger seat. Rachel started the car and they headed off to her parent's house in Chantry View Road.

The drive to her house took about 15 minutes. By now, it was dark, but the sky was clear. As they drove up the long driveway, Nick admired the dramatic effect of the uplights from the carefully placed ground-level spotlights illuminating the oak trees that lined the driveway and stood guard over the manicured gardens. The central trunks and larger branches of the stately trees thrust themselves defiantly and intimidatingly into the darkened sky.

Rachel parked her car in the driveway, and the two of them climbed out and entered the house through its imposing heavy-timbered front door. The large reception hall was lit by an expansive central chandelier, and in its far corner, the hall boasted a superb eight-foot-high Christmas tree. The tree was beautifully decorated in whites, silvers, and golds, and its branches were adorned with an array of tiny twinkling lights of white and red. The overall effect was simply enchanting.

Rachel took Nick by the hand and shouted, "Hi Mum and Dad. We are back. Come and say hello to Nick."

Lynne was the first to appear. She gave Nick a generous hug and told him how pleased she was to see him. Nick returned the embrace.

"Hi Mrs Dixon," he said. "It is so good to be back here in your lovely home. And your Christmas tree is simply stunning."

He was still holding the bouquet of flowers. Rather coyly, he outstretched his arm and gave them to Mrs Dixon.

"Oh Nick, those are lovely," she said. "And they match the Christmas tree perfectly. But please don't call me Mrs Dixon. My name is Lynne. From now on, please call me that. And I know Stuart would want you to call him by his first name as well."

"Sure thing," said Nick. "That would be my pleasure."

"Well, that is settled then," she said. "Stuart will be down here any minute now. I am just putting the finishing touches to dinner. Why don't you take your suitcase up to your room? Rachel can show you the way. Then the four of us can have a pre-dinner drink in the lounge."

"That sounds fine to me," said Nick. "Is that OK with you Rach?" said Nick.

That is the second time he has called me *Rach* thought Rachel. I like it. It sounds so intimate and makes me feel close to him.

"Absolutely," she said. "Come, I will show you where your room is. It is the same one you were in when you were last here."

Nick caught the cheeky glint in her eye.

She held her hand out to him, and the two of them went up the stairs to the first bedroom on the left. This was the same room in which they had first made love a few months earlier. That memory was blissful for them both. Nick placed his case on the bed, gave Rachel a tender kiss on her lips and the two of them went downstairs to join Lynne and Stuart for a drink.

During drinks, the lively conversation inevitably drifted back to the situation in Zimbabwe now that Robert Mugabe was Prime Minister. That certainly proved to be the case. Stuart asked after Nick's parents, Matthew and Brenda Sinclair. Although Nick had only been away from Zimbabwe for four months, he had often phoned his parents during that time. From these conversations, he had begun to sense a growing unease in his parents about what was likely to happen in Zimbabwe under Mugabe's leadership.

In answer to Stuart's question, Nick replied, "Mum and Dad have not spoken much about the country since I left back in late August. But I think Dad, in particular, is beginning to feel somewhat concerned about the direction Robert Mugabe is likely to follow. I definitely think some of the high hopes that he had when Mugabe first took power are beginning to fade. "

"That's an interesting observation," replied Stuart. "As you know I have had quite a lot of business dealings both with your father and with other businesspeople from Zimbabwe for many years. I follow political developments in that country very closely. Fortunately, I still have many close contacts who are well informed about what is going on there from both a political and business point of view."

"I would be very interested to learn what you have heard," said Nick.

Stuart's forehead creased as he thought about his reply. Then he said, "Well, as you know, Zimbabwe is an enigma. It has so much potential and so much going for it. Left to its own devices, I am sure the country would be able to do just fine. With the right leadership, it ought to be able to show the rest of the world that black Zimbabweans are more than capable of governing the country. But the people I have been talking to are extremely worried by the rapid change in power in the country, and also by the fact that many foreign countries seem to think they know better than Zimbabweans do about what is best for the country and its people.

"In fact, Nick, I have recently been delving a bit into the recent history of Zimbabwe and in particular about the transition from Ian Smith's RF[192] party to Robert Mugabe's ZANU-PF[193] party. In my research I came across a quote from Ian Smith that he made in March 1976. It really is quite telling. I have written it down."

He went to the writing bureau in the corner of the lounge and retrieved a notepad on which he had written Smith's quote.

Then he continued, "The media has often reported on Smith's infamous words when he said that he didn't believe in majority rule ever in Rhodesia, not in a thousand years. But that sentence was taken out of context. The media never tell you what he said both before and immediately after those oft-quoted words."

"I must admit I have ever heard the full context," said Nick. "Do you have it there?"

"I sure do," said Stuart. "Here, have a read."

Stuart handed the notepad to Nick, who then read out aloud the full quote which was as follows: -

'I have said before, and I repeat, we are prepared to bring black people into our government to work with us. I think we have got to accept, that in the future, Rhodesia is a country for black and white, not white as opposed to black and vice versa. I believe this is wrong thinking for Rhodesia. We have got to try to get people to change their way of thinking if they are still thinking like that. Such thinking is outdated in Rhodesia today. I don't believe in majority rule ever in Rhodesia, not in a thousand years. I repeat, that I believe in blacks and whites working together. If one day it is white, and the next day black, I believe we would have failed, and it will be a disaster for Rhodesia.'

"Well, that is extremely interesting," exclaimed Nick. "I had no idea."

---

[192] Rhodesian Front.
[193] Zimbabwe African National Union – Patriotic Front. ZANU-PF is a political organisation that has been the ruling party of Zimbabwe since independence in 1980.

"That's my point," said Stuart. "Most people think that Smith and his government were out and out racists. Certainly, that is the impression that the left-leaning media want to create. And I am sure we can all agree that much of the legislation which his government passed was definitely racist in its intent and effect. But I reckon his thinking was far more nuanced than that. Unfortunately, the British Government, and indeed, the American Government, cannot seem to grasp that."

Lynne interrupted him. "Stuart, I can see you're about to get carried away on one of your favourite topics — politics. However, dinner is ready and will spoil if I let you get on a roll. Let's head into the dining room, where we can continue this discussion."

Stuart chuckled. "You know me far too well darling. But I agree."

With that he took Lynne by the arm and led the way into the dining room.

Chapter 20 – Stuart Dixon's analysis of situation in Zimbabwe

The styling of the lavish formal dining room was ideally suited to the character of the Dixons' house and the generous proportions of the room.

In the centre of the room was a large, high-gloss, rectangular oak dining room table around which there were 12 chairs – four on each of the long sides of the table and two on each of the short sides. The chairs were upholstered in a light grey fabric with white trim.

Above the table was a statement crystal chandelier, adding to the refined opulence of the room. The chandelier hung from the white, decorative plaster-cast ceiling, which Nick guessed was at least ten feet high. At one end of the room stood a large fireplace with a white marble mantle and surrounds.

The room overlooked part of the manicured gardens through three floor-to-ceiling windows, filling one of the four walls. Drawn across each window were pleated dark grey velvet curtains that disappeared into recessed pelmets. The walls were painted white, but their visual scale was diminished by the clever use of dado rails and decorative wainscoting covering the lower third of the wall. The wooden panelling was painted in a white satin finish with a hint of grey.

The natural timber floorboards were stained with a dark-gloss finish. Much of the floor was covered by a grey-patterned rug, upon which the dining room table and chairs stood. The rug was carefully sized to ensure a three-foot border of dark-gloss timber floor remained uncovered, perfectly offsetting the rest of the room.

The styling of the room was completed by the addition of a classic display cabinet with glass doors showcasing Lynne's impressive collection of porcelain figurines, along with an oriental-styled sideboard that cleverly incorporated a hidden warming drawer.

Dinner began with a simple winter favourite — tomato soup with croutons. This was followed by another British classic — roast beef served with individually baked Yorkshire puddings.

While the main course was being eaten, discussion returned to the topic of Zimbabwe when Rachel said to her father, "Dad, what did you mean before dinner when you said that you thought Ian Smith's attitude to the blacks in Zimbabwe was not out and out racist, but more nuanced?"

Lynne sighed and raised her eyebrows. With a sigh she said, "Rachel, did you have to reopen that can of worms so soon?"

Stuart, ignoring Lynne's comment, replied, "Well, from what I have read, I think in the early days of his leadership, Ian Smith really did believe that neither the blacks nor the whites should exclusively rule the country. Instead, he thought the two races needed to rule the country together.

"The problem was how that could be done. Western democracies like Britain and America were insistent on the principle of *one-man-one-vote* being implemented straight away. But Smith knew that this would not work in Rhodesia. This was because back in the 1960s there was such a huge gap between the level of education of the white people and black people. The vast majority of black persons were unschooled and pretty illiterate. Smith knew that this education gap had to be significantly narrowed before the principle of *one-man-one-vote* would work. He also knew that this would take time. Back in the early 1960s, I think there was time enough for this gap to be bridged. But the trouble was that the RF[194] failed to wisely use the time they had available."

Stuart had grabbed Nick's attention. He had not heard this line of reasoning before.

"How do you mean?" he asked.

"Well, the RF came to power in 1962 essentially because the white electorate were concerned that the former ruling party, the UFP[195], would collude with the UK and allow the country to become independent under a system of *one-man-one-vote*. The RF, on the other hand, sought independence not under a system of universal franchise, but under a qualified franchise where the right to vote was linked to the attainment of specified income and educational thresholds. These thresholds were not based on race *per se*[196]. However, at that time in the country's development, very few black people met the requisite income and educational thresholds and were unlikely to do so in the foreseeable future."

"So, in a sense the RF was seeking to maintain white control of the country via the backdoor," said Nick.

"In a sense, I suppose you are right," said Stuart. "But I think it is also important to remember that these voting provisions, along with other important matters, had been approved via a constitutional referendum in 1961. So, when the RF came into power the following year, it really had a clear choice. It could, on the one hand, continue to *maintain the status quo* — that is, white control of the country, by implementing policies which were designed to ensure that the vast majority of the black population would never attain the requisite income and educational thresholds. Or, on the other hand, it could implement an intentional and deliberate *reform agenda* which would ensure significant numbers of black persons would be able to meet the

---

194 Rhodesian Front.
195 The United Federal Party.
196 Latin phrase meaning *in and of itself*.

required thresholds in a reasonable timeframe. Unfortunately, it chose the former.

"If it had chosen the latter, I believe this would have meant that the control of the country would have gradually transferred from the whites to the blacks. Although it is impossible to know, I also believe that if the RF had done this back in the early 1960s, there would never have been any need for UDI[197]; the Rhodesian Bush War would never have broken out, and the transfer of power from the whites to the blacks would have occurred in a much more orderly and manageable manner."

Rachel interjected, "So why do you think the RF chose *the maintenance of the status quo route* as opposed to the *reform agenda route*?"

"Well," said Stuart, "I think that was because they believed this would be more attractive to the white electorate, which I suppose it would have been. However, I think the RF failed to understand the mood of the electorate back in 1962. At that time, I do not believe the white voting public outrightly opposed African advancement — they were, in fact, supportive of it, *provided* that standards were not lowered. If the RF had chosen to pursue a *reform agenda* instead of a *maintain the status quo agenda*, I believe they could have taken the electorate on that journey with them.

"If they had done this, I believe the 1961 constitutional changes would have been accepted by many black nationalistic parties, which at that time had not yet become radicalised. I also think that, in such a climate, the UK would have been willing to grant independence based on the provisions of the new constitution. This was because adoption of the *reform agenda* would have enabled the RF to clearly demonstrate to Britain and the black population of Zimbabwe that it was serious about advancing black involvement in governing the country.

---

[197] Unilateral Declaration of Independence. The Government of Rhodesia declared UDI from Britain on 11th November 1965.

"However, by following a path of *maintaining the status quo*, the RF triggered two disastrous outcomes. **Firstly**, those on the extreme right of the political spectrum were emboldened by the RF's stance, causing the party as a whole to become more right-wing in its outlook. **Secondly**, the black nationalist parties became radicalised and quickly abandoned any talk of a qualified franchise.

"Consequently, the RF headed inexorably towards a showdown with Britain, which, as we all know, resulted in the RF declaring UDI. Once UDI was declared and Britain imposed sanctions on the country, the RF had to shift into crisis mode — government efforts had to focus on economic survival rather than African advancement.

"For their part, the black nationalist parties abandoned any idea of achieving change through peaceful methods and quickly moved to bring about change through armed conflict. Moreover, Britain found itself largely sidelined and unable to exert any meaningful influence in the country."

Stuart pondered for a moment and then continued, "Initially, the RF was quite successful in overcoming sanctions and ensuring that the country continued to function relatively normally. However, the black nationalist leaders quickly became far more radical and began to openly threaten the peace and stability of the country. When this occurred, the RF had no choice but to imprison many of them, causing many of the black nationalist parties to go underground and re-establish themselves in exile in Zambia, Mozambique, or Botswana. Outside of Rhodesia, numerous foreign powers were willing to lend them a helping hand — countries like Russia, China, North Korea, and Cuba, to name a few. Thus, the resultant Rhodesian Bush War was inevitable.

"I think it is fair to say that in the early days of the Rhodesian Bush War, the Rhodesian Security Forces did an excellent job of containing the effects and reach of the terrorists. However, when Mozambique gained independence in 1975 under Frelimo's[198] rule and South Africa,

---

[198] The Front for the Liberation of Mozambique.

under pressure from the American Secretary of State, Henry Kissinger, began withdrawing its support for the RF in July 1976, I'm afraid the final outcome for the country and the RF was sealed.

"The Smith government could neither win the war nor hold onto power. This meant that in September 1976, Smith was forced to accept the ultimatum carefully crafted by Kissinger in conjunction with South Africa, Britain, and the African Frontline States[199].

"That ultimatum required Smith to publicly confirm his acceptance of the principle of majority rule within two years and to agree that the RF would participate in the all-party negotiations, which would be held to establish the process for transferring power.

"As we all now know, it ultimately took about three and a half years for the all-party negotiations to be held and concluded, and for the first *one-man-one-vote* general elections to be held in the country. However, three and a half years is really no time at all for the black political leaders in the country to prepare for their roles in running and governing the country, especially considering that the Rhodesian Bush War continued for the first three years of that period."

"That's so awful and depressing," lamented Rachel.

"Yes, it is," said Nick. "But I think your Dad has summarised the position clearly and accurately. In fact, I think today is the first time I have ever heard the position so succinctly expressed."

He looked at Stuart and added, "I am also interested to hear what your sources are saying about the future for my country."

Stuart replied, "Well, based on the views I have gleaned from people I trust and who understand the politics and economics of the country far better than I do, I am afraid the outlook does not appear do be that

---

[199] These were a loose coalition of African countries from the 1960s to the 1980s committed to ending white minority rule in Rhodesia. They included Angola, Botswana, Mozambique, Tanzania, and Zambia.

good. In fact, their view of the future is somewhat dire. I hope they are wrong."

"I am too scared to ask," said Nick. "But what have you heard?"

Stuart replied, "The most surprising thing I have heard is that the outcome of the recent elections caught the British, American and South African Governments completely unawares. The advent of a government in Zimbabwe with strong Chinese and Russian inclinations, was never really considered a likely outcome. But now that this has occurred, all three countries are gravely worried."

"In what way?" asked Nick.

Stuart replied, "While the British and American governments are relieved that the open wound of the illegal Smith regime has now been healed, they fear that the cure — the emergence of a Communist-leaning government in Zimbabwe — might be far worse than the wound itself. They realise that China and Russia have gained influence and standing in southern Africa, which will quickly surpass any remaining influence that Britain or America might have. Their current assessment is that Russia poses a greater threat to their national interests than China. As a result, they are attempting to develop strategies to undermine Russia's support for ZAPU[200] without further strengthening China's backing of ZANU-PF[201]."

"From South Africa's perspective, their government is devastated that their withdrawal of support for Ian Smith did not garner any kudos for them from either the African Frontline States or from the international community in general. Nor has it brought them any relief in terms of the international community's condemnation of their apartheid[202] policies. Naturally, they are now extremely worried that they have a

---

[200] Zimbabwe African People's Union.
[201] Zimbabwe African National Union – Patriotic Front. ZANU-PF is a political organisation that has been the ruling party of Zimbabwe since independence in 1980.
[202] Apartheid is the Afrikaans word for *apartness*. It was a system of institutionalised racial segregation that existed in South Africa and South West Africa (now Namibia) from 1948 to the early 1990s.

government with both Chinese and Russian backers right on their doorstep.

"By comparison, the Government of the People's Republic of China is ecstatic. China had not expected their man, Robert Mugabe, to win the elections, let alone to win them with such a large majority. They now see their relationship with Robert Mugabe as being critical in terms of assisting them in their strategy of gaining a strong influence in South Africa, which has always been their main game.

"On the other hand, the Government of Russia is devastated that their man, Joshua Nkomo, did so badly in the elections. This has put a huge dent in their long-term plans of gaining a real influence in South Africa. I have been told that they are now trying to develop a strategy which will enable them to effectively narrow the wide gap that exists between them and China."

"Do you think these developments will negatively impact Zimbabwe's economy?" asked Nick.

Stuart thought for a moment and then replied, "From an economic point of view, the new Zimbabwean Government is likely to enjoy a honeymoon period, during which many countries from both the West and East will seek to curry favour with the new government by offering generous aid packages and other incentives. Mugabe is already significantly beholden to China for its support of ZANLA[203] during the war, so it seems quite likely that he will lean towards China.

"In addition, now that the Zimbabwean Government has, in the eyes of the world, been legitimised, many international companies and NGOs[204] will pivot away from the South African apartheid regime towards the new legitimised Zimbabwean Government. This will also work in favour of the country.

"From an economic point of view, it is indeed fortunate that the fundamentals of the country's economy remain sound despite the

---

[203] Zimbabwe African National Liberation Army. ZANLA was the military wing of ZANU.
[204] Non-government organisations.

prolonged period of economic sanctions following UDI. Equally, despite the longevity of the Bush War, the physical, civil, administrative, and judicial infrastructure of the country remains intact and in good working order. Hopefully, this will continue.

"I think Mugabe understands that for the next ten years or so, it will be extremely important for the country to retain the expertise of the white population while ensuring that the Africanisation of the labour force at senior executive levels occurs as quickly as possible. Therefore, it is likely that his current policy of racial reconciliation will be allowed to play out. However, if that begins to create political problems for him, it is probable that his attitude towards reconciliation with the white community will weaken and waver."

Rachel had been listening carefully to her father's considered comments. She asked him how strong he thought Mugabe's position was from a political point of view.

In response, Stuart replied, "Internally, Mugabe's political position is very strong, and it is likely to remain so. However, during the war, many promises were made to the black population, so he will need to manage their expectations carefully.

"I think it is also important to remember that Mugabe's internal popularity is likely to be targeted by external forces, especially the South Africans. South Africa now wants to destabilise Zimbabwe by any means possible. They are likely to try to provoke bad relations between the Shona and Ndebele tribes. The Chinese and Russians are also likely to attempt to outmanoeuvre each other, and they, too, will try to create tensions between these two tribes. Therefore, it is quite likely that significant tribal conflict will soon arise in Zimbabwe.

"I was also told that the South Africans have already infiltrated Zimbabwe's intelligence agency. Apparently, a number of Zimbabwe's CIO[205] agents are now double agents working for South Africa as well. This is going to significantly compromise any advice that the

---

[205] Central Intelligence Organisation.

Zimbabwean intelligence community provides to the new Zimbabwean Government."

Stuart paused. His dialogue still held the attention of Nick, Rachel, and Lynne.

He concluded by saying, "Given all the variables and uncertainties and despite some positives, the current situation in the country remains extremely complicated and precarious. Mugabe and his government have a difficult task. If they manage things carefully and diligently then, with a bit of luck, the country should be able to manage the transition of power relatively well.

"However, if they become reckless or careless, or if international events move against them, then it is quite possible that everything will unravel fairly quickly, and that Zimbabwe will become another failed African country. If that happens, Mugabe's legacy in the international community is likely to be not much better than Smith's."

He paused, and then concluded with these thoughts "I sincerely hope that does not happen, because the citizens of the country have already been through a hell of a lot. However, and more importantly, if Zimbabwe and its government are successful, their success will be a shining example to the rest of Africa. And Heaven knows, Africa needs every success story that it can find."

There was silence in the room.

This was eventually broken by Lynne when she said, "My goodness darling. I had no idea you knew so much about the country. I am really quite impressed."

"Ditto from me," said Nick.

"And me," Rachel chipped in.

"Well let's hope things turn out just fine for the country then," said Stuart. "Now what's for dessert?"

Chapter 21 – Nick and Rachel plan to visit Zimbabwe

Later that night and after Stuart and Lynne had gone to bed, Nick and Rachel were sitting together on the couch in the TV lounge watching *One Flew Over the Cuckoo's Nest*[206]. Rachel was curled up on Nick's lap and his arm was protectively wrapped around her shoulders. Neither Nick nor Rachel had seen the film before, but both had read the glowing reviews it had received in the USA and the UK.

Nick and Rachel both found themselves captivated by the thought-provoking plot of the film and by the amazing performances given by Jack Nicholson and Louise Fletcher. The film had a profound effect on them both, but particularly so on Nick.

After the movie finished, Nick said, "Jeez, Rach, watching that movie has made me realise how easy it is for those with power and authority to misuse them, causing so much injustice, and mental and physical suffering to people who have done nothing wrong. The movie, along with what your Dad said this evening, has really made me question a lot of Rhodesia's recent history, before it became Zimbabwe. I'm also worried about some of the other things your Dad said. If he's right, Zimbabwe could very easily unravel."

Nick's empathy struck a chord with Rachel. She kissed him on the cheek and said, "Would you like to talk about it?"

Nick pondered for a few seconds. He felt comfortable and safe with Rachel. He also realised he wasn't entirely sure how he felt about

---

[206] Refer to the Glossary for brief details of what the film is about.

certain things, but thought that talking through his feelings with her might help him untangle his thoughts. "Yes, that would be great," he said.

"So where do you want to start?" said Rachel. "I know very little about Zimbabwe apart from what I have heard from both you and Dad. It sounds an amazing place. I certainly would like to visit it one day."

Nick replied, "Yep, it sure is a wonderful place. But it is also an enigma. I would love to take you there to see it for yourself. I am planning to go back in June or July next year to visit my folks. Perhaps we can go together. We would both be on university vacations then."

"That would be wonderful," enthused Rachel. "Let's do it. Not only would I get the chance to visit Zimbabwe, but it would also be great to meet your folks. I am sure Mum and Dad would be supportive. It is safe, isn't it?"

"Well, I think so," said Nick. "From what I understand, the security situation in the country is now relatively stable. Following ZANU-PF's[207] victory in the elections this February, there was a lot of anxiety, especially among the white population. But Mugabe's policy of reconciliation seems to be holding, and the economic situation has improved. Still, I'm troubled by what your Dad was saying tonight, and I know my Dad is also concerned about the long-term future for the country."

"How do you mean?" asked Rachel.

"Well, do you remember when your Dad said that his sources were telling him that it was very likely that the South African Government, or the Russian or Chinese Governments, might try and stir up trouble between the Shona and Ndebele tribes?" asked Nick.

"Yes," said Rachel.

---

[207] Zimbabwe African National Union – Patriotic Front. ZANU-PF is a political organisation that has been the ruling party of Zimbabwe since independence in 1980.

"Well, those words of warning certainly struck a chord with me," said Nick." About this time last year, I was still doing my national service with the RAR[208]. The Zimbabwe-Rhodesian Government had just agreed to a ceasefire with the terrorist forces, and the country was preparing for general elections to be held in a couple of months' time. Under the terms of the ceasefire, the country's security forces, and Mugabe's and Nkomo's guerrilla forces had agreed to cease all combative operations.

"As a precursor to the elections, the guerrilla forces were in the process of moving into designated camps known as assembly points, scattered throughout the country. It was a strange time. Suddenly, all these terrorists were gathered in known and relatively confined locations. There was great temptation among some units of the Rhodesian Security Forces to break the ceasefire and strike a pre-emptive blow against the camps. However, the top brass had issued strict orders for all units to observe the ceasefire, and both sides were being closely monitored by the Commonwealth's Ceasefire Monitoring Force."

"Based on the information I was reading in the media and on the information that was being fed to us by our superior officers, I did not believe that either Mugabe or Nkomo were going to perform very well in the elections. And by that time, the country had its first black prime minister, who was a bloke called Bishop Abel Muzorewa, who supposedly held quite moderate political views. I had assumed his party, which was called the UANC[209], was going to win the elections, and quite easily so.

"However, I decided to find out what some of the black NCOs[210] in the RAR were thinking, and I ended up chatting with a corporal named Sipho Pukelo. As I've mentioned to you before, Pukelo was a fine soldier. He was from the Ndebele tribe, but he was admired and respected by all our men regardless of their particular tribe. Anyway,

---

[208] Rhodesian African Rifles.
[209] United African National Council.
[210] Non-commissioned officers.

when I asked him who he thought was going to win, I was stunned by what he said."

"What did he say?" asked Rachel.

"I remember very clearly what he said," answered Nick. "He was adamant that Mugabe was going to win the elections easily. I was absolutely convinced he was wrong. The first time I'd even heard Mugabe's name mentioned was a few months earlier during the Lancaster House Conference[211] that Britain had organised.

"I asked Pukelo why he thought Mugabe would win. His reply astounded me. However, upon reflection, his answer now makes perfect sense. He said that the black population of the country would largely vote on tribal grounds and, as Mugabe's tribe, the Shona, outnumbered Nkomo's tribe, the Ndebele, by three or four to one, Mugabe would win handsomely. He never even mentioned Muzorewa's name. The only names he mentioned were Mugabe and Nkomo.

"As it turned out he was entirely correct. Mugabe won 57 seats, Nkomo 20 and Muzorewa 3, with Smith winning the 20 seats which were reserved for the white voters.

"Historically, there has not been much love lost between the Shona and Ndebele people. Prior to white settlement, the two tribes were often at war with each other. Although this enmity did reduce quite significantly following white settlement, it still remained just below the surface.

---

[211] In August 1979, the British Government invited Bishop Abel Muzorewa, the Prime Minister of Zimbabwe-Rhodesia, Ian Smith, the leader of the Rhodesian Front and former Prime Minister of Rhodesia, the leaders of the Patriotic Front, Robert Mugabe and Joshua Nkomo, and other relevant political persons to participate in a Constitutional Conference at Lancaster House in London. The purpose of the Conference was to discuss and reach agreement on the terms of an Independence Constitution, to agree on the holding of elections under British authority, and to enable Zimbabwe-Rhodesia to proceed to lawful and internationally recognised independence, with the parties settling their differences by political means.

"I would imagine that if superpowers like Russia or China wanted to agitate these historical tribal animosities for their own purposes, it would be very easy to do so. And the white apartheid[212] South African Government will, I am sure, now do everything they can to try and destabilise Zimbabwe. The easiest way to do this will be to try and foster rivalry and hatred between the Shona and Ndebele peoples.

"The other thing which your Dad said at dinner which really made an impression on me, was when he said that the whole situation in the country could have had a very different outcome if the RF[213] had implemented an intentional reform agenda when they won the elections in 1962. He is dead right you know. I am not a particularly political person, but when I think of the way the RF handled themselves when they came into power, they definitely missed a significant opportunity to change the destiny of the country."

"Such as?" asked Rachel.

"Well, take education for example," said Nick. "I went to a wonderful senior school in Salisbury[214] called Prince Edward. It was a government school, yet it had facilities that were second to none. We had wonderful teachers, a well developed and broad curriculum, and sporting facilities that would have been the envy of any school in England, public or private. There were boarding houses for kids who lived in the farming areas, a great school hall, a wonderful gym, tennis, squash and basketball courts, a swimming pool, more sports fields than I could count, and an observatory — the school had everything. And all this was provided virtually free of charge to my parents. The only expense they really had was to buy school uniforms. Yet there was not a single black pupil in that school. Only white kids!"

"Gosh," said Rachel. "Why was that?"

---

[212] Apartheid is the Afrikaans word for apartness. It was a system of institutionalised racial segregation that existed in South Africa and South West Africa (now Namibia) from 1948 to the early 1990s.
[213] Rhodesian Front.
[214] The capital of Zimbabwe. Its name was changed to Harare in April 1982.

"Well, government schools were classified into different groups. The better government schools, such as Prince Edward, were known as Group A schools, and all these schools were in areas in which blacks were, by law, not allowed to live in. So, no matter how bright a black kid was, he or she could not practically enrol in any of the all-white government schools.

"Another bizarre thing was that whereas primary education had, since 1930[215], been made compulsory for white kids and free of charge, this was not the case for black kids. Those black kids who did have access to education found themselves in schools that were poorly funded and with very limited facilities. In fact, school education for black students was largely provided by mission schools and farm owners, not by the government. As far as the mission schools were concerned, the government put pressure on them to ensure that the curriculum that was offered to black pupils was practical and not academic in nature. This meant that apart from basic arithmetic and reading, the lessons were focussed on teaching black kids vocational skills. This was to prepare them for employment in unskilled or low-skilled jobs, on farms, mines, factories, or as domestic servants. Only about 45% of black kids went to primary school and, of those, less than 10% would go on to complete secondary school.

"I believe attempts were made in the early 1960s to reform the education system. One of these reforms was to implement free and comprehensive primary education for all kids, regardless of race. However, the RF dragged its feet on following through with this change, and it wasn't until 1966 that any serious efforts were made to implement the recommendation. But instead of providing free primary education for all, regardless of race, the policy as implemented was to offer free education to any child *within reach of a school*. Since most schools were in white areas, this did little to bring about any meaningful reform for black kids.

---

[215] Compulsory Education Act of 1930.

"Now, I have no idea how aware the black political leaders were of how cynical the RF were in implementing the reforms, but if they were, I'm sure they'd have been mightily pissed off," Nick concluded.

"Jeez, I see what you mean," Rachel said. "Mugabe certainly has a lot of historical wrongs to deal with."

"Yes, he does. I hope he is up to it," said Nick. "And there is another important matter that he will have to deal with, and that is the question of land ownership. As you may know, the question of land ownership has been a red-hot issue in Zimbabwe ever since an Act, known as the Land Apportionment Act, was passed in 1930. Under this Act, and subsequent amendments, 50% of the land in the country was reserved for white settlers, 30% for Africans, and 20% for commercial companies and the Rhodesian Government. This was despite the fact that the number of blacks in the country was at least 20 times the number of whites.

"Moreover, the land set aside for Africans was generally of poor quality and far from transport corridors and other essential services. The outcome of the legislation was entirely predicable — that is the overcrowding of Africans on native reserves, which had limited services and facilities. This destroyed the native reserve economy and limited the social or economic advancement of Africans. The Act ultimately led to a decline in agricultural production by the black people, which added to the growing inequality between the races. Within 20 years, the Land Apportionment Act had created a crisis in terms of overcrowding and ecological damage on the native reserves."

Rachel interjected and said, "That does seem grossly unfair."

"And things were no better for the black people living in urban areas. They weren't permitted to purchase land in the main residential areas, which meant land ownership in cities and towns was completely dominated by whites. The only land available for blacks to buy was in specially designated high-density township areas. But these townships were located far from the main industrial and residential areas in the cities. As a result, Africans living in these high-density areas had to travel long distances to get to work, and their employment was largely focused on providing goods and services to the low-density white urban centres."

"I feel ashamed to admit it, but prior to doing my national service, I had never even been inside an African house in the townships nor been into an African rural village. The nearest I ever got to seeing how the Africans lived was when I went into the servants' quarters[216] that my parents provided to our cook and gardener. These were very modest and were located at the rear of our garden."

Rachel brushed her fringe from her forehead to better reveal her sapphire-coloured eyes. She stretched out her long, denim-clad legs and looked lovingly into Nick's eyes. Nick's heart rate increased. He took Rachel's hand and lightly said, "Are you trying to distract me?"

"I don't know what gives you that idea," she chuckled. "But I do want to hear the end of what you were saying about land ownership in Zimbabwe. But make it quick. Then we can go upstairs."

"Now there is an invitation I don't want to refuse, so I will be quick. You may know that as part of the agreement that was reached at the Lancaster House Conference, the question of land redistribution was addressed. Mugabe and Nkomo were pushing for large-scale reform of the ownership of arable land. They wanted to be able to compulsorily purchase white-owned farms with such purchases being funded by Britain. Britain understood the need for land redistribution, but said any redistribution had to be subject to the principle of *willing buyer, willing seller*. This meant that the Zimbabwean Government could not compulsorily acquire occupied farming land but instead would be given the right of first refusal from any white farmer wishing to sell their land. The government would, however, have the right to compulsorily acquire *unoccupied* white farms, providing reasonable compensation was paid to the absent landholder. Britain told Mugabe and Nkomo that if they agreed to this, funds would be provided to assist with the buying of land from willing sellers.

---

[216] Servants' quarters were colloquially referred to as kias.

"These assurances weren't enough for Mugabe and Nkomo, and property rights became a major sticking point in the negotiations. Mugabe and Nkomo were determined that land reform shouldn't be so restrictive, and that the UK should fund the compulsory buy-out of land from white farmers generally. The British government was equally insistent that the constitution must fully protect land titles and minority rights. Following pressure from America, a verbal compromise was eventually reached. The British and American governments gave assurances that funds would be committed to assist with land reform, but any such acquisitions had to comply with the terms of the new constitution, which couldn't be altered for ten years."

"So, in a sense this difficult question has just been kicked down the road for the next ten years. After that, who knows what might happen. But, if at that time a large proportion of farming land still remains in white hands, I fear things may become very difficult."

Nick stopped talking, then added, "Gosh, it really is a complicated situation. I suppose when a nation has been held in subjugation for so long, any change is bound to be complicated."

"It sure is complex," said Rachel. "But I would still love to visit it next year — and especially with you. That thought is going to keep me excited for the next six months."

She paused and snuggled into Nick's arms. She placed her hand on his thigh and said, "Talking about excitement, why don't we quietly head upstairs to your bedroom. That room has some very fond memories for me."

Chapter 22 – Nick's first visit to London city

On the Saturday before Christmas, Rachel and Nick took the train into London to do some last-minute Christmas shopping. Although the day was icy cold, the sky was cerulean blue and cloudless, and this did much to lift the spirits of most Londoners.

This day was going to be Nick's first visit into London itself. Rachel knew the city well and had offered to plan the day, an offer Nick gladly accepted. However, Rachel had not shared any of her plans with him, other than mentioning they were going into London to do some Christmas shopping and for her to show him a few of the city's many sights. The fine weather, the closeness of Christmas, and the omnipresent bonhomie meant that Rachel could showcase London at its best. She was bubbling with excitement.

Rachel had told Nick that they needed an early start as she had planned a full day. They had left her folks' house in Guildford at 7:00 am and had driven to the Guildford Railway Station, where they caught the train to Waterloo.

While travelling on the overland rail service to Waterloo, Nick observed the passing scenery, though his impression of the landscape was less than favourable. The railway line wound through poorer neighbourhoods, with mile upon mile of small, cookie-cutter terraced houses, each with a postage-stamp-sized back yard that appeared untidy and overgrown. The exterior walls of the houses were rarely plastered or painted, creating a dull canvas of brick-reds and browns. Rooflines were scarred by disused chimneys, while the fences around the cramped gardens were often sagging or broken. There was little evidence of well-kept lawns, flower beds, or hedges. He imagined that from above, the scene would resemble rows of old, scratched dominoes, rather than the neat, green-hued English countryside that looked like a carefully stitched patchwork quilt.

From Waterloo Station, it was a short walk to the Waterloo Tube Station, where they hopped onto the Northern Line to the Tottenham Court Road stop.

Once they moved from the overland service to the underground service, Nick lost all sense of direction, and of course had no way of knowing what the streetscapes above might look like. From the many games of monopoly which he had played as a child, he did, however, recognise the names of three of the tube stations they stopped at – Leicester Square, Oxford Circus and Bond Street. On a monopoly board, these properties were the yellow and green coloured highly-priced properties, so he assumed the streets above must be smart and opulent.

Nick enjoyed studying the London underground map in their carriage to work out their route and the stops. After they had left the Bond Street stop, he had ascertained that their next stop was Marble Arch, but he still had no idea where they were headed.

"Come on Rach, where are we heading?" he queried.

"You have been patient, Nick," she replied. "You will be pleased to know that the next stop is ours."

She got up from her seat and took Nick's hand. Once the train had stopped, she and Nick stepped across the gap from the train to the platform and followed the signs to Marble Arch. Rachel explained that the Arch had taken nearly six years[217] to construct and had originally been located at the entrance to Buckingham Palace. However, in 1851, it was relocated to its present position in the north-east corner of Hyde Park at the Cumberland Gate.

---

[217] Construction of the Arch was completed in 1833.

"Hyde Park is just over there," Rachel said, pointing with her arm. She was wearing a baby blue cashmere jumper which highlighted her sapphire blue eyes exquisitely. On her slender wrist she was wearing a beautiful Longines watch. The round sunray blue dial was in a stainless-steel case. Sparkling diamonds were inset around the perimeter of the case, and the hour digits were marked with similar stones. The watch strap was an intricate stainless-steel chain-link mesh, which complemented the watch dial and case perfectly.

"Oh my gosh," exclaimed Nick. "What a beautiful watch." He took her hand and admired the jewelled timepiece.

"Why, thank you Nick," she said. "It was another present from my parents in February for my eighteenth birthday. I love it and only wear it on special occasions, like today."

She giggled and gave him a kiss on his cheek. "Now let's get to Speakers' Corner and see what is happening there today."

They walked along the paved pathway towards Speakers' Corner. Nick had heard of Speakers' Corner and looked forward to listening to some of the speakers. He had his arm around Rachel's shoulders, and she nestled comfortably into his caring embrace.

Nick already knew Rachel was 18 years old, but he did not know the date of her birthday, other than it was in February. "So, when is your birthday?" he asked.

"Well, I am a first of the month babe," said Rachel. "I was born on 1st February 1962. And when is yours?" she asked.

"I was born on 27th November 1960," said Nick. "So, I am just over a year older than you. My star sign is Sagittarius while you are an Aquarius."

"That's interesting," said Rachel. "My star sign is represented by the water healer, while yours is represented by the archer. Apparently, Aquarius is the last air sign of the zodiac. I think Sagittarius is a fire sign. I hope we will get on."

"Of course, we will," said Nick. "Fire and air are a powerful combination, aren't they? But look, it is getting busier. I think we must be getting closer to Speakers' Corner. I can see a couple of people on their soap boxes. Let's go and see what they are talking about."

As Christmas was only a few days away, it was not surprising that there were a number of persons who were talking about the birth of Christ and how His birth marked the way for humankind to be reconciled back to God. These speakers were often heckled by onlookers who were obviously persons of other faiths.

Other speakers were also speaking about the need for love and peace but not necessarily from a Christian perspective. They were instead focussing on the assassination of John Lennon[218], which had occurred a few weeks earlier in New York City. His death had stunned much of the world, especially the younger generations. From the speakers, Nick and Rachel learnt that John Lennon had been shot multiple times by a young man named Mark Chapman. Apparently, Mark Chapman had been incensed by John Lennon's lavish lifestyle and by the comments he had made in 1966, when he had claimed that the Beatles were more popular than Jesus. It was later to emerge that Mark Chapman claimed to be doing the will of God by assassinating John Lennon, and that in assassinating him, Mark Chapman was trying to emulate Holden Caulfield[219], the fictitious lead character in JD Salinger's book *Catcher in the Rye*.

There were also a number of speakers of Asian appearance who were berating the People's Republic of China's recently announced *One-Child Policy*[220]. The speakers claimed that this policy infringed upon the fundamental human right of people to determine their family size. A number of the speakers were urging the British Government to put

---

[218] John Lennon was the founder of the iconic British rock group, The Beatles.
[219] In the book, *Catcher in the Rye*, Holden Caulfield suffered from an all-consuming rage against adult hypocrisy and phoniness.
[220] The One-Child Policy was a program that was implemented nationwide by the Chinese Government in 1980 in order to limit most Chinese families to one child each. The policy was enacted to address the growth rate of China's population, which the Chinese Government viewed as being too high.

diplomatic pressure on the Chinese Government in an attempt to get that government to reverse its controversial policy.

Nick was astounded by the freedom of speech the speakers enjoyed, despite the presence of several uniformed policemen nearby. "It amazes me that people can say just about anything they want," Nick remarked. "That certainly wouldn't be allowed in my country. Censorship, in one form or another, has been in place in Rhodesia since the mid-1960s, and I'm sure it will continue under Mugabe. It seems to me that freedom of speech is strongest in countries with stable and inclusive governments, and most restricted in those places ruled by dictatorships or where the government isn't inclusive."

"Well, the British people highly cherish their right to free speech. I find it difficult to imagine any situation whereby the British people would allow the British Government to put significant limits on that freedom. I suppose our parliamentary traditions are stable and inclusive, so at least Britain supports your hypothesis," replied Rachel. "But let's move on. Our next stop is Buckingham Palace. It is about a 20-minute walk. We need to get there before 10:30 am to get a good spot to see the Changing of the Guard."

They headed south through Hyde Park, exited at Stanhope Gate, and continued down Park Lane. Just after an impressive five-star hotel called *45 Park Lane,* they turned left into Curzon Street, which they followed before turning right into an exotic sounding street called Half Moon Steet. They followed this street until it dissected a very busy road called Piccadilly. They crossed over Piccadilly using the pedestrian crossing and, walking in a south-easterly direction, entered a park called Green Park.

They exited Green Park on its southern boundary through the Canada Gate, crossed Constitution Hill, and followed the signs to Buckingham Palace. When they arrived, they were pleased to discover that it was not too busy. This allowed them to take a closer look at the very impressive Victoria Memorial which stood immediately in front of the main palace gates.

Rachel told Nick that the Victoria Memorial had been built to honour Queen Victoria and was dedicated by King George V in 1911. She explained that the monument stood nearly 25 metres tall and was sculpted from white marble by Sir Thomas Brock. At the top of the central plinth was a gilded angelic figure called Winged Victory, which stood on a globe, with several striking bronze figurines beneath it.

The central plinth featured statues on each of its four sides. Facing the Mall and looking north-east, was the seated Queen Victoria. She appeared to be waiting to greet all visitors to Buckingham Palace. On the three other sides of the plinth were the Angel of Truth, the Angel of Justice, and a statue of Motherhood, which was facing in a south-westerly direction directly towards the palace. At the four corners of the monument were more massive bronze figures. Rachel told Nick that these bronze figures represented Peace, Progress, Agriculture, and Manufacture.

Nick remarked on the poignancy of this symbolism and said, "This really is a very impressive memorial. It speaks volumes about both Queen Victoria and Britain."

Having marvelled at the beauty of the Victoria Memorial, they then moved towards the gates of Buckingham Palace and were able to get a splendid spot about ten metres directly in front of the palace gates. The two guards who were on guard duty in the palace's forecourt stood stoically still in front of their sentry boxes, resplendent in their scarlet-red uniforms and black bearskin head caps. Guard shifts would last for two hours, and during this time each of the two guards would be required to remain motionless but ever alert.

Rachel explained that the Changing of the Guard was the ceremony during which guard duties for the protection of Buckingham Palace and the nearby St James's Palace were handed over from one regiment of the Queen's Foot Guards[221] to another. The ceremony showcased

---

[221] The Queen's Foot Guards are senior infantry regiments responsible for guarding the Royal Family. They also perform other ceremonial duties but, at the same time, are combat soldiers.

quintessential English pageantry, as the outgoing regiment, known as *the Old Guard,* transferred responsibility for guarding the two palaces, along with the nearby Wellington Regimental Barracks, to the incoming regiment, known as *the New Guard,* for the next 24-hour period. The pomp and ceremony were underscored by marching music provided by a regimental brass band.

The entire ceremony lasted about 40 minutes. The carefully choreographed and precision marching of soldiers in their ceremonial dress, reminded Nick of his time during national service when, on certain important ceremonial occasions, his regiment had to parade on the drill square under the watchful and fearsome eye of the Regimental Sergeant Major. Nick remembered fondly how these parades were particularly enjoyed by the RAR[222] soldiers. They would literally spend days getting their uniforms washed, starched, and ironed so they were wrinkle-free with straight plumb-lined creases running down each trouser leg and along each arm sleeve. Then they would spit-and-polish their black boots until they gleamed like new unspoilt sump oil. The soldiers' innate sense of rhythm meant that marching drills came naturally to them, and very often would be accompanied by them singing their hauntingly beautiful regimental song, *Sweet Banana*[223].

After the Changing of the Guard ceremony had ended, Nick asked Rachel where the next stop was going to be.

"Well," said Rachel, "having heard you and Dad talk extensively about how the new Zimbabwe was created, I thought we should visit the place where all the discussions and negotiations occurred. Our next stop is Lancaster House. From what I understand, the future of Zimbabwe for the next 20 years will depend largely on what was

---

[222] Rhodesian African Rifles.

[223] Sweet Banana was a song that was created in 1942 and which was used by the Rhodesian African Rifles as its regimental marching song. When the RAR was disbanded in 1981 following the establishment of Zimbabwe, they sang the song for the last time as they marched through the streets of Bulawayo.

agreed upon there late last year. As a result of that agreement, the country will either mature and thrive or stagnate and unravel."

Rachel led the way back to Green Park and then through the park to Lancaster House. The short walk took them about 15 minutes.

Rachel had read up on Lancaster House, and during the walk through Green Park she told Nick that Lancaster House was originally known as York House. This was because its construction had been commissioned by the 'grand old' Duke of York in 1825. After the Duke died, the house was purchased by the Duke of Sutherland, whose family occupied the house from 1829 until 1912. During this time the house was the hub of social and political life for London's high society. In 1912 the house was purchased by Sir William Lever[224] who was from Lancaster. He renamed the building Lancaster House and gifted it to Britain in 1913.

Since then, the building had been the venue of many significant political events, including the signing of the agreement of independence for Malaya in 1956, and the transition of South Africa to a republic in 1961. And, as Nick already knew, it had most recently been the venue for the negotiation and signing of the Lancaster House Agreement[225], under which the warring parties in Zimbabwe-Rhodesia agreed to a ceasefire, which ended the Rhodesian Bush War and led to the country achieving internationally recognised independence as Zimbabwe.

Nick wanted to do a tour of the inside of Lancaster House, but when he and Rachel made enquiries, they were told that the house was not open to the public, other than on a few ad hoc special occasions. The concierge they spoke to did, however, give them some information about the house. He described it as a neo-classical mansion with fabulous Louis XIV style interiors, a stunning art collection, and a

---

[224] Sir William Lever, together with his brother, James Darcy Lever, were the original founders of the British manufacturing company Lever Brothers, which they founded in 1885.
[225] The Lancaster Agreement was negotiated between relevant parties during the period from 10th September 1979 to 15th December 1979. It was signed on 21st December 1979.

beautiful terrace and garden some of which Rachel and Nick could see from where they were standing. The concierge allowed them to look through the portico entrance into the Grand Hall, which opened up to reveal a sweeping staircase and balustrade, in the style of the Palace of Versailles just outside Paris. The concierge went on to describe other significant rooms in the mansion including the Long Gallery, the Music Room, the State Dining Room, the State Drawing Room, the Green Room, the Gold Room, and the Eagle Room.

Now that Nick had a small understanding of the grandeur of Lancaster House, he wondered how the Zimbabwe-Rhodesian dignitaries and black nationalist leaders who had participated in the Lancaster House negotiations, would have felt about deciding the future of their home country in such palatial surroundings.

Disappointed that they had not been allowed to tour the inside of the mansion, but appreciative of the fact that they had at least been able to see some of the surrounding gardens as well as looking into the Grand Hall, they decided to head off towards Regent and Oxford Streets to do their Christmas shopping.

To get to Regent Street, Rachel took them along a road called Stable Yard which ran between Lancaster House and Clarence House. From Stable Yard, they turned right into a road called Cleveland Row, and then left into St James Street. This road became Albemarle Street once it crossed Piccadilly.

By now it was nearly 1:30 pm. Rachel suggested that they stop for lunch at a famous historical pub called the Kings Head. This was located just off Albemarle Street in a road called Stafford Street.

The pub was heaving with people, but they were lucky to come across a table that was being vacated by an elderly couple. Rachel slipped into one of the vacant seats, while Nick made his way to the bar, where he ordered two pints of lager plus a chicken and mushroom pie for himself, and a fish pie for Rachel.

Over lunch, Nick thanked Rachel for having spent so much time planning the day. "It has been absolutely brilliant," he enthused. "You

the UNRAVELLING

have no idea how wonderful it has been to visit places which I have heard about but never seen. And the historical context you have added has further enriched the experience. You are a complete star."

"Well, you are definitely worth it," said Rachel. "I enjoy every second we are together." She leaned into him and gave him a loving kiss. He responded with an equally amorous caress.

After lunch, they agreed to part ways and meet again at 4:00 pm on Oxford Street, at the entrance to the Oxford Circus Tube Station. Nick wanted to buy Rachel a Christmas present, along with gifts for Stuart and Lynne. Similarly, although Rachel had already purchased Christmas presents for her family, she still needed to buy a gift for Nick and one for her long-time friend Claire, whose nineteenth birthday party they had attended earlier in the year.

Nick got to the Oxford Circus Tube Station entrance just before 4:00 pm, while Rachel arrived just after 4:00 pm. They were both carrying the wrapped spoils from their shopping sprees. They gave each other a big hug and then went into the station to begin their two-hour trip back to Rachel's parents house in Guildford.

That night over dinner, Nick and Rachel shared the details of their day's outing with Stuart and Lynne. Stuart was particularly impressed to find out that Rachel had made the effort to take Nick to Lancaster House as well as doing some research into its history.

"I had no idea you would be interested in Lancaster House and its history," Stuart said. "I wish you had let me know. It is managed by the Foreign & Commonwealth Office, and I know some very senior bureaucrats who work there. Given the fact that Nick is from Zimbabwe, I might have been able to organise for you to have been shown around the place."

"That would have been special," said Rachel. "But never mind — we may be able to do that some other time. The research I did into the Lancaster House Agreement, together with what Nick and you have taught me over the last few days, certainly helped me understand more about the complex negotiations that preceded the end of the

Rhodesian Bush War and the creation of the new Zimbabwe. I would love to visit it one day with Nick."

At Rachel's mention of a visit to Zimbabwe, Nick took her cue and jumped into the conversation. He looked at Stuart and Lynne and said, "In fact, Rachel and I have been talking about visiting Zimbabwe next year. We're thinking of going during our summer university vacs next year. Would that be OK with you both?"

Nick thought he saw a shadow of doubt fall across Lynne's face. But this was quickly replaced by an enthusiastic smile. "That would be wonderful," she said. "I have visited Africa a couple of times with Stuart and have always loved my trips there."

"That's true," enthused Stuart. "I am sure Rachel would enjoy every moment of such a trip. I certainly know Nick must be keen to see his parents and friends again. Going during your summer vacations seems like a sensible idea. Zimbabwe has an idyllic climate, and even in winter it is as beautiful as ever. I am tempted to go myself again with Lynne. It would be wonderful to catch up with Nick's father again."

There was a general buzz of excitement around the dining room table as the four of them began talking about the proposed trip. A month-long trip by Nick and Rachel was almost a certainty, while it began to seem quite likely that Stuart and Lynne might be able to join them for one or two weeks.

That night both Nick and Rachel retired to their respective bedrooms full of excitement. Their dreams that night were full of African imagery — both magical, and sometimes, frightening.

Chapter 23 – Nick's wish for a white Christmas comes true

Traditionally, Christmas Day in the Dixon household always began early, with Rachel waking at first light. She would creep downstairs, carefully nursing the wrapped presents for her parents under her arm, which she would place under the Christmas tree in the reception hall. The area beneath the tree would already be festooned with the presents her parents had positioned there before retiring to bed the night before. Rachel would switch on the air-conditioning in the reception hall to remove the chill from the air. She would then go into the kitchen to warm some mince pies and make a pot of tea for her parents and herself. Once these were ready, she would put some Christmas music on the turntable and go upstairs to wake her parents, who, more often than not, would already be awake.

The three of them would then come downstairs to enjoy a cup of tea and mince pies. Then *the present-opening ceremony* would start. First of all, her Dad would hand out all the presents. No one was allowed to open any of their presents until he had distributed them all. Then present opening would commence, with Rachel opening the first present of her choice. Once this had been opened, it would be her Mum's turn, then her Dad's. This cycle would be repeated until all the presents had been unwrapped. Following the *present-opening ceremony,* Stuart would clear up the scattered debris while Rachel and Lynne would prepare breakfast, the menu for which would have been decided on the previous day.

After breakfast, the family would go to the 10:30 am church service at their local church, St Saviour's Anglican church. After the church service, the family would return home and generally relax until after lunch, which was when preparations for their traditional Christmas dinner would commence with dinner starting at about 6:30 pm.

However, Christmas 1980 was somewhat different. Firstly, Nick was the Dixons' house guest, so he was included in all their comings and goings. Secondly, Rachel and Nick were rapidly falling in love, which meant that their preoccupation with each other tended to take priority over almost everything else. Finally, the weather in Guildford that year was abnormally cold during Christmas.

When Rachel had gone to sleep the previous night, she had done so with a sense of excitement and exhilaration. Consequently, it had taken her longer than normal to fall asleep. This was mainly due to the fact that she knew Nick was in the room just down the passageway from her room. She longed to be nestled up in bed with him and was tempted to breach her family's unwritten laws and sneak down the passage into his room once again. Despite the strong temptation, she had eventually fallen asleep without yielding to these enticements.

She had however woken earlier than normal, even for Christmas Day. Although it was still dark, the darkness was not complete, so she knew the first traces of light were not far away. She lay still, trying to pick out the sounds of the first birds to break the dawn silence. While she was pleasantly warm beneath her duvet, she knew it was a very cold morning. She purposefully exhaled, and there was now enough light for her to see her breath condense as a fleeting cloud before her eyes.

The sight of her breath forming a hazy mist in the air made her wonder if it had snowed overnight. She threw back her duvet, reached for her dressing gown at the end of the bed, and slipped her feet into her sheep's-wool-lined slippers. Wrapping the warm dressing gown over her cream-coloured satin camisole pyjamas, she walked to the large bedroom window overlooking the garden and slightly parted the curtains. Despite it still being half-light, she was thrilled to see that, overnight, there had indeed been a good fall of snow, blanketing the manicured lawns like a shroud of white icing sugar.

"How magical," she whispered. "Nick is going to love this." She opened her door and quietly tiptoed towards his closed bedroom door.

She opened the door. The curtains to Nick's room were still closed so the room was darker than the passage down which she had crept. Her eyes took an instant to adjust to the comparative darkness of the room. Once they had, she could quite easily make out the double bed in the centre of his room with his body beneath the duvet. She moved to the edge of the bed, slipped off her dressing gown and slippers, pulled pack his duvet and climbed under it next to his tantalising body.

Nick was only wearing a pair of sleeping shorts and a vest. Having discarded her dressing gown, Rachel's body had quickly become chilly. She burrowed in against his warmth and lay her head on his chest.

Nick was in the middle of a disturbing dream. He was back in Zimbabwe and Rachel was with him. He sensed they were in danger but was unsure what from. Indistinctively, he had pulled Rachel in towards him to protect her. He was holding her head tightly against his chest.

Rachel pulled back from Nick's tightened grasp, and this movement woke him up. He opened his eyes and relaxed immediately upon realising he had been dreaming and that Rachel was now beside him in bed.

He held her close, and she moulded herself into his embrace. "I have something I want to show you," she whispered. "Come and see. But be quiet. I don't want us to wake up Mum and Dad."

She climbed out of bed, and Nick followed. Her cream-coloured satin camisole nightwear accentuated her sleek figure. The cold air in the room sent a shiver down both their spines, and they spooned together for warmth. She led him to the bedroom window and pulled open the heavy curtains. By now, the growing morning light had largely chased away the darkness of the night. The snow-blanketed garden lay asleep before them, its surface as smooth and unblemished as the baize on a snooker table, while icicles hung like delicate jewelled necklaces from the leaves of the large oak trees that silently stood guard along the curved driveway. The scene he was gazing upon was picture-perfect, and for a few seconds, he was speechless.

"Oh my gosh Rachel. How beautiful. My first view of snow and a sight I shall not forget. Thanks for waking me up to show me it," he said in a soft voice.

Rachel shivered again with cold. Nick picked her up in his arms and carried her back to his bed. The duvet was still pulled back. He placed her down on the fitted white cotton sheet, lay down next to her and pulled the duvet back up over their bodies.

"I want you Nick," she whispered huskily. "But we will need to be quiet."

Nick slipped her camisole pyjama top over her head and did the same with his vest. Their bodies melted into one another, and they kissed deeply and passionately. Their hands and mouths explored each other intimately and unashamedly. They were both keen to make love, but neither of them was in a hurry. The discovery of each other was as pleasurable and erotic as the ultimate culmination. And when they did make love, their sexual intimacy was intense yet selfless, as they both sought to please the other. Their love making was all done in low whispers and with slow movements. Strangely, the need to be discreet and quiet added to the thrill of the whole sensual experience.

And when it was over their satisfaction was complete. They lay together in their nakedness and, in silence, rejoiced at what they knew they had found in one another.

After many minutes of complete contentment, Rachel eventually broke the silence by saying, "As much as I would like to stay here for a lot longer, I had better be a good girl and get the Dixon Christmas Show on the road. The first event is the *present opening ceremony*. Where have you put those presents you bought when we in London on Saturday? If you give them to me, I will take them downstairs and put them where they belong. You just stay here in your room and follow the cues as they are given. It is actually quite a lot of fun."

"I am intrigued," said Nick. He got out of bed, slipped on his sleeping shorts, and walked over to the built-in cupboard in his room. From its top shelf, he retrieved the three presents he had bought a few days earlier. He handed them to Rachel, who had put back on her camisole pyjamas, gown, and slippers. She tucked the presents under her arm and headed downstairs.

Nick soon caught the enticing smell of warming mince pies wafting upstairs from the kitchen. This was accompanied by the sounds of well-known Christmas carols coming from the turntable in the drawing room. Shortly afterwards, her dulcet voice called out, "Wakey wakey you sleepy heads. It's Christmas Day. And nature has given us a wonderful fresh fall of snow. Come and have a look."

Nick got out of bed, pulled on his track suit top and bottoms and went downstairs to the reception hall. Rachel was sitting alongside the tall Christmas tree. Next to her, there was a tea trolley laden with a plate of mince pies, jug of cream and a pot of tea.

Stuart and Lynne arrived just after Nick. Once tea had been poured and mince pies put onto side plates with big dollops of thickened cream, Stuart began the tradition of handing out the presents. True to form, no one was allowed to open any of their presents until they had all been dished out. Then it fell to Rachel to open her first gift.

Rachel played a bit of a charade, trying to decide which of her presents would be the first to be opened. But all along she had her eye on the box-shaped present that Nick had given her earlier from the cupboard in his bedroom. This had been carefully wrapped in midnight blue paper on which a gold leaf pattern had been printed. The wrapping was completed by the addition of a gold ribbon and a gift tag which read, 'To my darling Rach. I am such a lucky man. Yours for always. Love Nick.'

Rachel carefully untied the ribbon and took off the wrapping paper. Inside was a light grey and red box containing a Canon F-1n 35mm

SLR[226] camera. Nick had discovered that Rachel was a keen photographer but her camera was old and she needed a replacement. He had also heard her extol the virtues of the Japanese-made Canon cameras. When they had gone shopping on the prior Saturday, he had been lucky enough to stumble upon a top-end camera store in Regent Street as well as a salesman who was a whizz on everything to do with photography. The salesman was especially knowledgeable on the Canon brand. Apparently, the Canon F-1 was one of their best ever cameras. It had first been released in 1971. Since then, various minor modifications had been made to the original F-1 camera. In 1976 the new F-1n model was released. Apparently this included around a dozen or so modifications and improvements to the original model.

When Rachel opened the gift, she went wild with excitement. "Oh my goodness Nick. I could not have wished for anything else. It is beautiful. And the F-1n model has a whole lot of cool new features including a shutter speed of over $1/2000^{th}$ of a second. I cannot wait to try it out."

"Well I hope you get familiar with it quickly," said Nick. "When we go to Zimbabwe next year we are definitely going to go on a safari. So you will have lots of opportunities to take some really good pictures."

Nick was the next person to open the first of his gifts. He decided to follow Rachel's lead and opted to open the present that bore a gift tag from her. The words on the gift tag were simple, *'To my darling Nick. To our ongoing journey together. All my love. Rachel.'* The parcel itself was about the size of a small box of chocolates but twice the thickness. Nick had no idea what it might contain. He carefully removed the ebony black wrapping paper and white ribbon. Inside, was a malachite green leather box. The box had no markings on it other than an imprinted crown logo in the bottom right corner, which he immediately recognised as the Rolex logo.

"You haven't bought me a Rolex watch have you Rach?" he asked.

---

[226] SLR is the acronym for single-lens reflex.

"Yep, I sure have," she replied excitedly. She came over to him and sat on his lap. "I had no idea what to get you until we went into London on Saturday. You were so impressed by the Longines watch that Mum and Dad had given me for my 18th birthday that I thought I would treat you to something special as well. Open the box and have a look."

Inside the box was a beautiful Rolex Explorer 1016 watch. The watch had a black dial with a stainless-steel oyster strap and luminous white hands. Its design and engineering were sublime. Rachel told him that the watch itself had its origins in the watches that Rolex had supplied to Edmund Hilary and his expedition team in 1953 when they conquered Mt. Everest. Since then, there had been a number of changes to the watch to make it more suitable for everyday wear.

Nick loved it. He thanked Rachel with a heartfelt kiss and placed the watch on his wrist.

Rachel had bought her parents a joint present - a water colour painting by the landscape artist, William Heaton Cooper. Her parents loved the Lake District National Park in the north-west of England, and this was a painting of the Wast Water Lake in the western part of the national park. The gift was an instant hit.

Rachel's parents had bought Nick a new Dunlop squash bag, inside which was one of Dunlop's latest generation squash racquets. The racquet was not made of wood but of a composition of fibreglass and aluminium. The racquet head itself was no longer round but shaped like a tear drop. Nick's mate at Edinburgh University, Brian McKenzie, had recently purchased a similar racquet which he had allowed Nick to try out. The new design and materials meant that the re-engineered racquet could generate much greater power with less effort.

Nick was delighted with the gift. This was even more so given the fact that the weight of the racquet, the circumference of the handle, and the grip material, were exactly what he would have chosen if he were buying the racquet himself. When remarking on this to Stuart and Lynne, they confessed that Rachel had helped them in their selection. Rachel further confessed that she had liaised with Brian, who had told her exactly what to buy. Nick laughed and congratulated Rachel and her parents on their resourcefulness.

In deciding what to buy Stuart and Lynne for Christmas, Nick sought advice from Rachel. She informed him that her mum liked to collect Royal Doulton figurines. So, for Lynne, Nick purchased a porcelain figurine called *Christmas Parcel*. The figurine depicted a Victorian lady dressed in a long dark green coat, surrounded by presents and a small Christmas tree. Given the time of year, Nick felt the gift was appropriate. Fortunately, Lynne agreed — she loved it and placed it in a prominent spot in the large display cabinet in the lounge.

Rachel had also told Nick that Stuart had recently taken up birdwatching as a hobby. So Nick had bought him a pair of Bird & Stroud 10 x 42 waterproof binoculars. Stuart loved them and commented that not only would he be using them for birdwatching, but would also take them with him to Zimbabwe for game-viewing.

The rest of Christmas Day pretty much followed the script as outlined by Rachel. This included having breakfast, going to the local Anglican church service in the morning, playing board games and listening to the Queen's Christmas message in the afternoon, then enjoying a sumptuous traditional Christmas dinner in the evening. Nick also found half an hour to excuse himself from all the activities to allow him to phone his parents back in Zimbabwe and to wish them all a merry Christmas.

The two-week period following Christmas day raced by. Nick and Rachel were able to do much in and around Guildford. In addition, some friends of Lynne and Stuart had made their lovely holiday cottage available to the Dixon family. The cottage was in Windermere, in the Lake District, and the invite to use it had also been extended to Nick.

On Tuesday, 30th December, they drove up to the Lake District for a week. The weather remained cold, but fortunately it was reasonably clear and dry, at least during the day. They spent a lot of time enjoying bracing walks and appreciating the dramatic scenery that abounded.

This gave Rachel plenty of opportunity to start experimenting with her new camera.

As it was winter, there were few tourists about, making driving a pleasure. On the rare occasions when it did start to drizzle during their walks, they found it easy to locate an uncrowded pub with a cosy fire inside. They would settle at a table close to the fireplace, order some hearty English pub food for lunch, and easily while away an hour or so enjoying a drink or two, a delicious meal, and each other's company.

They returned to Guildford on Wednesday, 7th January 1981, after a thoroughly enjoyable holiday together. The time away had allowed Nick, Stuart and Lynne to get to know each other better. Fortunately, they had all enjoyed being together. Many stories were told and past experiences shared. By the end of the trip, Stuart and Lynne were captivated by Nick and he by them.

Rachel observed all this with growing pleasure. On the drive back to Guildford from Windermere, Rachel had commented on how well they had all got on. Everyone agreed and Lynne said that this augured well for their planned trip to Zimbabwe in six or seven months time.

Once back in Guildford, Nick had just over a day to prepare for his return trip to Edinburgh. Both he and Rachel busied themselves in different ways as they were dreading having to say goodbye to one another.

Saying farewell on Friday, 9th January 1981, was hard for both of them. However, they knew they could still talk over the phone every few days and that it wouldn't be long before Rachel could visit him again in Edinburgh.

More importantly, they knew it was only six or seven months before they would all be together again in a completely different part of the world.

This knowledge made the ache of their separation almost bearable.

Michael Chalk

Chapter 24 – Sipho transfers to 1RAR

Timeline – April 1980 to July 1980

You will remember that in June 1979, Corporal Pukelo's platoon had been involved in a firefight with a gang of terrorists in the Chimanimani area of Zimbabwe-Rhodesia. During the firefight, Corporal Pukelo had spectacularly slain the terrorists' stick commander, *Satani*, with a burst of fire from his MAG[227]. The slaying of Satani in such a dramatic manner had catapulted Corporal Pukelo's reputation amongst the other 3RAR[228] troops to unheralded heights.

At the time of the firefight, Corporal Pukelo had believed that the hostilities in Zimbabwe-Rhodesia would begin to subside following the general elections that had been held two months prior, but his optimism proved misplaced. These elections, which saw Bishop Abel Muzorewa become the country's first black prime minister, were supposed to end the Rhodesian Bush War and allow the country to regain international recognition after its illegal unilateral declaration of independence from the UK in 1965. However, neither peace nor recognition followed.

The 1979 general elections resulted from the 1978 Internal Settlement, negotiated between Ian Smith's government and moderate black nationalist leaders[229], including Muzorewa. While the agreements

---

[227] The Belgian designed Fabrique Nationale 7.62mm general-purpose machine gun. The MAG was standard issue for the Rhodesian Security Forces.
[228] 3rd Battalion of Rhodesian African Rifles.
[229] Black signatories to the Internal Settlement, signed on 3rd March 1978, included Bishop Abel Muzorewa, leader of the UANC, Ndabaningi Sithole, leader of a more

underpinning the Internal Settlement granted voting rights to all citizens over 18, they also preserved privileges for the white minority, including a ten-year veto on constitutional changes.

ZANU[230] and ZAPU[231] had boycotted the elections, which Pukelo interpreted as a lack of confidence on their part. Though international observers declared the elections to be generally free and fair, key players like the UK, US, and the African Frontline States[232] criticised them, calling the process flawed due to the exclusion of ZANU and ZAPU, both of which were still regarded as terrorist organisations by the government and thus banned. For their part, neither ZANU nor ZAPU recognised the Internal Settlement. Their leaders accused Muzorewa of collaborating with the illegal Rhodesian government, branding him and the other signatories to the Internal Settlement as *sell-outs*, and vowing to continue fighting until inclusive elections were held or a military victory was achieved.

Consequently, the Rhodesian Bush War against ZANLA[233] and ZIPRA[234] was still raging ferociously. This meant that the RAR[235] and all other units of the Zimbabwe-Rhodesian Security Forces were still heavily involved in deadly conflict.

In fact, the intensity of the armed conflict had ramped up considerably as both ZANLA and ZIPRA sought to gain the upper hand in their influence over the local population. The number of large incursions into the country by ZANLA and ZIPRA increased significantly, and as a consequence, large tracts of the countryside were now under the effective control of either ZANLA or ZIPRA.

---

moderate faction of ZANU, and Chief Jeremiah Chirau, a notable figure amongst Rhodesia's traditional black chiefs.

[230] Zimbabwe African National Union.

[231] Zimbabwean African People's Union.

[232] These were a loose coalition of African countries from the 1960s to the 1980s committed to ending white minority rule in Rhodesia. They included Angola, Botswana, Mozambique, Tanzania, and Zambia.

[233] Zimbabwe African National Liberation Army. ZANLA was the military wing of ZANU.

[234] Zimbabwe People's Revolutionary Army. ZIPRA was the military wing of ZAPU.

[235] Rhodesian African Rifles.

In response, the Zimbabwe-Rhodesian Security Forces intensified external strikes on the core support structures of ZANLA and ZIPRA in Mozambique and Zambia, respectively.

Within the country, the situation had become more complex following the election of the nation's first black prime minister. ZANLA, in particular, sought revenge against segments of the black population for supporting the UANC in the April 1979 general elections, leading to daily violent, sometimes barbaric, acts of intimidation against targeted individuals.

Amidst this increased frequency of terrorist activity, Corporal Pukelo found himself involved in several significant contacts with enemy forces.

In one of these, he was commanding the lead vehicle of a small convoy carrying RAR troops, when the rear vehicle was ambushed by approximately a dozen terrorists who were using RPG[236], RPD[237], and AK-47[238] small arms. The rear vehicle had been immobilized and the troops therein had taken a number of casualties. Corporal Pukelo immediately stopped his vehicle, which was out of the killing zone, and directed rifle-grenade fire onto the terrorists' position followed by an immediate clearance of the position. He showed a calm, professional approach and handled his men in an excellent manner throughout. His personal example, courage, and bravery motivated the troops in his vehicle to help in repelling the ambushers, who fled after having suffered six fatalities and a number of other casualties.

On another occasion, he was visiting friends in the TTLs[239] when a group of terrorists, suspecting he might be a member of the RAR, started questioning and threatening him. Using guile and cunning, he

---

[236] Rocket-Propelled Grenades.

[237] The RPD was a 7.62 x 39 mm light machine gun developed in the Soviet Union.

[238] This was a light automatic rifle developed in the Soviet Union by small-arms designer Mikhail Kalashnikov. The AK-47 was the preferred rifle of ZANLA and ZIPRA forces.

[239] Tribal Trust Lands. These were large tracts of land, usually sub-optimal, which were set aside for settlement by black Africans.

convinced them that he was not, and they then left him alone. However, with clever and wily tactics, he was clandestinely able to determine the area in which this enemy group was located. Thereafter, he returned to his base camp and directed RAR troops to this area resulting in a successful contact.

2nd Lt Nick Sinclair made sure that these exploits by Corporal Pukelo, coupled with his exemplary actions in the earlier firefight with the gang of terrorists in the Chimanimani mountains, were brought to the attention of his company's commander, Major Alan Lane.

In 1977, the RAR had commissioned its first-ever black officers, and subsequently had started a strategic drive to identify existing NCOs[240] who were considered to be *officer material*. In late 1979, Major Alan Lane met with Nick to see if he felt that Corporal Pukelo might be a suitable candidate to attend an officer training course.

Nick recommended him without hesitation.

Subsequently, Major Alan Lane met with Corporal Pukelo to gauge his interest in officer training and, if he was interested, to inform him that he would recommend to Army HQ that Pukelo be invited to attend such a course. Feeling honoured by the approach, Corporal Pukelo gladly gave his consent.

From April to August 1979, the country awaited recognition of the newly elected Zimbabwe-Rhodesian Government, led by Bishop Muzorewa, by the Carter administration in the United States and by the newly elected Conservative Government of Margaret Thatcher in Britain. However, Thatcher believed that any agreement that excluded Robert Mugabe and Joshua Nkomo was destined to fail. Consequently, rather than recognising Muzorewa's new government, Thatcher, under pressure from Nigeria and Australia, announced at the CHOGM[241] in Lusaka on 6th August 1979 that she would pursue a different course of

---

[240] Non-commissioned officers.
[241] Commonwealth Heads of Government Meeting.

action by advocating for another all-party conference to be held in London at Lancaster House.

The Lancaster House Conference[242] brought Nkomo and Mugabe back to the negotiating table with the new Zimbabwe-Rhodesian Government under the prime ministership of Bishop Muzorewa.

During this turbulent period, Corporal Pukelo did his best to keep track of political sentiments in his operational areas. By September 1979, he had ascertained that support for Bishop Muzorewa's UANC party had virtually vanished, primarily due to ZANLA's intimidation tactics and the charisma of Robert Mugabe.

He also began to realise that if ZANU and ZAPU were ever to contest a general election, the vast majority of rural Africans would vote along tribal lines. Consequently, when 2nd Lt Nick Sinclair sought his advice in late December 1979 about the upcoming general elections, scheduled for February 1980 under Britain's authority and supervision, Corporal Pukelo confidently advised him that Robert Mugabe would win easily, given that he was from the Shona tribe, which outnumbered the Ndebele tribe by three or four to one.

In early February 1980, Corporal Pukelo was advised that the recommendation by his company commander, Major Alan Lane, that he be invited to attend an officer training course, had been rejected by Army HQ. No reason had been given for the rejection. But in discussions he had with Major Lane and 2nd Lt Sinclair, it was apparent that they were both extremely disappointed and perplexed by the non-acceptance of their recommendation.

---

[242] In August 1979, the British Government invited Bishop Abel Muzorewa, the Prime Minister of Zimbabwe-Rhodesia, Ian Smith, the leader of the Rhodesian Front and former Prime Minister of Rhodesia, the leaders of the Patriotic Front, Robert Mugabe and Joshua Nkomo, and other relevant political persons to participate in a Constitutional Conference at Lancaster House in London. The purpose of the Conference was to discuss and reach agreement on the terms of an Independence Constitution, to agree on the holding of elections under British authority, and to enable Zimbabwe-Rhodesia to proceed to lawful and internationally recognised independence, with the parties settling their differences by political means.

However, this disappointment was somewhat mitigated by other news from Army HQ. While Pukelo's recommendation for officer training had not been approved, he was to be promoted to Platoon Warrant Officer (PWO), with the promotion taking effect after the results of the upcoming British-supervised general elections were announced.

His promotion to PWO[243] was officially announced on Tuesday, 1st April 1980, which was a few weeks before Zimbabwe's first official independence day celebrations, on Friday, 18th April 1980.

Then in early June 1980, PWO Pukelo was informed that, effective 1st July 1980, he would be transferred back to D Company 1RAR[244] in Bulawayo. One of his new responsibilities would be to assist in integrating ZANLA and ZIPRA cadres into the newly formed ZNA[245].

He received news of his promotion with a mix of pride and unease. He was deeply proud to have his skills as a professional soldier recognised in such a way, and he knew his parents, Mandla[246] and Nandi[247], would be equally proud.

Yet, a sense of unease lingered. While the traditions and daily garrison routines of the RAR had remained largely unchanged since Zimbabwe's independence, everyone knew that significant changes were imminent. What no one could predict was how these changes would unfold or how smoothly the integration of ZANLA and ZIPRA cadres into the new regular army would proceed.

History would soon reveal that the RAR would be involved in one of its most significant and successful battles since its re-establishment in 1940. Yet, despite this remarkable victory, history would also show that the RAR, in its entirety, was disbanded a mere ten months later, leaving many Zimbabweans of all races bewildered.

---

[243] Platoon Warrant Officer.
[244] 1st Battalion of Rhodesian African Rifles.
[245] Zimbabwe National Army.
[246] Mandla is a Ndebele boy's name meaning Power and Strength.
[247] Nandi is a Ndebele girl's name meaning Sweetness.

Chapter 25 – Integrating the Rhodesian Army & guerrilla forces

Timeline – June 1980

Sipho[248] was excited by his upcoming return to 1RAR[249].

He had been allocated a single man's quarters at the Methuen Barracks[250]. The barracks were located just outside Bulawayo and only about an hour's drive from the home of his parents, Mandla[251] and Nandi[252] Pukelo, at Inyathi Mission[253]. Both Mandla and Nandi were still employed at the Mission where Mandla was now the maintenance manager while Nandi was in charge of the school's kitchen. Sipho was very much looking forward to being able to spend more time with them.

Sipho arrived at the barracks on 30th June 1980. He had few possessions, so moving into his allocated single man's quarters was simple. The quarters comprised a bedroom, small kitchen, bathroom, and a sitting room. They were spartanly furnished, but the availability

---

[248] Sipho is a Ndebele boy's name meaning Gift.
[249] 1st Battalion of Rhodesian African Rifles.
[250] These were previously named the Heany Barracks.
[251] Mandla is a Ndebele boy's name meaning Power and Strength.
[252] Nandi is a Ndebele girl's name meaning Sweetness.
[253] The Mission had been established by the Reverend Robert Moffat in 1859. It is situated some 75 kilometres north-north-east of Bulawayo. Moffat was a member of the London Missionary Society, which had been established in England with the aim of spreading the knowledge of Christ among heathen and unenlightened nations.

of electrical outlets in all the rooms, plus plumbed hot running water in the kitchen and bathroom areas, was a definite bonus.

Over the next few weeks, he set out to make the quarters feel a little homier. He arranged to have the various certificates and photographs, which he had received while at 3RAR[254], framed, and then he hung these in his bedroom. He got permission from 1RAR's adjutant to replace the army-supplied metal-framed single bed in his bedroom and the two upholstered casual chairs in the sitting room. He caught the bus into Bulawayo and purchased a double bed, a two-seater sofa, and two casual armchairs from the Bulawayo branch of Nyore Nyore Zimbabwe Furnishers. Once these had been delivered to his quarters and put in place, he felt completely satisfied with his new home.

When he arrived at the barracks, he sought out Emanuel Wushe, the 1RAR sergeant his father had arranged for him to meet back in early 1970 when he had first expressed interest in becoming a soldier. It was largely due to his discussions and visits with Sgt. Wushe that Sipho changed his mind about joining ZIPRA[255] and instead enlisted with the RAR[256].

Emanuel Wushe had by now risen to the commissioned rank of captain. Given the fact that in 1980 there were very few black commissioned officers in the RAR, Emanuel Wushe's rise to the rank of captain was a testament to his professionalism and soldiering skills.

Emanuel Wushe had taken a real liking to Sipho when they had first met back in 1970. He was absolutely delighted when his cousin, Jacob Mpofu, had subsequently advised him that Sipho had successfully applied, and had been accepted, for enlistment into the RAR in 1972. Since then, he had closely followed Sipho's career with the RAR and was well aware of his brave and heroic service with 3RAR.

---

[254] 3rd Battalion of Rhodesian African Rifles.
[255] Zimbabwe People's Revolutionary Army. ZIPRA was the military wing of ZAPU.
[256] Rhodesian African Rifles.

Captain Wushe was again delighted to learn, some months ago, that Sipho had been promoted to the rank of Platoon Warrant Officer and was being transferred back to 1RAR.

Although the Rhodesian Bush War was now over, garrison activities at 1RAR in the middle of 1980 were still extremely busy. This was not due to any actual military action involving 1RAR but was rather associated with the far-reaching political changes that were occurring, specifically within the armed forces and more generally within the country.

A new entity called the Zimbabwe National Army (ZNA) had been formed in early 1980, shortly after Zimbabwe achieved its independence. The ZNA[257] was made up of various units from the Rhodesian Army that had existed before independence, as well as the former ZANLA[258] and ZIPRA cadres.

The government's declared aim was to integrate the ZANLA and ZIPRA cadres into the formal structures of the new ZNA. However, this was proving to be extremely difficult to achieve, especially within the RAR battalions.

The RAR officers, most of whom were white but whose number now included a few black officers, including Captain Emanuel Wushe, had held many formal and informal meetings to try and understand the impediments to the successful integration of ZANLA and ZIPRA cadres into the ZNA and, more importantly, to identify possible solutions to such impediments.

One of the more cynical senior white RAR officers, Major Simpson who was in command of C company at 1RAR, had coined a phrase which soon became common parlance within 1RAR.

This phrase was a play on the existing acronym of SNAFU which had been used for many decades by military personnel around the English-

---

[257] Zimbabwe National Army.
[258] Zimbabwe African National Liberation Army. ZANLA was the military wing of ZANU.

speaking world. SNAFU was the acronym for **S**ituation **N**ormal, **A**ll **F**ucked **U**p.

Major Simpson had used a variation of the acronym in his observation that the ZNA was suffering from *SNAFU'ness.* This phrase described the chaotic state of affairs that existed within the ZNA in 1980.

In Major Simpson's context the word SNAFU was the first letter of the following five words, which he said perfectly described what was going on in the ZNA at that time – **S**uperfluous manpower, **N**epotism, **A**fricanisation, **F**ear and **U**nprofessionalism.

When Sipho had arrived at 1RAR, he and Captain Wushe were discussing the current state of affairs in the ZNA. Captain Wushe had stated that the ZNA was suffering from *SNAFU'ness.* Sipho had no idea what this meant and asked Captain Wushe to explain. As the term *SNAFU'ness* was by then in regular use amongst the commissioned officers of 1RAR, Captain Wushe had no difficulty in explaining the phrase to Sipho.

"Well Sipho," he said, "**S** stands for *Superfluous manpower.* As you know, the ZNA is trying to integrate the troops from the former Rhodesian Army, plus the ZANLA and ZIPRA cadres, into one cohesive unit. This would have been hard enough to do in war time, but in peace time it is simply impossible. There are just too many troops to fill the required needs. Ignoring reservists, I have heard that at independence there was a total of about 55,000 troops and cadres under arms. The ZNA generals have estimated that, as a peacetime army, they only need a regular force of about 20,000 to 25,000 troops.

"**N** stands for *Nepotism.* I have already begun to notice that senior positions in the ZNA are not being filled based on merit but rather on loyalty to particular political leaders or factions. Military appointments should be apolitical, as the army is meant to support the government of the day, regardless of the ruling party. However, both Mugabe and Nkomo are attempting to appoint their supporters to the highest possible ranks within the ZNA. You may have observed that tribalism remains prevalent in both ZANLA and ZIPRA — the majority of ZANLA troops are Shona, while most ZIPRA troops are Ndebele. Given that the

Shona tribe is significantly larger than the Ndebele, this disparity results in more persons of Shona ethnicity occupying senior positions within the ZNA, despite both ZANLA and ZIPRA having roughly equal-sized forces.

"A team, from the United Kingdom, called BMATT[259], has been engaged by the ZNA to help with the integration of ZANLA and ZIPRA forces into the ZNA. BMATT had been following a policy whereby, if a ZANLA member was appointed to a senior position within the ZNA, then his 2IC[260] had to be a ZIPRA member, and vice versa. This was to try and prevent either of the two guerrilla forces achieving effective control of the ZNA. Regretfully however, Mugabe is now changing this policy as he wants the ZNA to be dominated by ZANLA personnel.

"**A** stands for *Africanisation*. The government has implemented a policy to rapidly promote black individuals into senior public service positions. The ZNA hierarchy is also required to follow this policy. Given that so few black soldiers held senior positions in the Rhodesian Army before independence, the policy is understandable. However, what is now happening in the ZNA is that black individuals are being appointed to positions they are not fully competent to hold. Moreover, as these appointments are increasingly based on political criteria, we are likely to see the ZNA being led by relatively inexperienced officers who are more loyal to ZANU[261] than to the elected government of the day

"**F** stands for *Fear*. There is still a significant amount of fear and anxiety about the country's future, particularly among the white community. This includes white members of the former Rhodesian Army, many of whom held senior positions. A number of them have already decided to leave the country, while most of the others are adopting *a wait-and-see* approach. Given the racial tensions that have existed since 1965, the senior hierarchy of the new ZNA is making minimal efforts to retain those white personnel who are thinking about resigning. The ZNA

---

[259] BMATT is the acronym for the British Military Advisory and Training Team.
[260] Second in Charge.
[261] Zimbabwe African National Union.

leadership seems to believe that their departure will facilitate the government's policy of Africanisation — and it will. However, what they fail to recognise is that the ZNA is also losing valuable knowledge and experience at a time when it desperately needs both. In my opinion, the ZNA should be doing everything possible to prevent this brain drain.

"And finally, **U** stands for *Unprofessionalism*. ZANLA and ZIPRA forces were trained as guerrilla fighters, with a focus on undermining and destroying the fabric of the country. They were not trained to maintain peace and stability or to defend the country from external threats. Regrettably, from what I've observed so far, neither ZANLA nor ZIPRA exhibit the qualities of professional soldiers. Their discipline is weak, their willingness to follow orders is questionable, and their commitment to professional soldiering is lacking."

Captain Wushe paused, and then concluded by saying, "So you see Sipho, the challenge we face is huge. I don't think either Mugabe or Nkomo really understand that the Rhodesian Army was apolitical and served the government of the day. That used to be the RF[262] led by Ian Smith, then the UANC[263] led by Bishop Muzorewa, now it is ZANU-PF[264] led by Robert Mugabe. They wrongly believe that the former Rhodesian Army was only loyal to Ian Smith.

"And when it comes to the RAR, both Mugabe and Nkomo are unsure where its loyalties will lie. This is because, unlike most other units of the former Rhodesian Army, the RAR consists entirely of black soldiers, while all its officers, with few exceptions, are white. Consequently, both Mugabe and Nkomo are unsure whether RAR's loyalties will be to Ian Smith or to Robert Mugabe or to Joshua Nkomo. You and I know that the RAR will always be loyal to the government of the day. The government today happens to be ZANU-PF. So that is where our

---

[262] Rhodesian Front.
[263] United African National Council.
[264] Zimbabwe African National Union – Patriotic Front. ZANU-PF is a political organisation that has been the ruling party of Zimbabwe since independence in 1980.

loyalties lie. However, if the people of Zimbabwe were to elect a different government, then our loyalties would shift accordingly."

Sipho got up and shook Emanuel Wushe's hands. "You are a wise man, Captain Wushe. Thank you for explaining these things to me. You are like a father to me and I feel blessed to know you."

Chapter 26 – Sipho's actions with 1RAR in Entumbane

Timeline – November 1980 to February 1981

Immediately following the independence of Zimbabwe, the officers of 1RAR[265] did their best to try and play a meaningful role in assisting with the integration of former ZANLA[266] and ZIPRA[267] troops into the ZNA[268]. However, they were consistently frustrated in their attempts to do so, due to political manoeuvrings by both ZANU[269] and ZAPU[270].

In 1980, the plan was for the new national army to comprise around 29 battalions divided into four brigades, with the 1st Brigade being based in Matabeleland and to which 1RAR would belong. However, to date, only half-hearted attempts had been made to integrate former ZANLA and ZIPRA soldiers into 1RAR. This was largely due to the deep mutual suspicions between Rex Nhongo, ZANLA's commander, and Lookout Masuku, ZIPRA's commander. Both commanders preferred to keep the core of their troops in separate encampments rather than risk integrating them into 1RAR.

Their suspicions and distrust were fuelled by inflammatory statements from the senior political leadership of ZANU and ZAPU. ZANU accused ZAPU/ZIPRA of being anti-Zimbabwean, while ZAPU alleged that

---

[265] 1st Battalion of Rhodesian African Rifles.
[266] Zimbabwe African National Liberation Army. ZANLA was the military wing of ZANU.
[267] Zimbabwe People's Revolutionary Army. ZIPRA was the military wing of ZAPU.
[268] Zimbabwe National Army.
[269] Zimbabwe African National Union.
[270] Zimbabwe African People's Union.

ZANU/ZANLA exhibited gross favouritism in appointments to senior positions within the government, army, and civil service.

Sipho[271] had already participated in two separate week-long induction exercises, which involved about ten senior ZANLA and ZIPRA field commanders. The aim of these exercises was to allow the former guerrilla field commanders to get to know each other better, and to enable them to become familiar with the formal structures and garrison activities of ZNA's 1st Brigade. Assistance in these exercises was being given by the BMATT[272] team from the United Kingdom.

These formal structures and garrison activities were largely a replication of what had been in place in the former Rhodesian Army. As the Rhodesian Army had been established in the colonial era, these structures and activities followed the British *spit-and-polish* traditions.

However, the ZANLA and ZIPRA field commanders generally viewed these activities as a waste of time and energy. Moreover, it quickly became clear that neither army's commanders regarded the other as their equal.

On the other hand, the 1RAR officers, especially the white officers, while not openly stating it, tended to regard both the ZANLA and ZIPRA field commanders as a motley crew of ill-disciplined upstarts!

Consequently, both of the induction exercises in which Sipho had been involved were abject failures.

The senior command of 1RAR was still trying to develop strategies to improve any future induction exercises when, in early November 1980, the tensions between ZANLA and ZIPRA troops flared up.

ZANLA and ZIPRA troops were encamped in separate yet adjacent holding camps before their attempted integration into the ZNA. These camps were located in a western suburb of Bulawayo known as Entumbane.

---

[271] Sipho is a Ndebele boy's name meaning Gift.
[272] BMATT is the acronym for the British Military Advisory and Training Team.

Shortly after the troops had moved into their respective holding camps, the Minister of Finance, Enos Nkala from ZANU, had made a political speech, in which he had stated that ZANLA would ultimately destroy ZIPRA. This comment infuriated the leadership of ZAPU/ZIPRA.

Enraged, the armed ZIPRA troops mobilised out of their holding camp in Entumbane and attacked the adjacent ZANLA camp. A fierce firefight ensued which lasted about four hours.

When fighting broke out, Captain Wushe assumed that 1RAR would be deployed to quell the fighting. However, the commander of ZNA's 1st Brigade ordered 1RAR to remain on standby, and instead chose to deploy approximately 280 men from the largely white-led BSAP[273] Support Unit to quell the violence and restore law and order.

Four hours after the firefight began, and only after personal intervention by Robert Mugabe, Rex Nhongo[274] and Lookout Masuku[275], officers from both guerrilla forces called a ceasefire.

Estimates of fatalities and casualties during the four-hour firefight were approximately 100 fatalities and over 500 casualties.

Sipho, like most other members of 1RAR, was not surprised by the outbreak of factional violence. However, he felt disappointed that the BSAP had been deployed to quell the unrest instead of 1RAR.

The black residents of Bulawayo, having endured years of violence during the Rhodesian Bush War, were devastated that factional and tribal violence between ZANLA and ZIPRA troops had erupted within a year of the war's end.

Many in the country's white community expressed sentiments like *"We told you so"* and *"Thatcher and Kissinger – this blood is on your hands."*

---

[273] British South Africa Police.
[274] Rex Nhongo was the commander of the Zimbabwe African National Liberation Army (the military wing of ZANU).
[275] Lookout Masuku was the commander of the Zimbabwe People's Revolutionary Army (the military wing of ZAPU).

Political commentators saw Mugabe's honeymoon period coming to an end and began speculating on what might happen next.

In the weeks following the violence that had erupted in November 1980, little improvement was seen. The ZANLA and ZIPRA troops who remained in their respective holding camps at Entumbane, believed that integration into the newly established ZNA was unlikely to happen. Even if it did occur, they still viewed themselves as being under the command of either Rex Nhongo or Lookout Masuku, and struggled to accept the concept of apolitical command structures. They were also sceptical of the *spit-and-polish* traditions of the former Rhodesian Army, which they saw as outdated and unwelcome symbols of their former British colonisers.

Consequently, many of these men simply deserted their respective holding camps and formed themselves into lawless tribal-based[276] gangs who roamed the countryside, intimidated and assaulted ordinary civilians, robbed stores, committed arson, and attacked white farmers.

At the same time, the coalition government Mugabe had formed at independence was rapidly fracturing. Deep suspicions between ZANU and ZAPU political leaders were widespread, and this distrust extended to the very top, with both Mugabe and Nkomo frequently defaming each other, both publicly and privately.

These tensions reached breaking point in January 1981 when Mugabe removed Nkomo from his position as Minister of Home Affairs and assigned him to a ministerial role without a specific portfolio. This move was widely perceived by Nkomo and his supporters as a demotion and a deliberate snub by ZANU. In particular, ZAPU/ZIPRA leaders viewed Nkomo's reassignment as further evidence that Mugabe was actively pursuing a policy of politically marginalising ZAPU.

---

[276] Either Shona based (former ZANLA cadres) or Ndebele based (former ZIPRA cadres).

Fearing ongoing marginalisation, the ZIPRA leadership began building up their forces. Very soon they had assembled over 6,000 troops, together with heavy armoury and artillery, at a place called the Gwaai River Mine[277], which was 245 kilometres to the north-west of Bulawayo, plus another large, armoured battle group at Essexvale[278], which was 45 kilometres south-east of Bulawayo.

Following the uprisings at Entumbane a few months earlier, and amid the ongoing tensions between ZANLA and ZIPRA, the white commander of 1RAR, Lt. Col. Mick McKenna, had taken precautionary measures to improve intelligence gathering. These measures included setting up an operational base in a beerhall at Entumbane plus establishing a string of observation posts on major roads leading in and out of Bulawayo.

On 8th February 1981, another serious incident involving ZANLA and ZIPRA troops occurred in Gwelo[279], the provincial capital of the Midlands Province. In this incident, ZANLA troops ambushed ZIPRA troops. In the ensuing firefight approximately 60 ZIPRA soldiers were killed while the remaining ZIPRA men fled into the bush.

Later that same day, reports of the incident reached ZNA's 1st Brigade in Bulawayo. This news triggered an intense firefight between the remaining ZANLA and ZIPRA forces in the two adjacent Entumbane holding camps. ZIPRA troop launched an attack on their ZANLA counterparts, killing around 60 and forcing the survivors to flee into the surrounding bush.

Fearing that this clash might spark a major civil war between ZANLA and ZIPRA, ZNA's 1st Brigade headquarters ordered 1RAR to intervene.

Based on intelligence received from the operational base which he had established at the beerhall in Entumbane, on the evening of 8th

---

[277] Now known as Gwayi River Mine.

[278] Essexvale is a small town in the Matabeleland province of Zimbabwe located approximately 45 kms south-east of Bulawayo. It is now named Esigodini.

[279] Gwelo was renamed Gweru in 1982. Gwelo is located 160 kms north-east of Bulawayo.

February 1981, Lt. Col. Mick McKenna deployed D company, under command of Captain Wushe, together with a troop of four armoured cars, which were formerly part of the Rhodesian Armoured Corps.

The armoured cars tore through the ZIPRA tents in the holding camp, killing many occupants and clearing the way for the follow-up D Company troops. Among them was PWO[280] Pukelo, who led his men with professionalism and bravery. Despite the fact that the enemy he was now fighting was comprised almost exclusively of ZIPRA soldiers of Ndebele ethnicity — his own ethnicity — PWO Pukelo displayed considerable courage and ferocity.

The operation was successfully completed within a couple of hours. It resulted in about 40 ZIPRA soldiers being killed and many more being captured, including two ZIPRA officers.

1RAR itself suffered no fatalities and only a couple of minor casualties.

However, in the days that followed, ZIPRA personnel used civilian vehicles to smuggle weapons and equipment back into the Entumbane area. In addition, ZIPRA troops from the earlier build-up near Bulawayo in Essexvale began discreetly making their way into the ZIPRA holding camp in Entumbane. This increase in troops and weapons was observed by 1RAR soldiers garrisoned at the operational base at the Entumbane beerhall and was reported to ZNA's 1st Brigade.

The ZNA 1st Brigade headquarters ordered 1RAR *not* to intervene.

Lt. Col. Mick McKenna obeyed these orders but, fearing another outbreak of hostilities between the warring ZANLA and ZIPRA factions, took immediate steps to ensure his troops could defend themselves if they became embroiled in any ensuring conflict, which he believed was imminent. He deployed C Company, under Major Simpson's command, to bolster D Company, and both units took up defensive positions around Entumbane.

---

[280] Platoon Warrant Officer.

Sure enough, within 48 hours, two major firefights, including one at Entumbane, erupted between ZANLA and ZIPRA troops.

The ZIPRA forces at Entumbane quickly overran the ZANLA forces at their holding camp, and then attacked C company. The commander of C company, Major Simpson, radioed ZNA's 1st Brigade for further orders and again was advised to not intervene but to retreat. Major Simpson advised that retreat was impossible as his men were surrounded. He requested that the commander of ZNA's 1st Brigade make urgent contact with 1RAR's commander, Lt. Col. Mick McKenna, so that more appropriate orders could be given.

A short time later, the commanders of C and D companies, Major Simpson and Captain Wushe respectively, received countermanding orders to take whatever measures were necessary to repel their attackers and break out of their positions. Both officers utilised every available resource to drive back their ZIPRA attackers, but the fight was intense, and they were heavily outnumbered.

In an effort to gain a decisive advantage, Major Simpson requested reinforcements from ZNA's 1st Brigade, along with air support in the form of a light bomber. This support was provided, allowing C and D companies to eventually turn the tide after nearly 20 hours of fierce battle.

Meanwhile, a ZIPRA armoured vehicle detachment left Essexvale, heading towards Bulawayo to join the fight. The convoy was spotted by one of the observation posts Lt. Col. Mick McKenna had set up along the road from Essexvale to Bulawayo. In response, Lt. Col. McKenna redeployed his troop of four armoured cars, supported by a platoon from 1RAR's A company, to intercept the convoy.

The ambush was laid on the outskirts of Bulawayo, and under the cover of darkness, the unsuspecting ZIPRA vehicles entered the trap. The ambush was sprung, and the ZIPRA armoured detachment was swiftly eliminated. The armoured troop, along with the soldiers from A company, were then redeployed to assist an ZNA relief column that had been mobilised to reinforce C and D companies.

By the evening of 12th February 1981, the uprising was quelled. C and D companies were relieved, ZIPRA ceased their attacks, and their armoured battle group at Essexvale surrendered to the ZNA.

The propaganda arm of Mugabe's Government did not want to overstate the seriousness of the rebellion. Hence they put the official count of those killed during the uprising at 260 people. However, witnesses and troops involved in the uprising placed the number of dead closer to 1,000 and with many more casualties.

1RAR and other units of the ZNA suffered no fatal casualties.

Historical military writers later asserted that this was likely the RAR's[281] greatest victory. Despite being significantly outnumbered and outgunned, they prevailed through superior professionalism, discipline, and intelligence gathering. These commentators also highlighted the irony that Mugabe's new government, which was meant to represent national unity, had been saved from the brink of civil war by ex-Rhodesian troops under white command.

The rebellion's defeat was also a defining blow to the military might of ZIPRA, a blow from which it never recovered. Many ZIPRA guerrillas, fearing retribution from the Mugabe Government, deserted en-masse and dispersed back into rural life amongst the people of Matabeleland.

The Battle of Entumbane marked the RAR's final engagement. While the battle reassured many in Mugabe's government, including Mugabe himself, that white RAR officers could be relied upon in future conflicts with ZIPRA or ZANLA dissidents, they regrettably failed to recognise that the same was true for the black RAR troops, particularly those of Ndebele ethnicity.

Due to this distrust, a decision was made to disband the RAR in its entirety in April 1981. White officers who chose to remain in the ZNA were reassigned to various other units, as were RAR troops of Shona ethnicity who were actively encouraged to stay with the ZNA. In contrast, RAR troops of Ndebele ethnicity did not receive the same

---

[281] Rhodesian African Rifles.

encouragement — in fact, it was made patently clear to these troops that their future prospects within the ZNA would be severely limited.

The ongoing tensions between the ZANLA and ZIPRA forces made Mugabe feel that his position as Prime Minister could again be threatened by an armed uprising of ZIPRA troops. He was also concerned about the ZNA's over-reliance on former white members of the Rhodesian Security Forces and BMATT to oversee the training and integration of the guerrilla forces into the newly created ZNA. Mugabe believed that these training and integration personnel were unlikely to comply with his goal that the ZNA should primarily comprise troops whose first loyalty was to him.

Accordingly, he decided to strengthen his military position within the country. To achieve this, he established a fifth infantry brigade consisting almost entirely of ex-ZANLA troops and field commanders, and predominantly of Shona ethnicity. Furthermore, unlike the ZNA's other four brigades, this unit would be armed and trained by a special North Korean[282] military mission, selected due to Mugabe's admiration for the dictatorial regime of Kim Il Sung, with whom ZANLA's senior leadership had enjoyed cordial relations since the early 1970s.

Interestingly, the 5th Brigade was not structured for conventional military operations. Instead it was a specialised counter-insurgency unit with specific responsibility for handling political dissidents, and reported directly to Mugabe as Prime Minister.

History would soon reveal that Mugabe, remaining fearful of ZIPRA, ordered the deployment of the 5th Brigade into northern Matabeleland in January 1983 to eliminate local ZIPRA dissidents. Unfortunately, this anti-dissident campaign quickly escalated into a brutal five-year genocidal campaign against the Ndebele people in Matabeleland, known as the *Gukurahundi*[283] massacres, which resulted in the deaths

---

[282] North Korea is the common name for the Democratic People's Republic of Korea.
[283] *Gukurahundi* is Shona expression which loosely translates to '*the early rain which washes away the chaff before the spring rains.*' It is estimated that during the *Gukurahundi* massacres, more than 20,000 people were killed, the vast majority of whom were of Ndebele ethnicity.

of over 20,000 individuals, the vast majority of whom were of Ndebele ethnicity.

The sanctioning of the *Gukurahundi* campaign and the failure to curb the unchecked violence and murder of innocent civilians by the 5th Brigade stand as some of the most shameful acts of the new ZANU-PF government and its leader, Robert Mugabe.

Chapter 27 – Sipho resigns from the ZNA

Timeline – May 1981

The proposed disbandment of RAR[284], and the persistent rumours that RAR *masodjas*[285] of Ndebele ethnicity were being overlooked in terms of their future advancement within the ZNA[286], came as a complete shock to Sipho Pukelo, especially after his very recent gallant action against the dissident ZIPRA[287] and ZANLA[288] troops at Entumbane.

Having served in the RAR for over eight years, he knew soldiering was his calling. It was everything he had ever wanted to do. Now, he found himself torn between continuing his career with the ZNA, despite the uncertainty surrounding his future, or resigning and embarking on a new path.

Uncertain what to do, he sought counsel from his friend and colleague Captain Emanuel Wushe. Emanuel was empathetic, yet forthright, in the counsel he gave Sipho.

In a soft but sombre voice, Emanuel said, "Sipho, you know I have the utmost respect for you as a RAR soldier. You've served the Regiment well, and with honour and distinction, which is why you now hold the rank of PWO[289]. If it were up to me, you'd be an officer by now. But things are changing quickly in the ZNA. Rumours are everywhere. I've

---

[284] Rhodesian African Rifles.
[285] *Masodja* is the Africanised word for soldier.
[286] Zimbabwe National Army.
[287] Zimbabwe People's Revolutionary Army. ZIPRA was the military wing of ZAPU.
[288] Zimbabwe African National Liberation Army. ZANLA was the military wing of ZANU.
[289] Platoon Warrant Officer.

heard that Mugabe sees the ZNA as his personal army, and so he's ensuring that only people close to him are promoted to senior positions. Future senior appointments — and by this, I mean all commissioned officers — will likely be made on purely political grounds. Right now, it seems Mugabe believes that any Ndebele officer is a potential threat, assuming their loyalty will be to Nkomo, not to him."

"Fortunately, I'm from the Shona tribe, so Mugabe's fears won't affect me as much. But I worry that it will be different for you, being Ndebele. I know many senior Shona officers in the ZNA, and unfortunately, they're starting to follow Mugabe's lead. If you're Ndebele, the ZNA is going to be a hard place to work — especially for someone like you, who is a natural soldier and leader. I hate to say it, but Shona officers will see you as a threat and will use your Ndebele background to discredit and undermine you. If you stay in the ZNA, I fear you'll be blocked and frustrated at every step of your career."

"So, before deciding to stay within the ZNA, it might be a good idea to see what other options may be appropriate for you," said Emanuel.

Sipho was quiet for a few seconds. Then he said, "I appreciate your frankness Emanuel. As I have told you before, you are like a father to me and I value your advice. I have always known how strong tribal bonds are in Zimbabwe. There is nothing wrong with that. But, when a person's tribal heritage starts to be used to set one Zimbabwean citizen against another, then that is wrong and dangerous.

"I would have thought our new Prime Minister would understand this. After all, he suffered greatly because of his race. Tribalism is just another form of racism. Yet now that Mugabe has power, it seems he's willing to use tribalism to secure his position if he must.

"I'm proud to be Ndebele, but I'm even more proud to be Zimbabwean. If I can't be both a proud Zimbabwean and a respected Ndebele within the ZNA, then I think it's time for me to leave and find a place where I'll be judged on who I am and what I do, not on my ethnicity.

"The RAR has always respected all its soldiers, regardless of their tribe — even under white rule. Now that blacks are in charge, it's tragic that this respect is being stripped away from Ndebele soldiers. Mugabe is unwise to stir up tribal tensions and jealousy within the army. If this unity unravels, the consequences will be dire. I can feel it deep down. It's time for me to find a new path."

True to his word, a couple of weeks later, Sipho gave notice that he wished to be released from the ZNA at the end of May 1981. No attempts were made to dissuade him from this decision, nor was he asked to delay his requested departure date.

Sipho only had modest savings and had no pension entitlements. His departure from the ZNA also meant that when he left the army, he would also lose access to his single man's quarters at the Methuen Barracks[290].

Since he was uncertain how long it might take to find alternative employment, he felt uneasy about where he would live if the hiatus dragged on. However, his concerns were alleviated when Emanuel assured him that, should accommodation become an issue, he was welcome to stay with him temporarily.

In addition, his parents had also invited him to come and stay with them for a few months at Inyathi Mission once he left the army.

---

[290] These were previously named the Heany Barracks

Chapter 28 - Sipho joins Mhuka Ranch as its anti-poaching manager

Timeline – July 1981

The Victoria[291] province is one of the five original provinces of Rhodesia. It is situated in the south-east part of the country and encompasses an area known as the lowveld[292].

The lowveld's climate can be exacting, particularly during the long, very hot, and humid summers. Conversely, the winters are short, comfortable and dry. Over the course of the year the temperature typically varies from 11°C to 33°C and is rarely below 8°C or above 38°C. The summer rains are sporadic and patchy, and the threat of drought is like a tangible gloom, which can hang heavily over the bush, for months on end.

Mhuka[293] Ranch is a 500 square kilometre property near the town of Chiredzi, some 195 kilometres south-east of Fort Victoria[294]. The ranch's landscape of grassland, bush, mopane forest, acacia woods, and ancient baobab trees was theoretically ideal for the grazing of animals. The property had been purchased shortly after the end of the Second World War by a pioneer rancher named Duncan Oliver. He had originally purchased the property to enable him to fulfil his dream of ranching cattle in the lowveld area of Zimbabwe. However, raising

---

[291] The Victoria province was renamed the Masvingo province in 1982.
[292] The term lowveld refers to low-lying, generally semi-arid region characterised by savanna or bushveld vegetation.
[293] A local word meaning animals or wildlife.
[294] Fort Victoria was renamed Masvingo in 1982.

cattle in the lowveld in the 1950s was fraught with difficulties. Apart from plagues of tsetse flies[295] and the threat of malaria, it was also extremely difficult to protect the cattle from a large number of wildlife predators including lion, leopard, hyenas, and wild dogs.

Another significant challenge was securing water in the drought-prone lowveld, a harsh and unforgiving environment without it. To improve water security, Duncan constructed several dams and weirs, the largest being Ingwe Dam. *Ingwe* is an African word meaning "leopard," a name Duncan chose in recognition of the many leopards inhabiting the kopjes[296] and rocky outcrops near the dam

The construction of Ingwe[297] Dam had been a game-changer for Mhuka Ranch as it ensured water security not only for the cattle but also for the abundant wildlife on the ranch.

Once water supplies were secured, Duncan's forward-thinking and hard work transformed the ranch over approximately 30 years from dry, desperate scrubland to verdant, well-treed grasslands where both cattle and wildlife thrived.

Surprisingly, there was an abundance of wildlife on the ranch. Duncan was an avid advocate for the conservation of wildlife, and had spent countless hours educating the local tribespeople on its value, and the need for it to be cared for with the same diligence as they cared for their cattle.

The ranch was located alongside the Gonarezhou[298] National Park. Its boundary with the park was unfenced, which meant that animals were able to cross unhindered between the two properties.

---

[295] Tsetse flies are a species of a blood sucking fly which are found in Africa. They can transmit sleeping sickness in humans and a similar disease, called nagana, in animals. If left untreated these diseases can be fatal.
[296] The word kopje is derived from the Afrikaans word koppie, which means a small hill.
[297] Ingwe is a local African word meaning leopard.
[298] Gonarezhou is a Shona word meaning *place of elephants*.

In the early 1970s, Duncan had run into financial difficulties as a result of a severe outbreak of anthrax on the ranch. The outbreak resulted in the death of many of his cattle. Faced with mounting bank debts, Duncan realised that he needed to find new ways to generate additional income.

He quickly recognised that the untapped potential from the wildlife on his ranch would be able to provide the solution to his financial problems. Consequently, he had taken the controversial decision to launch exclusive big game hunting safaris on the ranch.

These hunting safaris targeted the lucrative overseas professional hunters' market. With a longstanding penchant for big game hunting, Duncan quickly tapped into this niche. He made alterations to the main homestead by adding a self-contained guest wing to accommodate groups of up to ten adults. Additionally, he invested in a small airstrip on the ranch, significantly increasing accessibility for international clients who would fly into Salisbury[299] or Johannesburg on commercial airlines before chartering private flights to the ranch.

The hunting safaris were a spectacular financial success. Paradoxically, the wildlife, which was hunted and shot by the professional hunters, also provided the regular income stream that Duncan needed to enable him to safeguard the remaining wildlife on the ranch.

The number and breed of animals available for hunts were strictly regulated and monitored by Duncan and his staff. They were fully aware that, without sustainable hunting practices, the financial viability of the safaris would be short-lived.

Duncan was careful to ensure that the local tribespeople benefited from the hunting safaris, thereby fostering a strong custodial attitude towards the wildlife. To achieve this, a significant portion of the income generated from the hunting safaris was reinvested in the local villages, enabling improvements to the tribespeople's living conditions, which were still very basic at that time.

---

[299] The capital of Rhodesia. Its name was changed to Harare in April 1982.

Duncan collaborated closely with the village elders to determine how to allocate the available funds. Following these discussions, additional wells with diesel-powered water pumps were constructed in the two villages on the ranch, along with a toilet and shower block. A protective fence was erected around the perimeter of both villages, and three cattle dips were built on the grazing lands designated for the tribespeople's indigenous *mombies*[300]. Furthermore, the classrooms and sports fields at the local community school were upgraded, and two trained nurses were employed at the local clinic.

By receiving these tangible benefits from the profits generated by the hunting safaris, the tribespeople quickly came to understand why it was important for them to be diligent custodians of the wildlife on the ranch.

In addition, Duncan used part of the income from the hunting safaris to fund anti-poaching activities aimed at protecting the wildlife from a small number of rogue local poachers. Initially, these anti-poaching efforts were relatively low-key and purely reactionary in nature.

However, in the late seventies and early eighties the extent, and hence the costs, of these anti-poaching activities had to be ramped up considerably.

The driver behind the increase in poaching activities was ironically triggered by the commencement of the international CITES[301] convention on 1st July 1975. While the convention had the meritorious objective of protecting and conserving endangered species of animals and plants, it sought to achieve this by making the international trade of these animals and species illegal in signatory countries. As a result, the trade of items such as ivory, rhino horn, and leopard and lion skins became illegal in many parts of the world.

---

[300] This is the Shona word meaning cows or cattle.
[301] Convention on International Trade in Endangered Species of Wild Fauna and Flora. It is a multilateral treaty designed to protect endangered plants and animals. It came into force on 1st July 1975.

However, this prohibition did not halt the trade — instead, it pushed it underground. The black market for these items grew rapidly, along with the prices that people were willing to pay. Consequently, illegal poaching activities became far more prevalent and professional as international criminal gangs entered the market.

Paradoxically, the increase in poaching activities was also stimulated by Zimbabwe's independence in April 1980. Independence brought an immediate end to hostilities between the former Rhodesian Security Forces and the ZANLA and ZIPRA guerrilla forces. Consequently, rural areas were no longer patrolled by the Rhodesian Security Forces, and local tribespeople faced no threat of violence or torture for refusing to support the marauding ZANLA[302] or ZIPRA[303] guerillas.

Unfortunately, the absence of uniformed men carrying FNs[304] or AK-47s[305] in the bush created opportunities for criminals, who now perceived poaching as far less risky than when armed soldiers or insurgents were present everywhere

The establishment of Zimbabwe's first democratically elected government quickly transformed the country from a pariah state into a legitimate member of the international community. This change, accompanied by the dramatic cessation of hostilities throughout the country, opened a lucrative window of opportunity for international tourism. Global operators once again viewed Zimbabwe as a safe and desirable holiday destination, highlighting attractive offerings such as

---

[302] Zimbabwe African National Liberation Army. ZANLA was the military wing of ZANU.
[303] Zimbabwe People's Revolutionary Army. ZIPRA was the military wing of ZAPU.
[304] This was a light automatic rifle designed in Belgium and manufactured by FN Herstal. The FN was the standard issue rifle for the Rhodesian Security Forces.
[305] The AK-47 was developed by the Soviet Union and was the preferred light automatic rifle of the ZANLA and ZIPRA forces.

the Victoria Falls[306], the Great Zimbabwe Ruins, the Matopos, and the Eastern Highlands[307].

Duncan was acutely aware of how these changes were likely to be positive game-changers for Zimbabwe's tourism industry. However, he also had a nagging feeling that as more countries became signatories to the international CITES treaty, it would significantly impact the long-term sustainability of his hunting safari business. So, being both a pragmatist and shrewd businessman, and a passionate advocate for wildlife, he had decided to expand his existing cattle ranching and game hunting businesses by adding wildlife and photographic safaris.

In pursuit of this diversification strategy, he had already constructed one secluded luxury lodge which overlooked the Ingwe Dam, and was in the process of building two more. He had also constructed an elephant hide at the dam, as well as half a dozen bird hides that were located at strategic points around the ranch.

Duncan was acutely aware of the rapid escalation of illegal poaching activities, particularly targeting rhinos and elephants, in the countries to the north of Zimbabwe. He feared that a similar surge might occur in Zimbabwe, including at Mhuka Ranch. The large herds of elephants and rhinos that often transversed the ranch made them tempting targets for poachers. He was also apprehensive that if international criminal gangs became involved in poaching in his area, it could undermine the progress he had made with the local tribespeople in fostering their role as responsible custodians of wildlife.

Recognising the importance of wildlife to the future of his business and the lack of effective protection for these assets, Duncan decided to recruit a qualified individual to establish and manage a professional anti-poaching unit on the ranch. With many ex-soldiers leaving the army following independence in April 1980, he felt reasonably

---

[306] Victoria Falls, or *Mosi-oa-Tunya* (which means The Smoke That Thunders) is one of the seven natural wonders of the world.
[307] The Eastern Highlands is a mountainous area on the border of Zimbabwe and Mozambique. It extends for about 300 kilometres from north to south and includes the Inyangani Mountains, the Vumba Mountains and the Chimanimani Mountains.

confident that he could attract someone with military experience for this role. To assist in this endeavour, he engaged a Bulawayo-based recruitment company, Hays Employment Agency (Hays), to help secure the right candidate. Hays helped him specify the necessary skills and experience for the position and conducted an advertising campaign in the *Bulawayo Chronicle*[308] during the first two weeks of June 1981.

By the end of June, Hays had shortlisted three potential candidates for this role, one of whom was Sipho[309] Pukelo.

Hays arranged for the three potential candidates to be interviewed by Duncan in the boardroom of Hay's Employment Agency in Fort Street, Bulawayo on Tuesday, 30th June 1981.

The last of the three candidates to be interviewed was Sipho Pukelo.

By now, Sipho had left the RAR[310], but was still living in Bulawayo where he was boarding with his good friend, Emanuel Wushe.

Duncan and Sipho quickly established a strong rapport. Duncan's brother had been a major at 1RAR[311] in the mid-1960s, and this provided them with a common point of interest. Duncan was extremely impressed by Sipho's military credentials and was struck by his genuine desire to protect and conserve Zimbabwe's wildlife. Additionally, Sipho could start in his new role almost immediately and was well connected with ex-RAR soldiers. Duncan believed this pool of individuals would be ideal candidates for potential anti-poaching rangers when Sipho was ready to expand his team.

From Sipho's perspective, he was impressed by how Duncan had expanded the ranch's business model to include wildlife and photographic safaris, as well as his plans to protect the wildlife on the ranch.

---

[308] *The Chronicle* was published in Bulawayo and mostly reported on news affecting the Matabeleland area in the south of the country. It was first published in 1894.
[309] Sipho is a Ndebele boy's name meaning Gift.
[310] Rhodesian African Rifles.
[311] 1st Battalion, Rhodesian African Rifles.

Duncan informed Sipho that construction of the senior ranger's house would commence soon — its location had already been pegged out on the northern side of Ingwe Dam. Until its completion, the senior ranger would be accommodated in the self-contained guest wing annexed to the main homestead. They had also begun building a barrack room for approximately a dozen rangers, which would be situated close to the senior ranger's house.

Duncan also mentioned that he had recently signed a six-year agreement with an organisation called the Frankfurt Zoological Society. Under the agreement, the Society would be providing financial and other assistance to Duncan to help him establish a black rhino breeding and release program on the ranch.

At the end of the interview, Duncan indicated to Sipho that if he wanted the job, it was his, but that he would need to make a definite decision, one way or another, by the end of the week. Sipho had replied that he did not need any time to think about the offer, and that he was prepared to accept the position there and then. He also indicated that he would be able to start on Monday, 13th July 1981.

The two men shook hands with genuine affection. Duncan said that Hays Employment Agency would send Sipho a letter of employment for him to sign and that he would look forward to welcoming him onto the ranch on Monday, 13th July.

By the time the discussions were concluded it was nearly lunchtime, so Duncan invited Sipho to join him for a celebratory drink and light lunch at the nearby Bulawayo Club. The Club had been established in 1895 as a gentlemen's club along the lines of similar gentlemen's clubs in London, Cape Town and Johannesburg. The Club had relocated to its current premises at the corner of 8th Avenue and Fort Street, in 1934.

Sipho had heard of the Club but had never been inside it. Prior to Zimbabwe's independence, membership of the Club was restricted to Bulawayo's social elite, and so its membership was comprised almost exclusively of white male members. Members were allowed to take visitors into the Club, but the strict dress codes and other discriminatory restrictions, meant that blacks would have rarely been allowed to enter the Club as patrons.

Now that Zimbabwe had achieved independence, racial restrictions no longer applied. However, the Club was still very conservative in its approach and outlook, and so most of its members were still white males.

Sipho and Duncan entered the Club through a white-pillared entrance portico. Sipho was immediately struck by the architecture and grandeur of the beautiful colonial building. He felt he was stepping into a different era. As one entered the Club, the hustle and bustle of Bulawayo's lunchtime rush disappeared and was replaced by a sense of tranquillity and calmness. The main lobby was surrounded by mahogany wood panelling, artefacts from the country's colonial past, old prints and paintings of the town, and photos of past members including Cecil John Rhodes.

From the lobby, there was a grand mahogany staircase leading to the upper floor. The walls on either side of the staircase were adorned with paintings or photographs of historical figures from the country's past, including an original charcoal drawing of King Lobengula Khumalo[312] and Queen Lozikeyi Dlodlo[313]. The sight of these impressive drawings of Sipho's ancestors made his heart leap with joy.

The two men were greeted by a friendly receptionist, who obviously knew Duncan. Once Duncan had signed Sipho in as his guest, she led them to the open-air courtyard known as the Atrium. There, she handed them over to an impeccably dressed waiter in black trousers, a long-sleeved white shirt with a red tie, a black waistcoat, and highly polished black shoes.

The Atrium was surrounded by a wide marble-tiled veranda, where a table had been reserved for them. It was adorned with a crisp, white-

---

[312] King Lobengula Khumalo (1845 to circa 1894) was the second and last official King of the northern Ndebele people.
[313] Queen Lozikeyi Dlodlo (c 1855 to 1919) was one of the favourite wives of King Lobengula and a senior queen until 1893.

starched tablecloth. A large jug of cold water, complete with ice and lemon, had already been placed on the table, together with two crystal tumblers. Their waiter pulled out their chairs, each embossed with the Bulawayo Club's logo on the leather-covered arms, and presented them with leather-bound menus that bore the same emblem.

Sipho and Duncan both ordered a Lion[314] lager along with a steak roll, served with chips and salad. They then spent a lively hour chatting about future plans for Mhuka Ranch.

At times during lunch, Sipho almost had to pinch himself to confirm he wasn't dreaming. He could scarcely believe that he, a simple black rural person raised and educated at a mission school, was now enjoying lunch at the elite Bulawayo Club with Duncan Oliver, a respected white member of the country's business community. Moreover, he had just been offered — and accepted — a job with Duncan as the anti-poaching manager for Mhuka Ranch, taking on this role at an exciting time in the ranch's growth and development.

His luck seemed almost too good to be true. Surely nothing could happen to unravel his good fortune.

---

[314] Lion lager is one of Zimbabwe's top selling beers.

Chapter 29 – Johannes plans Operation Nzou

Timeline – July 1977

You will remember that in June 1977 Sergeant Johannes du Toit had illegally crossed into the Mozambican border town of Malvernia[315] and met with the Portuguese *businessman* Santiago de Costa. At the end of their meeting, Johannes had told Santiago that he would soon get back to him with further details about their new *business venture*.

Ordinarily, Johannes' word was not something one would place much trust in. However, in this instance, driven by his own selfish and unworthy desires, Johannes made a conscious decision to follow through on any promises he had made to Santiago.

Accordingly, upon his return from Malvernia to the RLI[316] field camp near Buffalo Range, Johannes began seeking out the relevant individuals he thought he would need to establish his and Santiago's newly agreed poaching enterprise.

Johannes initially thought he would need four or five spotters, along with two shooters. Both spotters and shooters had to be people Johannes trusted implicitly — preferably, individuals who had either witnessed or heard of his psychopathic tendencies and thus would be unlikely to double-cross him, fearing his violent and dangerous retribution.

---

[315] The town's name was changed to Chicualacuala in 1975 shortly after Mozambique's independence from Portugal.

[316] Rhodesian Light Infantry. This was an infantry regiment and was one of the country's main counter-insurgency units during the Rhodesian Bush War.

The spotters' role was to keep a close ear to the ground, identifying the locations of elephant and rhino herds. Once a herd was found, the spotter would contact Johannes via radio and use agreed code words to relay the location. Ideally, these spotters would be active-duty members from either the RLI or the Selous Scouts[317], stationed close to where Johannes was operating.

At present, Johannes was working with 1 Commando RLI in the south-eastern part of the country, near the Mozambique border and adjacent to Gonarezhou[318] National Park. The spotters' active-duty status was crucial, as it meant they were mobile and able to cover large tracts of land. Additionally, having spotters from different operational units would ensure wider territory coverage.

Johannes had mentally identified two RLI troopies[319] and two Selous Scouts as ideal candidates for the role of spotters. He and Santiago had calculated that, until they had a clearer idea of the market price for poached ivory and rhino horn, they could afford to pay the spotters a monthly retainer of Rh$200[320], plus Rh$400 per animal successfully poached as a result of their spotting.

Given the modest pay and conditions for junior regular servicemen in the Rhodesian Army, Johannes was confident that any spotters he approached would view the proposed remuneration favourably.

As expected, Johannes' approaches to the four individuals he had identified were successful. During their recruitment, he was careful to emphasise the absolute necessity of keeping the details of their

---

[317] The Selous Scouts were a special forces unit of the Rhodesian Army. It was mainly responsible for infiltrating the black majority population of Rhodesia and collecting intelligence on insurgents so that they could be attacked by regular elements of the Rhodesian Security Forces.

[318] Gonarezhou is a Shona word meaning *place of elephants*.

[319] Colloquial term meaning a regular member or national serviceman of the Rhodesian Army.

[320] The Rhodesian dollar at that time was regarded as a strong currency even though it was not freely tradeable on the foreign exchange markets due to international sanctions against Rhodesia. During the period October 1977 to March 1980 one Rhodesian dollar had the nominal pegged rate of US$1.50.

arrangement strictly confidential. He also made it crystal clear that any breach of this confidentiality would result in severe consequences, not only for them but for their loved ones.

Reports from his spotters started flowing almost immediately. These reports indicated that large herds of elephants were traversing the northern areas of the Gonarezhou National Park and heading further north. That year, the winter rains in the lowveld[321] had been virtually non-existent. Consequently, Johannes and the spotters assumed that the elephant herds were heading further north in search of better grazing and water, and, in so doing, were having to travel quite significant distances.

Based on these reports, Johannes decided that initially he would concentrate solely on hunting for elephants. Their numbers at that time were large, and hence they would be easier to locate than the far rarer rhino crashes.

In relation to shooters, Johannes reckoned that, to begin with, he would attempt to recruit two shooters. He had in mind two ex-RLI troopies[322] with whom he had previously served. They were cousins named Gary du Plessis and Jeremy du Randt who were currently living in Fort Victoria[323].

Gary had been dishonourably discharged from the RLI for insubordination to his superior officers, while Jeremy had recently left the RLI after completion of his second four-year sign-on period. Johannes knew that both men were excellent marksmen and had better than average tracking skills.

The two men were currently working as bounty hunters for the owner of a large, 800 square kilometres cattle ranch, which was 50 kilometres to the south of Fort Victoria. The ranch owner was facing a significant

---

[321] The term lowveld refers to low-lying, generally semi-arid region characterised by savanna or bushveld vegetation.

[322] Colloquial term meaning a regular member or national serviceman of the Rhodesian Army.

[323] Fort Victoria was renamed Masvingo in 1982.

problem from ZANLA[324] guerrillas who were regularly rustling his cattle, and violently intimidating his farm employees and their families.

As bounty hunters, the cousins were each being paid Rh$3,000 per dead guerrilla, half of which was paid by the ranch owner with the other half being paid by the Rhodesian Army. To claim their bounty, all they were required to do was to produce the right ear of the slain guerrilla as well as his AK-47[325] rifle.

For the shooters, Johannes and Santiago had calculated that they could offer a retainer of Rh$200 per month, plus Rh$3,000 for each animal killed and detusked. By aligning the kill fee with the bounty being paid for a dead guerrilla, they believed this would provide a strong incentive for shooters to join their operation. As with the spotters, this figure was only an initial estimate until they had a clearer understanding of the market price for poached ivory.

Johannes' approach to the two shooters proved successful. As with the spotters, he made it abundantly clear that maintaining strict confidentiality was crucial, and he left no doubt about the catastrophic personal consequences the shooters would face if they ever breached that trust.

In early July 1977, Johannes contacted Santiago via radio to inform him that their plans were progressing well. He anticipated launching their first poaching expedition in mid to late August. This would give Santiago six to eight weeks to arrange the retrieval of the ivory from an agreed location in Mozambique and transport it to Beira[326], where it would be shipped to markets in south-east Asia, after paying bribes to the relevant customs and shipping officials in Beira.

He also informed Santiago that, to simplify accounting, it would be easier if he handled the payment of the spotters' and shooters' fixed

---

[324] Zimbabwe African National Liberation Army. ZANLA was the military wing of ZANU.
[325] The AK-47 was developed by the Soviet Union and was the preferred light automatic rifle of the ZANLA and ZIPRA forces.
[326] Beira is on the east coast of Mozambique and is the capital and largest city in the Mozambican province of Sofala.

monthly retainers. In return for covering this ongoing expense, he proposed adjusting their profit-sharing arrangement to 55% for him and 45% for Santiago, instead of the previously agreed 50/50 split. Santiago agreed in principle but requested a review of these percentages at the end of 1977. Johannes accepted this.

Johannes was pleased to learn that Santiago had already made progress on several matters that had been assigned to him. First, he had initiated contact with his port, shipping, and customs connections in Beira. The only remaining step was for him and Johannes to decide how much they were willing to offer these corrupt officials to ensure their cargo would be shipped to south-east Asia without inspection. Second, Santiago had identified an *import/export* agent in Beira, who represented several buyers in Hong Kong and China. Subject to agreeing on prices, these buyers were eager to purchase African elephant ivory to meet the growing demand for African ivory from customers in Hong Kong and mainland China

Based on the information they had gathered, Johannes and Santiago estimated the street value of African ivory in Hong Kong and mainland China to be around US$1,500 per kilogram. They agreed their sale price to buyers in Asia should be no less than 50% of this value, resulting in a target sale price of US$750 per kilogram of ivory. The buyers or their agents would be required to pay this amount in cash when the ivory was delivered in Beira. Additionally, they agreed that any handling commission payable to the agent should not exceed 5% of the sale price.

The tusks of an adult elephant typically weigh around 25 kilograms each, meaning a pair would weigh approximately 50 kilograms. Therefore, for an average pair of tusks, they calculated their sales revenue at 50% of US$75,000, or US$37,500 per animal.

With this estimate in mind, they agreed the maximum amount they would be willing to pay in bribes to customs, shipping, and port officials would be US$2,000 per pair of tusks. Santiago would attempt to negotiate lower amounts with relevant officials but could not exceed the US$2,000 limit without first liaising with Johannes.

Johannes informed the two shooters that, since this was their first poaching sortie, they would strictly limit their kill to elephants. To assist in planning, they decided it would be sensible for the shooters to temporarily relocate from the cattle ranch in Fort Victoria, where they were currently working, to establish a bush camp at a camping ground called Hlaro on the southern bank of the Lundi River[327].

The Hlaro camping ground was about 80 kilometres from Chiredzi via rough dirt roads. As it was the dry season, there was minimal risk of getting bogged down in mud. However, there was always a chance of getting stuck in soft, dry river sand, so it was fortunate that Jeremy had a 1975 four-door Series III Land Rover equipped with a winch.

They would also take shovels, chains, and a chainsaw, which would be useful for removing any trees and for detusking the elephants they shot. Getting permission to take a couple of weeks off from their usual jobs as bounty hunters on the cattle ranch was not an issue, as neither Gary nor Jeremy had taken leave for over 12 months. Additionally, the ranch owner was going to be holidaying in Europe for six weeks from mid-August, so he was relatively relaxed about their absence for a couple of weeks.

Assuming the poaching sortie was successful, they still needed to determine how to transport the ivory from Gonarezhou National Park into Mozambique. After considering various options and discussing them with Santiago, they concluded that the most practical solution would be to load the ivory into their Land Rover at the Hlaro bush camp. From there, they would drive along a dirt road running south of the Lundi River, which ended at the confluence of the Lundi and Sabi Rivers[328] — approximately 50 kilometres away.

The confluence of the Lundi and Sabi Rivers is, in fact, a floodplain that would likely be impassable by vehicle. However, it was about two kilometres from the Mozambican border, and according to the 1:500

---

[327] The Lundi River was renamed the Runde River in 1985.
[328] The Sabi River was renamed Save River in Zimbabwe in 1985. But it was still called the Sabi River in Mozambique.

maps they studied, it was just a further two kilometres to a dirt road in Mozambique that began just after the floodplain. This road then followed the southern bank of the Sabi River to a place in Mozambique called Massangena, approximately 70 kilometres away.

They planned to rendezvous with Santiago in Mozambique at the beginning of this dirt road. The two shooters would transport the ivory on foot from the confluence of the rivers to this rendezvous point, a total distance of about four kilometres. While they reckoned they could each manage one tusk weighing about 25 kilograms, they knew they would struggle if it were any heavier. Consequently, they decided to construct a sling designed to carry two tusks, which they would carry between them, with one person at the front of the sling and the other at the back.

Santiago planned to travel from Malvernia to Massangena, where he would stay until he received radio confirmation from Johannes that the poaching sortie had been successful. He would then drive to the floodplain to rendezvous with the two shooters.

The ivory would be loaded onto Santiago's vehicle, and he would then drive to Beira, which was about 350 kilometres away. Upon arrival in Beira, the ivory would be crated in a small wooden container and delivered to the import/export agent, who would work with the corrupt shipping, port, and customs officials to ensure the ivory was safely loaded onto a ship for its onward journey to Hong Kong.

Johannes and Santiago had already established VHF[329] two-way radio communications between themselves. To assist in communication with the shooters, Johannes pilfered an army VHF radio from his RLI base camp and arranged for its delivery to the two shooters in Fort Victoria. He then assigned agreed call signs to the shooters and added them to the radio network established between himself and Santiago.

By Thursday, 25th August 1977, Johannes and Santiago were satisfied that all relevant arrangements were in place to initiate their first

---

[329] Very high frequency.

poaching sortie. It was agreed that Johannes would assume control of all operational matters of the hunt and that the operation should commence as soon as possible.

They gave the operation the code name Operation *Nzou*[330].

---

[330] *Nzou* is a Shona word for elephant.

Chapter 30 – The execution of Operation Nzou

Timeline – late August 1977

Johannes was still receiving regular reports from his spotters, confirming that large elephant herds were being sighted as they traversed Gonarezhou[331] National Park, moving in a northerly direction. In response, he radioed the two shooters, Gary and Jeremy, and asked them to swiftly proceed to the Hlaro camping ground on the Lundi River[332] and set up the previously agreed bush camp. He asked them to radio him once they had established the camp.

Two days later, Johannes received a radio message from the two shooters, informing him that they were now on site and had established the camp. On the same day, he received another report from one of his spotters that a large elephant herd was in the vicinity of the Hlaro camping ground. The spotter gave Johannes the locstat[333] coordinates of the sighting, which he then transmitted to Gary and Jeremy. He ordered them to locate the elephant herd as quickly as possible, and then shoot, kill, and detusk no more than three elephants. Once they had completed this initial part of their mission, he instructed them to radio him .

The Hlaro camping ground is located on the southern bank of the Lundi River. From the camp that Gary and Jeremy established, they looked out across the riverbed onto the very dramatic backdrop of the

---

[331] Gonarezhou is a Shona word meaning place of elephants.
[332] The Lundi River was renamed the Runde River in 1985.
[333] Ordnance survey map reference.

Chilojo[334] cliffs. Their campsite was situated at a point where the riverbed was relatively narrow — about 100 metres wide and appearing to be mostly dry. The campsite was well-shaded by an acacia tree, under which they parked their dust-covered Land Rover. They pitched their tent alongside the Land Rover, built a campfire, and dug a long drop[335].

Despite its beauty, from what Gary and Jeremy could ascertain, they were the only two persons in the camping ground. This was hardly surprising, considering the remoteness of the location, and the fact that that tourists had generally abandoned the more isolated areas of the country because of the raging Rhodesian Bush War.

It was sunset by the time Gary and Jeremy had finished setting up camp. It was too late to start searching for the elephant herd. So, instead, they opened a couple of ice-cold Lion[336] lagers, cut up some sticks of impala biltong[337], unfolded their camp chairs, and enjoyed the spectacular deepening oranges and reds of the sunset.

On the opposite side of the riverbed, a large pool of muddy river water attracted various animals. Using their binoculars, Gary and Jeremy identified buffalo, impala, nyala, zebra, baboons, and a few crocodiles, along with plenty of birdlife. While they did not see any lions, they heard plenty of them that night. Their deep, throaty roars and growls reverberated through the shooters' spines. Before retiring for the night, the shooters removed their 0.458 high-calibre hunting rifles from the Land Rover and took them into their tent. The knowledge that their rifles were close at hand helped them get some sleep, though it was somewhat disturbed by the ongoing sounds of the lions.

Gary and Jeremy woke at dawn, when the gathering morning light was just beginning to snuff out the darkness of the night. The outside air temperature was decidedly cool, but they knew that by 9:00 am, the

---

[334] The Chilojo cliffs are a spectacular 30 km stretch of red and white-banded sandstone columns that stretch along the shoreline of the Lundi River.
[335] A pit latrine.
[336] Lion lager is one of Rhodesia's top selling beers.
[337] Biltong is a form of dried, cured, and spiced meat that originated from South Africa.

day would have warmed up to about 20°C. Gary lit the campfire and boiled a kettle of water, which he used to brew a pot of tea. He also placed a frying pan onto the hotplate above the fire and fried up some bacon, eggs, and tomatoes for breakfast.

After they had eaten breakfast, Jeremy radioed Johannes for an update on the elephant herd's location. Fortunately, Johannes had just received a report from his spotter stating that the herd was still in the vicinity of Hlaro, and he provided the updated locstat details to Jeremy. Jeremy pinpointed the location on their 1:500 map — the coordinates indicated that the herd was about six kilometres to the south-east of their camp. Based on the information that Johannes had been receiving over the last couple of weeks, he and Gary guessed it was reasonable to assume that the herd would be heading in a northerly direction. If this was correct, it meant the herd would have crossed the Lundi River about four kilometres downstream from where they were.

After a quick discussion, they agreed that their best course of action would be to follow the riverbed downstream. The riverbed was largely dry, so they were confident they could pick up the herd's tracks if it had crossed the river.

The latest locstat reference was about an hour old. Elephants can easily travel three to four kilometres per hour in the bush, even when stopping frequently to graze. Jeremy reckoned it was quite possible that the herd could already have a seven-kilometre head start on them.

Gary and Jeremy quickly tidied up their campsite, locked their Land Rover, and donned their backpacks, which included the small chainsaw they had brought with them. They retrieved their high-calibre rifles and the tusk sling they had constructed in Fort Victoria[338], loaded their ammunition into the pouches on their webbing, and headed off downstream, following the river.

---

[338] Fort Victoria was renamed Masvingo in 1982.

In order to keep their packs as light as possible, they had decided to leave the VHF two-way radio back at camp. They knew that they would have to return to the camp with the tusks to pick up their vehicle before heading to the agreed rendezvous point. They figured that if they radioed Johannes upon their return to the camp to confirm the outcome of the hunt, this would still give him plenty of time to make radio contact with Santiago at Massangena and instruct him to start making his way to the agreed rendezvous point.

Both men were fit and not burdened with excessive weight, allowing them to make good progress. Within an hour, they found the place where the herd had crossed the river. The crossing was at a spot that featured another large pool of muddy river water near the northern bank. There was plenty of evidence of elephants having rolled in the mud. Judging by how much the mud had been churned up, they guessed it was quite a large herd. Moreover, imprinted in the mud were some very large elephant footprints. This buoyed Gary and Jeremy, as it indicated that the herd contained some big animals, and big animals meant big tusks!

About two hours later, they caught up with the herd. It was moving away from the river and was still heading in a northerly direction. As the elephants were moving away from the river, this indicated that they were probably moving towards a known water supply, probably a man-made dam, or perhaps a waterhole which was being fed by an artesian water source.

Both men were tired, hot, and thirsty. However, the sight of the elephant herd some 300 metres away, got their adrenaline pumping and lifted their energy levels. They stopped to take some deep gulps of water from their water bottles, and to have a quick discussion about what their plan of attack was going to be.

The herd was grazing beneath a small copse of trees. Between Gary and Jeremy and the elephants were numerous other trees and bushes that provided ample cover.

Elephants have very good senses of hearing and smell but rather poor eyesight. Since Gary and Jeremy were downwind from the herd and there was good cover between them and the elephants, they reckoned that, with a bit of luck and by remaining quiet, they might be able to creep within 40 metres of the herd without being spotted.

Once they were close enough, they would identify their target culls. They decided to try to shoot only two animals, selecting the largest ones they could see. Obviously, the herd would scatter at the sound of gunfire, so they planned to shoot simultaneously, which meant they needed to stay close together. Once they had selected their targets and had the animals in their telescopic sights, Gary would quietly count down to the *squeeze trigger moment* by saying, "Three, two, one, squeeze." This would ensure they both fired their rifles at the same time, hopefully hitting both targets before the herd scattered in panic.

In the event that the herd panicked and scattered in their direction, it would be open slather, with both men making as much noise as possible and firing as many bullets as they could.

Before they started their stealthy approach towards the herd, Gary reminded Jeremy that the most vulnerable spot on an elephant's body was along an imaginary line between their two ear holes.

Having secured any loose items on their webbing, they began to creep forward towards their target. The trick here was to be slow, steady, and silent. But it was painfully slow, taking them a good 20 minutes to get within about 40 metres.

They crouched behind two young rain trees[339], which were only about three metres apart. At this close range, they could clearly see the elephants' long eyelashes and every detail of their highly textured skin, with all its wrinkles, creases, and divots.

Using sign language, they identified their two target culls — a large male bull elephant and a large female cow. These two animals both

---

[339] The Rain Tree or Apple-Leaf Tree. The botanical name is Philenoptera Violacea. The name Rain Tree is derived from the fact that the tree can become infested with a spittlebug, which causes apparent rain to fall from the tree.

bore magnificent tusks and were standing close together, peacefully grazing on the leaves of the trees above them.

Gary whispered, "I will take the bull, and you take the cow. Take aim and say 'ready' when you have her in your sights."

A couple of seconds passed. Jeremy hissed, "Ready."

Gary whispered, "Three, two, one, squeeze."

Two loud cracks rang out across the bush as one. Neither Gary nor Jeremy heard the shots, nor did they feel the kick of their rifles into their shoulders. Their eyes and minds were intently focused on the animals that had been in the crosshairs of their telescopic sights. The angle at which the bull elephant was standing meant Gary had aimed his shot almost straight at its left ear hole. In contrast, the cow was facing Jeremy, so his shot was aimed just above its eyes, along the imaginary line between its two ear holes.

Although neither shooter had heard the sound of the gunshots, they certainly heard the distinctive *thwack* as their 0.458 calibre bullets struck their targets, bursting through the elephants' skin and skull, effectively destroying the back half of their brains.

Both shots were perfect.

For an instant, both animals quivered. Then, the agony of the bullets entering their brains contorted their faces into a terrible image of torture and pain. Gary could swear he heard an audible groan come from the large bull.

Then, both animals fell to their knees and collapsed onto their sides. As their enormous bodies hit the sandy soil, the ground trembled, and a visible cloud of dust was thrown up.

Both slaughtered animals lay motionless on the ground.

A fleeting moment of silence followed.

The herd had witnessed their patriarch and matriarch slain by an invisible but malevolent power that might strike again at any moment.

With this unseen threat looming over them, they initially bunched together to form a tight protective cluster. However, some of the younger calves panicked, throwing their trunks into the air and letting out heart-rending trumpet calls before fleeing with their large ears flapping out from the sides of their heads.

The protective instincts of their mothers kicked in, and they too stampeded after the calves, fortunately fleeing in a direction away from Gary and Jeremy.

Gary and Jeremy remained motionless behind their rain trees.

The bulls mulled around for about ten seconds, unsure of what or on whom they could unleash their anger, fear, and loss. But soon, they too strode off in the direction of the panicked cows and calves, which were now about 150 metres away.

Gary and Jeremy stayed behind the rain trees for a full five minutes before venturing out. By then, a few mopane flies were already buzzing around the slain animals' eyes.

"We need to move quickly," said Gary. "It won't be long before some of the braver bulls return to see what has happened to these two. And soon vultures will start circling, signalling to all and sundry that something is amiss. I know it's highly unlikely, but I don't want to be around if some over-zealous ranger comes to investigate."

Neither Gary nor Jeremy had ever detusked an elephant before. They needed to act quickly, so rather than trying to hack the embedded tusks from the elephants' jaws, they opted to use the chainsaw to cut through each tusk as close to its base as possible. In doing so, they realised they would leave a portion of the tusk still embedded in the jaws of the lifeless animals, but they decided speed was more important than precision.

The greatest difficulty they faced in removing the tusks was manoeuvring the massive bodies into a position where they could get a good purchase between the chainsaw and the tusks. In its death throes, the bull had fallen in a position that did not significantly obstruct access to its tusks. However, the cow had fallen onto her right side, making it tricky to remove the left tusk. Removing the right tusk proved even more challenging, as they needed to roll her head over. The weight was too great for them to manage unaided, so they cut two stout branches from nearby trees and rolled a small rock from the riverbed to the side of the cow's head. They placed the branches under her head and over the rock, using them as levers to shift the dead weight.

Removing the tusks was hot, strength-sapping work, and it took the men nearly an hour and a half to complete. Despite using the chainsaw to cut through the tusks rather than hacking them out, a lot of blood was still spilled, making the process messy.

By the time they had removed all four tusks, vultures were circling overhead, and it wouldn't be long before fearless, carrion-seeking hyaenas joined them on the ground.

It was now mid-afternoon, and they estimated it would take at least two hours to walk back to camp. Their original plan had been to transport two tusks at a time using the two-man sling they had constructed. Since they would need to make three one-way trips, this meant another six hours of bushwalking ahead.

They experimented with using the sling to carry two tusks but quickly found it easier for each of them to place one tusk over their shoulder instead. Even though they estimated the cow's tusks weighed about 30 kilograms each and the bull's around 35 kilograms each, this method proved more manageable.

Abandoning the sling, they burned it and buried the ashes. Each man then lifted one of the cow's tusks onto his shoulder, carried them about 400 metres from the slaughter site before caching them under some bushes near a baobab tree that they could easily locate again.

Returning to the site, they retrieved the bull's tusks, placed one on each of their right shoulders, and began the long trek back to camp.

The walk took about two and a half hours. Other than the gruelling weight of the 35-kilogram tusks, combined with their rifles, backpacks, and webbing, they encountered no problems. Still, despite their fitness, both men were aching and drenched in sweat by the time they reached camp.

With only about an hour of daylight left, they realised there wasn't enough time to return to the baobab tree, retrieve the cow's tusks, and make it back before dark. Besides, neither of them was keen on trekking through Gonarezhou National Park at night, especially after hearing the lions on their first evening. They also knew the cow's tusks were well concealed and should be safe. Consequently they decided to retrieve the tusks the following day and use the night to rest and recover.

Gary retrieved the VHF[340] two-way radio from the Land Rover and contacted Johannes. He gave Johannes an update on their progress and explained their plan to retrieve the cow's tusks. Johannes approved of the plan and said he would notify Santiago to be at the rendezvous point by 4:00 pm the next day.

That night, despite the ever-present, menacing sounds of lions in the darkness, both men slept well. They rose early the next morning, and after enjoying a mug of tea, and bacon and egg sandwiches slathered in tomato sauce, they set off to retrieve the cow's tusks. Without any tusks to carry, their progress was swift. They easily located the baobab tree and had recovered the cow's tusks by 10:30 am.

Hundreds of vultures were now circling above the slaughter site, tempting the two men to return to it and see how much flesh had been stripped from the carcasses. However, realising this curiosity would serve no purpose, they hoisted the tusks onto their shoulders and began the two-and-a-half-hour hike back to camp.

Both men were hot and tired when they arrived, but they wanted to get to the rendezvous point without delay. They loaded their gear into the Land Rover, including the four tusks, which they covered with a tarpaulin in the rear of the vehicle. After doing a final sweep of the camp to ensure no incriminating evidence was left behind, they set off.

---

[340] Very high frequency.

They found the dirt road to the south, which followed the Lundi River to just before its confluence with the Sabi River. Although the distance was only about 50 kilometres, the poor condition of the road meant the drive took an hour. By 2:30 pm, they had found a suitable place to park the vehicle, remove the bull's tusks and their rifles, and ensure the cow's tusks remained concealed beneath the tarpaulin. After locking the vehicle, they began the four-kilometre trek to the rendezvous point, each carrying one of the bull's tusks.

They had allowed 40 minutes for the walk, but it ended up taking 50 due to several detours they had to make while crossing the waterlogged floodplains. When they reached the rendezvous at 3:20 pm, Santiago had not yet arrived. They agreed Gary would wait, with the bull's tusks, for Santiago's arrival at the rendezvous location while Jeremy returned to fetch one of the cow's tusks from the Land Rover.

Santiago arrived just before 4:00 pm, and Jeremy returned with the cow's first tusk about 40 minutes later. Gary then offered to retrieve the second tusk, and by 5:45 pm, all four tusks had been weighed, photographed, and loaded into Santiago's vehicle. The combined weight of the tusks was 135.5 kilograms, slightly higher than their original estimate of 130 kilograms.

Not wanting to stay overnight in Mozambican territory, Gary and Jeremy decided to make the return trek to their vehicle in the fading light. Once there, they bivouacked on the banks of the Lundi River, planning to drive back to Fort Victoria the next morning.

Santiago opted to drive back to the town of Massangena, where he would find a place to stay for the night before embarking on the 325-kilometre trip to Beira[341].

He arrived in Beira late the next day. After booking into a small motel, he phoned the buyer's Beira-based agent, informing him that he had arrived with the goods and intended to deliver them the following day. Santiago advised that he would be delivering 135.5 kilograms of goods.

---

[341] Beira is on the east coast of Mozambique and is the capital and largest city in the Mozambican province of Sofala.

At US$750 per kg, this meant that he was expecting to receive US$101,625 payable in cash in US$100 bills. From this figure, the agent's commission of 3.5% and other agreed expenses would need to be deducted.

The agent explained that he couldn't organise such a large sum on such short notice and would need 48 hours to arrange payment.

Santiago had no choice but to accept the delay. They agreed the ivory would be delivered and paid for on Friday, 2nd September, at 10:00 am, at the agent's office on Eduardo Mondlane[342] Avenue in Beira's CBD[343].

As agreed, the meeting took place on Friday, 2nd September. The agent handed Santiago a bundle of US dollar bills and provided a hand-written receipt for US$95,500, a copy of which can be seen in Appendix 1. The agent advised Santiago there was no need for him to stay any longer, as the shipment needed to be consolidated into a 24-foot container with other cargo destined for Hong Kong. The agent assured Santiago he would handle the remaining matters.

After counting the bills to confirm the amount, Santiago shook the agent's hand and left, satisfied that everything had gone smoothly.

The next day, Santiago returned to Malvernia[344] without any problems despite the long drive. Early the next morning, he radioed Johannes to report that everything had gone according to plan and that he was back in Malvernia with the net proceeds from their first poaching operation.

Johannes requested a detailed breakdown of how the figure of US$95,500 had been calculated. He was pleased to see that the ivory weight on the receipt matched the information provided by Gary and

---

[342] Eduardo Mondlane was the President of the Mozambican Liberation Front (Frelimo) from 1962 until his assassination in 1969.
[343] Central Business District.
[344] The town's name was changed to Chicualacuala in 1975 shortly after Mozambique's independence from Portugal.

Jeremy. Johannes told Santiago he would prepare a final financial reconciliation of the venture and get back to him.

The following day, Johannes radioed Santiago to inform him that the net profits from their initial venture were US$84,707, with their agreed shares being US$46,589 and US$38,118, respectively. He provided Santiago with the relevant details[345] to allow him to do his own reconciliation.

Johannes said he would return to Malvernia within a week. Once his plans were finalised, he would radio Santiago to arrange a meeting in Malvernia, where he would collect his US$46,589 profit share from the funds Santiago was holding.

_____

[345] See reconciliation at Appendix 2.

Chapter 31 – Settling up with Santiago de Costa

Timeline – September 1977

Johannes had organised R&R[346] leave over the weekend beginning Saturday, 10th September 1977. On the preceding Monday, he radioed Santiago to inform him that he would be returning to Malvernia[347] on the 10th September and suggested they meet at Santiago's house at around 1:00 pm. Fortunately, Santiago was available and readily agreed to the meeting.

Johannes then radioed Gary and arranged to meet him and Jeremy in the bar at the Great Zimbabwe Hotel, just outside Fort Victoria[348], on Sunday, 11th September, at about 1:00 pm. He informed them that the purpose of the meeting was to celebrate the success of their first poaching sortie and to pay them their agreed retention and success fees.

On the 10th, Johannes made the three-hour drive from his base camp near Buffalo Range to the town of Vila Salazar[349], on the Rhodesia-Mozambique border. In recent weeks, there had been a significant increase in military presence in the town, due to the likelihood of it being used as a staging base for further cross-border raids into Mozambique by the Rhodesian Security Forces.

---

[346] Rest and Recuperation.
[347] The town's name was changed to Chicualacuala in 1975 shortly after Mozambique's independence from Portugal.
[348] Fort Victoria was renamed Masvingo in 1982.
[349] The town is now named Sango.

To avoid raising any undue suspicions, Johannes decided to arrive in town wearing his RLI[350] military fatigues. He also planned to adopt the same strategy for making the illegal entry into Mozambique that he had successfully used on his first visit to Santiago in Malvernia.

Consequently, as he had done two months earlier, Johannes crossed into Mozambique on foot. He first removed his military fatigues and placed them in the boot of his vehicle, and then changed into casual civilian clothes he had brought with him. Once again, he took his Browning semi-automatic handgun, concealing it in an underarm holster beneath his casual jacket, and set off on the short three-kilometre walk to Santiago's house in Malvernia.

He crossed into Mozambique using the same hole in the perimeter fencing that he had cut during his first crossing. Surprisingly, this had not been repaired, leading Johannes to assume it still had not been discovered.

Being careful to keep himself concealed, he arrived at Santiago's house just after noon. He surveyed the house for a full 30 minutes before approaching the front door and knocking. A short time later, Santiago opened the door, and the two men shook hands warmly. Santiago led Johannes into the lounge and offered him a beer, which he gladly accepted.

The two men engaged in small talk for about five minutes. Johannes mentioned that he couldn't stay long, as his driver would be picking him up in town at around 1:40 pm. Santiago understood and said he would fetch Johannes's share of the profits from the safe in his study.

He excused himself to retrieve the money. Santiago's departure from the lounge made Johannes nervous, and he reached beneath his jacket to ensure that his Browning handgun was still securely in place.

---

[350] This is the acronym for the Rhodesian Light Infantry. This was an infantry regiment of the Rhodesian Army which was formed in 1961 at the Brady Barracks in Bulawayo. It was relocated a year later to the Cranborne Barracks in Salisbury, where its headquarters remained for the rest of its existence. The RLI became one of the country's main counter-insurgency units during the country's bush war.

Fortunately, Santiago returned shortly after and handed over a bundle of US bills to Johannes.

Johannes counted the wad of money to ensure it totalled US$46,589. He then asked Santiago to briefly summarise how his dealings with the agent in Beira had panned out, which Santiago duly did. The two men congratulated each other on the success of their inaugural mission. Johannes said his farewells, shook Santiago's hand, and mentioned that he would be in touch once he was ready to begin planning their next mission. He then left.

Santiago returned to the lounge and reflected on how easy it had been for him to earn the tidy sum of US$38,118. He certainly looked forward to his next interaction with Johannes.

Stealthily, Johannes returned on foot to Vila Salazar, where he changed back into his military fatigues. By now, it was mid-afternoon. He knew that it was at least a five-hour drive from Vila Salazar to Fort Victoria. Not wanting to be rushed for time on the next day, he decided to leave that afternoon and head for the small town of Rutenga, roughly midway between Vila Salazar and Fort Victoria.

He arrived in Rutenga just after dusk. Fortunately, there was a room available at the small motel just outside the town. He checked in, ate a light meal in the modest dining room, and then retired to his bedroom to listen to the radio before going to bed.

After breakfast, he headed for the Great Zimbabwe Hotel. The well-maintained tarred road from Rutenga to Fort Victoria allowed him to make good progress, and he arrived at the hotel by 11:00 am. The hotel was only 700 metres from the Great Zimbabwe Ruins[351]. Johannes had not visited the iconic ruins for more than ten years, so he took the opportunity to do a whirlwind tour of them.

---

[351] The Great Zimbabwe Ruins is the name of the stone ruins of an ancient city known as Great Zimbabwe. The ruins are located just outside Fort Victoria (now called Masvingo). People lived in Great Zimbabwe from around 1100 but abandoned it in the 15th century. The city was the capital of the Kingdom of Zimbabwe, which was a Shona trading empire. Zimbabwe means "stone houses" in Shona.

He paid his admission fee at the entrance to the national park and then took a quick walk around the Great Enclosure. The outer wall of the Great Enclosure was approximately 250 metres in circumference, with a maximum height of just over ten metres. An inner wall ran alongside part of the outer wall, forming a narrow parallel passage about 50 metres long. This passage led to a ten-metre-high tower known as the Conical Tower.

Apart from their mystical aura, the remarkable feature of both the outer and inner walls of the Great Enclosure and the Conical Tower was that they were built from roughly hewn granite blocks, entirely without mortar. Johannes recalled learning that the Great Enclosure had been constructed during the 11th and 12th centuries by the ancient ancestors of the Shona tribe. He also knew that the original purpose of the Conical Tower remained unknown, though historians surmised it may have served as a symbolic grain bin or perhaps as a phallic symbol.

After viewing the Great Enclosure, he made the steep and arduous climb up to the Acropolis[352], believed to be the spiritual and religious centre of the city. It is the oldest part of the site, covering some 4,500 square metres, with archaeologists suggesting that the first stones were laid there in the 10th century.

Johannes would have liked to spend more time exploring the Acropolis, but as it was approaching 1:00 pm, he decided to make his way back to the bar at the hotel. Gary and Jeremy were already waiting for him. They greeted each other warmly and sat down on the hotel's veranda to enjoy a braai[353] lunch and a couple of cold beers, which Johannes treated them to.

After lunch, Johannes gave each of them Rh$3,597.50[354], covering their shooters' and retention fees for July and August, plus reimbursement of incidental expenses. They then bade each other

---

[352] The Acropolis is now known as the Hill Complex.
[353] Braai is the Afrikaans word for a BBQ.
[354] Refer Appendix 2.

farewell, with Johannes saying he would be in touch once he was ready to launch their second mission.

He drove back to his RLI base camp near Buffalo Range, while Gary and Jeremy returned to the cattle ranch where they worked, just outside Fort Victoria. That night, once Johannes was back at the base camp, he reflected on how well the operation had gone and how profitable it had been. He looked forward to future operations.

His only concern was the extent of Santiago's control over the collection of the sale proceeds and the subsequent handover of Johannes' share. This concentration of power in Santiago's hands troubled him, as it created a vulnerability that Johannes knew he needed to address. However, he was unsure how to resolve the issue just yet. Instead of dwelling on it, he pushed the thought to the back of his mind, confident a solution would emerge in time.

Chapter 32 – Johannes flees Rhodesia

Timeline – September 1978

During the 12 months leading up to August 1978, Johannes and his team of spotters and shooters successfully carried out six more poaching raids. The *modus operandi*[355] of these illegal operations remained largely unchanged. Elephants were still the sole targets, and their tusks were still removed using a chainsaw. The transport of the tusks from the slaughter sites to the Mozambican port of Beira[356] remained under Santiago's control, as did his responsibility for collecting payments from the Beira-based agent — a matter that continued to trouble Johannes.

The team of spotters had expanded from four to seven, with the addition of two more from the RAR[357] and one from the Selous Scouts[358]. Gary du Plessis and Jeremy du Randt remained the only shooters, but they were now much more reliant on the revenue they were earning from their poaching activities. This was because the Rhodesian Government was no longer part-financing any payments to guerrilla bounty hunters, fearing international outrage and political embarrassment if these arrangements were ever to become public.

---

[355] This is a Latin phrase meaning *method of operating*.

[356] Beira is on the east coast of Mozambique and is the capital and largest city in the Mozambican province of Sofala.

[357] Rhodesian African Rifles.

[358] The Selous Scouts were a special forces unit of the Rhodesian Army. It was mainly responsible for infiltrating the black majority population of Rhodesia and collecting intelligence on insurgents so that they could be attacked by regular elements of the Rhodesian Security Forces.

Although the *modus operandi* of the poaching sorties had not changed significantly, the operations themselves had become more fine-tuned and efficient. As a result, Gary and Jeremy no longer limited the number of culls per sortie to just two or three elephants. On their most recent hunt, they had shot and killed six animals.

The increase in the number of elephants killed per hunt had been facilitated by the addition of silencers to their 0.458 high-calibre hunting rifles, which significantly reduced the noise of gunfire. This noise reduction meant that the elephant herds, particularly the younger calves, did not panic and flee immediately when the rifles were fired.

To manage the larger volume of ivory and expedite the detusking process, it had become standard practice to hire two porters for each hunt. Initially, Johannes had opposed involving outsiders, but Gary and Jeremy assured him they knew a few local villagers who could be trusted to keep the details of the hunts absolutely confidential. The cost of engaging the porters was minimal[359], and their help reduced the time spent detusking and transporting the ivory. These time savings lowered the risk of discovery, and so Johannes ultimately agreed to their involvement.

Despite the assurances given by Gary and Jeremy regarding the reliability of the recently added porters, Johannes remained justifiably concerned that the increasing number of participants in each hunt heightened the risk of exposure. His fears were, in fact, eventually realised — though not because of a leak from the porters, but from one of the new spotters.

The last spotter Johannes had engaged was a Selous Scout named Fritz Viljoen. Johannes had worked with Fritz several times during Fire Force operations in south-east Rhodesia in 1977 and 1978. These operations involved both 1 Commando RLI[360] and the Selous Scouts. Johannes had

---

[359] Rh$30 per day per porter.
[360] Rhodesian Light Infantry. This was an infantry regiment and was one of the country's main counter-insurgency units during the Rhodesian Bush War.

been impressed with Fritz's soldiering skills and his cold-blooded efficiency in eliminating the enemy.

In early 1978, Johannes had approached Fritz to see if he would be interested in joining his elephant-spotting team. He informed Fritz that these activities were not authorised by anyone in the army and would need to remain completely confidential and top secret. In return, Fritz would earn a minimum of Rh$200[361] per month, which would help cover the rent for his lavish accommodation in Salisbury[362]. Johannes also warned him that any disclosure of these arrangements would result in severe consequences.

Fritz Viljoen agreed to be involved and had been working as a spotter since March 1978.

In early September 1978, Fritz was on R&R[363] leave from the Selous Scouts. He returned to his luxurious mess[364] in Greystone Park[365], which he shared with four other blokes. It had been months since he had last been in Salisbury, and he looked forward to catching up with his friends, relaxing by the pool at the shared house, playing tennis on its all-weather court, and socialising with young women.

While in Salisbury, Fritz had a few favourite pastimes that helped him stay grounded. One was taking his beloved Rhodesian Ridgeback, Huckleberry, for walks in the vlei[366] of Greystone Park. Another was riding his motorcycle — a second-hand 1975 Yamaha XT 500 adventure bike that he had recently purchased and kept garaged at the mess. Although he hadn't had much time to ride it yet, he planned to use his R&R to explore the rolling hills of Umwinsidale, north-east of Salisbury.

---

[361] At the time 1Rh$ was worth about US$1.50.
[362] The capital of Rhodesia. Its name was changed to Harare in April 1982.
[363] Rest & Recuperation.
[364] Shared house.
[365] An upmarket suburb of Salisbury, about 15 kilometres north-east of Salisbury CBD.
[366] A vlei is an Afrikaans word meaning low-lying marshy ground covered with water during the rainy season.

On Saturday, 9th September, Fritz headed into Salisbury's CBD[367] to meet up with friends at a local bar before going to the Archipelago Restaurant and Night Club in Baker Avenue. The first stop was the Twelve Thousand Horsemen bar at the Monomatapa Hotel, which had opened four years earlier. Located on Park Lane, the hotel had become a popular spot for younger people in Salisbury and a favourite haunt of soldiers on R&R leave.

That Saturday was like any other, except for the presence of numerous local and international journalists in the bar. They had come to Salisbury to report on the downing of Air Rhodesia Flight 825[368], which had been shot down the previous Sunday[369] by a SAM-7[370] missile launched by a group of ZIPRA[371] terrorists.

The flight was a scheduled passenger service from Victoria Falls to Salisbury. Of the 56 people on board, only 18 survived the crash. As shocking as the shooting down of a civilian aircraft was, an even more horrifying fact was that 10 of the 18 survivors were subsequently shot, bayoneted, or bludgeoned to death at the crash site — either by the ZIPRA terrorists who launched the missile or by another ZIPRA group in the area.

Among the 48 victims, 11 were children, and 23 were women.

Joshua Nkomo, leader of ZAPU[372], publicly claimed responsibility for the attack in a BBC[373] interview shortly after the incident. When questioned on television, he laughed and asserted that the aircraft was being used for military purposes, making it a legitimate target. However, he denied that his forces were involved in the subsequent massacre of the survivors.

---

[367] Central Business District.
[368] The downed aircraft was a Vickers Viscount.
[369] Sunday, 3rd September 1978.
[370] This is a Soviet built surface-to-air missile which is launched from the shoulder.
[371] Zimbabwe People's Revolutionary Army. ZIPRA was the military wing of the ZAPU.
[372] Zimbabwean African People's Union.
[373] British Broadcasting Corporation.

Nkomo's claim that the plane was being used for military purposes was flatly denied by Air Rhodesia, the Rhodesian Army, and Ian Smith himself. Moreover, his denial that ZIPRA forces were responsible for the subsequent massacre directly contradicted witness accounts from the eight survivors.

On Friday, 8th September, a memorial service had been held at Salisbury's Anglican Cathedral. The service, conducted by the Dean of Salisbury, Reverend John de Costa, was a powerful and emotional ceremony attended by more than two thousand mourners packed into the Cathedral.

During the service, the Dean declared, "*Nobody who holds sacred the dignity of human life can be anything but sickened by the events surrounding the downed Viscount.*"

Describing the plight of those who survived the crash, he continued, "*The horror of the crash was bad enough. But for this to be compounded by murder of the most savage and treacherous kind leaves us stunned in disbelief and fills us with revulsion. This bestiality, worse than anything in recent history, stinks in the nostrils of heaven.*"

Anger and anxiety within the white community were already at fever pitch before the memorial, but after the service, tensions rose even higher — and not only among the white population. For example, Sergeant Pukelo learned about the incident through the media. As the details emerged — particularly the fate of the survivors and the fact that many of those killed were women and children — his disgust for the wanton brutality of the ZIPRA forces deepened. He was also devastated by the potential damage this would inflict on the Ndebele nation's reputation.

While at the Twelve Thousand Horsemen, Fritz struck up a conversation with a couple of British journalists who had just arrived in the country to cover the downing of the Air Rhodesia civilian flight. They were also eager to hear how Rhodesian soldiers felt about the current situation in the country.

Fritz had already had about half a dozen beers, making him relatively unguarded in his answers. He told the journalists that, in his view, neither ZANLA[374] nor ZIPRA was fit to govern, and this absolutely included the leaders of both parties — Robert Mugabe and Joshua Nkomo respectively. He went on to boast about serving in the Selous Scouts and the significant role this unit was having in combating ZANLA and ZIPRA guerrillas.

Fritz mentioned that he was currently on R&R leave, enjoying some downtime in civvy[375] street. He also explained to the journalists how the Selous Scouts used observation posts (OPs) to clandestinely monitor activities in rural villages, often for weeks, to gather valuable information about the potential presence of terrorists nearby. This information would then be relayed back to base, where Fire Force units would be deployed to eliminate the terrorists in the area.

When asked how they managed the boredom of such long surveillance, Fritz said that Selous Scouts were trained for this type of duty, rotating OP[376] tasks among the team hourly. He then added that he was now also required to report on any movement of elephant or rhino herds that occurred close to the OP, and that this new task had helped to negate any potential boredom.

One of the journalists raised an eyebrow and asked, "That's interesting. Why would that information be required?"

Fritz immediately realised he had been too loose with his words. In an attempt to salvage the situation, he replied, "I'm not sure, but I think the army is collaborating with the Department of National Parks[377] to monitor elephant and rhino movements. This collaboration helps the Department provide greater protection for the herds against illegal poaching activities."

---

[374] Zimbabwe African National Liberation Army. ZANLA was the military wing of ZANU.
[375] The expression *civvy street* refers to life and activities which were not connected with the Rhodesian armed forces.
[376] Observation Post.
[377] The full name is the Department of National Parks and Wildlife Management.

This explanation seemed to satisfy the journalists, who commented on how refreshing it was to see government bodies working together in such difficult circumstances. The conversation soon moved on to other topics, and Fritz thought nothing more of his slip of the tongue.

However, unfortunately for Fritz, he and the two British journalists were seated next to a table occupied by a well-connected local journalist, Tony Miller. Tony had been listening carefully to the three men's conversation and was concerned that the young Selous Scout might be disclosing too much information to the British journalists, who were generally anti-Rhodesia and everything it stood for.

Fortunately, this did not turn out to be the case. However, when Fritz mentioned his newly assigned task of reporting on elephant and rhino herd movements and that this intelligence was being relayed to the Department of National Parks, Tony knew that any liaison between the Rhodesian Army and the Department was highly unlikely. His journalistic instincts *smelt a rat* and he decided to investigate this further.

First thing on Monday morning, Tony set out to verify whether the Rhodesian Army was indeed monitoring the movements of elephant and rhino herds and relaying this information to the Department of National Parks to assist with its anti-poaching efforts. If this was true, which he doubted, he wanted to learn more about the Department's efforts to combat poaching.

Tony was friendly with Captain Eric Morley, the adjutant of the RLI's 1st Battalion, based at its headquarters in the Cranborne Barracks, south-east of Salisbury. He called Eric to share what he had overheard on the prior Saturday and to verify its accuracy. Tony relayed what he had heard the young Selous Scout named Fritz say at the Twelve Thousand Horsemen bar. He then asked Captain Morley if he could confirm whether the RLI or the Selous Scouts were indeed monitoring the movement of elephant and rhino herds and passing that information on to the Department of National Parks.

Captain Morley replied, "From what you've told me, it seems what you overheard was purely hearsay. I can assure you that the army has far more pressing matters on its hands than monitoring elephant and rhino movements in the country. If the Department of National Parks needs that sort of information, it will undoubtedly implement the relevant procedures to gather it. But this is of no interest to the army."

After hanging up, Captain Morley leaned back in his chair, a worried look on his face. The conversation he had just finished reminded him of a radio signal he had seen a couple of weeks earlier from the RLI's base in Buffalo Range. It was from someone called RSM[378] Sandy McLeary, expressing concerns about rumours circulating among his troops that one of their number was involved in illegal poaching activities, and that suspicion had fallen on someone named Sergeant Johannes du Toit.

This suspicion was purely circumstantial, and was based on the fact that Sergeant du Toit had recently made several expensive purchases, including a new S-class Mercedes Benz manufactured in South Africa, which had been imported into Rhodesia. Such a purchase was well beyond a sergeant's pay grade. Additionally, at that time, the country's foreign currency reserves were extremely limited, and strict currency controls were in place. Therefore, even if Sergeant du Toit had the funds for such a purchase, it was highly unlikely that, without the payment of bribes, he would have received the necessary foreign currency permits to enable him to buy the required South African rand to pay for the car.

Captain Morley promptly phoned the Buffalo Range base camp and asked for RSM McLeary. Fortunately, he was available, and the two men had a detailed discussion about Sergeant du Toit. Captain Morley relayed what the journalist had overheard and inquired whether there could be any connection between the rumours circulating at Buffalo Range about Johannes du Toit's potential involvement in poaching activities and the alleged claim by a Selous Scout named Fritz that he was now monitoring the movement of elephant and rhino herds, and passing this information on to one of his superiors.

---

[378] Regimental Sergeant Major.

RSM McLeary acknowledged that it was definitely possible, especially as there didn't seem to be any other explanation for du Toit's recent lavish lifestyle. While the RSM attested to Johannes's soldiering skills, he also mentioned a ruthless streak in his nature that disturbed many of his fellow servicemen. He noted that although Johannes tended to be a loner, he had recently become close to a couple of troopies[379] who now also seemed quite flush with money. It was therefore possible that the three men were collectively involved in some kind of poaching activity.

Captain Morley thanked RSM McLeary for his time, and asked him to keep their discussion private while he conducted further investigations.

Two weeks passed without any further word from Captain Morley. This prompted RSM McLeary to take matters into his own hands by confronting Johannes directly about the rumours. He also intended to question him about how he could afford his recent expensive purchases.

A few days later, Johannes du Toit happened to be back at the base camp in Buffalo Range. Fire Force sticks were being rotated, giving him a few free days in base camp. RSM McLeary seized the opportunity to confront Johannes about the troubling matters.

The meeting did not go well. Johannes vehemently denied any involvement in poaching or any other illegal activities and demanded to know who was making such allegations. The RSM deflected the question, stating that the allegations had not come from the RLI but from another army unit.

In response to the RSM's inquiries about his new car, Johannes angrily retorted that this was none of RSM McLeary's bloody business, and then he stormed out of the office.

---

[379] Colloquial term meaning a regular member or national serviceman of the Rhodesian Army.

Following this heated meeting, Johannes returned to his temporary quarters to decide on his next steps. He realised that any future poaching hunts had to be postponed and that purchasing the new vehicle had been a grave mistake — it had drawn unwanted attention to him and had obviously raised some jealousies among his fellow servicemen. More worryingly, he knew that if he was required to explain how he had been able to afford his luxury car, there was no way he could provide an explanation that would stand up to scrutiny.

He also needed to determine who had spilled the beans about his poaching activities. He quickly ruled out the two shooters and four spotters who had been with him from the start — this left him the porters or the three new spotters as the likely culprits.

The porters, being villagers, would have had no, or very limited, contact with RLI troopies, so he dismissed them. That left the two new spotters from the RAR or Fritz Viljoen, the new spotter from the Selous Scouts. The RAR spotters were unlikely candidates since they were black soldiers who, to Johannes's knowledge, had not been involved in any Fire Force activities and thus had no ties to RLI troopies.

So, the most likely culprit was Fritz Viljoen, the newest spotter recruit and a white Selous Scout, who, by chance, had recently been on OP duties with a RLI section.

Johannes realised he had to act quickly. His instincts warned him that the the *shit would soon hit the fan!*. He decided his best course of action was to skip the country for a few months until the situation cooled down.

With two days remaining before his new Fire Force rotation commenced, he spent the night packing his essential belongings from his temporary quarters into his Mercedes Benz. This included a small locked metal trunk filled with American dollar bills, his Rhodesian passport, and other important documents related to his business venture with Santiago de Costa, as well as files for each of the shooters and spotters he had engaged. He also packed his RLI-issued FN[380] rifle and a VHF[381] two-way radio he had pilfered from the signals store.

At dawn the following morning, he left Buffalo Range and drove 230 kilometres south towards Beitbridge, arriving by 10:30 am, where he completed customs and immigration formalities without any issues.

He then headed for Pretoria where he knew a number of people he could stay with for a few months while the dust settled.

One of the first things he did when he arrived in Pretoria was to access Fritz Viljoen's personal file. From this, he was able to find Fritz's address in Greystone Park. He then called a drug dealer he knew who lived in Arcadia, which was a popular 'goffel'[382] suburb in Salisbury. This man's name was Rudi. Rudi was a thug who made a living out of terror and extortion. His criminal activities occurred mainly in Salisbury but occasionally had extended into South Africa.

Johannes had first met Rudi as a youngster before he joined the army. They had however stayed in touch over the years and Johannes had occasionally engaged Rudi's services when he needed to make a strong point with recalcitrant persons.

Johannes provided Rudi with Fritz's address in Greystone Park. He explained that Fritz was a Selous Scout who had double-crossed him and needed a stern lesson. Johannes offered Rudi US$2,000 if he could locate Fritz, tell him he had come with a gift from Johannes, and then beat him within an inch of his life. Additionally, if Rudi could harm, wreck, or destroy anything else that was important to Fritz during the assault, Johannes promised to pay him another US$1,000.

Rudi agreed to take on the assignment. He said that once the assignment was completed he would post relevant photographic evidence to Johannes. Johannes said that upon receipt of such

---

[380] This was a light automatic rifle designed in Belgium and manufactured by FN Herstal. The FN was the standard issue rifle for the Rhodesian Security Forces.
[381] Very high frequency.
[382] Goffel was a Rhodesian derogatory term used to describe persons who were of mixed-race.

evidence, he would post Rudi's fee, in cash, to any address Rudi gave him.

The two men exchanged address details and then hung up.

Four weeks later, Johannes received an envelope through the post. The envelope bore Rhodesian postage stamps. Inside were four black and white photographs. Two of the photographs showed a very badly beaten-up Fritz on the bed in some bedroom. On one of the bedroom walls was a mirror on which was written, in blood, the words '*Love from J.*'

The third picture was of a burnt-out Yamaha motorcycle in a garage while the fourth was of a dog's decapitated head floating in a swimming pool.

Johannes smiled to himself.

The next day, he placed 40 US$100 bills into an envelope and sent it by registered post to the address in Johannesburg that Rudi had provided. He then phoned Rudi in Salisbury and, using their pre-agreed codes, advised Rudi that '*the pigeons had been released*' and added that '*an additional chick had been included in the release.*'

A week later, he received a call from Rudi, who confirmed that '*the pigeons had arrived*' and thanking him for the additional chick.

Chapter 33 – Nick and Rachel en route to Zimbabwe

Timeline – 31 July 1981

Rachel reached across her seat, took Nick's hand and excitedly said, "Oh Nick, this is so wonderful! I cannot believe that I am finally going to Africa and will be able to see for myself some of the places you have been telling me about over the last year."

Nick squeezed her hand, and said, "I am excited to be going home. And returning with you by my side is going to make everything so much more enjoyable."

It was Friday, 31st July 1981, and Nick and Rachel were on a British Airways flight from London to Johannesburg. Thanks to an upgrade gift from Rachel's parents, they were flying business class. They had been in the air for just over two hours having taken off from London Heathrow at 6:20 pm. They were due to arrive at Johannesburg's Jan Smuts International Airport at 7:25 am on Saturday morning. From Johannesburg, they were scheduled to take an SAA[383] flight at 1:00 pm to Victoria Falls, arriving there at 2:45 pm. They would then be spending four nights at the world-renowned Victoria Falls Hotel.

On Wednesday, 5th August, they would fly to Salisbury[384] with Air Zimbabwe, where they would be staying with Nick's parents who lived in the beautiful suburb of Ballantyne Park. Nick's younger brother, Russell, was expected to return from the University of Cape Town on Friday, 7th August. He, too, would be staying in the family home in

---

[383] South African Airways.
[384] The capital of Zimbabwe. Its name was changed to Harare in April 1982.

Ballantyne Park, and Nick was looking forward to catching up with him. Nick and Rachel planned to be in Salisbury for twelve days, and apart from reconnecting with his family, Nick was also excited about reacquainting himself with his many friends there.

On Monday, 17th August, they would then head off on a road trip that would encompass Bulawayo, Rhodes Matopos National Park, a photographic safari at the Mhuka[385] Ranch just near Chiredzi, and then to Vumba and Inyanga in the Eastern Highlands[386], before heading back to Salisbury. The road trip would cover about 1,700 kilometres. Their timetable was a bit loose, but all in all, they expected to be away for about two weeks. The only hard deadlines they had were 21st August when they were due to arrive at Mhuka Ranch, and 27th August when they were meeting up with both sets of their parents for a three-night stay at the luxurious Troutbeck Inn in Inyanga, before returning to Salisbury.

Nick had organised the entire trip, which had taken many weeks of effort and planning during which itineraries had changed on several occasions.

Nick had desperately wanted to take Rachel to see the Victoria Falls but getting her parents to agree to this had been difficult. Although Zimbabwe had now been independent for nearly 18 months, ZIPRA's[387] downing of Air Rhodesia's flight 825 from Victoria Falls to Salisbury on 3rd September 1978 had left deep and lasting scars on the psyche of the country's population. These fresh wounds were reopened and significantly deepened when, a mere five months later, ZIPRA guerrillas perpetrated an almost identical incident. On this occasion, the guerrillas used a surface-to-air missile to shoot down a Viscount 782D

---

[385] A local word meaning animals or wildlife.

[386] The Eastern Highlands is a mountainous area on the border of Zimbabwe and Mozambique. It extends for about 300 kilometres from north to south and includes the Inyangani Mountains, the Vumba Mountains and the Chimanimani Mountains.

[387] Zimbabwe People's Revolutionary Army. ZIPRA was the military wing of ZAPU.

aircraft shortly after its take-off from Kariba. In the ensuing crash, the entire crew and 59 passengers perished[388].

These two incidents had shaken both Air Rhodesia and the country to their core, and had all but crippled the tourism industry in the country. Fearing further attacks, 50 flight attendants had resigned from Air Rhodesia. Additionally, the significant decline in passenger numbers meant that Air Rhodesia itself had cancelled its domestic service to Victoria Falls, Wankie and Kariba, as well as its twice-weekly international service from Salisbury to London, and its twice-weekly roundtrips between Johannesburg and Victoria Falls.

Mercifully, following Zimbabwe's independence[389] in April 1980, the Rhodesian Bush War had come to a welcome and sudden end, and the tourism industry was gradually recovering. However, lingering fears and doubts about the wisdom of flying to and from Victoria Falls still persisted. Initially, Rachel's parents shared these concerns. At Nick's insistence, Rachel's father, Stuart, sought advice from his contacts in the Foreign and Commonwealth Office in London regarding the safety of flying to Victoria Falls. Fortunately, the Foreign and Commonwealth Office assured Stuart that there was no longer any risk of passenger airlines being targeted by official or renegade military units anywhere in Zimbabwe. Based on this advice, Stuart relented.

Following Stuart's agreement to allow Rachel to fly to Victoria Falls, Nick himself started having misgivings about including the Falls in the itinerary, despite various assurances he had received from friends still living in Zimbabwe. These concerns came and went like the ebb and flow of the tide. It was only after Nick decided to take his talisman—the Bronze Cross of Rhodesia, awarded to him in August 1980 — on their holiday that his misgivings evaporated and were replaced by a

---

[388] On 12th February 1979 a SAM-7 surface-to air-missile destroyed Flight 827 killing all 59 persons on board. The plane was a Viscount 782D which had originated in Victoria Falls on route for Kariba and then onto Salisbury. The plane had been shot down shortly after its take-off from Kariba.

[389] The United Kingdom granted Zimbabwe independence on 18th April 1980. This was following general elections based on a universal franchise, which had been held in February 1980 and which resulted in victory for ZANU-PF, led by Robert Mugabe

deep sense of assurance that their trip to Victoria Falls would be one to remember, and for all the right reasons.

Just when the itinerary for the trip appeared to be final, a last-minute change was made in early July 1981 when their four day stay at Mhuka Ranch, near Chiredzi, had been added. Nick had in fact never even heard of Mhuka Ranch. However, a strange set of circumstances had occurred in the months of May and June, which made it seem as though their visit to the ranch had been predestined.

As things were to subsequently play out their visit to the ranch did, in fact, prove to be definitively fateful.

When Nick had received his national service call-up papers in January 1979, a very good school friend of his named Michael Ripley, had also received his. Both Nick and Michael had applied for acceptance for officer training, at the School of Infantry in Gwelo[390]. Both had been accepted, and both had passed out of the School of Infantry as Second Lieutenants. Nick had been posted to 3RAR[391] in Umtali while Michael had been posted to 1RAR[392] in Bulawayo. The two young men had kept in touch during and after their national service. Michael knew that after Nick's demobilisation, he had gone to the University of Edinburgh to study business and economics. In turn, Nick knew that Michael had gone to the University of Cape Town to study medicine.

In March 1981, Nick received a letter from Michael, giving him all his news. Nick had received the letter in Edinburgh at a time when, in spite of his blossoming relationship with Rachel, he was feeling particularly homesick for Africa.

In his letter, Michael had talked about the political changes that were occurring in Zimbabwe following independence. He also advised Nick that 3RAR, the battalion to which Nick had been posted following completion of his officer training course, had ceased to exist in January 1981. At that time, it was required to relinquish the RAR shield and

---

[390] Gwelo was subsequently renamed Gweru in April 1982.
[391] 3rd Battalion of Rhodesian African Rifles.
[392] 1st Battalion of Rhodesian African Rifles.

name, and had become the 33 Infantry Battalion within the ZNA[393]. Michael advised that the same destiny awaited both 1RAR and 2RAR, both of which were to be disbanded in April 1981.

Michael went onto to say that in August 1980, at about the same time that he and Nick were being demobbed from the army, Nick's 3RAR colleague, Corporal Sipho[394] Pukelo, had been promoted to the rank of PWO[395] and had been transferred to Michael's former battalion, 1RAR.

Michael knew that Nick had a lot of respect for Sipho, but he was unsure if Nick was aware of Sipho's subsequent distinguished service with 1RAR, particularly during the Battle for Entumbane. So, in his letter, Michael briefly outlined Sipho's achievements at 1RAR.

Although Nick knew about Sipho's transfer to 1RAR as a PWO, he was unaware of his subsequent accomplishments and was grateful to Michael for bringing him up to date. Recognising Sipho as a professional and skilled soldier, Nick was not surprised by his achievements while serving with 1RAR. He began to wonder what Sipho might do once 1RAR was disbanded. Given Sipho's track record, Nick assumed he would be commissioned and absorbed into the ZNA, where he would undoubtedly have a long and distinguished career.

Nick did not regard these revelations as mere happenstance. Since they had occurred while he was still planning his trip to Zimbabwe with Rachel, he felt compelled to contact Sipho to see if they could meet. Consequently, he phoned Michael in Cape Town and asked if he could find Sipho's contact details and send them to him.

Michael reached out to Captain Emanuel Wushe, whom he knew from his time with 1RAR. 1RAR had now been merged into ZNA's 11 Infantry Battalion and was still headquartered in Bulawayo. Captain Wushe informed Michael that tribal prejudices within the ZNA had led Sipho to decide to leave the organisation. His last day of duty would be 31st May, and on 13th July, Sipho would begin his new role as the anti-

---

[393] Zimbabwe National Army.
[394] Sipho is a Ndebele boy's name meaning Gift.
[395] Platoon Warrant Officer.

poaching manager at a cattle ranch called Mhuka Ranch, just outside Chiredzi. Captain Wushe also mentioned that Sipho would be spending part of the period from 1st June to 12th July with him in Bulawayo.

Michael had conveyed all this information back to Nick, and had also provided Nick with Emanuel Wushe's telephone number. Nick had phoned the number on several occasions from Edinburgh, and to his delight, had eventually got through. Even more fortuitously, Sipho happened to be in when Nick got through and Emanuel Wushe had passed the telephone handset over to him.

Sipho confirmed everything Nick had learned from Michael and expressed how much he was looking forward to starting at Mhuka Ranch on Monday, 13th July 1981.

For his part, Nick told Sipho that he was now at the University of Edinburgh in Scotland and had met a wonderful lady named Rachel Dixon. He mentioned that he and Rachel would be visiting Zimbabwe at the end of July 1981 and planned to take a road trip around much of the country, including Bulawayo and the Matopos. He asked Sipho if there was any chance of them catching up in Bulawayo.

Sipho explained that arranging a meeting in Bulawayo would be difficult, as he would have just started his new job and would be living at Mhuka Ranch, near Chiredzi. However, he added that his new employer was starting photographic safaris at the ranch. He mentioned that one luxury lodge had already been built and that two more would soon follow. Sipho wondered if he and Rachel would like to visit him at the ranch, saying that he would check if the lodge was available for their stay. As an enticement, Sipho added that he had heard the wildlife at the ranch was spectacular and that the weather in the lowveld was at its best in August and September.

Nick discussed this possibility with Rachel. She was thrilled, both at the prospect of going on a photographic safari in the south-east of Zimbabwe, and meeting Sipho, about whom Nick had spoken with much admiration and affection. For his part, Sipho had discussed the availability of the lodge with Duncan Oliver, the owner of the ranch, and the possibility of Nick and Rachel being paying guests there.

Fortuitously, the lodge was available and Duncan encouraged Sipho to try and persuade Nick and Rachel to visit, promising that he would personally make it his business to ensure that they were both treated like royalty.

After a few more phone calls, arrangements between Nick and Mhuka Ranch were finalised, with their booking being for arrival on Friday, 21st August and departure on Tuesday, 25th August.

Nick's musings were interrupted when the British Airways hostess brought him and Rachel the menu for the evening meal. She topped up their champagne glasses and took their dinner orders. Rachel leaned over and gave Nick a tender kiss on the cheek. She was in heaven, eagerly anticipating their arrival in Johannesburg, followed by their SAA flight to Victoria Falls, which she knew was one of the seven natural wonders of the world.

Dinner arrived shortly after. Both its presentation and taste were superb, befitting business class standards. They enjoyed another two glasses of champagne as Nick captivated Rachel with stories of the Zimbabwean bush, its magnificent wildlife, and its warm, welcoming people.

After dinner, they stretched out in their luxurious business class seats and enjoyed six hours of restful sleep before landing in Johannesburg.

Chapter 34 – Nick and Rachel transit through Johannesburg

Nick and Rachel disembarked at Johannesburg's Jan Smuts International Airport at 7:30 am on Saturday, 1st August. Rachel was pleasantly surprised at how modern, sophisticated, and efficient everything was. They followed the signs to customs and were politely directed by an airport staff member to the relevant queue. The queue moved quickly, and before long, they were called to an arrivals booth, where a customs official diligently inspected and stamped their passports and entry visas. Then they proceeded to the baggage hall to collect their two large suitcases from the revolving carousel.

After they had safely retrieved their suitcases, they made their way to a comfortable restaurant in the airport terminal where they enjoyed a hearty South African breakfast of mealie meal porridge followed by fried eggs, boerewors[396], and tomatoes.

While Rachel and Nick had been making their way around the expansive halls of the airport, Nick had been cautiously scanning the walls and doorways for the ubiquitous *Whites only* or *No Blacks* signs. He knew that these would make Rachel feel uncomfortable and was wondering how he was going to explain them to her. Surprisingly, he saw none, which was unexpected. Subsequently, he discovered that while apartheid[397] was still the official policy of the South African

---

[396] Boerewors is a type of spicy sausage which originated in South Africa.

[397] Apartheid is the Afrikaans word for apartness. It was a system of institutionalised racial segregation that existed in South Africa and South West Africa (now Namibia) from 1948 to the early 1990s.

Government, since 1979, the government under Prime Minister PW Botha[398] had begun implementing measures to sanitise the more petty and uglier aspects of apartheid. This included the removal of all apartheid-related signage from any significant government building which was likely to be in the international community's public eye. This obviously included Jan Smuts International Airport.

Nick and Rachel's SAA[399] flight to Victoria Falls was due to take off at 1:00 pm. They made their way to the SAA check-in desk, where they were served by an attractive young lady with a strong Afrikaans accent. While she was checking them in, she engaged in small talk with Rachel. She was delighted to learn that this was Rachel's first trip to Africa and offered to upgrade them both to business class. Rachel was thrilled and commented to Nick that this augured well for the rest of their trip.

They still had more than an hour before they needed to head to their departure gate. Rachel wanted to wander around the many boutique shops in the airport. Nick, on the other hand, wanted to catch up on local Zimbabwean news. He said he would buy a newspaper and have a coffee while Rachel did her shopping. Rachel concurred, and they agreed for her to meet him at the coffee shop in about half an hour.

Nick purchased the latest edition of the Financial Gazette, a respected weekly Zimbabwean newspaper focusing on business, finance, and politics. First published in 1969, the paper was easily recognisable by its distinctive pink-coloured recycled paper.

Nick knew that the Rhodesian economy had historically been strong but had taken a downturn between 1975 and 1979 due to the Rhodesian Bush War, rising international oil prices, and two years of severe drought. However, with strong agriculture, mining, and

---

[398] Pieter Willem Botha was a South African politician who was the last Prime Minister of South Africa from 1978 to 1984 and its first executive state president from 1984 to 1989.
[399] South African Airways.

manufacturing sectors, the fundamentals were still sound when the new ZANU-PF[400] government came to power in April 1980.

According to the Financial Gazette's economic analysis, the economy had performed well during the first 15 months after independence, with real growth exceeding 20%. This impressive growth was driven by the resumption of normal economic activity after the end of the war, increased employment as military call-ups[401] ended, and a surge in imports following the lifting of international sanctions.

The new government's economic policy centred on *growth with equity*, a principle reflected in its first two pragmatic yet socialist-leaning budgets. The economy the government inherited was capitalist in nature, designed to benefit the former white ruling class. One of the new government's central policies was to end all racial discrimination, and one of its first steps was to ensure equal access to state institutions for all citizens, regardless of race. Consequently, the government's first two budgets prioritised health, education, and high-density housing. In addition, it was reforming the country's industrial relations system by granting greater powers to trade unions.

As far as the financial health of the economy was concerned, the article in the Financial Gazette noted that since April 1980, there had been a big jump in imports, mainly funded by drawing down on reserves and taking out short-term loans. Unfortunately, this surge in imports wasn't matched by an increase in exports, leading to a hefty balance of payments deficit. To tackle this issue, the government had raised sales tax, import duties, and interest rates, while also implementing measures to control the money supply.

Nick's recent studies in business and economics at the University of Edinburgh helped him grasp some of the macroeconomic issues the

---

[400] Zimbabwe African National Union – Patriotic Front. ZANU-PF is a political organisation that has been the ruling party of Zimbabwe since independence in 1980.
[401] By 1978, all white men up to the age of 60 were subject to periodic call-up to the army; younger men up to 35 years in age were required to spend alternating blocks of six weeks in the army and at home. These mandatory call-ups had posed a considerable burden on the country's workforce.

new government was facing. While he didn't claim to be an expert, he felt that, given the political upheaval that brought ZANU-PF to power, it was currently doing a reasonable job in managing the economy.

He was also smart enough to understand that for things to significantly improve, the new government would have to juggle a few tricky priorities. One of these was managing people's hopes for a brighter future while being realistic about what the country could actually afford. Another challenge was retaining the experienced white professionals in the country while promoting black employees into senior roles in both the public and private sectors as quickly as possible.

It was also vital to ensure that the newly elected or promoted officials — many of whom were still learning the ropes — didn't abuse their power or fall into corruption. Plus, the government needed to move towards a socialist system without losing the positive aspects of the Western democratic framework it had inherited.

Keeping social harmony was another important matter, especially after the recent bloody civil war. Care had to be taken to ensure that old tribal rivalries, some of which had been simmering since the late 19th century, didn't flare up again.

Nick was pondering these matters when Rachel reappeared.

She was excited and smiling. She ran up to Nick holding a duty-free customs bag, and said, "You will never believe what I have just bought!"

She rummaged into the bag and pulled out two boxes — one containing a wide-angle lens and the other a telephoto lens — for the Canon F-1n camera that Nick had given her for Christmas.

"These are just what I needed," she said. "I cannot wait to use them at Mhuka[402] Ranch."

---

[402] A local word meaning animals or wildlife.

Nick gave her a big hug. "I am sure you will be using them long before we get to Mhuka Ranch," he said. "But they have just called our flight. You can show me all their cool features on the plane."

With that he took her hand and they headed towards the departure gate.

Chapter 35 – Nick and Rachel visit Victoria Falls

Rachel and Nick's SAA[403] flight from Johannesburg to Victoria Falls touched down at the small rural airport just after 2:45 pm on Saturday, 1st August. The flight had been without incident, and Nick felt a wave of relief wash over him. During the flight, there were moments when he had reached into the pocket of his jeans to touch the black velvet pouch containing his Bronze Cross of Rhodesia. The feel of the medal offered him a modicum of reassurance that their journey to Victoria Falls would be safe.

Rachel, too, had felt a twinge of anxiety during the flight. She had read numerous heart-wrenching accounts of the downing of Air Rhodesia flights 825 and 827[404] just over two years earlier. Today, their flight had been full of excited passengers, most of whom she imagined were tourists eager to see the Victoria Falls, or to give it its correct name in the Lozi language, *Mosi-oa-Tunya*[405]. She thought the same excitement would have been felt by the passengers aboard the two civilian Vickers Viscount aircraft that were tragically shot down by ZIPRA[406] guerrillas in the final years of the Rhodesian Bush War. Although she knew little about Zimbabwe and knew no one from the country besides Nick, her

---

[403] South African Airways.

[404] Both these flights were scheduled civilian flights that were shot down by surface to air missiles fired by ZIPRA troops. Air Rhodesia flight 825 was shot down on 3rd September 1978 whilst Air Rhodesia flight 827 was shot down on 12th February 1979.

[405] *Mosi-oa-Tunya* is the local Lozi name for the Victoria Falls. It means *The Smoke that Thunders*.

[406] Zimbabwe People's Revolutionary Army. ZIPRA was the military wing of ZAPU.

mind recoiled at the thought of the horror endured by those who had been aboard the two ill-fated flights.

Nick and Rachel collected their hand luggage from the overhead lockers and made their way to the front of the plane. They thanked the airflight crew and carefully made their way down the passenger steps from the door of their aircraft to the hot bitumen of the airport's apron.

At the bottom of the steps, Rachel paused, taking in her surroundings. Her bright blue eyes sparkled with excitement and anticipation. She was struck by the cerulean expanse of the cloudless sky and the vastness of the land before her. It would take time for her eyes and mind to adjust to these unfamiliar horizons. Everything felt alive with nature, almost untouched by the human presence she was so used to in Europe. The sun warmed her face and shoulders, and as she lifted her chin to sniff the air, she caught a faint scent of dust from the nearby bushland, mingled with the cool, clean breeze.

Nick looked across at Rachel and was once again struck by her understated beauty and elegance. She wore an oat-coloured cashmere V-neck cardigan over a soft white short-sleeved cotton blouse, which was tucked into high-waisted, olive-green linen tapered trousers. Her shoes were soft-leather, mid-heeled khaki ankle boots that enhanced her height and the length of her legs. The sleeves of her cardigan were gathered just below her elbows, revealing a simple yet elegant gold bracelet on her right wrist and a white fashion watch on her left.

Nick went over to her, put his arms around her waist, and gave her a firm but gentle embrace. "Welcome to Victoria Falls," he said. "The airport is not much to write home about, but I know you are going to love the hotel, and the Falls themselves will simply blow your mind away."

Rachel wrapped her arms around his neck and said, "My mind is already in a whirl. This place is so unlike anywhere I've been to before. It's like being on another planet. I know I'm going to love it. I can't wait to get to the hotel. Let's go and collect our luggage."

With that they followed the people in front of them into the modest terminal building. After their passports and Rachel's visa had been checked by an immigration official, they collected their luggage and exited the terminal to find the shuttle bus service to the Victoria Falls Hotel.

In addition to Nick and Rachel, four other hotel guests were aboard the bus. All four were black South Africans visiting Zimbabwe for the first time, drawn to the country following the end of the Rhodesian Bush War.

The bus driver was a large, jovial, middle-aged Ndebele man who introduced himself as Mbuso[407]. He explained that it was about a 25-minute drive to the hotel and that if they were lucky, they might even see some wildlife on or close to the road.

He told the passengers about the swift recovery of the tourism sector in Victoria Falls following the end of the Rhodesian Bush War. In the early 1970s, international tourist numbers to the Falls averaged approximately 375,000 annually. However, by 1979, this figure had plummeted to a mere 80,000, the lowest level since 1963. This decline in international visitors was primarily attributed to various terrorist incidents[408] that had occurred in and around Victoria Falls, though he chose not to elaborate. He noted that in 1980, the number of international tourists had rebounded to 238,000, with expectations for that number to rise to 320,000 in the current year. Additionally, he mentioned that the town of Victoria Falls was growing rapidly, expanding from a population of 3,500 in the mid-seventies to about 8,000 in 1980.

Mbuso had just begun sharing some of the history of Victoria Falls when he slowed down and pointed to the right, about 40 metres ahead. Standing in the long grass among a few acacia trees was a small herd of elephants. He pulled off the road and turned off the engine.

---

[407] Mbuso is a Ndebele boy's name meaning Leader.
[408] These incidents included hostile attacks on the railway line, police camp, airport buildings, civilian air flights, and a number of hotels including Peters Motel, Elephant Hills Hotel and the Victoria Falls Hotel itself.

The herd emerged from the grass, crossing the road just 30 metres in front of their stationary vehicle. It consisted of six elephants, including a young calf that, to everyone's delight, decided to roll over and take a dust bath on the road verge. Rachel excitedly pulled out her Canon camera from her backpack and managed to capture several excellent shots with her newly purchased telephoto lens.

A little further down the road, they spotted zebras and baboons, and caught a fleeting glimpse of a magnificent kudu bull standing motionless beside some tall bushes just off the road. The bull posed for a few brief seconds before snorting into the air and disappearing back into the bush without a trace.

Once the kudu bull had disappeared, Mbuso restarted their shuttle bus and resumed his narration about David Livingstone's discovery of the Falls in 1855.

Mbuso told the passengers that David Livingstone had given the Falls the name *Victoria Falls* in honour of the Queen of England at that time, Queen Victoria[409]. He also said that in describing the Falls, David Livingstone had written that, *'No one can imagine the beauty of the view from anything witnessed in England. But scenes so lovely must have been gazed upon by angels in their flight.'*

He explained that these words and other writings by David Livingstone were subsequently responsible for bringing the existence of the Victoria Falls to the modern world's attention.

All this was, of course, already known to Nick. However, Mbuso mentioned something about David Livingstone that Nick was completely unaware of. In 1866, 11 years after his first sighting of Victoria Falls, Livingstone returned to Africa for a third and final time, this time to try to discover the source of the Nile.

Ill health and misadventure thwarted Livingstone's quest. However, during his final African expedition, which ended with his death in 1873,

---

[409] Queen Victoria was Queen of the United Kingdom and Ireland from 20th June 1837 until her death in 1901.

he had several interactions with Arab slave traders on the eastern shores of Lake Tanganyika[410], near an Arab settlement named Ujiji[411]. What Livingstone witnessed during these encounters horrified him and fuelled his determination to alert the Western world to the ongoing existence of the slave trade in that part of Africa, despite its supposed abolition by the colonial powers controlling or influencing the countries bordering the lake.

According to Mbuso, in one of David Livingstone's many letters to the editor of the New York Herald, he wrote, '*And if my disclosures regarding the terrible Ujijian African slavery should lead to the suppression of the African East Coast slave trade, I shall regard that as a greater matter by far than the discovery of all the Nile sources together.*'

Nick later learned that Livingstone's many letters, books, and journals had indeed sparked public support for the abolition of slavery in Africa. Consequently, he had received much of the credit for the eventual end of slavery along the east coast of Africa.

Shortly thereafter, their shuttle bus arrived at their hotel. The entrance to the hotel's grounds was marked by a cream-coloured arch built atop four stone pillars, two on each side. The arch bore the inscription, *The Victoria Falls Hotel*.

They drove under the arch and along a tarred driveway that led to the hotel entrance. The driveway meandered through a large park filled with beautifully landscaped gardens. Built in Edwardian style, the hotel featured solid brick inner and outer walls, ornate decorative details, and spacious rooms with high ceilings. It first opened in 1904, aimed at

---

[410] Lake Tanganyika is one of Africa's great lakes. The lake is shared by four countries – Tanzania (previously named Tanganyika and before that German East Africa), the Democratic Republic of the Congo (formerly the Congo and before that Zaire), Burundi (formerly part of the colony known as Ruanda-Urundi) and Zambia (previously named Northern Rhodesia).

[411] Ujiji is a historic town located in the Kigoma region of Tanzania. It is the site of the famous meeting in November 1871 when Henry Stanley, who at the time was on an assignment commissioned by the New York Herald, found David Livingstone and reputedly uttered the famous words, "Dr Livingstone, I presume?"

attracting wealthy passengers travelling to Victoria Falls on the newly constructed railway line, which entered Rhodesia from Plumtree in the south-west and exited at Victoria Falls in the north-west, after passing through Bulawayo and Wankie. The line was intended to be part of the ambitious Cape to Cairo Railway[412], a visionary project designed to connect the length of Africa from South Africa's Cape Town in the south to Egypt's Port Said in the north.

They were met at the hotel entrance by a portly doorman dressed in a bright red jacket, blue trousers, white-gloved hands, a tall black hat, and shiny black shoes. His jacket and top hat were decorated with hundreds of travel pins and badges given to him by guests from around the world.

He introduced himself as Odwell, a name which both delighted and amused Rachel. Rachel asked him if he would mind being photographed with her, a request to which he gladly agreed. Consequently, Nick took a picture of a beaming Odwell standing alongside a smiling Rachel.

Following the camera shoot, they checked in at reception. From there, a slimly built porter took them to their luxurious bedroom on the first floor. It was now late afternoon, and too late for them to visit the Falls. Instead, Nick suggested they go down to the hotel's terrace to enjoy a cup of tea with scones and jam.

From the terrace, they had a direct view of the Victoria Falls bridge, which was approximately two kilometres away. The view to the bridge was eastwards across the hotel's manicured gardens and then along

---

[412] The original proposal for a Cape to Cairo railway was made in 1874 by Edwin Arnold, then the editor of The Daily Telegraph in London. The project was never completed due to financial restraints, international political disagreements, and the advent of WWI. Imperialist and entrepreneur Cecil Rhodes had been instrumental in securing the southern African states in the late 19th century for the British Empire and envisioned a continuous 'red line' of British dominions from north to south.

Victoria Fall's second gorge[413] to the bridge. The bridge itself was situated some 350 metres to the south of and below the Victoria Falls.

The Falls were not visible from the terrace, but their ceaseless spray enveloped a large part of the bridge in a misty cloud. The bridge had been the brainchild of Cecil John Rhodes[414], who had instructed his engineers, *'To build the bridge across the Zambezi where the trains, as they pass, will catch the spray of the Falls.'*

As they sat on the terrace enjoying their cup of tea and scones, Rachel looked across to Nick and said, "Gosh if the rest of Zimbabwe is anything like this, I certainly can understand why you love this country so much. I cannot believe how friendly everybody has been and how beautiful everything is."

She then rather coyly said, "All this beauty is making me feel quite amorous. After we have finished tea I would like to go back to our room and make love to you."

The thought of making love in such a sublime setting made them both finish their tea and scones with the minimum of delay. Once they were back inside their bedroom, Nick opened the windows and curtains to let in the cool breeze, and to allow the muffled roaring sounds of the Falls to fill the room. As their room was on the first floor, there was no danger of them being espied by passing staff or guests.

Nick lifted Rachel's blouse over her head and then unhooked her delicate lacy bra. He undid the belt of her trousers and pulled them down to reveal her sexy knickers. She looked deeply into Nick's eyes. He had taken off his shirt and Rachel's hand touched his chest and her fingertips slightly massaged his erogenous zones.

---

[413] The entire volume of the Zambezi River pours through the First Gorge's 100 metre-wide exit for a distance of about 150 metres, then enters a zigzagging series of gorges designated by the order in which the river reaches them. Collectively the seven gorges are known as the Bakota Gorge.

[414] Ironically, Cecil John Rhodes never visited the bridge. He died on 26th March 1902 before construction of the bridge began in 1904. Construction of the bridge was completed on 11th April 1905.

He pulled down her knickers and lay her face up on the bed. He placed tender kisses along her inner thighs which were trembling with readiness and desire.

Nick put his manhood into her womanhood and gently began to move with her. Her movements quickly gathered pace and she arched her hips up into him. She became wild and her breath became short as did his.

Their large bed creaked but not enough to be off-putting.

Nick placed his hands on the headboard and pushed himself deeper into her. In a bid to get as much of him as she could, Rachel lifted both her legs into a near vertical position and placed her calves over his shoulders.

"Gosh," she moaned, "that is perfect."

Nick and Rachel came at almost the same time. Their coming brought them both down from their climax and then they crumpled like a sandcastle. They collapsed into each other. But they were still locked together and their kisses were still deep, moist, and long. Then suddenly, their passion ebbed. They disentangled themselves and lay back on the bed. Neither of them attempted to cover any part of their nakedness.

They lay like that for several minutes. Rachel eventually broke the comfortable silence by saying, "If that is my African welcome, I wish we had come here months ago!"

Nick laughed. A while later they showered together enjoying the sight of each other's naked bodies. Then they dressed and went downstairs to enjoy an intimate evening meal together.

Chapter 36 – Mosi-oa-Tunya

The next morning they woke early. Rachel was extremely excited as today she would be seeing *Mosi-oa-Tunya*[415] for the first time. She had no idea what to expect but was sure that she would not be disappointed.

By now, she had become accustomed to the muffled roaring sound of the nearby Falls that echoed around most parts of the hotel. She had also become used to the ever-present cloud of mist that hung over the unseen void into which the mighty Zambezi River disappeared, as its waters crashed over the precipice of the chasm that marked the border between Zimbabwe and Zambia.

They ate a hurried breakfast, and then headed along the clearly marked pathway from the hotel to the Falls. They both had waterproof ponchos with them and, naturally, Rachel also had her camera and lenses. On advice from Nick, she had carefully wrapped these into a plastic bag to protect them from the mist that Nick had assured her would saturate them both, and everything in their possession that was not waterproofed.

They entered the Victoria Falls National Park through the Visitors' Centre, which was situated close to the western end of the Falls. Nick wanted Rachel's first sighting of the Falls to be as dramatic as possible. He had therefore decided that the most stunning viewing point would

---

[415] *Mosi-oa-Tunya* is the local Lozi name for the Victoria Falls. It means *The Smoke that Thunders*. The Lozi people live primarily in south-west Zambia and surrounding countries.

be the one that overlooked the *Devil's Cataract,* which was also at the western end of the Falls.

Although this viewing point did not give a complete panoramic vista of the *Main Falls,* it had the advantage that it was hardly ever shrouded in mist. So Nick surmised that this would give Rachel a dramatic first view of the Falls as well as providing wonderful photo opportunities.

They walked along the bitumen path through a wooded area towards the viewing point. With no mist or rain, they had not yet donned their ponchos. Nick was holding Rachel's hand as they rounded a bend and descended a well-maintained path to the viewing point. When Rachel first saw the Falls, her grip tightened around his hand. She stopped, standing in silence as she absorbed the breathtaking sight before her. Although this section of the Falls was the lowest, she was astonished by the force of the torrents of water crashing over the precipice, falling 60 metres into the turbulent river below. From this vantage point, Rachel could also gaze eastward towards the line of the *Main Falls* and the raging waters below.

Nick explained to her that the waters of the Victoria Falls did not drop into an open basin but instead fell into a chasm, which varied in width from 25 to 75 metres. This chasm had been formed by the sheer drop of the Falls on the one side, and by the wall of rock of approximately the same height on the other side. The narrow chasm, combined by the extensive width of the Falls of nearly 1,600 metres, and the enormous volume of water that cascaded over the precipice, helped explain the irresistible power and majesty of the Falls.

Nick explained that the chasm's only outlet was a narrow channel, which exited the barrier wall at a point about three-fifths of the way along its length from the western end of the Falls. This outlet was less than a 100 metres wide and 150 metres long. Through this narrow and short channel, the entire volume of the mighty Zambezi River was being forced.

At the end of the short exit channel was a deep pool of water known as the *Boiling Pot,* into which the raging torrents of water churned and raged before travelling another 250 metres and flowing beneath the

Victoria Falls bridge. This was the bridge they had viewed while sitting on the terrace of the hotel.

Rachel was captivated.

In awesome wonder she said, "No wonder David Livingstone had said that it was impossible to imagine the magnificence of the Falls from anything witnessed in England. They are incredible and their beauty is unsurpassed."

She removed her camera from its waterproof wrapping, adjusted various settings, and took a multitude of photographs. She hoped these images would forever capture and remind her of the wonderful scenes she was now witnessing.

After about ten minutes, Nick suggested they walk a short distance away from the Falls to see David Livingstone's statue. They would then return to the bituminised pathway that followed the southern side of the *Main Falls*, allowing Rachel to fully appreciate just how wide and high the Falls were.

It was only a short walk to David Livingstone's statue which stood on the western bank of the Falls. The bronze statue showed a stoic looking David Livingstone gazing towards the *Devil's Cataract*. According to the plaque beneath the statue, the effigy had been designed by a Scottish sculptor named William Reid Dick and it had been unveiled in 1934 by Howard Unwin Moffat[416]. The statue afforded more photographic opportunities for Rachel, with her favourite composition being a picture of a smiling Nick standing beneath the 4-metre-high monument.

From the statue, they returned to the paved path that ran along the solid-rock southern wall of the chasm into which the Zambezi River fell. Interspersed along this pathway were several viewing points, from where visitors could gaze directly at the *Main Falls*, spanning approximately 1,600 metres in length. The path meandered through a

---

[416] Howard Unwin Moffat was a nephew of David Livingstone. He had been premier of Southern Rhodesia from 1927 to 1933.

heavily wooded area known as the *Rain Forest*, named after the heavy mist, which enveloped the region throughout the year. As they progressed, the mist intensified and soon fell like rain. The increased precipitation required both of them to don their ponchos. Despite the glorious sunny day, Rachel found it challenging to take photographs along the pathway due to the heavy mist — almost like rain — coming from the Falls.

The *Rain Forest* was a tapestry of every imaginable shade of green. They stopped at each viewing point along the way. Rachel was surprised by how unprotected these lookouts were. If they were so inclined, there was nothing stopping them from stepping off the paved pathway, walking right to the edge of the chasm, and gazing down at the raging river some 100 metres below. One slip of the foot could result in a deadly fall onto the rocks. The frequent, unguarded hazards were unlike anything she had ever encountered in Europe. The thrill of danger sent her adrenaline pumping, filling her with a profound sense of being alive.

The pathway continued until it reached the exit gorge, through which the mighty river was squeezed and forced amidst much protestation. The pathway opened up into a grassy heath and on to a viewing point known as the *Corner Viewpoint*. From here, you could look across the chasm and onto the eastern extremity of the Falls. This was known as the *Eastern Cataract* and was entirely on the Zambian side of the river.

From the *Corner Viewpoint,* Nick and Rachel returned to the Visitors' Centre, near which they found a small café. There, they both enjoyed an ice-cold vanilla milkshake while sitting in the café's gardened area, which was filled with colourful birds the breeds of which Rachel had never seen before. There were even a few brazen monkeys who waited for someone to drop a morsel of food onto the lawned area. The monkeys would, quick as a flash, snatch up the food treasure and then excitedly scurry away with the treasure firmly clutched in their little hands.

By now, it was just after midday. Unbeknownst to Rachel, Nick had arranged a 30-minute flight over the Falls. The service, aptly named

The Flight of Angels, had commenced only a year earlier in response to the rising number of international and domestic visitors. Operated by a company called United Air Carriers, it flew out of a small airfield named Spray View, located just outside the town of Victoria Falls. Their flight was scheduled for 2:30 pm, and Nick had arranged for them to be picked up from the hotel at 1:15 pm.

"Hey Rachel, I have another surprise for you today. But first, we need to get back to the hotel. We're being picked up at 1:30 pm, so we'd better get going," he said.

"Oooh, I love surprises," said Rachel. "Let's get moving. We don't want to be late."

They made their way back to the hotel, had a quick shower, and were in the hotel's lobby area by 1:15 pm. At 1:30 pm their transport arrived. Apart from Nick and Rachel, there was another couple and their teenager daughter who were visiting from the United States of America.

Everyone introduced themselves. The teenage girl was named Amy, and her parents were Dennis and Sally. Amid the lively chatter, Rachel learned that the surprise was a flight over the Falls. Nick explained to Rachel that he had never seen the Falls from the air but had heard that the only way to truly appreciate their vastness and magnificence was from above.

At the airfield, they were met by a representative of United Air, who explained the procedure for the flight. They would be flying in a six-seater, twin-engine Piper Aztec light aircraft, so all six seats would be occupied. The representative informed them that the aircraft would complete two clockwise and two anti-clockwise loops over the Falls, allowing everyone on board to enjoy a full view of the Falls and the Zambezi River, both before and after it plunged into the massive natural chasm that cut across the river. He added that there was a good chance they might spot some wildlife from the air, particularly elephant or buffalo herds.

Their pilot, a middle-aged man named Philip, then introduced himself and escorted them to the aeroplane, which was parked outside a hangar near the runway. Once everyone had boarded, the plane taxied to the runway, preparing for take-off into the wind — something that Nick knew was ideal. Within 20 seconds of accelerating down the runway, they were airborne.

The window layout of the Piper Aztec provided them all with excellent views of the river and bushland below. Philip pointed out several landmarks as they flew. About five minutes later, they were soaring above the Falls. Both Rachel and Nick were awestruck by their vastness and breathtaking beauty.

Looking down into the chasm that split the river, it appeared as though a giant had slashed a mighty gash right across it. The river cascaded into this rift, trapped by the solid rock walls behind and ahead. About three-fifths of the way along, it seemed as though the same giant had carved a short escape passage, followed by a series of zigzagging cuts on the downstream side of the Falls. The furious river, in a raging attempt to break free, crashed through these zigzags, only finding freedom after a turbulent journey of roughly 100 kilometres.

From their bird's-eye view above the Falls, the passengers in the plane were thrilled by the grandeur and ferocity of the landscape below. They truly felt like angels in flight.

All too soon, the flight was over, and they were back on the ground. However, the brief experience would stay with them for many years to come. Each time Nick or Rachel looked back at the photographs they had taken from the air, they felt the same thrill they had on that first Sunday in August 1981.

On Monday, Rachel wanted to explore the small town of Victoria Falls. She was particularly interested in visiting the street traders' stalls and the more upmarket shops, where all manner of crafts and arts were displayed. The wood, soapstone, serpentine, and malachite carvings were especially impressive, as were the traditional beadwork and paintings.

Rachel was particularly taken by an abstract painting by an artist called Shadreck Ndlovu. It was called *Fantasy Illusion* and was painted in oils on canvas. The canvas size was 90 by 120 centimetres. The colours of the painting were various shades of yellow, red and blue. The artist had been able to create an interesting finish and texture to the work by the clever addition of various lines of poetry, which he had delicately etched into the painted work with a graphite pen.

Rachel wanted to purchase the painting as a gift for Nick's parents to thank them for allowing her and Nick to stay with them on the Salisbury[417] leg of their trip. She asked Nick if she thought they would like it. Nick had no hesitation in endorsing her suggestion.

"They will both love it," he said. "They have quite a large entrance foyer to their house and I think it will look perfect there. The walls in the entrance hall are large so they will easily be able to take that painting."

Rachel asked the shop owner how much the picture cost. He replied saying it was Zim$800[418]. Rachel thought that was quite reasonable, but before she could respond, Nick intervened and began to haggle with the shop owner. Nick offered him Zim$350, and after some back-and-forth, they finally settled on a price of Zim$450[419]. The shop owner carefully rolled and wrapped the canvas which Rachel then placed under her arm, delighted with her purchase.

Tuesday was their last full day at the Falls. It was another beautifully warm and sunny day. They decided to spend the morning at the hotel's gym where they would complete a workout session. Thereafter, they intended to relax for a few hours at the hotel's glorious swimming pool. In the afternoon Nick had booked a couple of seats on the

---

[417] The capital of Zimbabwe. Its name was changed to Harare in April 1982.
[418] From the beginning of 1981 the value of the Zimbabwean dollar started to depreciate against the US dollar. By August 1981, Zim$1.00 was worth about US$1.10. This was from its high at independence in April 1980 when Zim$1.00 was worth about US$1.50.
[419] In August 1981 this was equal to about US$495.

Zambezi Sunset Cruise, or *Booze Cruise* as it was more colloquially known as, which departed at 4:00 pm.

They woke reasonably early and headed to the well-equipped gym, where they completed an energetic cardio and weight workout session that lasted about an hour. Afterward, they showered and enjoyed a late breakfast on the hotel's terraced veranda.

After breakfast, they returned to their room and changed into their swimwear. Nick put on a T-shirt, while Rachel slipped on a brightly coloured silk kimono over her bikini. They each grabbed the book they were reading and headed to the pool.

Being a weekday and still relatively early, the pool was quiet, and they easily found two sunbeds beneath a large market umbrella. They had just removed their outer coverings and applied sun protection when a middle-aged waiter appeared, seemingly out of nowhere. He asked if they'd like something to drink, and they both ordered soft drinks, which arrived shortly afterward in tall, attractive plastic tumblers. The waiter apologised for the plastic tumblers, explaining that the hotel didn't allow glassware near the pool since most guests were likely to be barefoot. Nick and Rachel agreed that it made sense and thanked him for the drinks. Then, they lay back on their sunbeds, soaking in the warm sunshine and admiring the pristine swimming pool.

Unbeknownst to Nick and Rachel, ZANU-PF[420] was also holding a conference at one of the hotel's conference facilities that day. Nick would later learn that the conference was being attended by senior ZANU-PF party members, who were discussing the next steps following the successful ZIMCORD[421] conference held in Salisbury earlier in the year.

---

[420] Zimbabwe African National Union – Patriotic Front. ZANU-PF is a political organisation that has been the ruling party of Zimbabwe since independence in 1980.
[421] ZIMCORD stands for the Zimbabwe Conference on Reconstruction and Development. The conference was held in 1981 during the period 23 March to 27 March. At the conference 31 nations and 26 international agencies had pledged just over US$1.45 billion in economic aid to Zimbabwe over a three-year period.

Just before the lunch break, some of the conference delegates had left the conference room and had gone to the bar to order a drink. Some of the delegates had moved away from the bar and had taken their drinks to the swimming pool area, where they were enjoying their drink and a cigarette.

The waiter who had earlier served Nick and Rachel at the pool, had been given the unenviable job of advising these delegates that glassware was not allowed in or around the pool, and requesting that they transfer the contents of their glasses into a plastic tumbler.

The waiter approached one of the delegates standing near Nick and Rachel's sunbeds. Nick overheard the waiter explaining that, to minimise the risk of broken glass, glasses were not permitted in the pool area. The waiter then politely asked the delegate if he would mind transferring his drink into a plastic tumbler, which he had ready on his tray.

The delegate was a portly, middle-aged black man in his late forties. He was extremely annoyed by the waiter's request to transfer the contents of his glass into a plastic tumbler. In a loud voice, he told the waiter he had never heard such a ridiculous policy before and that there was no way he would comply.

The waiter refused to back down and advised the delegate that if he did not comply, the waiter would have no alternative but to ask him to leave the pool area.

At this point the delegate became noticeably belligerent and angry. He started shouting at the waiter, and said, "Who do you think you are? Do you know who I am? I suggest you just go on your way. If you do not, I will speak to the management of this hotel and make sure you lose your job."

The outburst from the delegate had aroused Rachel from her nap. She sat up and asked Nick what was going on.

"I am afraid you're about to see a nastier side of Zimbabwe," replied Nick. "Just watch. Let's see how this plays out."

The waiter still did not back down. He advised that he was just doing his job and that he had been asked by the hotel's management to make sure that glassware was not taken into the pool area.

The delegate got even more angry. "I can see and hear that you are Ndebele," he shouted at the waiter.

The waiter replied, "Yes I am. But I am not sure what that has got to do with me asking you to pour the contents of your glass into this plastic tumbler."

The delegate's face became even more enraged. "You idiot. You and the rest of your tribe are worthless and irrelevant. We are going to destroy you?"

With that, he shoved the waiter, who fell backwards into the pool.

Nick leapt up from his sunbed and approached the enraged delegate. He exclaimed, "Hey, steady on there Mister! The guy is just doing his job. He just wants to make sure that glasses are not accidentally broken in or near the pool. You have no right to act like that. I suggest you apologise to him."

By now the bedraggled waiter had climbed out of the pool and was standing next to Nick.

"And who the bloody hell are you?" said the delegate. "You stupid interfering *murungu*[422]. Don't you understand you lost the war. We now own and run this country and we will run it how we want."

Nick was not the kind of person who would be inclined to back down in such a confrontation. The situation was likely to quickly escalate when fortunately, another delegate, who had also been outside around the pool, intervened and took the first delegate by the shoulder.

"Come on Minister," he said. "I think we need to get back to the conference venue. Don't waste any more of your valuable time on this trivial matter."

---

[422] *Murungu* is the Shona word for a white person.

With that, he led the Minister back towards the conference facility.

The waiter turned to Nick and said, "Thank you, Sir, for trying to help. That man is one of the new fat cats in government. He is a nasty piece of work. I am sorry he has ruined your morning."

"That's no problem," said Nick. "I am glad his colleague intervened and took him away. I was about to give him a good hiding."

"That would not have been a good idea but I would have enjoyed seeing it," said the waiter. They both chuckled and shook hands.

The waiter said he would like to offer him and Rachel lunch on the house and asked them what they would like. Nick and Rachel were happy to accept.

The incident left both Nick and Rachel feeling a little frazzled. Nick couldn't help but feel that if the Minister's actions typified what was happening within ZANU-PF, the prospects for maintaining harmony between the country's different races and tribes seemed bleak. He was also extremely perturbed by the Minister's throwaway comment that the government intended to destroy the Ndebele nation.

However, Nick was determined to not let the incident spoil the rest of their day, especially their late afternoon booze cruise on the Zambezi.

By the time they had finished the complimentary lunch, which came with a gin and tonic, they had both put the matter behind them.

The next morning after breakfast, Mbuso, the driver who had picked them up from Victoria Falls Airport on the previous Saturday, arrived at the hotel to take them back to the airport for their flight to Salisbury.

Chapter 37 – Nick and Rachel arrive in Salisbury

Nick and Rachel had taken off from Victoria Falls Airport at 10:00 am on Wednesday, 5th August. They had finished their light morning breakfast, and the friendly Air Zimbabwe cabin crew were now serving tea and coffee prior to the aircraft's descent into Salisbury[423] Airport.

Rachel was both excited and a little bit apprehensive about meeting Nick's parents and his younger brother, Russell. She leaned across to Nick and said, "I know very little about your brother. Why don't you tell me a bit about him?"

"Sure thing," said Nick. "You'll love him. He's an absolute charmer with a wonderful sense of humour. He's an outdoorsy kind of guy — he loves his sport and enjoys camping, fishing, and hiking. He was born in February 1963, so he's just over a year younger than me. I'm really looking forward to seeing him again. The last time I saw him was back in September last year when I flew out of Salisbury to the UK. At that time, he was in upper six at Prince Edward School, preparing for his A-Level[424] exams at the end of November.

"He was always very passionate about African wildlife. When he was at school, he wanted to join the Department of National Parks[425] in Zimbabwe. However, with the situation in Zimbabwe looking rather precarious, Mum and Dad instead persuaded him to go to university

---

[423] The capital of Zimbabwe. Its name was changed to Harare in April 1982
[424] A-Levels were the Advanced Level of school examinations. It was conferred as a school leaving qualification to senior school pupils as part of the Cambridge International General Certificate of Education.
[425] The full name is the Department of National Parks and Wildlife Management.

after he had finished school. So he's now at the University of Cape Town. He started there in February 1981 and is doing a three-year Bachelor of Science degree, majoring in environmental and geographical sciences and geology.

"He was a bit apprehensive about doing a university degree as he never really saw himself as the academic type. But, judging from his recent letters, he's really enjoying UCT[426]. He likes his course, loves the social life, and has made loads of new friends. He's mentioned a South African girl named Yvonne — they seem keen on each other. He's also started getting involved in student politics, which surprised me."

"What about national service?" asked Rachel. "I thought it was compulsory."

"Well, it was," said Nick. "But it was abolished by Robert Mugabe shortly after Zimbabwe became independent in April 1980. I'm not sure when the last intake of servicemen happened, but it definitely didn't apply when Russell left school at the end of 1980."

"That was fortunate," said Rachel. "I bet he was pleased."

"Yes, he was. As was the whole country, especially my Mum," laughed Nick. "She always dreaded the idea of me or Russell doing national service, and her fear only grew as the Rhodesian Bush War intensified."

"I don't blame her," said Rachel. "I would have been worried stiff. You said Russell has become involved in student politics at UCT. What do you mean?"

Nick replied, "Well, I'm not sure, actually. All I know is that in his letters, he talks a lot about how students view the political situation in South Africa. UCT has always been regarded as one of South Africa's more liberal universities, yet by law, it was reserved exclusively for whites. Nonetheless, according to Russell, many of its students are

---

[426] University of Cape Town.

fiercely opposed to the government's apartheid[427] policies. He says they are quite militant and openly challenge all symbols of the government's authority.

"He told me that this militancy really picked up momentum after the 1976 Soweto[428] uprising. Now there are frequent student protests against laws like detention without trial, censorship, and restrictions on freedom of speech. There's also a growing student movement to end compulsory conscription of white men into the South African Defence Forces."

"Your brother sounds like an interesting guy. I'm looking forward to meeting him," said Rachel.

Before their conversation could progress any further, the pilot announced that they would soon be landing and asked the cabin crew to prepare the plane for landing.

A short time later, the plane landed smoothly and taxied to the apron area just in front of the passenger terminal. Nick and Rachel disembarked via the passenger boarding stairs and walked across the airport apron into the terminal building, making their way to the baggage collection area. As they did so, Nick saw his mother, Brenda, waiting just near the baggage carousels.

"Look, there's my Mum," said Nick. "Let me introduce you to her."

Nick walked towards his mother and gave her a warm hug, which she returned in kind.

Rachel looked on. Brenda was an attractive woman, who Rachel guessed would be in her early forties. She had a slim figure and golden-

---

[427] Apartheid is the Afrikaans word for apartness. It was a system of institutionalised racial segregation that existed in South Africa and South West Africa (now Namibia) from 1948 to the early 1990s.

[428] The Soweto uprising was a series of demonstrations and protests led by black school students in South Africa that began on the morning of 16th June 1976. It is estimated that up to 20,000 students took part in the demonstrations. They were met with fierce police opposition which resulted in approximately 176 students being killed and many more being injured.

brown hair, fashionably cut in a shoulder-length bob. She was wearing a knee-length denim skirt and a white chambray shirt. Her shapely arms and legs were healthily tanned.

"Oh, it's so good to see you at long last," Brenda said. "You have no idea how much your Dad and I have missed you. And this must be Rachel, I assume?"

Brenda turned towards Rachel and gave her a warm kiss on the cheek, which she returned.

"Welcome to Salisbury," said Brenda. "I've heard so much about you from Nick. It's wonderful to finally meet you. It's going to be so nice having another woman in the house for the next week or so. You'll be able to help me keep Nick, Russell, and their father in order."

They both chuckled.

"I'm so looking forward to spending some time with you and Mr Sinclair," said Rachel. "I'm not sure we'll have much success in keeping Nick in line, and I can't comment on Russell and Mr Sinclair. But heck, we'll give it our best."

They laughed again. Brenda then got serious and said, "Now, Rachel, what is this Mr and Mrs Sinclair business? I absolutely insist you call me and Matthew by our first names. Please promise me you will."

Rachel smiled. "That will be my pleasure, Brenda," she said. The two of them then engaged in small talk while Nick went to retrieve their cases from the baggage carousels.

After picking up their luggage, they made their way to Brenda's car. Brenda tossed the keys to Nick and said, "You can drive. I'm sure Rachel would like to see the sights, so she should sit in the front seat with you. I'll enjoy being a passenger for a change."

"Fine," said Nick. "I see you have a new car. When did you get it?"

"About six months ago," Brenda replied. "Since independence, there's been an abundance of new cars coming into Zimbabwe. Dad finally persuaded me to trade in my old Peugeot 404. I'm so glad he did — I'm loving my new Alfa Romeo."

"Well, it looks pretty nice," said Nick. "But let's get going. I'm looking forward to showing Rachel around."

Matthew and Brenda Sinclair lived in the pretty north-eastern suburb of Ballantyne Park, about 21 kilometres from the airport. They had moved there just after Nick completed his O levels.

Nick drove along Airport Road in a northerly direction until he reached Glenara Avenue, where he turned right. They continued on Glenara Avenue until reaching Enterprise Road, were he turned right again. They proceeded along Enterprise Road to the Ridgeway North intersection, where they turned left. From there, they turned right into Nigel's Lane.

As they drove, Rachel tried her hardest to take in all the new sights while also listening carefully to Brenda's conversation from the back seat. Brenda asked about her course at Oxford University and wanted to know about her parents. The two of them engaged in animated conversation, with the occasional interjection from Nick.

Rachel remarked on how modern and well-maintained the roads were. Nick agreed but noted that there seemed to be far more cars on the road than when he last visited Salisbury, just over a year ago. Brenda added that many believed the increase in traffic was due to an exponential rise in untrained black drivers who had obtained their licences by bribing officials.

The drive along Airport Road took them through light-industrial areas. Once they turned onto Glenara Avenue, the streetscape changed to residential. Rachel was surprised by the large gardens and bemused by the many street vendors at major road intersections, selling vegetables, firewood, or carved artefacts.

Brenda explained that unemployment was high in Salisbury, and due to the country's limited social security system, people were compelled to find any means to earn a few dollars. If that failed, begging or theft often became the only alternatives. Consequently, house burglaries were quite common, despite the various security measures homeowners had in place, such as burglar bars, alarms, guard dogs, and security walls.

When they were on Enterprise Road, Brenda explained that it was one of the main arterial roads connecting the north-eastern suburbs to the city. These suburbs were considered the more affluent suburbs and, prior to independence, had been exclusively occupied by whites. However, since independence, a new wealthy upper class of black politicians, civil servants, and businessmen had emerged, and many of these black families had purchased houses in the north-eastern suburbs.

Rachel was curious to know if this shift in demographics bothered Brenda but was unsure how to ask without seeming insensitive. Fortunately for her, Nick raised the subject, saying, "Mum, have you noticed any change in the dynamics in the north-eastern suburbs since independence?"

"That's an interesting question," said Brenda. "Right before and after independence, many white people felt anxious about the future, which led to a lot of properties being put on the market. Every time one of these properties was bought by a black family, nearby white neighbours felt a twinge of anxiety. However, I believe this was mainly due to fear of the unknown — after all, black families had never been allowed to live in these areas before. However, apart from the occasional incident, black families have settled in well and have been reasonably well accepted by their neighbours."

"What kind of incidents have occurred?" asked Rachel.

"Oh, just some minor irritations, really. We haven't seen any ourselves, but I've heard of black families digging up their front gardens to plant maize. Some homes have also become overcrowded with extended family members from rural areas living alongside the main household. But these are exceptions, not the norm," said Brenda.

Once they turned left off the Enterprise Road into Ridgeway North, Rachel immediately noticed a marked change in the houses lining the road. The properties were far more opulent and gracious. Most of the blocks were either walled or hedged — and on all four sides. The verges were lawned and beautifully maintained, adorned with flowering shrubs. It was also clear that the gardens behind the walls or hedges were park-like, featuring large trees, flowering shrubs, well-manicured lawns that resembled golf fairways, and paved driveways. Many of the homes had swimming pools and/or tennis courts.

"My goodness," said Rachel. "The houses and gardens look beautiful."

"Yes," replied Nick. "That's true. In this part of Salisbury, the homes and gardens are wonderful. This is largely due to the excellent climate that Salisbury enjoys and, historically, the incredibly low costs of both land and labour.

"Most people in these suburbs will have at least one full-time servant and a full-time gardener. Zimbabweans love their gardens and enjoy spending time outdoors, so their gardens are an important part of life. Unlike in England, where only very wealthy families can afford nice homes and gardens, in Zimbabwe, a much higher percentage of families can afford attractive residences, albeit historically most of these families have been white," Nick explained.

They had just turned off Ridgeway North into Nigel's Lane. Nigel's Lane was a cul-de-sac, and Matthew and Brenda lived at number 15, at the end of the street. Their property was walled and gated. Brenda asked Nick to press a button on a remote control pad in her car. He did so, and the gates silently glided open to reveal a paved driveway leading to a large double garage on the right-hand side of the house, under the main roof.

The house was set back about 30 metres from the gate. The front garden was lawned and featured a large jacaranda tree that bore beautiful purple flowers from October to December. On the left side of the house was an all-weather tennis court. The lawn in front wrapped around its left side, creating a grassy area between the house and the tennis court. This lawn extended into the back garden, where Nick mentioned there was a swimming pool and an entertainment area.

Nick pushed another button on the remote control pad, opening the roller door to the garage. He drove the car inside, and the three of them got out. Nick had just started to remove their two large suitcases from the boot when a middle-aged black woman, dressed in a maid's uniform, appeared. Upon seeing Nick, she clapped her hands in excitement, then cupped them together in the traditional African manner and said, "Aaah, Master Nick. Makadiiu uye mangwanani. Ndave nenguva refu ndisina kukuonai[429]."

Nick replied, "Mangwanani, Dorothy. Maswera sei[430]? Yes, it's been just over a year since I was last home. You look well. Let me introduce you to my girlfriend."

Nick put his arm around Rachel's shoulders and said, "Rachel, this is Dorothy. She has worked for Mum and Dad for more than ten years."

Rachel extended her hand and shook Dorothy's hand. "It's so nice to meet you, Dorothy."

"Medem, munogamuchirwa[431]," replied Dorothy. She then looked at Nick and, with a twinkle in her eyes, said, "Akanaka![432]"

Nick laughed and said, "Iwe uri right chaizo[433]. But no more Shona. Rachel will think we're talking about her!"

Nick, Rachel, and Brenda went inside while Dorothy took their suitcases.

"I'm sure you would love a cup of tea," said Brenda. "Dorothy will bring us one shortly. In the meantime, let me show you around. Nick, why don't you go and say hello to Dennis? I know he's looking forward to seeing you."

Rachel looked puzzled. "Who is Dennis?" she asked.

---

[429] Aaah Master Nick. Good day and good morning. I haven't seen you in a long time.
[430] Good morning, Dorothy. How have you been?
[431] Madam, you are welcome.
[432] She is beautiful.
[433] You are absolutely right.

"I'm sorry," replied Brenda. "He's our gardener. Now, why not come with me? I'd like to show you around the house."

Nick went to find Dennis. He wasn't sure how long Dennis had worked for his parents, but he suspected it was even longer than Dorothy's service. When Nick was a young boy, Dennis had spent a lot of time teaching him and Russell how to make catapults and use them to shoot the many doves that roosted in their trees. Dennis also used to play soccer in the back garden with the two boys, teaching them how to dribble and strike a soccer ball. Nick had always held him in high regard.

Nick found Dennis cleaning the pool. The two men greeted each other like old friends and exchanged pleasantries. Once the niceties were out of the way, the conversation turned to more serious matters. Nick was curious about how Dennis viewed the new political situation in the country, so he asked him what he thought of the new government.

"Baas[434], I'm very happy that I could finally vote in my country," Dennis replied. "I voted for Robert Mugabe because all the black leaders said we should. When Mugabe became Prime Minister, he promised us many things — freedom, peace, and equality. Like many black people, I thought this would mean better jobs, pay, housing, schools, and clinics. But nothing has changed for me. We just have a different Prime Minister now. Democracy gave us the vote, but we still don't know if life will be any better for us than it was under Mr Smith or Bishop Muzorewa."

"Thanks for being so honest with me, Dennis. Time will tell, I guess. We'll just have to wait and see," answered Nick.

Nick excused himself and joined Rachel and Brenda, who were sitting on the veranda overlooking the pool. Dorothy had brought them a pot of tea and some crunchies that Brenda had baked the day before.

---

[434] Baas is a word derived from Afrikaans and means boss or master.

Rachel looked up and said, "Nick, your Mum has been showing me around the house. It's absolutely gorgeous. And Dorothy is lovely."

Brenda interjected, "Rachel has given us an absolutely stunning painting from Victoria Falls. The artist is Shadreck Ndlovu, whom I've heard of. I think it will look wonderful in the entrance foyer."

Nick looked knowingly at Rachel and grinned.

After morning tea, Nick and Rachel unpacked. Dorothy had left Nick's suitcase in his bedroom, while Rachel's case was placed in one of the two guest bedrooms. As Nick unpacked, he couldn't help but grin when he realised how both his and Rachel's mothers were quite decorous about sleeping arrangements for unmarried couples. However, he appreciated that this consideration would prevent any awkward moments between them. Besides, Rachel and he still seemed to find time to enjoy intimate moments together whenever the opportunity arose!

The rest of the day was spent relaxing at home. Brenda spent a lot of time with Rachel, telling her about the various plants and trees in her impressive garden and describing the habits of some of the bird species that regularly visited.

While all of Brenda's descriptions were interesting, the one that strangely stuck in Rachel's mind was that of the black and white *butcher bird*. Brenda told her that the *butcher bird* belonged to the shrike family, and that the species found in Zimbabwe was the southern fiscal[435]. According to Brenda, the butcher bird, like ravens, is a meat-loving species. She explained that their common name — the *butcher bird* — was derived from their gruesome feeding method. When they caught prey, including small birds, they would hang it from a branch or thorn and hack away the meat with their sharp, hooked beak, much like a butcher using a cleaver. Any uneaten meat was left impaled on the thorn or twig, where the butcher bird would later return to feed.

---

[435] The butcher bird's taxonomical name is *Lanius Collaris*.

In the late afternoon, Nick and Rachel decided to have a game of tennis. Nick had been a reasonable tennis player at school. Unbeknownst to him, so had Rachel. They were both a bit rusty, as neither had picked up a tennis racquet while at university. However, they quickly found their groove and enjoyed a pleasant set of tennis together.

They were both quite competitive, and Nick suggested that, in order to even up the match, he would give Rachel a 15-point start in each game. Rachel accepted his generosity and ended up winning the set six games to four.

As they walked off the court, he playfully said to Rachel, "Well, that is the last time I'm going to be a gentleman to you!"

She dug him in the ribs and said, "Serves you right. Don't underestimate me!"

Brenda had told Nick that Matthew, his father, would be home at about 5:30 pm, and for dinner, she would be cooking one of Nick's favourite meals — beef stroganoff and rice.

The sun was rapidly sinking, and with the disappearing sun, the temperature was also dropping. As they were both feeling a little chilly, Nick suggested they go inside to take a shower and then enjoy a drink in the lounge before Matthew arrived.

Chapter 38 – Nick and Rachel's first few days in Salisbury

Matthew arrived home at 5:45 pm. He parked his car in the garage and wandered into the lounge, from where he heard chatter. Inside, he found Nick, Rachel, and Brenda sitting in front of the fire, enjoying a drink.

Nick stood up and gave his father a warm hug. "Hi Dad, it's good to see you again," he said. "You're looking well."

"Well, just look at you, my boy," replied Matthew. "So nice to see you again. And this must be Rachel."

Rachel stood and extended her hand to Matthew. They shook hands, and she said, "I've heard so much about you from both my Dad and, of course, from Nick. It's so nice to meet you in person."

"The pleasure is all mine," replied Matthew. "As you know, I've had some business dealings with your father before. I am really looking forward to catching up with him during his and Lynne's forthcoming visit to Zimbabwe. But we can chat more later. Please excuse me for a few minutes while I go and have a shower and change into something more comfortable."

Matthew left the lounge. Brenda also excused herself and went to the kitchen to organise a few things with Dorothy, leaving Nick and Rachel alone.

"Nick, I know that our fathers have had some prior business dealings, but I have absolutely no idea what your Dad does. Can you enlighten me?" asked Rachel.

"Well, I'm sure Dad will tell you himself. But basically, he heads up the country's Tobacco Marketing Board, or TMB for short. Tobacco is one of the country's leading agricultural exports, and the TMB[436] is a statutory body that controls and regulates the marketing and exporting of the country's tobacco. When the country was subject to international trade sanctions, including the export of Rhodesian tobacco, I know Dad worked with your father and others to find ways and means to ensure Rhodesian tobacco still found its way into British and American markets. I don't know much about the details, but I'm sure Dad will be able to tell you more."

"I bet he has some interesting tales to tell," said Rachel. "However, I think I'd better go and find your Mum to see if there's anything I can do to help."

With that, Rachel went off to find Brenda. Nick was now by himself in the lounge and took the opportunity to read the current edition of the daily newspaper, The Herald[437]. He quickly leafed through the paper but stopped to read an editorial piece that examined the new government's industrial relations record since coming to power.

According to the article, at independence, the government had pledged to benefit workers through policies designed to end discrimination in the workplace, raise workers' living standards, narrow the income gap between low and high-income earners, and generate employment growth. Since coming to power, the government had made some progress. Discriminatory provisions in various pieces of industrial relations legislation had been removed, the promotion of blacks in the public sector had been accelerated, pressure was being put on private enterprise to promote blacks to managerial levels, minimum wage legislation had been introduced to

---

[436] Tobacco Marketing Board.
[437] The Herald is the country's foremost national paper. Its origins date back to 1891.

improve wages for the lowest-paid workers, and, in an attempt to reduce the income gap between low and high-income workers, the government was just beginning to tinker with the concept of legislating wage increases for salaried employees.

However, in recent months, there had been widespread labour strikes. The cause of these strikes was the perceived slow pace of real reform to the current industrial relations system, which was essentially still capitalist in nature and dominated by a white-controlled private sector. Initially, the government had been sympathetic to the strikers' cause. However, when the strikes started to adversely affect national production, the government intervened and ordered the strikers to return to work. When the strikers failed to heed this order, the government used the police to break up the strikes and arrest the most militant *trouble-makers*.

The government faced heavy criticism for its actions but justified its opposition to the strikes by emphasising the harm they caused to the country's economic development. It argued that allowing the industrial relations chaos to persist would hinder national recovery after the recent Rhodesian Bush War and jeopardise the security of the new majority-rule government. To put an end to the strikes, the government adopted tactics similar to those used by the previous white government. Workers were told that their interests were subservient to the national interest, and that if they continued to strike, the police would be used to break the strikes and arrest the strikers.

The editorial piece left Nick feeling that the new government was beginning to show its true colours regarding workers' rights. Workers' rights would be respected, but only provided that such respect did not adversely affect the national economic interest. However, if the national economic interest were threatened, workers would be told to wind their necks in!

During dinner, Matthew reminisced as he recounted some of the details of the sanction-busting deals he had concluded with Stuart in the late 1970s. Nick had never been privy to much of the information

Matthew disclosed that night, and some of it came as quite a surprise to him.

For example, Matthew told Rachel that sanctions against Rhodesia had significantly hampered the country's tobacco exports. He explained that in the first year after UDI[438], the volume of tobacco produced by Rhodesia fell by half, and its export value plummeted by two-thirds. Prices had fallen alarmingly as the TMB was forced to sell the tobacco *under the counter* at heavily discounted prices. Despite these rock-bottom prices, the TMB still found it difficult to secure buyers. Consequently, large stockpiles of unsold tobacco built up.

To make matters worse, sanctions meant that tobacco farmers were forced to pay a premium for any agricultural equipment or machinery they needed to import. To keep the tobacco industry viable, the government was compelled to pay subsidies to tobacco growers. As a result, by 1980, the tobacco sector had lost billions of dollars. While most larger growers were able to survive the sanction years, this was not the case for smaller growers. Matthew mentioned that in 1965, there had been over 3,000 registered tobacco growers in the country; however, by 1980, only about half that number remained.

Nick had always assumed that sanctions against Rhodesia had been relatively ineffective. However, in light of what his father was now saying about their impact on the tobacco industry, he wondered whether this was also the case in other sectors of the economy.

"So, Dad," he said, "overall, do you think sanctions had much effect in forcing the Smith government to eventually agree to a transfer of power to the black nationalist parties?"

"Well, that is a question that I expect will be debated much in the years ahead," Matthew replied. "Many people believe that the effect of sanctions was limited and that it was the strength of the guerrilla forces, as well as the heavy diplomatic pressure from Western powers and South Africa, which were primarily responsible for the transfer of

---

[438] Unilateral Declaration of Independence. The Government of Rhodesia declared UDI from Britain on 11th November 1965.

power to the blacks. They fail to mention the economy. The reality was that by the late 1970s, the country was facing significant economic difficulties, and in my view, these economic challenges absolutely played a definitive role in the government's decision to agree to a transfer of power.

"I've also heard it said that these economic difficulties were due more to the global economic recession and the increasing cost of waging the war, rather than the effect of sanctions. That's certainly partly true. But that's not to say that sanctions were ineffective. We need to remember that Rhodesia endured sanctions for 15 years. That's an awfully long time for any economy, especially a small one like Rhodesia's, to battle against sanctions. I believe that over the long term, sanctions certainly had a part to play in forcing the government to agree to a transfer of power. The fact that the economy survived for so long is remarkable. The country owes its resilience to the ingenious sanction-busting schemes developed by Rhodesian businesses, as well as the invaluable support, guidance, and assistance that people like Rachel's father were willing to provide."

With that, Matthew raised his glass and said, "Here's a toast to Stuart and Lynne. I cannot tell you how much I am looking forward to catching up with them in three weeks' time."

They all raised their glasses, saying, "To Stuart and Lynne."

The recognition and acknowledgment that Matthew had given to her father made Rachel feel very proud. It also made her feel extremely close to Nick's parents.

The meal Brenda had prepared was delicious. Beef stroganoff and rice were served as the main course, followed by rhubarb crumble. Brenda proudly mentioned that the rhubarb was from the garden and had been freshly picked by Dennis that day. Both courses were accompanied by a bottle of Merlot wine from South Africa, bearing the label *Nederburg*. Rachel, who had never tasted South African wines before, remarked on the Merlot's exceptional quality.

After dinner, Dorothy came to clear away the plates. Rachel stood up from the table and said, "Thank you, Dorothy. Let me give you a hand."

Dorothy looked puzzled and a little embarrassed, leaving Rachel wondering if she had upset her. Fortunately, Brenda noticed what was happening and came to Rachel's rescue by saying, "That's very kind of you, Rachel, but Dorothy has this covered. I think we'll all go into the lounge for a cup of tea or coffee. What would you like?"

"I'd love a cup of tea," said Rachel.

Nick, Brenda, and Matthew all requested coffee and gave their orders to Dorothy, who then disappeared into the kitchen to prepare the drinks and handle the washing-up.

The rest of the evening played out as delightfully as the entire day had been. Unfortunately, Matthew had to leave for work at 7:00 am the next morning, so at 10:45 pm, he and Brenda excused themselves and went to bed.

Nick and Rachel remained in the lounge, chatting. During their conversation, Rachel asked Nick why Dorothy had been embarrassed when she offered to help clear the dishes and do the washing-up. Nick tried his best to explain but failed miserably. The best he could come up with was that it was not the done thing! His explanation left Rachel even more confused, but she decided not to press her curiosity further.

Rachel also asked about the plans for the next day. Nick hinted that it would be a surprise but mentioned they would start by visiting one of his favourite cafés for breakfast.

Rachel snuggled up to him. "You know I love surprises. I'm sure tomorrow is going to be wonderful, just like today has been."

"I hope so," said Nick. "After such a full day, you must be tired. And there's no chance of any nookies[439] in my folks' house, as all the

---

[439] Slang term for sexual intercourse.

bedrooms are in the same wing. So perhaps we should both head off to our respective bedrooms."

"Scaredy cat," she teased, chuckling. "But I agree."

They shared an intimate goodnight kiss. Nick whispered into her ear, "So you think I'm a scaredy cat, do you? What do I need to do to prove I'm not?"

He flirtatiously moved his hand onto her thigh.

Rachel was sorely tempted to play along but thought better of it.

"Unfortunately, that'll have to wait until we're alone together in the Matopos," she said. "So, before I change my mind, I'm going to bed."

She pecked him on the cheek and headed off to the guest bedroom. Nick watched her walk down the passage, then locked up, set the burglar alarm, and went to his bedroom.

The next morning, at 7:15 am, Rachel was still dozing in bed when she heard a soft knock at her door. Thinking it must be Nick, she smiled to herself and sat up.

"Come in," she said alluringly.

To her surprise, it was Dorothy who appeared at the door, carrying a tea tray with a pot of tea and the morning newspaper.

"Good morning, Madam Rachel," she said. "I hope you slept well. *Baas*[440] Nick asked me to remind you that he's taking you out for breakfast and would like to leave by 8:30."

She placed the tray on Rachel's bedside table and then asked if she would like the curtains opened.

"Why, thank you so much," replied Rachel.

Dorothy opened the curtains and then left the room.

---

[440] *Baas* is a word derived from Afrikaans and means boss or master.

What a curious thing, thought Rachel. But rather nice, just the same! She looked out through the slightly open, burglar-barred windows. The morning air was sharp and cool, but the sun was bright and already quite high. The sky was blue, with only a light breeze — she knew it was going to be another spectacular day. She lay back in bed, feeling incredibly lucky and happy.

Rachel took her time reading the paper and enjoying her tea. She then had a soothing bath, dressed in a comfortable but stylish outfit, and went to find Nick. She found him on the veranda, reading the newspaper and enjoying a cup of tea.

He looked up and said, "Hi, honey. You look nice. I hope you slept well. I thought we'd go to one of my favourite coffee places — it's nearby, in the Borrowdale Shopping Centre. Mum said we can use Russell's car, which is still here. Apparently, he decided not to drive it down to Cape Town, so we have the use of it until he arrives on Friday."

"That sounds great," she said. "I'm actually quite hungry."

A short time later, they said goodbye to Brenda and headed off to a little café called *Hit the Spot* in the Borrowdale Shopping Centre. Rachel was pleasantly surprised by the variety of shops and how well presented they were, all seemingly well-stocked with high-quality goods at reasonable prices.

During breakfast, Nick told Rachel he needed to go to Barclays Bank on First Street in the city. He said he'd try to park close by as this would allow him to show her around the CBD[441].

After breakfast, they headed along Borrowdale Road towards the city, passing a heavily guarded residential property. Nick explained that the property, formerly known as *Independence House*, had been the home of the former Prime Minister of Rhodesia, Ian Smith. When the country was renamed Zimbabwe-Rhodesia in 1979, the new Prime Minister, Bishop Abel Muzorewa, moved in and renamed it *Dzimbahwe*[442].

---

[441] Central Business District.
[442] Dzimbahwe means *House of Chiefs* in Shona.

However, the Bishop's residency was short-lived, as he was required to vacate the house following Zimbabwe's establishment under Robert Mugabe in April 1980.

Once again, Rachel was surprised by the well-organised, modern roads. As a main arterial route from the north-eastern suburbs, Borrowdale Road was busy, yet the traffic flowed smoothly, with drivers following the road rules and signs.

At the intersection of Borrowdale Avenue and North Avenue, they turned right and, after a kilometre, left onto Second Street, entering the CBD and parking near the corner of Second Street and Union Avenue. From there, they walked a short distance to First Street.

Nick explained that First Street had once been a major road but was transformed into a pedestrian mall some years ago. Now it was the city's leading shopping area. Rachel could see why it was so popular — the former bitumen road was now a beautifully paved pedestrian mall, wide and spacious, with well-maintained plants, benches, and carefully pruned trees offering shaded areas. Sophisticated shops and commercial offices lined both sides.

It was mid-morning, and the mall was bustling with cheerful shoppers and workers, the majority of whom were black. Rachel commented on this, and Nick agreed, noting that there seemed to be many more black people in the city than he remembered from a year ago.

They soon reached Barclays Bank, which was near a large, upmarket department store named Barbours. Nick suggested that while he was in the bank, Rachel might enjoy exploring Barbours. He said that there was a lovely tearoom on the second floor where they could meet in 30 minutes.

While Nick was at the bank, Rachel explored the department store, spending most of her time in the Ladies Department. She was pleasantly surprised by the variety of fashion wear available at reasonable prices, and this was also true of the other departments she briefly visited.

After about half an hour, she made her way to the tearoom, where Nick was already waiting. He had ordered a pot of filtered coffee, served in a silver coffee pot with a matching jug of cream. He asked Rachel what she would like, and she ordered the same.

As they chatted over coffee, Rachel remarked, "You know, Nick, this store is more British than most places in Britain! It reminds me of the TV show *Are You Being Served*[443]! I half expected to bump into Mr Humphries or Mrs Slocomb!"

Nick grinned. "Yes, Barbours has been a real institution among white shoppers in Salisbury for many years. I'm not sure how popular it will be with black shoppers, but it still seems much the same as I remember it. Rather charming, isn't it?"

"Just lovely," said Rachel. "Speaking of British things, didn't you say you and Russell attended a very British school? What was its name again?"

"Prince Edward School. Although it's a government school, it's run very much like a private British boys' boarding and day school," Nick replied.

"It would be interesting to see it," said Rachel. "I went to Guildford High School in the UK, a private girls' school with both day students and boarders. I'd love to compare the two schools."

"The school is quite close," Nick said. "If you're interested, we can drive past on the way home."

"Hmm, that would be interesting," said Rachel. "Do you think we'd be allowed in?"

"What for?" asked Nick.

---

[443] *Are You Being Served* was a British sitcom that aired on the BBC from 1972 to 1985. The series followed the adventures of the staff from the retail ladies' and gentlemen's clothing departments in a fictional upmarket UK department store called Grace Brothers.

Rachel replied, "Oh, I don't know — it would just be interesting to see how a private boys' school is run here in the middle of Africa compared to back home. I find it hard to believe there would be much similarity."

Nick raised an eyebrow. "You've seen how British this department store is. Prince Edward School is similar — it is very British! If you're really interested, we could look around. I was a prefect there, and I'm sure many of my teachers are still around. I planned for us to have lunch at the Royal Harare Golf Club[444], but we could stop by the school on the way if you'd like."

"Absolutely," replied Rachel.

After coffee, they returned to Russell's car and drove to the school, which was only about ten kilometres away. Nick parked in the parking area, and they walked past the hall to the administration offices. Luckily, Mrs Jacobson, the headmaster's secretary whom Nick had known well, was still working there.

She was delighted to see Nick again and even more so when he introduced Rachel. She assured him they were welcome to explore the school but requested that they avoid entering any classrooms without prior permission from the teachers.

Nick began the tour by showing Rachel the main school quadrangle, the oldest part of the school. As they walked around, they encountered several schoolboys who politely took off their hats and said, "Morning, sir; morning, ma'am."

The students they met included both black and white boys. Nick reminded Rachel that the school had historically been exclusively for white students. However, after independence in 1980, it was opened to all races. He was quite surprised at how many black boys there appeared to be at the school already but pleased to see them showing

---

[444] The Club had changed its name to Royal Harare Golf Club at independence in 1980. Prior to that, it was called the Royal Salisbury Golf Club.

the same respect to adults that had been the norm during his own time there.

From the quadrangle, Nick took Rachel to the Beit Hall, named after the Beit Trust[445], which funded its construction in 1931. As the hall was empty, Nick was able to show Rachel the paintings of past headmasters and other memorabilia adorning its walls.

Next, they visited the gym and basketball courts before following a charming bituminised road to the School Chapel[446]. Large jacaranda trees lined both sides of the road, their branches forming an intricate 180° arched canopy overhead. Nick explained that in summer, the trees would bloom with purple flowers, and when these blossoms fell, the road would be magically transformed into a soft carpet of purple.

They passed the main rugby field, *The Jubilee*, and the Tuck Shop on its northern side before reaching the three impressive boarding houses — Rhodes House, Selous House, and Jameson House. Nick mentioned these could house up to 250 boarders.

Continuing the tour, they stopped at the on-site hospital and swimming pool, ending with a walk along the road that separated Prince Edward School from the neighbouring Allan Wilson High School. Nick explained that this road was part of the school's cross-country course. Although he hated cross-country running, participation was compulsory, so he had no choice but to endure the event for each of the six years he was at the school.

After thanking Mrs Jacobson for the tour, Nick and Rachel headed to their car and drove to the Royal Harare Golf Club for lunch. Nick explained that the Club was colloquially referred to as *Royal* or *The*

---

[445] The Beit Trust was established in 1906 by the will of Alfred Beit. Alfred Beit was an Anglo-German gold and diamond magnate. Income from the Trust was used for infrastructure development in the former Northern and Southern Rhodesia. The purposes for which the Trust's income could be used were later modified by the Trustees to include university education and research in those countries as well as in Malawi.

[446] The School Chapel had been completed and dedicated in 1953.

Royal and was the country's premier golf club, ranked among the world's top 50 golf courses outside the United States in 1979.

The drive to Royal took only ten minutes. Nick turned to Rachel, smiling, and said, "Well, darling, I hope traipsing around Prince Edward School wasn't too dull. I'd love to hear how it compares to the British schools you know."

Rachel replied, "It was quite an eye-opener! The facilities were impressive, especially for a government school. They're certainly on par with all of our better schools in England, except perhaps Eton and Harrow, which are of course private institutions. From what I saw, I completely understand now why you said it was run along the lines of a British private school."

"That's what I thought," said Nick. "Discipline was very strict, especially in the boarding houses, and I'm sure traditions like skivvying were copied from England. I loved my time there, and being a day scholar I was spared from some of the bullying that boarders experienced in their junior years. When we moved to Ballantyne Park, there was some talk that Russell and I might have to change schools as were no longer zoned for Prince Edward School. However, Dad was able to pull a few strings, and we were permitted to remain at the school even though we were no longer in the right zone. I am very grateful to him for that."

Soon they arrived at Royal Harare Golf Club. With a good sense of direction, Rachel realised they were near Robert Mugabe's residence. Nick confirmed this and pointed out that from certain locations in the car park, they could see into the grounds of Mugabe's property.

Nick parked Russell's car and looked around the car park, which seemed to be filled with many high-value luxury vehicles — many more than he remembered from his last visit. He had heard that many of the country's new black political and business leaders had become members of the Club after independence, and judging by the number of luxury cars, he realised that this must be true.

Nick took Rachel up to the bar, which overlooked the practice putting greens and the 9th and 18th holes. The setting and layout were sublime, and Rachel could easily understand how the Club had gained its substantial reputation.

Since they had eaten a sizeable breakfast, they decided to have only a light lunch and did not go into the dining room. Instead, they ordered a steak pie and salad, enjoying them on the open-air veranda that wrapped around the bar. Quite a few of the waiters recognised Nick, and they shook his hand heartily and welcomed him back home.

As it was just after 1:00 pm, the lounge, dining, and veranda areas were busy. Just as Nick had predicted in the car park, many of the patrons were well-dressed black individuals. Nick was pleased to see that these new members were abiding by the Club's dress code.

Nick ordered a beer to go with his lunch, while Rachel chose a gin and tonic. With the sun high in the sky, the temperature on the veranda was perfect. They enjoyed their lunch and sipped their drinks unhurriedly, content to be in one another's company and to soak in the tranquillity of the beautiful golf course stretching out before them.

After lunch, they decided to head home and spend the afternoon by the pool, soaking up more of the delicious sunshine. They returned to their car and drove back along Borrowdale Road. They had just crossed the intersection of Borrowdale and Churchill Roads when they suddenly heard a cacophony of sirens. Nick looked in his rear-view mirror and saw a kaleidoscope of flashing lights.

"What the hell?" he exclaimed.

He slowed down but did not stop. The next minute, three BMW motorcycles with flashing lights and police livery roared alongside his car. The police riders angrily gesticulated at him, and one was even brandishing a revolver. Nick slowed right down and pulled off the road. A few seconds later, more motorcycles raced by with sirens blaring, followed by about half a dozen black vehicles with darkened windows and a couple of Landcruisers full of heavily armed soldiers. Rachel felt anxious and wondered what was happening.

Nick had no idea what was going on but noticed that all the other nearby cars had also stopped. Once the convoy had passed, the other stationary vehicles pulled back onto the road and continued on their way. Nick followed suit.

"I have no idea what that was all about," he said. "I'll have to ask Mum."

When they arrived back at the house, Nick and Rachel recounted the incident to Brenda. She looked a little sheepish and said, "I'm so sorry, Nick. I should have warned you. The motorcycles and vehicles are part of Robert Mugabe's motorcade. They accompany him whenever he travels on the roads. Locals have nicknamed his motorcade *Bob Marley and the Wailers*. Other vehicles are required, by law, to pull off the road until the motorcade has passed. It really is ridiculous and quite dangerous. There have already been several accidents — they drive so fast and so close together, it's only a matter of time before someone is killed."

"I thought as much," said Nick. "I can understand a police escort, but such a large one, with a whole platoon of armed soldiers, seems bloody ridiculous. Mugabe must be really scared of being assassinated or something. It certainly gave Rachel a fright."

That night, Rachel recounted the story to Matthew. Matthew echoed Nick's sentiments and hoped the incident hadn't unsettled her.

"Absolutely not," said Rachel. "I enjoyed the little excitement. I'm beginning to learn that when in Zimbabwe, you always need to be ready for the unexpected. And it seems that the unexpected quite often happens! It makes life interesting. Speaking of the unexpected, when do you expect Russell to arrive back home? I'm really looking forward to meeting him."

Chapter 39 – Russell Sinclair arrives in Salisbury

Russell was scheduled to land at Salisbury[447] Airport on Friday, 7th August, at 12:00 noon. Unfortunately, Brenda had a prior engagement that couldn't be changed, so it had been agreed that Nick and Rachel would pick him up instead.

Nick and Rachel arrived at the airport approximately 15 minutes before Russell's SAA[448] flight was due to land. They headed to the upstairs viewing area, which offered a good vantage point overlooking the runways. It was another beautiful day, so they sat on the outside decking area, enjoying a cold beer.

Shortly after 12:00 noon, the SAA aircraft touched down and taxied towards the passenger terminal, coming to a halt on the apron area. Passengers emerged from the aeroplane, descended the passenger steps onto the apron, and then made their way towards the terminal.

Nick and Rachel scanned the disembarking passengers, trying to spot Russell. Nick soon saw him and pointed him out to Rachel. Once Russell had disappeared into the terminal, Nick and Rachel made their way downstairs to wait for him near the international arrivals gate.

It didn't take long for Russell to appear. As soon as he saw Nick, a broad smile lit up his face. The two young men hurried towards each other and embraced warmly.

---

[447] The capital of Zimbabwe. Its name was changed to Harare in April 1982
[448] South African Airways.

"It's so good to see you," said Nick. "I like the long blonde hair. It's a change from the short back and sides we had to have at Prince Edward."

Russell smiled. "You're looking good too," he said to Nick. "Except for the pasty-coloured skin. We'll have to get you out into the Zimbabwean sun!"

"Rachel and I have been trying to do that since we arrived," said Nick. "Let me introduce you to her."

Russell and Rachel welcomed each other with a hug and a kiss on the cheek.

"It's lovely to meet you," said Russell. "I've heard a lot about you."

"Likewise," said Rachel. "And I won't argue with you about getting more of this glorious weather. It's absolutely sublime."

"You bet," replied Russell. "After being away from Salisbury for just over eight months, I've come to appreciate just how wonderful the weather is here."

After some more casual conversation, they made their way to the car and headed for Ballantyne Park.

That afternoon, Nick and Russell played tennis while Rachel sunbathed and started reading a South African classic, Jock of the Bushveld[449], which she had borrowed from Brenda's extensive home library.

At dinner that evening, Russell faced a barrage of questions about his university course, life in Cape Town, and his girlfriend, Yvonne. The Sinclair family had always been transparent with each other, and this trait continued during dinner. Rachel found their openness refreshing, and she soon became engaged in the candid but sensitive conversation taking place around the table.

---

[449] Jock of the Bushveld was written by Sir James Percy Fitzpatrick and first published in 1907. It is a true story about Fitzpatrick's travels with his dog, Jock, a Staffordshire Bull Terrier cross.

Russell expressed enthusiasm for his Bachelor of Science degree, particularly the courses with an environmental focus. He had developed a friendship with one of his lecturers, Mr Francois Swanepoel, who was an endangered species biologist. Mr Swanepoel had been researching the disappearance of black and white rhinos from the wilds of Africa. He believed that without significant intervention from central and southern African nations, both species would cease to exist in the wild within the next two or three decades.

Russell stated that his discussions with Mr Swanepoel about the existential threat to rhinos had definitely reinforced his desire and determination to pursue a career in African wildlife conservation and management.

Rachel changed the subject and playfully asked him about Yvonne. Russell, once again, was open and willing to share. He explained that he had met Yvonne at UCT[450], where she was studying marine biology. They were both the same age and had met at a social event organised by Mr Swanepoel. They had been dating for a little over three months, and both were committed to the relationship, hoping it would lead to something more significant and permanent.

The discussion was bound to shift to politics. This change was, in fact, sparked by Matthew when he asked Russell how students generally viewed the current South African government's apartheid[451] policies and whether Russell thought apartheid was under threat.

Russell replied, "Dad, the entire apartheid system in South Africa is on the brink of collapse. It can't survive much longer. Apartheid is detested by blacks, Indians, coloureds, and even many whites. Only the Afrikaners still cling to it, and even they know the end is near. External pressure against apartheid is relentless, and internal resistance is

---

[450] University of Cape Town.
[451] Apartheid is the Afrikaans word for apartness. It was a system of institutionalised racial segregation that existed in South Africa and South West Africa (now Namibia) from 1948 to the early 1990s.

growing. I imagine it will be dead and buried before the end of the century."

"The South African government is also concerned about the influence Zimbabwe will now have on internal South African politics. South African black nationalists have been emboldened and empowered by what they have seen has happened here. I know Mugabe is under pressure to allow the ANC[452] and other black nationalist groups to establish external military bases in Zimbabwe, and it wouldn't surprise me if that happens."

Debate, discussion, and laughter continued until just after midnight. Since it was Saturday the next day, nobody was in a rush to go to bed. Eventually, however, everyone excused themselves, with Russell being the last to head to bed.

On Saturday afternoon, Nick, Rachel, and Russell went to watch club rugby at Old Hararians Sports Club, where Old Hararians (or Old Boys, as they were colloquially referred to) were playing against Old Georgians[453]. Nick explained to Rachel that Old Hararians was established in 1922 as the alumni association for Prince Edward old boys. The Old Hararians Sports Club had been built in the 1960s and was located quite close to the school on Drummond Chaplin Road. Today, it was one of the country's main social and sporting clubs.

The warm winter afternoon and clear skies had drawn a large crowd of spectators to the game. Both teams were near the top of the Mashonaland rugby union league, so the match was fiercely competitive, with Old Boys eventually beating Old Georgians 19-17.

Nick, Russell, and Rachel thoroughly enjoyed the game. Rachel was surprised by the scarcity of black players in the two teams and asked Nick why this was the case. He explained that rugby, along with cricket,

---

[452] The African National Congress is one of the oldest and most well-known liberation movements in South Africa. It was founded in 1921 and played a central role in the fight against apartheid.
[453] Old Georgians is a sporting club which was established for former pupils of St George's College in Salisbury.

had played a central role in the early white Rhodesian culture. These sports had been imported when the country was first settled by pioneers from the United Kingdom. Rugby and cricket had brought the small and scattered white population together and, especially before UDI[454], provided a link back to the mother country, the United Kingdom. These were the two most popular sports at the elite, all-white senior schools in Rhodesia, where black students were unable to enrol. As a result, black people had limited exposure to these particular sports.

Nick went on to express the hope that, with the outlawing of racial discrimination in all sectors of the country, including education, in the coming years more black students would be enrolled in the previously white-only senior schools. He believed that this would, in due course, pave the way for increased participation by black players in rugby and cricket.

After the game, Nick, Russell, and Rachel went to the bar at the Old Boys Sports Club for a few drinks. The bar was bustling, with both white and black patrons. Nick and Russell caught up with several friends, and Rachel made an immediate impression with her good looks, friendly demeanour, and engaging manner.

Spontaneously, they decided to have dinner at the Club and enjoyed steak, chips, and salad on the veranda outside the bar before heading home around 7:00 pm.

During the drive home, they animatedly discussed the enjoyable afternoon. However, Nick cast a shadow over the conversation when he said to Russell, "The one thing that troubled me was how many people I talked to expressed serious thoughts about leaving the country. When I asked why, they said they were already seeing signs that Zimbabwe was heading towards becoming another failed African state, and if that were the case, they had no intention of sticking around."

---

[454] Unilateral Declaration of Independence. The Government of Rhodesia declared UDI from Britain on 11th November 1965.

"I've heard that sentiment for years," said Russell. "However, I'm sure most whites will stay. The country has so much potential now that it's been welcomed back into the international community."

"I agree that the potential is there," said Nick. "But what worries me is that a lot of expertise and know-how still remains predominantly with the whites. It will take time for that knowledge and expertise to be transferred to the blacks. With the dwindling number of white people in the country, every departure creates a gap. I fear that if the gaps become too large, the entire system might start to unravel. The system can tolerate and manage a few departures, but if that trickle becomes a flood, I don't believe there's enough expertise to effectively fill the gaps."

"I think you're overthinking things," said Russell. "What do you think, Rachel?"

"That's a tough question," said Rachel. "I've only just arrived in the country, so I'm unqualified to express an opinion. But my Dad shares similar concerns to what Nick has expressed, and he has a good understanding of the country. I genuinely hope he and Nick are wrong about the country potentially unravelling because, from what I can see, it has so much to offer. It shouldn't be allowed to fail."

"Dear me," said Nick. "I obviously shouldn't have opened that Pandora's box. Perhaps we should change subjects. Have I told you that Russell and I are taking you to the Imire Game Reserve on Monday and that later in the week we are going camping at Lake McIlwaine?"

"No, you haven't," Rachel replied. "Those are two more wonderful surprises, and as you know, I love surprises."

Chapter 40 – Exploring Imire Game Park & Lake McIlwaine

Timeline – 10 August to 14 August 1981

Imire[455] Game Park is located in the Wedza district of Zimbabwe, 100 kilometres east of Salisbury[456] on the road to Umtali[457]. It was established as a wildlife conservancy in 1972 by a man named Norman Travers.

During the Second World War, Norman had served with the British Army and rose to command a tank regiment. While in battle against a German Panzer tank unit, one of his tanks took a direct hit. Norman had jumped into the blazing tank to extract one of his men, an act for which he was subsequently awarded the Military Cross.

After the war, Norman joined thousands of British war veterans seeking a better life and emigrated to Southern Rhodesia, where he initially farmed tobacco in the rolling hills of the Wedza District.

However, by the late 1960s, Norman had become bored with conventional agriculture and started exploring ways to combine farming with his real passion — wildlife conservation. This pursuit led him and his wife, Gilly, to establish Imire Game Park in 1972.

The first wildlife introduced to the 4,000-hectare property was impala, but by the early 1980s this had expanded to include lions, giraffes,

---

[455] Imire is the Shona word for meeting place.
[456] The capital of Zimbabwe. Its name was changed to Harare in April 1982.
[457] Umtali was renamed Mutare in 1982.

waterbuck, kudu, sable, eland, zebra, wildebeest, hyena, warthogs, and two recently orphaned female elephant calves.

As Imire Game Park was close to Salisbury and accessible via the main road to Umtali, it offered visitors an easy way to experience an African safari without having to contend with significant travel and logistical challenges.

While the wildlife offering was more limited than what one might expect on a full African safari, Nick thought a visit to Imire would be an ideal way to give Rachel a taste of what an African wildlife safari could offer.

Nick, Rachel, and Russell left for Imire Game Park early on Monday, 10th August and arrived just before 8:30 am. Upon arrival, they were greeted by Gilly Travers, who took the time to share the history of Imire and her and Norman's vision for its future. Initially established as a small-scale game park, Imire's convenient location made it an attractive destination for visitors from Salisbury. Their long-term goal, however, was for Imire to evolve into a fully-fledged wildlife conservancy that worked in harmony with both the tourism industry and the local community.

Gilly explained that wildlife could only be fully protected if such protection was endorsed by the local community. Without such endorsement, human activities would continue to be in conflict with wildlife conservation, and human needs would ultimately prevail. Accordingly, Imire was using some of the funds generated by its game park to support programmes designed to benefit the local community. Gilly also hoped that as Imire expanded, it would create more employment opportunities for the local population.

Rachel was interested in learning more about how Imire benefitted the local community, so she asked Gilly to explain what Imire was doing from a community perspective.

Gilly explained that funds from Imire's Game Park had already been used to build a maternity clinic, a community library, an education centre, and a community vegetable garden. She added that within the next year, Imire hoped to establish a training centre, which would provide adults in the local community with skills to help them start sustainable, home-based micro-businesses or improve their prospects of finding employment in the formal sector.

Russell found Gilly's talk especially interesting. He asked her if Imire was currently doing anything in relation to the protection of rhinos, and shared with her the concerns of Mr Swanepoel, his lecturer at UCT[458] and an endangered species biologist.

Gilly replied, saying, "Your question is, in fact, quite serendipitous. Norman and I are both extremely concerned about the extent to which rhino poaching is currently occurring throughout most parts of southern and central Africa. We believe it is only a matter of time before such escalation is seen here. As we speak, there are discussions underway between the Zimbabwean Government and various environmentally aware organisations regarding the establishment of specific rhino breeding and protection conservancies across Zimbabwe.

"We are hopeful that these discussions will lead to some concrete outcomes, including Imire potentially being established as one such conservancy. If that happens, it would definitely be something that Imire would be immensely proud to be part of.

"Rhinos are one of Africa's flagship mammals. They also support various lesser environmental ecosystems, so if we preserve rhinos, then those other ecosystems will also be preserved. Conversely, if the rhinos are wiped out, then those other ecosystems will also be destroyed."

After Gilly's fascinating introductory talk, they walked to the main homestead, where they enjoyed a hearty breakfast. Breakfast was served by a waiter with the bizarre name of *Go Away*. He was a jovial fellow with a very dry sense of humour. He told Rachel that his mother had named him *Go Away* because he was the youngest of seven children and so she didn't have much time to look after him!

---

[458] The University of Cape Town.

Following breakfast, Gilly introduced them to their guide for the day. His name was *Lovemore*. He was a lovely young Shona man with a bright and open face and an appealing, calm, and gentle manner.

Their first activity for the day was to help *Lovemore* feed the two young elephant calves. *Lovemore* explained that the two calves had been orphaned during a controlled elephant cull in the Wankie National Park. The cull had gone horribly wrong when the mothers of both calves had been shot in error. The Department of National Parks[459] had rescued the calves and had approached Imire to see if they would be prepared to take on the responsibility of raising the two young animals until they were old enough to be released back into the wild. *Baas*[460] Travers had agreed.

Lovemore explained that both animals had been sedated and then trucked to Imire. As each calf weighed over 100 kilograms, this had been a significant and complex logistical operation. The animals had arrived at Imire approximately three months ago and had been weak and malnourished on arrival. Responsibility for looking after the young animals, including hand-feeding them three times a day, was shared between *Lovemore* and three other animal handlers. Each calf drank between 12 and 15 litres of specially formulated milk daily, and this would have to continue until the calves were about 15 months old. *Lovemore* explained that all you had to do was to put the teat from a two-litre bottle of the specially formulated milk, into the animal's mouth. The calf would then hold the bottle in its trunk, tilt back its head, and suck from the teat until the bottle was empty. It would then drop the bottle and wait expectantly for the next.

Nick, Russell, and Rachel each took a turn in feeding the calves. They were all initially a bit tentative, but the calves were by now well-trained and used to the routine. It was fascinating to watch how each calf took the teat of the bottle into its mouth, wrapped its trunk

---

[459] The full name is the Department of National Parks and Wildlife Management.
[460] *Baas* is a word derived from Afrikaans and means boss or master.

around the bottle, and then tossed its head back while sucking and slurping at the teat.

It was great fun for them all, but especially for Rachel who, prior to her visit to Zimbabwe, had never before seen a live elephant other than at circuses.

After feeding the elephants, they proceeded with another feeding activity. They were each given some acacia branches with fresh green leaves to feed to two semi-tame giraffes, which were kept in an enclosed paddock close to the main homestead. Rachel was surprised at how long and blue a giraffe's tongue was. It was also incredibly prehensile and sticky, and the giraffes had no difficulty using their tongues, almost like fingers, to grasp and hold leaves and twigs.

After the animal-feeding activities, they went on a game drive. The wildlife at Imire was accustomed to having Land Rovers in close proximity, so *Lovemore* was able to drive their Land Rover right into the middle of the various antelope herds they encountered. Even the pride of lions they saw did not seem to be bothered by their presence. Consequently, Rachel was able to get some marvellous wildlife photos with her Canon camera, a Christmas gift from Nick.

Lunch was served while they were out on the game drive. It consisted of cold meats, salads, and some ice-cold drinks, which had been kept chilled in an ice-packed portable cooler box. Although the food was simple, it was tasty and more than sufficient.

After lunch, *Lovemore* drove them to the Markwe Caves, where they were shown rock art painted during the Stone Age by early hunter-gatherer Bushmen who once inhabited the area. *Lovemore* explained how the Bushmen made their earthy-coloured paints by mixing plant extracts, eggshell, natural chalk, and sometimes even blood. The early artists used their fingers, porcupine quills, and bird feathers to paint their scenes onto the granite walls of the cave. The scenes generally comprised various species of animals depicted in simplistic form.

By now it was late afternoon. *Lovemore* drove them back to the homestead where they thanked Gilly Travers for putting on such a splendid day. They then drove back to the Sinclair's house in Ballantyne Park.

The next few days were spent visiting various friends and other places of interest in and around Salisbury, and in preparing for their camping trip to Lake McIlwaine[461]. Russell was taking the lead in organising the camping trip. This was both due to his inherent love of camping and also because he was calling in a few favours from a good school friend of his named Neville McIntosh.

Neville and Russell had been in the same class at Prince Edward School. Neville's father had been, and still was, a Chief Superintendent in the BSAP[462]. Neville's father was friendly with Russell and Nick's father, Matthew. Through this contact, Russell had been able to get access to the Police Club at Lake McIlwaine.

The Club was open to all senior serving members of the BSAP and to their guests. Facilities at the Club included a well-maintained camping and caravan park with powered sites, a swimming pool, a small clubhouse with kitchen, catering, and bathroom facilities and, most importantly, a small marina and launch ramp.

Neville's father kept a small 16-foot aluminium speedboat with a Mercury four-horsepower outboard motor moored at the marina. He had kindly agreed to make this available to Russell and Nick. Russell was thrilled with this offer, as it meant that they could enjoy some decent fishing.

On Wednesday, 12th August, they loaded Matthew's trailer with everything they would need for their camping trip, including two tents, camping chairs, fuel for the boat, gas lights, fishing gear, bait, food, beer, cold drinks, and cooler box. They hitched the trailer to Russell's vehicle and headed for the lake, which was some 50 kilometres away.

---

[461] The lake was named after Sir Robert McIlwaine, a former judge of the High Court of Rhodesia and founder of Southern Rhodesia's soil and water conservation movement. It was renamed Lake Chivero in 1982.
[462] British South Africa Police.

When they arrived, they encountered some difficulties with the Club's gatekeeper, who was initially hesitant to let them in. Russell explained that they were personal guests of Chief Superintendent McIntosh, who would be quite displeased if he learned his guests had been turned away at the gate. Fortunately, mentioning the Chief Superintendent's rank and offering the gatekeeper six beers for his trouble did the trick, and they were allowed to enter the Club without further issues.

They found a suitable site beneath some msasa trees, where they pitched their tents and set up camp. Their chosen site was within easy walking distance of the Club's facilities and the marina, which was a relief to Rachel, who had been told, in jest, by Russell that they would have to dig a long drop[463] for a toilet and that the only bathing facilities would be in the swimming pool or in the lake.

Their gift of six beers to the gatekeeper had also brought him around. While they were setting up camp, he approached them and told them he had arranged for them to have access to the small cold room in the clubhouse. This earned him another six beers and the promise of a bonsella[464] of Rh$20.00[465] if he continued to look after them well during their stay.

The gatekeeper told him that his name was Bruce and that he would be honoured to look after them. To demonstrate his willingness to please, he offered to take all their perishables and drinks to the Club's cold room. His offer was accepted without hesitation.

In the late afternoon they filled the boat's fuel tank with petrol, stocked the cooler box with some ice-cold beers, and went out on the lake. It was a beautiful afternoon with hardly any breeze. They ventured some 200 metres from shore and then dropped the boat's small anchor.

---

[463] A pit latrine.
[464] Bonsella is an Afrikaans word meaning *showing thanks with a gift*. The word was in common use by both whites and blacks in Zimbabwe.
[465] In August 1981, Zim$1.00 was worth about US$1.10.

Russell informed them that the lake was well-stocked with fish, including common grass carp, tigerfish, black bream, green-headed bream, and yellowfish. Bream were best for eating, while tigerfish were prized for game fishing. They decided to fish for bream, hoping to catch enough to cook fresh for dinner.

Russell advised them on the best tackle and bait for bream, helping Rachel set up her rod while Nick prepared his own. He explained that the best spot for catching bream was closer to shore. However, the nearer one was to the shore, the greater the risk of contracting bilharzia[466]. He and Nick had been exposed to it countless times, so the risk was of little concern to them, though he knew Rachel might feel differently — hence his cautious approach.

Nick opened a beer for each of them. Russell raised the anchor, and they let the boat drift over the lake's mirrored surface, their three rods hanging in the water. They enjoyed each other's company, savouring the beautiful setting as the fiery-scarlet sun slowly descended towards the lake's western shore.

Luck was on their side, as the fish were biting. Rachel was the first to get a nibble, and although she lost it in her excitement, it wasn't long before the others began to get bites as well. They successfully landed a dozen bream, six of which were large enough to keep. After removing the hooks, they released the smaller fish back into the water.

They returned to shore in the failing light, pleased with their haul. To their surprise, Bruce was waiting at the launch ramp to meet their boat. He told them he'd started their campfire and offered to clean and descale their catch, promising to deliver the prepared fish back to their campsite. Delighted by their luck, they gladly agreed.

Before returning to the campsite, they picked up a few more beers and fresh salad vegetables for their evening meal from the clubhouse.

---

[466] Bilharzia is also known as snail fever. It is a disease caused by parasites (known as schistosomes) carried by freshwater snails. In parts of Africa, it is endemic.

By the time they got back to their camp it was almost dark, but the glow from the campfire cast enough light to help them find their way around their tents and campsite. Nick lit two of the gas lamps, while Russell and Rachel made the salad and buttered some rolls.

True to his word, Bruce arrived a short time later with the fresh bream, which he placed on the BBQ grill above the campfire. Nick invited Bruce to stay and have dinner with them, and he was delighted to accept. The four of them sat around the campfire, drinking beers, enjoying their meal, and learning more about each other.

Bruce told him that he had worked as a gatekeeper at the Club for the last six years. He was from a small rural village near Hartley[467], where his parents still lived.

Russell asked him what he thought about the recent political changes in Zimbabwe.

Bruce replied, "*Baas*, I am pleased that the war has ended and that, at long last, I was able to vote in the elections last year. But I am very worried about my future. Already, a lot of the white policemen have come and taken their boats from the marina. They have told me that they are going to live in South Africa. The Club has become very quiet, even during weekends. And when senior policemen do come with their families over the weekend, the new black police officers and their families treat me very badly. They do not look after the Club either. They leave all their rubbish around the pool or in the campsite. If I did not pick it up, it would just be left there."

"I am sorry to hear that," said Rachel. "I am sure things will improve. The new police officers just need to be given time to get used to their new positions, powers, and responsibilities."

---

[467] Hartley is located about 50 kilometres south-west of Lake McIlwaine. In 1982 it was renamed Chegutu.

"I hope you are right, madam," said Bruce. "But I still worry. I think they will get used to their new powers, but I am not so sure about them getting used to their new responsibilities!"

A short time later, Bruce excused himself. Nick and Russell cleared up the plates and took them to the kitchen in the clubhouse to wash, while Rachel tidied up the campsite. Once the men returned, they spent a while chatting around the campfire, pondering Bruce's fears and concerns for the future. After about an hour they all retired to their respective tents.

Nick woke early the following morning, just as the sun was beginning to warm the cold morning air. He lay still in his sleeping bag, enjoying the feel of Rachel's sleeping bag next to his own. He was still delighting in the sounds and smells of the early morning when he suddenly became aware of the smell of smoke and the slight crackle of burning logs.

"What the hell?" he muttered. He climbed out of his sleeping bag, being careful not to disturb Rachel. He shivered in the cold morning air and pulled on his tracksuit top and bottoms. Then he crawled out of the tent.

To his surprise, he was confronted by Bruce, who was tending the fire. Above the fire was a grill on which a metal kettle was close to boiling.

"Good morning, *Baas* Nick," said Bruce. "I hope you slept well. I'm making tea for you. When you're ready, let me know, and I'll come and cook breakfast for you, *Baas* Russell, and Madam Rachel."

"Well, thank you very much," said Nick. "That wasn't expected. It's very kind of you."

By now, Russell had also emerged from his tent, and the two brothers enjoyed their mugs of tea that Bruce had prepared. Bruce also made a mug of tea for Rachel, which Nick took into their tent. She was awake, and he kissed her on the cheek, telling her that Bruce had made her a cup of tea and would soon be returning to cook breakfast.

"Goodness me," she said. "Why on earth has he done that?"

"Beats me," said Nick. "But who's complaining? He must be very keen to earn his bonsella!"

Once they had all finished their tea, they headed to the clubhouse to freshen up while Bruce cooked eggs, bacon, tomatoes, and toast on the grill over the campfire. They all agreed that breakfast prepared over an open fire somehow tasted much better than the same meal served in a restaurant.

After breakfast, Bruce insisted on clearing away the plates and taking them to the kitchen area in the clubhouse to wash.

"He is jolly accommodating," said Rachel. "Do you think he has any sort of hidden agenda?"

"Somehow, I don't think so." said Nick. "It is weird I know. But it seems to me that he knows the way of life he has known for so long may be coming to an end. He is just hanging onto the past as he is frightened of the unknown."

Later that morning, the three of them drove into Lake McIlwaine's Game Park. The game park was just over 1,800 hectares in size and had opened in 1962. It held a wide variety of game and birds, many of which had originally been brought in from Lake Kariba during Operation Noah[468]. On their drive they saw many different animals including rhinos, giraffes, zebra, impala, kudu, sable, baboons, and vervet monkeys.

Birdlife was abundant as well. Nick and Russell were able to identify kingfishers, fish eagles, cormorants, doves, weavers, and lilac-breasted rollers. Rachel was stunned that such a variety of wildlife and birds was on display so close to Salisbury. She again took many photos and was

---

[468] Operation Noah was a wildlife rescue operation on the Zambezi River which lasted from 1958 to 1964. The operation was necessitated by the flooding of the Kariba Gorge following the construction of Kariba Dam. The operation was led by Rupert Fothergill. It is estimated that approximately 6,000 animals, birds and snakes were rescued and relocated.

very glad that she had left the United Kingdom with a plentiful supply of 35mm film.

They got back to the Club just after 2:00 pm. Rachel prepared ham and tomato sandwiches with mustard for lunch, after which they spent the afternoon lying by the pool and soaking up the warm winter sun.

For the evening meal, Nick and Russell used the kitchen facilities in the clubhouse to prepare a pot of minced-beef meatballs in Bolognese sauce, which they served with spaghetti and baby garden peas. This was washed down with two bottles of *Nederburg* Chardonnay wine from South Africa.

To their surprise, Bruce did not appear that evening.

However, much to their delight, he made a reappearance the following morning. He once again offered to cook them breakfast, which this time comprising mealie meal porridge followed by scrambled eggs on toast.

They needed to return to Salisbury shortly after lunch, so decided to spend the morning fishing. Once again, they decided to go after bream. They agreed that any fish they caught they would leave with Bruce, assuming they saw him before they left. Russell was again responsible for the choice of tackle, bait, and fishing spots. Once again, they had success and ended up landing eight bream, all of which were large enough to keep.

Nick also received a bite that he assumed was from a tigerfish. However, the tackle and rods they were using weren't suitable for tigerfish, and, unsurprisingly, the fish escaped. In its escape, it displayed the aggressive and cunning nature for which tigerfish are famous.

They returned to the marina by about 1:00 pm and were delighted to find Bruce there, who was equally pleased to be gifted with the bream. Bruce helped them clean the boat, break camp, and reload the trailer.

By 2:30 pm, they were ready to leave. Nick paid Bruce the agreed bonsella of Rh$20.00, plus an additional tip of Rh$20.00. Bruce was ecstatic and shook Nick and Russell's hands, expressing the hope that he would see them back at the Police Camp soon. He respectfully bowed his head to Rachel and wished her a safe trip back to the United Kingdom.

With that, they drove out of the Camp and headed back to Salisbury.

On Saturday and Sunday, Nick had to finish making preparations for his and Rachel's 1,700-kilometre road trip, which would take them to Bulawayo, the Matopos, Mhuka[469] Ranch in Chiredzi, the Vumba and Inyanga[470] in the Eastern Highlands[471] before their return to Salisbury.

In his initial planning, Nick intended to ask Russell if they could borrow his car, which Russell had left behind in Salisbury when he went to UCT. However, after running his plans past his father, Matthew expressed concern about using Russell's car due to its age. Matthew also mentioned that he thought some of the travelling in and round Chiredzi would be on dirt roads and suggested that a 4WD[472] vehicle might be preferable.

Nick agreed but told Matthew that he did not have access to a 4WD vehicle. Matthew kindly said he could arrange for Nick to use a 4WD Toyota Land Cruiser J40 series from work.

Matthew had already organised insurance cover for the vehicle. However, Nick could only pick it up from the TMB offices in Salisbury on Saturday, 15th August.

This was the first thing Nick had to do when they returned to Salisbury. He then needed to plan his route and discuss it with Rachel, as well as confirm their accommodation bookings at Maleme Dam, Mhuka

---

[469] A local word meaning animals or wildlife.

[470] Inyanga was renamed Nyanga in 1982.

[471] The Eastern Highlands is a mountainous area on the border of Zimbabwe and Mozambique. It extends for about 300 kilometres from north to south and includes the Inyangani Mountains, the Vumba Mountains and the Chimanimani Mountains.

[472] Four-wheel drive.

Ranch, Leopard Rock Hotel, and Troutbeck Inn. All these matters were settled by Sunday, 16th August.

Consequently, when he and Rachel went to their respective bedrooms on Sunday night, they did so with the exciting anticipation of being alone together for the next 13 days while visiting some of Zimbabwe's loveliest locations.

Chapter 41 – Nick and Rachel travel to Maleme Dam

Timeline – 17 August 1981

Nick and Rachel woke up just before 6:00 am on Monday, 17ᵗʰ August. The previous night, they had packed their provisions into the Toyota Land Cruiser, which Matthew had generously made available to them. Therefore, on Monday morning, all they had to do was shower and put their suitcases in the car. Nick also carefully placed the black velvet pouch containing his talisman, the Bronze Cross of Rhodesia, in the glove box.

They had said their farewells to Matthew, Brenda, and Russell the previous night, knowing they would be leaving early and not wanting to disturb them. However, Brenda woke up shortly after they did and came to say goodbye. She had prepared a flask of hot tea to go with the picnic breakfast they had packed the night before. She wished them a safe journey and stated how much she was looking forward to the reunion of their two families at Troutbeck Inn on Thursday, 27ᵗʰ August.

By 6:15 am, they had left the Sinclairs' house in Ballantyne Park and started their 475-kilometre trip to the Rhodes Matopos National Park in the south-west of the country. It took them a good 45 minutes to bypass Salisbury[473] and find their way to the main road to Bulawayo. The day was cool, but the sky was cloudless, as was typical for this time of year.

---

[473] The capital of Zimbabwe. Its name was changed to Harare in April 1982.

As they travelled along the main road to Bulawayo, Rachel remarked on how well-maintained it was. It had recently been resurfaced, so it was smooth and even. The line markings were bright and clear, with cats' eyes installed on the sharper bends. The road shoulders had been widened and resurfaced, and the grass on the verges had been cut short. The quality of the road was definitely not what Rachel had expected.

Rachel also marvelled at the extensive stands of maize visible from the road, which stretched on for kilometre after kilometre. Nick told her that maize was the country's staple food crop and that, apart from drought years, the country consistently produced far more maize than was consumed domestically, allowing for substantial exports each year[474].

After about three hours, they passed through the large rural town of Que Que[475]. Shortly thereafter, Nick suggested they pull off the main road at the next lay-by to enjoy their picnic breakfast. At that time in the country's development, lay-bys were primarily constructed for the benefit of holidaymakers, particularly those travelling long distances to South Africa. These lay-bys were well-maintained, featuring shady trees, concrete tables and benches, and facilities for disposing of rubbish. Occasionally, subsistence farmers from nearby villages would set up pop-up stalls to sell their locally grown vegetables and fruit to passing travellers.

The lay-by that Nick and Rachel pulled into just after Que Que was exactly as described above, albeit without a pop-up stall. Rachel removed the cold beef and tomato rolls, hard-boiled eggs, and apples from the cooler box. She and Nick were quite peckish by then, so the picnic fare was eaten hungrily. The food was washed down with mugs of hot tea from the flask Brenda had prepared.

---

[474] In the 1970s, apart from in two drought years, annual exports of maize were in excess of 400,000 metric tons per annum.
[475] Que Que was renamed Kwekwe in 1982.

A couple of vervet monkeys were hanging around the rubbish bin, hoping to scavenge some scraps. Nick made their task a little easier by tossing a few apple cores to the small primates. The monkeys chattered excitedly as they picked up the cores in their tiny hands and crammed them into their mouths. Rachel watched with a satisfied grin, reflecting on how different these lay-bys were compared to the ugly, bituminised truck stops dotted along the motorways back home in England.

After breakfast, they returned to their vehicle and continued their journey. The next large town they passed through was Gwelo. Nick mentioned to Rachel that the School of Infantry was located there, and it was where he had successfully completed a three-month officers' training course as part of his national service.

From Gwelo, they continued to the city of Bulawayo, arriving just before 1:00 pm. Nick told Rachel that Bulawayo was the capital of Matabeleland and the second largest city in the country. The city had its origins in the mid-19th century, when the king of the Ndebele nation, King Lobengula[476], built his royal kraal there. After white settlement, soldiers from the British South Africa Company invaded Bulawayo. King Lobengula fled with his followers, first detonating a munitions cache and setting fire to the royal kraal. Later that year, Leander Starr Jameson declared Bulawayo a settlement under the rule of the British South Africa Company and, as directed by Cecil John Rhodes, the new pioneer settlement was founded on the ruins of King Lobengula's former royal kraal.

Nick wanted to take Rachel somewhere special for lunch, so he decided on the Bulawayo Club. The Bulawayo Club was a distinguished gentlemen's club with stunning architecture. The present clubhouse, built in 1934, had become an iconic meeting place for Bulawayo's social, political, business, and farming leaders.

---

[476] King Lobengula Khumalo (1845 to circa 1894) was the second and last official King of the northern Ndebele people.

As they drove through Bulawayo's CBD[477] to the Club, Rachel noticed how wide the roads were, especially considering the relatively low volume of traffic they appeared to be carrying. She commented on this to Nick, who explained that the city's main roads had first been designed and constructed when ox-drawn carts were still the primary means of transportation. When the roads had initially been laid out, the city planners specified that the roads needed to be wide enough to allow a cart drawn by a span of 16 oxen to turn around using a one-point turn.

Unbeknownst to Nick, his friend and colleague from 3RAR[478], Sipho Pukelo, had also lunched at the Bulawayo Club a month or so earlier with Duncan Oliver, following his acceptance of the position of anti-poaching manager on Duncan's Mhuka[479] Ranch, just outside Chiredzi.

Whereas Sipho had been thrilled by the charcoal drawings of his ancestors, King Lobengula and Queen Lozikeyi Dlodlo[480], that adorned the walls of the Club, Rachel was more intrigued by the photographs of the early white pioneers in the new English colony.

"I wonder what on earth would have made people like Cecil John Rhodes want to leave their homeland in the northern hemisphere to explore southern Africa," she said. "I know his health played a part in his parents' decision to send him to warmer climes as a young man, but it must have been daunting to find oneself in such a foreign place and culture."

"I guess it was the spirit of adventure and the unknown that he found attractive," said Nick. "When you are young and as ambitious as he was, any sacrifices he may have had to make would have seemed insignificant."

---

[477] Central Business District.
[478] 3rd Battalion of Rhodesian African Rifles.
[479] A local word meaning animals or wildlife.
[480] Queen Lozikeyi Dlodlo (c 1855 to 1919) was one of the favourite wives of King Lobengula and a senior queen until 1893.

"I suppose so," said Rachel. "However, I do wonder why and how he thought he could impose British beliefs and culture on the local people in this part of the world. The two cultures had absolutely nothing in common — there was not even any historical connection between the peoples of Britain and the indigenous tribes of southern Africa."

"Well, that is part of the mystery of the man," said Nick. "I know it seems arrogant and paternalistic today, but back in the 1870s, Rhodes genuinely believed that the English race was the foremost race in the world, and that the more of the world the English could inhabit, the better it would be for humanity. However, the history of the 20th century proved him wrong. Nations simply are not willing to be ruled by foreign powers, especially when such a power has been imposed upon them against their collective will and is vastly different from what they had known before."

After lunch, they returned to their vehicle and headed south for the Maleme Dam, which was in the Rhodes Matopos National Park, some 50 kilometres from Bulawayo. The road from Bulawayo to the national park was tarred and initially passed through scrubby farmland, with the occasional homestead stubbornly clinging to the ground as its occupants desperately tried to eke out an income from the unforgiving soil. However, after about 30 kilometres, they passed a pretty lake called Lake Matopos, and from that point onwards, there was a distinct change in the landscape.

The trees grew greener and denser, as did the long grass alongside the road. However, the most striking change in the scenery was the appearance of rocky outcrops composed of enormous granite boulders, haphazardly clustered together. Occasionally, the boulders appeared to be delicately balanced atop one another, as if arranged by the unseen hand of some mythical giant. In the nooks and crannies between the boulders, the occasional tree or bush thrived, where the vagaries of nature had conspired to place a seed in a slight indentation in the rock, allowing enough water and soil to accumulate for the seed to germinate and grow.

These rocky outcrops were the homes to a huge array of birds, lizards, snakes, mongooses, dassies[481], baboons, and small buck as well as the occasional leopard or cheetah.

Rachel was intrigued by the landscape in general, but particularly by the rocky outcrops. She asked Nick to tell her more about the area.

"Well," said Nick, "archaeologists have been able to establish that the area was originally inhabited by the San, or bushmen, about 2,000 years ago. They were hunters and gatherers, but they also loved to decorate the rocks and caves with their rock paintings. I believe there are over 3,000 registered rock art sites in the national park. The style of the paintings is very similar to the ones we recently saw near Imire[482] Game Park. However, many of the paintings in the Rhodes Matopos National Park are far better preserved than those at Imire. I believe that the most extensive paintings can be found in a cave called the Inanke Cave, which contains beautiful friezes of giraffes, elephants, and kudu. Archaeologists have also found many historic artefacts and primitive tools in the area, with some dating back to 320 AD."

"That is amazing. The area definitely has a mystical feel about it," said Rachel.

"You are quite right," said Nick. "The grandeur and stillness of the Matopos hills have existed for centuries and continue today. Many rituals, mystical trance ceremonies, and other religious activities have historically been performed in the Matopos. Before the colonial era, the Matopos hills were the stomping ground of the oracle and spiritual leader of the Ndebele people, a man named Mlimo. Mlimo is said to have used a cave called the Silozwane Cave as a shrine. I have never been to it, but I believe it is quite impressive. If we have time, we might go and see it.

---

[481] These are also known as the rock hyrax or rock rabbit. They are a medium-sized terrestrial mammal native to Africa. An adult dassie can weigh up to 5 kgs.
[482] Imire is the Shona word for meeting place.

"The Matopos hills were also the site of the famous indaba[483] between the white settlers and Ndebele leaders in 1896, which marked the end of the Second Matabele War. Hostilities began when the Ndebele revolted against the British South Africa Company's unwanted rule in Matabeleland. Mlimo, their spiritual leader, was blamed by the white settlers for inciting much of the anger that led to the rebellion. He had convinced the Ndebele that the white settlers, who numbered about 4,000 by then, were responsible for the drought, locust plagues, and rinderpest[484] disease ravaging Matabeleland at the time. The war concluded with the reported assassination of Mlimo by Frederick Burnham, an adventure-seeking scout from America's Wild West who had emigrated in 1893 to join Rhodes' fledgling pioneers in Rhodesia."

"That is so interesting," said Rachel. "If we have time, I would love to visit Silozwane Cave."

By now, they had arrived at the entrance to the national park. The entrance was marked by a small stone-walled building with a thatched roof. On either side of the building was a six-foot-high double gate — the gate on the left was for vehicles entering the park, while the one on the right was for vehicles exiting. They paid their park entrance and accommodation fees and were given a map of the area along with the keys to the lodge they had booked.

The lodge was situated on a large granite outcrop on the western banks of Maleme Dam, which was about 20 kilometres away and accessible by well-maintained dirt roads. To get to the lodge, they had to drive across a low dam wall at the southern end of the dam. The water level of the dam was about 30 centimetres below the top of the dam wall, so they had no difficulty driving across the narrow wall.

The lodge had been constructed using natural rocks from the surrounding area, topped with a thatched roof that also extended over the spacious veranda. Inside, the accommodation comprised two

---

[483] An indaba was the name given by the local tribespeople to collective meetings of chiefs and headmen.
[484] Rinderpest, also known as cattle plague, is a disease which can be fatal. It is caused by the rinderpest virus, which primarily affects cattle and buffalo.

bedrooms, each with its own bathroom, alongside a kitchen, dining room, and lounge. The lodge was fully equipped for self-catering, and also featured a BBQ area built on a granite ledge below, complete with a woodpile and wrought-iron tables and chairs.

The whole site was beautifully secluded. From the lodge, you looked down onto the Maleme Dam and then across the water to extensive well-treed kopjes[485], which no doubt were teeming with all sorts of wildlife and creatures, and perhaps some caves and rock art paintings.

"Oh, this is beautiful," exclaimed Rachel. "Not a soul in sight and such a stunning view. I'm sure we will have the best time here."

They unpacked their provisions into the well-equipped kitchen, transferring meat, drinks, and dairy products from the ice-packed cooler box to the fridge. The fridge was powered by gas, as were the lights. Hot water for the lodge was supplied by an external iron boiler heated by a wood fire, with a large pile of wood stacked beside it. The fire was already lit, and the water was steaming. Guest instructions indicated that the large gas cylinders were refilled weekly, while a housekeeper would attend to the lodge daily, in the morning and evening, to tend to the boiler fire.

By the time they had stocked the kitchen and unpacked their suitcases, it was late afternoon. Nick suggested they take a stroll along the dam's shoreline to the dam wall and then return to the lodge. He reckoned this would be a distance of about two kilometres. After their walk, they could enjoy a sundowner on the veranda before preparing their BBQ supper.

From the veranda, they followed a rough path down to the dam, where they picked up a well-worn walking track around its edge. It was a still afternoon, with not a breath of air, making the dam resemble a mirror. About five metres from the shoreline lay the skeletal remains of a large dead tree, with a solitary fish eagle perched high on one of its bare branches.

---

[485] The word kopje is derived from the Afrikaans word *koppie,* which means a small hill.

Nick and Rachel stopped to scrutinise the impressive bird. The plumage on its head, breast, and tail was milky white, while the feathers on its back were a distinctive chocolate brown. The eagle had intimidating but ever-alert large dark eyes and a fearsome hooked grey beak. Its beak and eyes were surrounded by an orange-yellow cere, and its large feet were equipped with vicious-looking talons.

As they watched the magnificent bird, it suddenly took off from its perch and swooped down towards the water's surface. Just before it reached the water, the eagle outstretched its wings and pushed its feet forward, causing its body to almost stall just above the dam's surface. In a deft movement, its powerful talons snatched a large fish from the water, and with a few strong beats of its wings, it broke free from the pull of the water, the fish firmly grasped in its talons.

Despite its bulky catch, the fish eagle swiftly and gracefully flew over the water to another spot further down the dam. It landed on the forlorn structure of another lifeless tree, its prize still securely clasped in its talons. From its new perch, it let out its distinctive piercing cry, which to Nick and Rachel seemed like its victory whoop.

"That was so beautiful to watch," whispered Rachel. "What a pity I did not have my camera with me."

"Yes, that was great," agreed Nick. "I don't believe fish eagles visit this area often, so we were very lucky."

The sighting of the fish eagle meant they had to cut their walk short, as they didn't want to be wandering around the dam in the dark. They returned to the lodge just as the last light was fading. Nick lit the gas lights, opened a couple of beers, and took them outside to the veranda, where Rachel was sitting. By now, the cicadas and frogs had joined together in their regular evening flash mob chorus for the local bush creatures. Their chorus had a distinctively African feel — a sound that Nick knew well. For Rachel, however, this was not the case. She found the chaotically organised melody mesmerising.

The darkened sky was pierced by thousands of pinpricks of light from the Milky Way and constellations like Scorpio and Aquila. The nearly full moon, together with the stars, cast an eerie glow over the dam's dark surface. The rocky hills loomed as heavy black shapes on the horizon, while the occasional, chilling glint from the eyes of a nocturnal predator flickered momentarily in the distance.

Nick used the bright beam from a hand-held torch to help him light the BBQ. He then went into the kitchen to prepare the meat and salad, while Rachel continued to absorb the sights, sounds, and smells of this strange yet magnetic landscape in which she found herself.

After they had eaten dinner and done the washing up, they enjoyed an intimate shower together before heading into the bedroom, where they snuggled beneath the sheets and duvet. Although the night was cold, Rachel asked Nick to leave the windows and curtains open so she could enjoy the sounds of the African bush, as well as the spectral gloom from the moon and night sky.

They hugged each other close, the warmth from their naked bodies keeping them snug. However, it did not take long for their passion to override any need to keep warm. They tantalised and teased one another with their exploring hands and mouths. When they were both ready, they made love passionately and earnestly.

When it was over, it did not take long for their bodies to feel the chill once again. They snuggled back together beneath the duvet and fell asleep in each other's embrace.

As if in unison, the African bush hushed and quietened.

Life seemed good and as it should be

.

Chapter 42 – Nick and Rachel explore the Matopos National Park

Nick and Rachel were setting out on an early morning game drive in the Rhodes Matopos National Park. Nick aimed for an early start, as he wanted Rachel to experience the African bush at dawn — an experience which, in his estimation, was without comparison.

Their alarm rang shrilly at 5:45 am. They quickly showered and dressed in warm clothes. Nick made tomato and boerewors[486] rolls using cold leftovers from the previous night's meal. By 6:20 am, they were in the Landcruiser, ready to set off before sunrise.

The day before, Nick had studied the map they were given when they entered the park. It indicated a large vlei[487] a few kilometres west of their lodge, with a well-used dirt road running alongside it. He switched on the Landcruiser's headlights and quickly found the road. They followed it for a couple of kilometres until they reached the point where the road veered north-west.

This point marked the beginning of the vlei. According to the map, the vlei stretched for at least 500 metres to the right of the road, descending into a gulley. Nick spotted a track off to the right of the dirt road and carefully manoeuvred the Landcruiser onto it for about 100 metres. He then parked the vehicle, facing east — towards the direction of the rising sun.

---

[486] Boerewors is a type of spicy sausage which originated from South Africa.
[487] A vlei is an Afrikaans word meaning low-lying marshy ground covered with water during the rainy season.

Once the sun appeared on the horizon, they could see that the vlei became marshy as it neared the gulley. About 150 metres away, shallow surface water began to glimmer as the rising sun's rays caught its surface. A large shroud of mist hung about a metre above the water due to the cold air. The combination of the rising sun, surface water, and mist refracted the sunlight, producing an amazing array of reds, oranges, and yellows.

The early morning bird and animal life was starting to stir, bringing the usual sounds back to the quietened African bush. On the horizon, silhouettes of thorny acacia trees became visible. The whole scene was sublime — one that Rachel would remember for years to come. Fortunately, she had brought her camera. After fiddling with the shutter speed and aperture dials to accommodate the low light, she busily snapped away at the unforgettable landscape.

Suddenly, Nick raised his hand and put his finger to his lips to quieten her. He pointed ahead at about two o'clock. Rachel strained her eyes but saw nothing for several seconds. Then, the distinctive shape of a male lion emerged from behind a low-lying clump of bushes. She held her breath, not daring to make a sound. It was a massive black-maned male lion, slowly meandering past their vehicle, a mere 15 metres away. He seemed aware of the vehicle but untroubled by it. With each purposeful and deliberate step, his paws — big as dinner plates — made no sound as they softly touched the ground. He took one last look at the vehicle, swished his tail, flicked his ears, and then disappeared into the bush.

"Oh my God," exclaimed Rachel. "That was magical."

"We were certainly lucky to catch that sight," said Nick. "I wonder where the rest of his pride is?"

They remained still for another 15 minutes or so. A large herd of zebras entered the vlei and walked down to drink. Nick wondered whether the lion would be attracted by the herd, but it was moving together in a tight pack. This formation meant that even if the lion was still nearby, its interest in the herd was doubtful, as there were no obvious weak points in its ranks.

Once it became apparent that the lion would not be returning to investigate the zebra herd, Nick slowly edged their vehicle out of the vlei and back onto the dirt road. They followed the dirt road until they came across another rough track, which looked as though it had recently been used by other game-viewing vehicles. They turned onto the track and were immediately rewarded when they encountered a small confusion of wildebeest. In close proximity to the wildebeest was a journey of giraffes. Nick managed to position their vehicle within 20 metres of the animals. They then switched off the engine and watched, spellbound, as the animals slowly made their way through the bush, following an ancient route that only they could discern.

The game viewing continued in this manner for several hours. They did not see any animals while on the dirt road, but each time they ventured off onto a rough track, they were soon rewarded. Besides the lion, zebra, and wildebeest, they also saw impala, kudu, sable, and ostrich, as well as a whole variety of birdlife, including many types of birds of prey, guineafowl, bustards, doves, and nightjars.

They returned to their lodge just before noon. By now, the day had warmed, and they were glad to be back in the lodge, where they could enjoy a cold drink, a light lunch, and a rest. The morning had been a wonderful success, and they had been fortunate to see just about every animal they had hoped to see, other than rhinos and leopards.

Just after 3:30 pm, they set off from the lodge for their late afternoon game drive. According to information received at the park entrance, the western areas of the park held a large population of white rhinos, which tended to stay in those areas while grazing. Conversely, sightings of black rhinos were far less common, as only a few remained in the park and, being more timid than their white counterparts, they usually avoided open spaces.

Based on this information, they headed for Mpophoma Dam, located in the western part of the park, about 20 kilometres from their lodge. Once again, the road was a dirt road, but it had been well-graded and was relatively easy to drive on. As they did not have many hours of daylight left, they stayed on the dirt road and did not venture onto any of the rougher tracks they encountered.

Just before reaching Mpophoma Dam, they passed an ablution block. They both needed a toilet break, so Nick stopped the car and went to the Gents while Rachel made her way to the Ladies. When Nick entered the Gents, he was shocked to find that the interior had been significantly vandalised. The metal urinal trough had been ripped from the wall and left on the concrete floor, while the white ceramic toilet pan had been smashed and lay in pieces on the ground. Graffiti covered the whitewashed walls, much of it written in Ndebele, which Nick could neither read nor understand. However, there were some English phrases, including one that read, "Nkomo is a sell-out and Mugabe is a dog. We need a new Khumalo[488] king."

Nick was dismayed both by the words and the vandalism, especially in this iconic tourist destination. He hoped that the Ladies' toilets hadn't suffered the same fate.

When he returned to the car, he informed Rachel about the state of the Gents' toilets. She reassured him that, fortunately, the Ladies' toilets, while rather dirty and without toilet paper, were still functioning and usable.

As they were talking, another vehicle pulled up at the ablution block. Inside were two white men. Nick told them about the state of the Gents' toilets and suggested they might want to use the bush instead. He also asked if they had come across any rhinos. The men excitedly informed them that they had just seen a pair of rhinos grazing in an open savannah area just off the dirt road, about half a kilometre ahead.

Nick thanked them gratefully, started the Landcruiser, and he and Rachel set off to try to find the animals.

---

[488] The last official king of the Ndebele people was King Lobengula Khumalo who died circa 1894.

A short way down the road, they came across the two white rhinos, which were about 20 metres off the road, contentedly feeding on the short grass. Both animals had their heads and squared lips lowered to the ground as they grazed. Each rhino sported two large horns, with the front horn being roughly twice the size of the rear horn.

Rachel was stunned by the rhinos' enormous size[489]. She was also astonished that, despite their prehistoric frames and undeniable power, they moved quite elegantly and gracefully. The folds in their tough grey hides made it appear as though they were wearing specially fitted suits of leather armour. As she took picture after picture, she readily understood why rhinos, together with elephants and lions, had become the emblematic icons of the African wilderness.

In their preoccupation with the rhinos, they lost track of time. It was only when Nick noticed the quickly fading light that he realised they ought to be heading back to their lodge. He quietly reversed the vehicle away from the rhinos and back onto the dirt road. Due to the fading light, Nick needed to turn on his headlights, the beams of which helped him navigate the quickly disappearing road. They returned to their lodge just after 6:00 pm, by which time it was quite dark.

Fortunately, the housekeeper had, as required, come to the lodge in the late afternoon to tend to the fire beneath the outside hot water boiler. Consequently, the water was steaming hot by the time they returned.

Nick lit the gas lamps, unpacked the vehicle, and then he and Rachel shared a shower. Once they had showered, Nick poured a gin and tonic for both of them and then helped Rachel prepare the evening meal, which consisted of grilled steak coated with a delicious marinade, roasted razorback potatoes, carrots, and peas.

Over dinner, they reminisced about the extraordinary events of the day, all of which had been remarkable apart from the vandalised toilet

---

[489] An adult male white rhino can weigh over 2,500 kilograms.

block and graffiti. The graffiti, in particular, left an uneasy and troubling feeling in Nick's mind.

Over breakfast the next day, they decided to visit World's View. Rachel had heard of the site but was unsure of what it was, so she asked Nick to tell her about it.

In response, Nick replied, "The site is, in fact, a graveyard. Cecil John Rhodes, Leander Starr Jameson, Allan Wilson, and the other men of his doomed patrol, as well as several other leading white settlers, are buried there. The entire location is a giant granite dome, with some very large boulders at its summit. From the top, there is a magnificent 360° view over the rugged mass of the Matopos hills.

"I understand that when Rhodes first came across the site, he was profoundly moved both by the view and the haunting sound of the wind as it blew across the valley below and up onto the boulder-strewn granite dome above. It was Rhodes who gave the site the name *The World's View*, and he subsequently chose it as the place he wanted to be buried. For centuries, the local Kalanga people had also been awed by the mysticism of the site and had named it *Malindidzimu*, which means *The Hill of Benevolent Spirits*."

World's View was about 11 kilometres from the lodge. It took them about 20 minutes to drive there. They parked in the car park at the foot of the granite dome. Near the car park was a Visitors' Centre, a small building of natural rock with a thatched roof. Inside, there were various displays providing a brief historical overview of Cecil John Rhodes and his colonisation of Rhodesia. Nick was surprised that the information still cast Rhodes in a positive light. He knew that for many in the new Zimbabwean government, Rhodes epitomised everything that was wrong with British imperialism. He wondered how long it would be before the information about Rhodes was re-written to reflect the perspective of the colonised people, rather than that of the colonisers.

From the Visitors' Centre, they made their way up the gentle ascent to the peak of *Malindidzimu*[490]. The granite dome they were walking on was very large — probably as big as three cricket ovals. The surface was splattered with the greens and oranges of centuries-old lichen growth. In some places, soil had accumulated in shallow circular indentations in the granite, some as large as four metres in diameter, where beautiful soft green clumps of wild grasses were growing. The low clumps of grass swayed in unison as gentle breezes flowed up, down, and across the large granite dome.

Rachel observed dozens of colourful lizards lying on the rock, soaking up the sun, before quickly scurrying away when a careless foot came too close for comfort.

At the summit of the dome, there were at least 30 large boulders that looked as if they had been used by giant mythical creatures to play a game of marbles or something similar. The graves of Cecil John Rhodes and Leander Starr Jameson were situated among these boulders. Each man had his own separate grave, yet the graves were positioned close to each other and shared a striking resemblance. Chiselled into the solid granite, the grave holes were sealed with rectangular granite lids. Bronze plaques were securely bolted onto these lids. The plaque atop Rhodes' grave bore the inscription, *"Here lie the remains of Cecil John Rhodes,"* while the one atop Jameson's grave was similar, reading, *"Here lies Leander Starr Jameson."*

About 100 metres past the graves and lower down the granite dome, there was a memorial to the Shangani patrol. The memorial was an oblong, flat-topped structure about ten metres tall, made from granite cut from a nearby kopje[491]. On each of the memorial's four sides, there was a bronze panel depicting the members of the patrol. At the base of the memorial was a granite viewing platform bearing the inscription, *"To Brave Men."*

---

[490] The Hill of Benevolent Spirits. This was also named by Cecil Rhodes as The World's View. The latter name is the better-known name.
[491] The word kopje is derived from the Afrikaans word koppie, which means a small hill.

The memorial also included another dedication that read, *"Erected to the enduring memory of Allan Wilson and his men who fell in fight against the Matabele on the Shangani River on 4th December 1893. There was no survivor."*

Rachel spent quite some time perusing the memorial to the Shangani Patrol. "This really is quite impressive," she said. "Can you tell me more about it?"

"Sure," said Nick. "From what I remember from our school history lessons, the patrol consisted of members of the British South Africa Company and was commanded by a man named Allan Wilson. Do you remember the school next to Prince Edward School that I pointed out to you? It was named after Allan Wilson. Anyway, Allan Wilson's patrol was a forward scouting patrol for a larger column of men who were tracking and trying to capture King Lobengula after he had set fire to and fled from his royal kraal in Bulawayo in early November 1893.

"The patrol did not, however, catch up with King Lobengula until 3rd December 1893. They had crossed the Shangani River and bivouacked for the night close to where they believed Lobengula and his fleeing people were encamped. However, during the night, there were heavy rains, and the Shangani River rose, making it impassable.

"Early the next morning, the Matabele forces, comprising some 3,000 warriors, surrounded the patrol. Wilson ordered three of his men to try to covertly re-cross the river and head back to Bulawayo to get reinforcements. The Matabele troops attacked the remaining 34 men of the patrol, who were heavily outnumbered. The men fought to the last one standing. When their ammunition ran out, the battle turned to hand-to-hand combat. All 34 men were slaughtered, but only after inflicting heavy casualties on the Matabele. The patrol's last stand achieved a prominent place in the British public's imagination and subsequently in Rhodesian history.

"I understand that the remains of the patrol's members were originally buried in the ruined city of Bulawayo. However, Rhodes later wrote into his will that he wished for the patrol to be re-interred alongside him here at World's View after he died. Rhodes' wishes were carried out in 1904, two years after his death."

"That certainly is a gallant story," said Rachel. "I can understand why it became embedded in the public's imagination. The story reminds me of Custer's Last Stand[492] against the Sioux and Cheyenne Indians in the American West."

Before returning to their lodge, they decided to travel the short distance back to the park's entrance. They wanted to visit Silozwane Cave the next day, but since it was outside the national park, Nick was unsure how to get there. Consequently, he wanted to see if they could hire a guide or park ranger who would be able to take them. Fortunately, a park ranger was available and agreed to pick them up from their lodge at Maleme Dam at 9:00 am the next day.

The park ranger arrived in his Land Rover shortly after 9:00 am the next day and introduced himself as Themba, a name Nick recognised as Ndebele.

The drive to Silozwane Cave took about two hours. The cave was located outside the national park, in the Silozwe rural area, and passed by a number of quintessentially African villages that were quite beautiful.

One of the most striking villages nestled at the foot of a large granite dome, comprising approximately a dozen mud huts with thatched roofs and a few concrete-block rectangular buildings with tin roofs. The upper halves of the huts' exterior walls were painted burnt orange, while the lower halves were dark brown. All the rectangular buildings were whitewashed. A well-constructed one-metre-high fence surrounded the village, and the grass within was green and recently cut, giving it a smart and tidy appearance.

---

[492] This was the Battle of Little Bighorn which took place on 25th and 26th June 1876 along the Little Bighorn River in the Crow Indian Reservation in south-eastern Montanna Territory, USA.

They also drove past Silozwe Primary School, which was signposted by a low concrete wall adorned with a mural of granite boulders and acacia trees. The mural was framed by a hand-painted arch carrying the words "*Co-operation, Devotion, Success.*" However, the most charming aspect of the school was the handsome, smiling faces of the young children who waved excitedly at the occupants of the Land Rover.

All the children were smartly dressed, complete with socks and shoes — a rarity in those days for black schoolchildren in rural areas. They looked so neat and cheerful that Rachel asked Themba to stop so she could take some pictures. As soon as she took out her camera, their happiness exploded, and some even broke into a spontaneous African tribal dance.

Rachel was delighted, as were Nick and Themba. Once they had left the school behind, Themba said, without any prompting, "Those young children are the future of this country. They will know nothing of the terrible conflict this nation has endured over the last decade, nor of the sacrifices their parents have made. I just hope the new government and some hot-headed young men don't let them down.

Nick was surprised by Themba's comment and asked him what he meant.

Themba thought for a moment before replying, "As a park ranger, I meet many Zimbabweans, both black and white. The black Zimbabweans I meet are usually from either the Shona tribe or my own, the Ndebele. The Ndebele are proud and want to play a meaningful role in the new Zimbabwe. Many Ndebele served in the former Rhodesian Army, and most of the ZIPRA[493] guerrillas were Ndebele. Before independence, they were promised significant roles in the new Zimbabwean National Army. Unfortunately, that promise has not been kept. They see Shona-speaking soldiers receiving good

---

[493] Zimbabwe People's Revolutionary Army. ZIPRA was the military wing of ZAPU.

positions in the ZNA[494], while very few Ndebele soldiers have been given similar opportunities."

"Lots of these men are now unemployed, angry, and bored. They blame the new government for not looking after them and Nkomo for not standing up to Mugabe. Because they are not welcomed in the new national army, many are talking about forming a new Ndebele army and even their own nation. There is talk of a revolution against Mugabe. And it's not just idle talk. If Mugabe and Nkomo don't start working together to ensure the Ndebele nation is given proper recognition in the new government, I think things might boil over."

Nick was very interested in what Themba had to say. He shared his experience of the vandalism and graffiti that he and Rachel had seen in the toilets at Mpophoma Dam. He also recounted the tribal prejudices his friend and colleague, Sipho[495] Pukelo, faced when trying to transition from the RAR[496] to the ZNA, which led him to quit in disgust.

Themba and Nick continued their conversation in this vein for a while longer, with Rachel occasionally chiming in with questions or observations.

A short time later, they arrived at Silozwane Cave and parked in the car park. Themba pointed out a nearby granite hilltop, explaining that this was where the cave was located. They followed a path through the bush towards the granite hilltop. The walk was relatively easy until they reached the base of the hill, where the gradient became steep and quite strenuous. By the time they reached the top, Nick and Rachel were breathing heavily, and their T-shirts were damp with sweat. In contrast, Themba was still breathing normally, and his khaki-coloured T-shirt showed no tell-tale sweaty patches.

From the summit, the view across the Matopos hills was expansive, uninterrupted, and quite spectacular. The cave itself was extraordinary, appearing as though someone had carved a large hollow

---

[494] Zimbabwe National Army.
[495] Sipho is a Ndebele boy's name meaning Gift.
[496] Rhodesian African Rifles.

at the base of the enormous granite mound. The cave entrance was about eight metres wide and stretched back into the granite dome for at least ten metres. The smooth walls of the cave were adorned with beautiful primitive rock art, depicting various traditional hunting and village-life scenes. These included delicate drawings of giraffes, rhinos, antelopes, and other wild animals native to the area. The rock art also featured large *stick-drawings* of people, rendered in dark red ochre, with some as tall as one and a half metres.

After exploring the walls of the cave for about half an hour, they began the walk back to the car park. The descent was much less strenuous but still hard on the knees.

Once back at Themba's Land Rover, they enjoyed cold drinks and oranges that Themba had packed into the vehicle before heading back to their lodge.

They arrived at their lodge in the mid-afternoon. Nick settled up with Themba, and the two shook hands, wishing each other well. Themba hopped back into his Land Rover and disappeared down the dirt road, back towards the national park's main entrance.

Nick and Rachel enjoyed a cup of tea and a biscuit on the veranda before preparing their vehicle for the next leg of their trip to Mhuka[497] Ranch near Chiredzi. They hoped to be on the road by 9:00 am the following day, Friday, 21st August.

---

[497] A local word meaning animals or wildlife.

Chapter 43 – Nick and Rachel travel to Mhuka Ranch, near Chiredzi

Timeline – 21 August

It was Friday, 21st August.

Nick knew it would be a long drive to Mhuka[498] Ranch — about seven hours. However, given that it was August, he also knew that the weather in the lowveld[499] would likely be at its most benign, with the average temperature for the month being around 25°C.

By 9:00 am, they had packed up their Toyota Land Cruiser and checked out of their lodge at Maleme Dam. They took the Matopos Road back into Bulawayo, arriving at 10:00 am, by which time the early morning traffic had eased.

From Bulawayo, they headed in an easterly direction on the A6 to Chiredzi. The trip to Chiredzi would take about six hours and would take them through the small country towns of Essexvale[500], Balla Balla[501], Shabani[502], Mandamambge, Ngundu and Triangle.

Much of the countryside they travelled through consisted of typical scrubby lowveld grassland, scattered with mopane, acacia, and baobab trees. The topography was well-suited for cattle ranching, and as a

---

[498] A local word meaning animals or wildlife.

[499] The term lowveld refers to low-lying, generally semi-arid region characterised by savanna or bushveld vegetation.

[500] Essexvale was renamed Esigodini in April 1982.

[501] Balla Balla was renamed Mbalabala in April 1982.

[502] Shabani was renamed Zvishavane in April 1982.

result, there were some enormous cattle ranches in this part of the country. However, many of these had been seriously neglected during the Rhodesian Bush War and required significant investment to restore them to full productivity.

As they travelled through the sparse countryside, Rachel was particularly intrigued by the baobab trees, with their smooth, grey-pink, fluted trunks. Nick explained that baobabs stored water in their trunks and branches, which helped them survive long periods of drought. This ability to store water also contributed to their exceptional longevity[503], which is why they were sometimes colloquially called the *Tree of Life*.

At this time of year, the trees were devoid of leaves, and their tangled, bare branches resembled roots. Rachel remarked that they looked as though they had been planted upside-down, and Nick agreed. He explained that the trees' peculiar appearance had made them part of ancient tribal beliefs. Some tribes in the Zambezi Valley believed that the gods had regarded the baobab trees as being too proud and upright. To teach them a lesson, the gods uprooted the trees and replanted them upside-down!

The countryside started to change completely when they were about 50 kilometres from Chiredzi. From this point, the barren, dry landscape gradually gave way to acres and acres of green, chequered fields of irrigated sugar cane.

Nick explained to Rachel that the transformation of this part of the lowveld was rooted in local folklore dating back to the 1920s. It all began when a Scotsman named Thomas MacDougall acquired a large tract of land in what is now known as the Triangle and Hippo Valley Estates.

MacDougall initially used the land for cattle ranching. However, when his venture failed, in 1923 he turned his attention to the irrigable potential of the rich alluvial soils in the northern section of his

---

[503] Carbon-dating has put the age of some baobab trees in Zimbabwe at over 1,000 years old.

property. He constructed the Jatala Weir across the Mtilikwe River, diverting water through two hand-hewn tunnels, each about 450 yards long, carved through solid rock over a period of seven years. From there, an eight-mile-long canal carried water onto his paddocks.

By 1931, MacDougall had completed this impressive engineering feat, marking the beginning of the lowveld's great irrigation revolution. Discipline and order were imposed on the wilderness, and the once dry and barren land began its transformation into one of the country's most fertile farming areas, producing sugar cane, citrus, and wheat.

With this agricultural development came western concepts of planning and community. The dry bush morphed into a vast, rectangular patchwork of irrigated fields and neat estate townships, complete with schools and health clinics. As the estates expanded and the sugar mills increased production, they provided much-needed revenue, particularly after UDI[504], when mineral revenues declined due to the international sanctions imposed on the illegal Smith regime.

Of course, the folklore surrounding this irrigation revolution often omitted to mention the less glamorous details — the appropriation of land, exploitation of labour, and the environmental damage caused by such large-scale development.

Nick told Rachel that although agricultural development had provided jobs for many, deep resentments remained, especially among the local Shangaan tribespeople. They were angry about how their land had been commandeered for agriculture, leading to the displacement of entire villages and the loss of traditional burial sites. The Shangaan were a minority group whose interests had largely been ignored by the white Rhodesian Government. Nick said that he suspected this marginalisation would continue under the new black government, which was dominated by Shona and Ndebele members of parliament.

When they reached Chiredzi, they bypassed the town centre and continued along the A10. About seven kilometres later, they crossed a

---

[504] Unilateral Declaration of Independence. The Government of Rhodesia declared UDI from Britain on 11th November 1965.

bridge over the Chiredzi River, and after another ten kilometres, they turned right onto a dirt road, following the signs to Mhuka Ranch.

After two kilometres on the dirt road, they arrived at the ranch just before 3:00 pm. They drove up the dusty driveway to the open security gates of the fenced main homestead and parked in the designated area. Shortly after, they were met by a man who introduced himself as Duncan Oliver, along with his daughter-in-law, Jenny Oliver.

Duncan, though elderly, appeared fit. Nick estimated him to be in his late sixties. His face was tanned and wrinkled from both age and years of worry, but his bright, clear eyes contrasted with his weathered features. He had a full head of dark brown hair, heavily silvered at the edges. Despite having spent most of his adult life in the harsh climate of the lowveld, his movements were still sharp, unaffected by arthritis or injury.

Jenny, in her late twenties, was introduced as the wife of Duncan's youngest son, Mark Oliver. She had a slender, athletic build and short blonde hair styled in a no-nonsense, easy-to-maintain cut. Her bright emerald eyes and warm, open expression immediately endeared her to Nick and Rachel.

After introductions, Duncan excused himself, leaving Jenny to show them around the main homestead before taking them to the lodge where they would stay.

Jenny stepped forward and said, "You must both be tired after your long drive from Bulawayo. Before I show you around the main homestead, please come inside for a cold drink. After that, we can drive to the lodge where you can unpack and freshen up. Tonight, we'll have dinner in the guest wing of the main homestead. Duncan, two of his sons, and Sipho[505] will be joining us."

She looked at Nick and continued, "Sipho tells me that you spent some time with him at 3RAR[506] during the Rhodesian Bush War. He has a

---

[505] Sipho is a Ndebele boy's name meaning Gift.
[506] 3rd Battalion of Rhodesian African Rifles.

high regard for you, and we're grateful to have him on board here at the ranch. You know we've recently employed him as our anti-poaching manager. Although it's still early days, from what we've seen, he's going to be a great asset."

Nick replied, "Yes, I met Sipho during my national service. I was posted to 3RAR in Umtali[507], where Sipho was a corporal in my platoon. He was an excellent soldier and performed admirably in some tricky situations. At the end of the war, he was promoted to platoon warrant officer and transferred to 1RAR[508] in Bulawayo. He continued to serve with distinction, especially in the battle for Entumbane in early 1981. I'm sure you'll find him to be an exceptional employee. I am looking forward to catching up with him."

Jenny showed Nick and Rachel around the main homestead. It was a large, rambling solid-brick Rhodesian farmhouse, surrounded on all sides by a wide veranda. The rooms were expansive and high-ceilinged, with ceiling fans to circulate air and keep them cooler, particularly during the long, oppressive summer months. The eastern side of the house was shaded by large leafy trees, which further helped in maintaining a cool temperature. The house was comfortably but modestly furnished. The enormous kitchen included a massive walk-in pantry and a large AGA oven that Jenny said had been imported from the UK in the early 1960s. The main homestead featured three bathrooms, each with both a bath and shower, serving its four bedrooms.

On the northern side of the house, a guest wing had been added. Jenny explained that this wing was generally used by the ranch's hunting guests and their families. One of the bedrooms was currently occupied by Sipho while his house was being built[509].

Compared to the main homestead, the guest wing was more modern and furnished to a higher luxury standard. It included three large

---

[507] Umtali was renamed Mutare in 1982.
[508] 1st Battalion of Rhodesian African Rifles.
[509] The anti-poaching manager's house was being built on the northern side of Ingwe Dam.

double bedrooms, each with its own en-suite bathroom, plus a dormitory-style bunkhouse that could sleep another four or five people. The guest wing had its own entrance hall, lounge, dining room, kitchen, and business/office area. The lounge overlooked a well-designed garden, which included a large, fenced swimming pool.

The three bedrooms in the guest wing were accessed via a long passageway. As they walked down it, Jenny pointed out the bedroom Sipho was temporarily using. The door to his room was ajar, and Nick glanced in, smiling at how neat and tidy it was. A couple of brass coat hooks were on the wall near the bathroom, and hanging from one was Sipho's RAR[510] green beret, with its distinctive badge incorporating a Matabele shield, crossed spears, and knobkerrie[511].

During the tour of the homestead and guest wing, Jenny shared some details about the Oliver family. Duncan Oliver was the family patriarch. Born in England in 1912, just before the First World War, he came to South Africa with his parents in 1923. He migrated to Southern Rhodesia in 1933 and turned to cattle ranching. His ventures in cattle ranching were interrupted by the Second World War. He had volunteered in 1940 and served with the Allied Forces in both East Africa and North Africa. After being demobilised in 1945, he returned to Southern Rhodesia.

He bought the land that now comprised the ranch in 1948. At the time of purchase, it was barren scrubland. However, over the last 30 years or so, he transformed the property into a thriving business comprising cattle ranching, wildlife conservancy, big game hunting safaris, game viewing, bird watching, and photographic safaris.

In addition to the main homestead, guest house, and swimming pool, the property included a small airfield, various dams (the largest of which was Ingwe[512] Dam), a compound for the ranch's workers and

---

[510] Rhodesian African Rifles.
[511] A knobkerrie is a wooden club with a large knob at one of its ends. Traditionally, they were used by South African tribespeople for throwing at animals or for clubbing an enemy's head.
[512] Ingwe is a local African word meaning leopard.

their families, barns, cattle dips, a farm shop, a workshop, an elephant hide, six bird hides, one luxury lodge overlooking Ingwe Dam, two rhino bomas, and a rhino holding pen that was nearing completion.

Jenny also explained that they were currently building a house for Sipho and constructing barrack rooms for approximately a dozen rangers. Once these projects were completed, they planned to build two more luxury lodges.

Jenny mentioned that Duncan had married a woman named Margaret van Zyl in 1947, just before purchasing Mhuka Ranch. Unfortunately, he was now widowed, Margaret having died tragically in June 1978 after contracting rabies from a farm dog that bit her while she was trying to free it from a poacher's snare.

Duncan and Margaret had three sons. The eldest, Timothy, was born in 1948 and had migrated to South Africa in January 1980 together with his wife and two young children. They had settled in the Orange Free State, where Timothy was trying to replicate what his father had established in Zimbabwe.

The middle son, Hamish, was born in 1949 and remained unmarried. He lived on the ranch and, along with Duncan, was responsible for the big game hunting and cattle ranching operations.

Jenny was married to the youngest son, Mark, who was born in 1950. They married in May 1980, shortly after Zimbabwe achieved independence. Although they did not have children yet, they were trying. They lived in their own house on the ranch and were responsible for the new wildlife and photographic safari ventures, including the construction of three luxury lodges overlooking the Ingwe Dam. The first of these was already completed and was where Nick and Rachel were staying during their visit.

After the tour of the main homestead and guest wing, Jenny said she would show them the way to their lodge, which was about seven kilometres away.

They made their way back to where they had parked their Land Cruiser upon arrival. Jenny climbed into her vehicle and drove out of the fenced compound, with Nick and Rachel following closely behind.

Chapter 44 – Nick and Rachel settle into Ukuthula Lodge

Access between the main homestead and Ukuthula[513] Lodge was via a good dirt road that ran in a southerly direction for about eight kilometres. At this point, one turned left into a narrow access road that approached the lodge from its rear elevation.

On the lodge's right-hand side, there was a double carport, into which Nick and Rachel pulled, parking next to Jenny's vehicle.

From the carport, a paved pathway led to the lodge's entrance door. The lodge's walls were constructed from natural stone, and the roof had been beautifully thatched. The solid wooden entrance door opened into a generous foyer, decorated in a rustic-safari style. From the foyer, a few steps descended into a large open-plan lounge and dining area.

This space was marvellously decorated in an African safari style, featuring large African soapstone carvings, comfortable couches and easy chairs, a large fireplace, and stunning African art. The floor, made of highly polished concrete, was dyed in soft browns and clay hues. Large handmade woollen carpets adorned the floor, showcasing bold symmetrical patterns in earthy oranges and browns.

The lounge looked out onto a spacious deck with sunbeds and umbrellas. Access to the deck was through large wooden French doors along the entire northern wall of the lounge. The deck encircled a

---

[513] Ukuthula is the Zulu word for calmness or silence.

beautiful infinity swimming pool, tiled with blue mosaic tiles imported from Spain. This area also included a bar and a fire pit.

The lodge was beautifully presented, but the crowning glory was the view from the deck, looking northward over Ingwe[514] Dam. The dam, considerable in size, was surrounded on three sides by heavily treed kopjes[515]. There wasn't a breath of wind, and in the late afternoon sun, the dam glistened like the emerald green plumage of an African sunbird. The sounds of the surrounding bush provided the perfect soundtrack to complete this magical setting.

Jenny led them back into the lounge and down a light-filled passage branching off from the lounge's western wall. This was the bedroom wing, containing two luxurious bedrooms, each with en-suite bathrooms. The room where they would stay featured a king-size four-poster bed and a light grey leather sofa. Its north-facing windows offered stunning views across the dam. The bedroom's furniture and decor were muted and romantic, contrasting with the African safari styling in the lounge and dining areas. Their room boasted its own external deck, accessible via a sliding French door on the northern wall.

The en-suite bathroom featured a free-standing bath and a large double shower. A glass-paned skylight, set into the thatched roof above the bath, was designed to allow guests to gaze up at the star-studded African night sky while soaking in a hot bath.

"Wow," gasped Rachel. "This is magnificent. I couldn't have imagined anything as beautiful or peaceful as this."

"Thank you," replied Jenny. "We've worked very hard to create the perfect setting for the lodge. We named it *Ukuthula*, the Zulu word for calmness or silence. Our architect, builder, and interior design team from Bulawayo have been wonderful. Most of the on-site work has been done by local Shangaan craftsmen, who have turned out to be

---

[514] Ingwe is a local African word meaning leopard.
[515] The word kopje is derived from the Afrikaans word koppie, which means a small hill.

quite exceptional. The lodge opened just a couple of months ago, and you and Nick will be our fifth group of guests.

"Before I leave you, I'd like to introduce you to the two staff members who will be taking care of you during your stay. I think they're in the kitchen. Just give me a minute while I find them."

With that, Jenny headed for the kitchen. She reappeared shortly thereafter with the two staff members, Samson and Beauty, whom she introduced to Nick and Rachel.

Samson was the cook and waiter, and also responsible for the firepit at night and the lounge fire in the colder weather. He was a tall, middle-aged man with dark ebony skin and a broad, jovial smile.

Beauty was the housekeeper, looking after cleaning, laundry, and tea-making. She was petite, shy, and very pretty, likely in her mid-twenties.

Nick and Rachel shook hands with them. Samson returned their handshakes with confidence, while Beauty's was quite deferential in comparison.

Before Jenny left, she reminded them that the three of them would be dining in the guest wing at the main homestead later that evening, where they would be joined by Duncan, Mark, Hamish, and Sipho[516]. She asked them to arrive at the main homestead just before 7:00 pm for pre-dinner drinks, then bade them farewell and headed off in her car.

Samson offered to fetch their luggage from their Land Cruiser. Beauty asked if they would like a cup of tea while unpacking. Rachel replied that would be lovely, and Beauty disappeared into the kitchen to prepare the tea and sandwiches.

Once Samson and Beauty had left, Rachel wrapped her arms around Nick's neck and gave him a passionate kiss. "This is awesome, Nick. I couldn't have wished for anything else."

---

[516] Sipho is a Ndebele boy's name meaning Gift.

He returned her affection with a loving hug.

They were interrupted by a knock at the door. It was Samson, returning with their luggage, closely followed by Beauty, who carried a tea tray with fine bone china cups and saucers, a silver teapot, a silver jug of cold milk, and a silver sugar bowl filled with golden-brown demerara sugar crystals. The tray also held a fine bone china plate of delicate cucumber sandwiches.

Rachel squeezed Nick's hand in delight.

Nick thanked both Samson and Beauty, who then left them to unpack and freshen up.

After unpacking, Nick and Rachel stepped onto the decking area to enjoy their tea and cucumber sandwiches, letting the calm beauty of the Ingwe Dam and the surrounding kopjes soothe their eyes and minds.

Once they finished their tea, they changed into their swimming costumes and took a dip in the enticing swimming pool. By now, the sun was low in the sky, the evening air was cool, and the water felt decidedly cold. After a few minutes, they climbed out and wrapped their soft, large towels tightly around their shoulders. Earlier, Samson had lit the fire in the firepit, and the flames were now glowing invitingly. Drawn by the fire's heat, they sat around it until they felt warm again.

The sun quickly sank below the western shores of the dam, and darkness began to envelop Ukuthula Lodge. As the darkness deepened, the lodge's lights and the gas lamps on the decking seemed to beckon the wildness of the bush into the safety and warmth of the haven the Olivers had created.

Hand in hand, Nick and Rachel left the firepit and returned to their bedroom. Beauty had already closed the curtains and turned down their sheets. The young lovers enjoyed a hot shower together before dressing for dinner.

Once they were ready, they went to say goodbye to Samson and Beauty, who said they would see them the next morning.

Nick and Rachel stepped into their Land Cruiser and headed for the main homestead. They arrived just before 7:00 pm, drove through the open security gates, and parked. From there, they walked along the illuminated paved pathway to the guest wing, which led them around the heavily treed eastern side of the main homestead to the guest wing's separate entrance. The door was ajar, and music could be heard coming from the lounge area. They stepped into the entrance hall, where Jenny greeted them with a warm embrace.

"I hope you've made yourself at home at Ukuthula," Jenny said.

"We certainly have," Rachel replied. "The lodge is gorgeous. I think we'd like to stay there forever."

Jenny chuckled. "Duncan, Hamish, Mark, and Sipho are already here. Come and say hello to everyone."

Nick and Rachel followed Jenny into the lounge. Duncan stepped forward and shook hands with both of them, introducing them to his two sons, Hamish and Mark. Both men were imposing, with their father's good looks and the lean, strong build of men accustomed to outdoor ranch life. The brothers shook Nick's hand warmly and gave Rachel a polite peck on the cheek.

Duncan glanced around the room, searching for Sipho. However, Sipho had already spotted Nick and was approaching with his hand outstretched. The two men greeted each other with a firm handshake.

Sipho knew Nick's Ndebele was basic, but was also aware how important it was for RAR[517] officers to be able to greet their troops using traditional African expressions.

"Sawubona[518]," he said.

---

[517] Rhodesian African Rifles.
[518] Sawubona is the Ndebele word meaning *Hello*.

"Yebo[519]," Nick replied.

"Kunjani[520]?" asked Sipho.

"Ngiyaphila[521]," Nick responded.

Sipho chuckled. "I see you still remember a few of the phrases we taught you at 3RAR[522]."

Nick grinned. "Ah, Sipho, I always knew my Ndebele was terrible, but you guys were too polite to laugh at me. It's great to see you. You're looking well."

"Thanks, *Ishe*[523]. You're looking good too, and browner than I expected! I thought after a year in the UK, you'd have the pale skin of the English," Sipho teased.

"Don't get me started on the UK," Nick said, laughing. "It's a world apart from here. But, as you know, I was lucky enough to meet the most wonderful woman there. This is Rachel. Let me introduce you."

Rachel leaned forward and hugged Sipho. "It's so nice to finally meet you," she said. "Nick has spoken of you often. I'm glad you two could reconnect on this trip."

Sipho smiled and told Rachel how much he and the 3RAR soldiers had admired and respected Nick, adding that he was delighted Nick and Rachel had accepted his invitation to visit Mhuka[524] Ranch.

"I'm glad we did," Rachel said. "From what little we've seen so far, it feels like it is one of Zimbabwe's hidden gems."

"It certainly is," Sipho replied. "I'm looking forward to showing you both around tomorrow."

---

[519]Yebo is the Ndebele word meaning *Hi*.
[520] Kunjani is the Ndebele word meaning *How are you?*
[521] Ngiyaphila is the Ndebele word meaning *I am fine thank you*.
[522] 3rd Battalion of Rhodesian African Rifles.
[523] *Ishe* is a term of respect used by RAR soldiers when referring to their officers.
[524] A local word meaning animals or wildlife.

Suddenly, the sound of a tinkling glass came from the corner of the lounge. Duncan was tapping his wine glass with a spoon to get everyone's attention. The chatter died down.

"Thank you, thank you," Duncan began. "The cook has let us know dinner is ready. But before we sit down, I'd like us all to raise our glasses to our newest guests, Nick and Rachel — and to our latest permanent acquisitions, the Two Ronnies."

Laughter rippled around the room, except for Nick and Rachel, who exchanged confused glances.

Duncan glanced at Nick and Rachel and said, "I can see from your puzzled expressions that no one has told you about the Two Ronnies yet. They're our first two black rhino bulls, which arrived by truck from the Zambezi Valley two days ago. They're currently in a couple of bomas and will stay there until we can move them into the adjacent holding pen. This is a significant achievement for Mhuka Ranch, and we're thrilled to share it with you both."

The room erupted in spontaneous applause. Nick and Rachel, caught off guard by the news, quickly joined in the excitement. Glasses were raised in a toast to the Two Ronnies.

They all took their seats at the dining table. Nick sat between Sipho on his left and Hamish on his right. Across from him, Rachel was seated between Mark and Jenny, with Duncan at the head of the table.

"Well, that was quite an announcement," Nick said to Hamish. "Congratulations to you all."

"Thanks," Hamish replied. "Dad and the team have worked hard to make this happen. I don't know if you're aware, but rhinos in Zimbabwe are in grave danger from poachers. Since independence last year, the poaching threat has escalated. It's not just local tribespeople hunting opportunistically anymore. We suspect organised criminal syndicates with international connections are driving the increase.

"These poachers are highly organised and skilled, often using high-calibre rifles to bring down large animals. Dad anticipated this would happen, which is why he created the position of anti-poaching manager. We're fortunate to have Sipho leading the charge. We need to shift from a reactive approach to a proactive one, and we believe Sipho is the right person to make that happen."

Nick looked concerned. "I've heard about rhino poaching, but I didn't realise it was this severe. But if Sipho's leading the efforts, I'm confident he'll do an outstanding job."

"Thanks for the confidence," Sipho said. "I've still got a lot to learn about rhinos, but I do understand the mindset of professional poachers. They're ruthless, so we need to be just as determined in our response. There's a lot of work ahead, but we hope to have our first rangers in place within the next month or so.

"We're currently building barrack-style quarters for them. The rangers will probably start working before the barracks are finished, so they'll stay in tents initially. I'm developing a rigorous training programme for them, drawing from the discipline and team-building techniques we learned in the RAR. I'm committed to building the best anti-poaching squad in the country."

"That's an ambitious plan, Sipho. How serious is the poaching threat here in the lowveld?[525]" Nick asked.

Sipho nodded towards Hamish. "I think Hamish is better suited to answer that."

Hamish jumped in to answer, "Things have developed much more quickly than we anticipated, and not in a good way. For years, the Rhodesian Bush War acted as a deterrent to organised criminal gangs setting up poaching operations here in Zimbabwe. But that's changed, and the threat is very real now.

"There are some prominent environmentalists who have been closely monitoring rhino numbers across southern and central Africa for

---

[525] The term lowveld refers to low-lying, generally semi-arid region characterised by savanna or bushveld vegetation.

decades. They've shown that, in this region, the number of rhinos lost to poaching has risen dramatically over the last ten years. More worryingly, in the last two years alone, there's been a significant spike in poaching here in Zimbabwe.

"These environmentalists are now working with the IUCN[526] and the Department of National Parks[527]. A specialised unit has been formed to advise on how to protect and preserve Zimbabwe's rhino populations. Based on their recommendations, the government has agreed to establish rhino conservancies across the country. These conservancies will be protected zones to which vulnerable rhinos can be relocated.

"The idea is to move rhinos from high-risk areas to these conservancies, where breeding programmes will hopefully be developed. As rhino populations grow, we can reintroduce them to areas where they've been depleted. But a lot of this depends on how well the conservancies perform. A key measure of success will be how effectively poaching is controlled. We're hoping that the anti-poaching strategies we're developing here at Mhuka Ranch could serve as a model for the other conservancies in Zimbabwe.

"Mhuka Ranch was approved as a rhino conservancy last year. We've set aside 50 square kilometres for rhino conservation, and with our good grazing and water resources, the ranch's ecological carrying capacity[528] for rhinos has been estimated at between 50 and 75 animals.

"We've been allocated 10 rhinos initially, to be delivered over five weeks. These animals will be closely monitored for about six months. If all goes well, we'll receive another 25. The goal is to increase the herd from 35 rhinos to around 70. Once we reach that number, we'll use

---

[526] International Union for the Conservation of Nature. This is an international organisation working in the field of nature conservation and sustainable use of natural resources.
[527] The full name is the Department of National Parks and Wildlife Management.
[528] The ecological carrying capacity is the estimated maximum number of rhinos that can be sustainably supported by the resources of a specific area at a level where births tend to balance out deaths.

about 20 rhinos to help repopulate other areas, bringing us back to our core herd of 50. This cycle of growing the herd and then restocking other regions will continue."

Nick interrupted, "You mentioned things had developed more quickly than expected. What do you mean by that?"

"Well," Hamish began, "we originally expected the first animals to arrive in early 1982. But about a month ago, the specialised unit I mentioned earlier contacted us, asking if we could accept our first two black rhinos within a month due to a sudden surge in poaching activity in the Zambezi Valley.

"Since then, we've been working flat out. We built two bomas, each capable of holding one rhino. They're small, about 30 square metres each, with sturdy walls made from gum poles concreted into the ground. They share water and feeding troughs, and there are shaded areas to protect the animals from the sun.

"The two bomas open into a holding pen, which is almost finished. It's about the size of a cricket oval, with water and feeding troughs, and surrounded by a stout six-foot-high electrified fence. Some large trees in the pen will provide shade for the rhinos.

"The Two Ronnies arrived on Wednesday, 19th August. Ideally, they should only stay in the bomas for a couple of days before being moved to the holding pen. But since it's not quite ready, they'll likely stay in their bomas until Monday, then be transferred to the holding pen for up to four weeks. After that, they'll move to the release paddock for another month before being allowed to roam freely across the full conservancy, which covers about 50 square kilometres.

"The release paddock is about two acres big and is next to the holding pen. It'll be fenced with standard farm-grade fencing. We're still putting up the fences and setting up water and feeding troughs, and we aim to finish these tasks in the next fortnight.

"We're expecting eight more rhinos to arrive over the next four weeks, with the next delivery being two females to keep the Two Ronnies company. So, as you can imagine, we're very busy at the moment."

"How on earth were the animals transported from the Zambezi Valley?" Nick asked.

"Luckily, we didn't have to handle that," Hamish explained. "The specialised unit took care of it. The animals were darted in the wild with anaesthetic darts and loaded into custom-made metal crates. A specially designed hoist mounted on a Land Rover was used to load the crates onto two trucks. These trucks, along with the Land Rover and hoist, were driven to Mhuka Ranch overnight. During the journey, the rhinos were given an antidote to bring them out of their deep anaesthesia but were kept lightly sedated with a tranquiliser."

"When the trucks arrived, they were driven directly into the bomas using a rough access track we'd built. We had a vet on site, and once the animals were inside the bomas, they were once again lightly anaesthetised. The crates were then hoisted off the trucks and onto the ground. Once the doors were opened, the vet notched the animals' ears, rounded off the tips of their horns, and fitted collars with radio transmitters and transponders.

"Finally, the vet administered another antidote. The rhinos quickly woke up, staggered out of the crates, and immediately got angry. Both started head-butting the walls of the bomas, but fortunately, the structures were robust enough to withstand the battering. After about 30 minutes, the rhinos calmed down and began grazing."

Sipho chimed in, "Considering it was the ranch's first time receiving rhinos, the whole operation went smoothly. In fact, it was pretty slick. Duncan and Hamish deserve all the credit for planning it so well."

"Good to hear," Nick said. "It's great to see serious efforts being made to protect rhinos. They're iconic and should be considered a national treasure."

Over dinner, the conversation turned to the challenges facing the new Zimbabwean Government. Hamish expressed concerns about its ability to manage the economy. Both rural and metropolitan populations had high expectations, fuelled by the rash and unrealistic promises made by black nationalist leaders during the Rhodesian Bush War. Hamish doubted the government could deliver on these promises and feared how the people would react when their hopes were dashed.

On the other hand, Sipho voiced his worries about the growing discontent among young Ndebele men. When Nick asked what was causing this, Sipho explained, "Well, Nick, you know the Ndebele nation takes great pride in its military heritage. So, when the Rhodesian Bush War intensified, many Ndebele men either joined ZIPRA[529] or, like me, enlisted in the Rhodesian Security Forces. Generally, Ndebele young men like the discipline of military life and thrive on the camaraderie they find in the army.

"After the general elections in February 1980, despite ZAPU[530] not doing as well as we had hoped, ZIPRA soldiers expected to be absorbed into the new ZNA. Similarly, those of us in the Rhodesian Security Forces expected to be offered comparable roles in the ZNA[531].

"But that hasn't happened. Mugabe has quickly politicised and tribalised the ZNA. To many of us, it feels like the ZNA is becoming an army for the Shona, not for the Ndebele. So now, many Ndebele men who fought in the war have lost their sense of identity and purpose. They're angry and disillusioned. I hear talk about them wanting to rise up against the ZNA and try to seize power. It's worrying."

"Geez," Nick said, "that does sound serious. Are you sure it's not just idle talk?"

"I don't think so, Nick. These men seem pretty determined. And now that the ZNA is closed off to them, there aren't many other employment options. Some may turn to petty crime, but there are definitely more motivated individuals talking about forming militias and opposing the government. It's serious."

---

[529] Zimbabwe People's Revolutionary Army. ZIPRA was the military wing of ZAPU.
[530] Zimbabwe African People's Union.
[531] Zimbabwe National Army.

"Hell, that's troubling," Nick replied. "If historical tribal tensions between the Shona and Ndebele flare up again, that could be dangerous. Do you think it could happen?"

"It's a real possibility," Sipho said. "Many Ndebele men are pushing for it, and I've heard rumours that the ZNA is preparing for it. We saw what could happen during the Entumbane uprisings[532] earlier this year. That could easily happen again. I'm grateful I've been able to continue in a military-related role by leading the anti-poaching squad here at Mhuka Ranch. I've been very fortunate."

After dinner, Nick and Rachel thanked the Olivers for a lovely evening. Sipho walked them to their car, mentioning that he had kept his weekend free and was available both Saturday and Sunday to show them around the ranch, including introducing them to the Two Ronnies. They agreed to meet him at the guest wing at 10:00 am the next morning.

Nick and Rachel then drove the short distance back to Ukuthula Lodge. During the drive, Rachel told Nick how much she had enjoyed the evening. Jenny and Mark had shared a lot about the work being done on the ranch, as well as their efforts to support the local community.

"I really admire what they're doing here," she said. "They're making a real difference, not only in terms of wildlife conservation but also in improving the quality of life for the local people. They've financed classroom upgrades, sports fields, and employed two resident nurses at the community clinic. They've also installed wells with diesel-powered water pumps in both villages on the ranch, built cattle dips, and made paddocks available for grazing the local tribespeople's cows.

"When I see Mum and Dad in a few days, I'm going to tell them all about it. Maybe Dad would be willing to make a substantial financial donation to the ranch — it's certainly a worthy cause."

---

[532] The Entumbane uprisings took place in January and February 1981 around Bulawayo when ZIPRA and ZANLA troops clashed over political differences. The uprising was crushed by the ZNA who heavily relied on forces from the former Rhodesian Security Forces.

"That would be terrific," Nick said. "Do you think he would?"

"Absolutely," Rachel replied. "This is exactly the kind of project Dad admires."

By then, they had arrived at Ukuthula Lodge. Samson and Beauty had thoughtfully left the entrance light on, making it easier for Nick and Rachel to find their way from the carport to the door.

They unlocked the door and stepped inside. Thanks to the glowing embers in the fireplace, the lodge was warmer than the chilly night air outside. A light had been left on in the passage to the bedrooms, and Beauty had placed a chocolate on each of their pillows.

"Gosh, those two are so thoughtful," Rachel said.

They brushed their teeth, changed into their pyjamas, and snuggled into their enormous four-poster bed. The warmth of their bodies soon dispelled the coolness of the bed linen, and they lay in each other's arms, feeling safe and at peace.

Little did they know that their drive back to the lodge had been watched by prying, malevolent eyes.

Chapter 45 – Johannes loiters in South Africa

Timeline – October 1978 to May 1981

You may recall the fiery meeting between RSM[533] Sandy McLeary and Sergeant Johannes du Toit on Wednesday, 27th September 1978. During that meeting, RSM McLeary accused Sergeant du Toit of involvement in illegal poaching activities — an accusation Sergeant du Toit flatly denied. When RSM McLeary questioned how Sergeant du Toit could afford a new Mercedes-Benz and its importation into Rhodesia, the Sergeant angrily replied that it was none of his "bloody business" and stormed out of the office.

The meeting left RSM McLeary furious and certain that du Toit was involved in something nefarious, although he knew du Toit would never admit to it. Resolving to find proof, McLeary planned to confront him again once he had concrete evidence.

RSM McLeary was well aware that du Toit was a loner who didn't bother cultivating friendships. In fact, du Toit's bullying and manipulative nature made most people wary of him. However, as a sergeant in the RLI[534], he wielded a degree of formal power, especially over the RLI troopies[535], and wasn't afraid to use it for his own benefit.

Despite his solitary nature, rumours had been circulating around the Buffalo Range base camp in recent months that du Toit had grown

---

[533] Regimental Sergeant Major.
[534] Rhodesian Light Infantry.
[535] Colloquial term meaning a regular member or national serviceman of the Rhodesian Army.

close to a couple of RLI troopies who also seemed to have an unusual amount of money. This raised suspicion, and the RSM was convinced there was a crooked connection between the three men. Determined to uncover the truth, he resolved to identify and interview the two troopies.

On Monday, 2nd October, before the RSM had the chance to investigate further, he received a report that Sergeant du Toit had failed to report for duty. His absence had created a manpower issue on the Fire Force rotation that began that day. The report also stated that du Toit's car was missing from the base and that he had cleared his personal belongings from his quarters.

Now, RSM McLeary was certain that Sergeant du Toit was up to no good. He assigned another competent NCO[536] to the Fire Force rotation for the week and immediately phoned Captain Morley, the adjutant at RLI headquarters at Cranborne Barracks in Salisbury[537].

After a few rings, the phone was answered by the rather officious voice of Captain Morley, who said, "Captain Morley here. Can I help you?"

"Morning, Captain. This is RSM McLeary. Sorry to disturb you. You may recall we spoke a few weeks ago about some rumours circulating around our base camp — allegations that one of our men, Sergeant Johannes du Toit, was involved in illegal poaching activities."

"Of course, I remember," replied Captain Morley. "Unfortunately, I haven't had a chance to look into it yet. The shooting down of Air Rhodesia Flight 825[538] by ZIPRA[539] guerrillas has caused a real shitstorm here. The top brass have been in emergency meetings all week, trying to figure out how to protect future civilian flights from such despicable and cowardly attacks."

---

[536] Non-commissioned officer.
[537] The capital of Rhodesia. Its name was changed to Harare in April 1982.
[538] Air Rhodesia Flight 825 was a scheduled passenger flight that was shot down by ZIPRA guerrillas on 3rd September 1978 shortly after take-off from Kariba.
[539] Zimbabwe People's Revolutionary Army. ZIPRA was the military wing of ZAPU.

"I can imagine the pandemonium," said RSM McLeary. "I know you have a lot on your plate, but I thought I should update you. I interviewed du Toit last week regarding the allegations. He reacted badly and denied everything. To make matters worse, today he failed to report for his Fire Force rotation — his FN[540] rifle and car are missing, and he has cleared out his quarters."

"Shit," said Captain Morley. "That bloody bastard. What do you intend to do now?"

"Well, we don't have any actual proof of his involvement in anything irregular yet. I was planning to interview the two troopies he's become friendly with — the ones who've also been throwing money around lately. Maybe they'll spill the beans. I still intend to do that. But now that du Toit has gone AWOL[541], I think we need to inform the Military Police. The CO[542] of Buffalo Range has already been briefed."

"OK, that sounds good to me. I'll report the matter to the Military Police and make sure you're copied in."

"Roger, Sir. Will do. Have a good day," replied RSM McLeary.

Over the next two weeks, RSM McLeary made it a priority to identify and interview the two troopies. Once he had identified them, he confronted them with the allegations. Both men initially denied any irregular contact with Sergeant du Toit or involvement in any illicit activities. However, when the RSM threatened to cancel their R&R[543] leave for the next six months unless they came clean, the troopies cooperated. They admitted that they had been providing du Toit with information on elephant herd movements since August 1977, intelligence they had gathered while on OP[544] duties.

---

[540] This was a light automatic rifle designed in Belgium and manufactured by FN Herstal. The FN was the standard issue rifle for the Rhodesian Security Forces.
[541] Absent Without Leave.
[542] Commanding Officer.
[543] Rest and Recuperation.
[544] Observation Post.

When asked what they had gained from this, the troopies first denied receiving any benefit. But when the RSM pressed the matter further, demanding to know how they were financing their lavish spending during R&R, they finally confessed. They stated they had each been paid Rh$50[545] per month by du Toit for the intel[546]. They claimed not to know what du Toit did with the information and failed to disclose that they were also receiving an additional Rh$400 for any animal that was successfully poached as a result of the information they had provided.

Despite these partial admissions, no disciplinary charges were brought against the two RLI troopies. Their superiors viewed their actions as minor indiscretions. Furthermore, the demands of the Rhodesian Bush War at the time meant that every able-bodied serviceman was crucial to the fight against the guerrillas, leading the troopies' superiors to rationalise that, on balance, their actions could be overlooked.

As promised, Captain Morley referred the matter to the Military Police for further investigation. However, their inquiries turned up nothing. Due to incompetence on the part of the Military Police, no checks were made with border officials at Beitbridge to determine whether Sergeant du Toit had left Rhodesia and entered South Africa around the time in question.

Regarding the severe beating that Selous Scout Fritz Viljoen suffered at his home in Greystone Park[547] in early October 1978, his housemates had taken him to Andrew Fleming Hospital in Salisbury for treatment, and he was slowly recovering. Moreover, the bloodied message[548] inked on the mirror in Viljoen's bedroom by his unknown assailant left him with no doubt about who was responsible. Consequently, fearing for his life, he had reported the incident to the Borrowdale Police merely as a home burglary with assault. When questioned about the bloodied message, the decapitation of his dog, and the burning of his

---

[545] They were in fact each being paid Rh$200 per month.
[546] Intelligence information (often military in nature).
[547] An upmarket suburb of Salisbury, about 15 kilometres north-east of Salisbury CBD.
[548] Refer chapter 32. The message read *Love from J*.

motorcycle, Viljoen provided no explanation and did not identify anyone who might have held a grudge against him.

Given the strain on police resources at the time, further investigations were minimal, and the case was eventually closed as an unsolved *burglary with aggravated assault causing serious bodily harm.*

As for Johannes du Toit, after being AWOL for 30 consecutive days, his military records were updated to show that he was presumed to have deserted. If apprehended, he would face a court-martial, and if found guilty, he could face a lengthy prison sentence for desertion.

When Johannes initially went AWOL, he had naively assumed he might only need to lie low in South Africa for up to six months before returning to Rhodesia.

He hadn't fully decided on his course of action if he did return, but he wanted to keep that option open. This would allow him to potentially revive his business dealings with Santiago de Costa, Gary du Plessis, and Jeremy du Randt.

After a few weeks in Pretoria, Johannes reached out to all three men. His first call was to Santiago de Costa. After a couple of attempts, he got through and explained that he had suffered a minor heart attack. He reassured Santiago that he was recovering well but had been advised by his cardiologist to take it easy for at least six months to ensure a full recovery. Santiago expressed sympathy, wishing him a speedy recovery, and Johannes promised to update him on his health sometime after Easter 1979.

Next, Johannes called Gary du Plessis in Fort Victoria, explaining that one of his new spotters had made careless remarks while on R&R leave in Salisbury, sparking suspicions about Johannes' possible involvement in illegal activities. He told Gary he had decided to leave Rhodesia hastily but hoped to return in about six months once the dust settled. Johannes reassured Gary that the suspicions were focused solely at him and that he had already ensured that the spotter was appropriately punished for his indiscretion. He ended the call by saying he would contact Gary again around Easter 1979 and asked him to pass the message on to Jeremy. Gary expressed regret over the sudden turn of events and said he looked forward to resuming their business activities soon. He also agreed to inform Jeremy.

As the weeks and months passed, Johannes began to fully appreciate the seriousness of his situation, especially the real possibility of facing arrest and court-martial for desertion if he returned to Rhodesia. Meanwhile, early 1979 reports in the South African press painted an increasingly bleak picture for Rhodesia. It became evident to Johannes that South Africa's political leaders had decided to abandon Rhodesia, optimistically hoping that their actions would be rewarded by the African Frontline States[549] easing their pressure on South Africa regarding its apartheid[550] policies.

The withdrawal of SADF[551] personnel, aircraft, and other military support from Rhodesia signalled to Johannes that the Rhodesian Security Forces now had little hope of prevailing in the Bush War. In his mind, this meant that either Robert Mugabe, Joshua Nkomo, or some other equally unappealing figure was likely to become the future leader of Rhodesia. Unable to imagine returning under such leadership, he began to explore other options.

Initially, Johannes thought his easiest path would be to enlist in the SADF. He was pursuing this option in early 1979 when, to his surprise, a potential return to Rhodesia started to seem feasible.

This unexpected possibility emerged in April 1979, when general elections were held in Rhodesia and won by the UANC[552] under Bishop Abel Muzorewa's leadership. Following the elections, on 1st June 1979,

---

[549] These were a loose coalition of African countries from the 1960s to the 1980s committed to ending white minority rule in Rhodesia. They included Angola, Botswana, Mozambique, Tanzania, and Zambia.
[550] Apartheid is the Afrikaans word for apartness. It was a system of institutionalised racial segregation that existed in South Africa and South West Africa (now Namibia) from 1948 to the early 1990s.
[551] South African Defence Forces.
[552] United African National Council.

a government of national unity took office with Muzorewa as Prime Minister, and the country was renamed Zimbabwe-Rhodesia.

To Johannes, Muzorewa's victory appeared to have sidelined the communist and socialist agendas of ZANU[553], led by Robert Mugabe, and ZAPU[554], led by Joshua Nkomo. Johannes thought that Muzorewa's more moderate government might offer a relatively secure future for the whites in the country.

However, Johannes remained uncertain about the risk of arrest and court-martial for desertion if he returned. To test the waters, in July 1979, he discreetly began inquiring about the possibility of returning to Zimbabwe-Rhodesia.

His first call was to his two associates, cousins Gary du Plessis and Jeremy du Randt, in Fort Victoria[555]. They were pleasantly surprised to hear from him. During their conversation, Johannes mentioned that he was considering returning in light of Zimbabwe-Rhodesia's improved political conditions. However, given his prolonged absence from the RLI, he feared being regarded as a deserter and sought their opinion on the likelihood of an arrest warrant.

To Johannes's astonishment, Gary and Jeremy quickly dismissed his perception of political improvement. They informed him that neither Mugabe nor Nkomo had recognised the April election results, labelling Muzorewa and his government as Ian Smith's stooges. Furthermore, neither the OAU[556] nor the international community acknowledged Muzorewa's government, which was now being pressured to return to the negotiating table with ZANU and ZAPU.

According to Gary, the country was *fucked*. ZANU and ZAPU were waging war more fiercely than ever. Muzorewa's government was ineffectual, and major powers like Russia, China, England, and the

---

[553] Zimbabwean African National Union.
[554] Zimbabwe African People's Union.
[555] Fort Victoria was renamed Masvingo in 1982.
[556] The Organisation of African Unity (1963 to 2002). The OAU was superseded by the African Union in 2002.

United States were circling like vultures, eager to exploit whatever emerged from the chaos. South African Prime Minister PW Botha[557] and his predecessor BJ Vorster[558] were despised by the white community for their perceived betrayal of Rhodesia. The white population and its defence forces felt despondent, with no clear vision of the future.

Gary and Jeremy added that they were still engaged in anti-cattle rustling operations near Fort Victoria, but their earnings were modest, and they longed for the return of the *good old days*. However, given the political instability and Johannes's current situation, they doubted whether that was ever likely to happen.

Johannes agreed but added that he would keep in touch, recognising that the situation in Zimbabwe-Rhodesia was fluid and that new opportunities might arise in the future. He then tried to call Santiago de Costa in Malvernia. Initially, the line was dead, but after several tries, he finally got through. Santiago was happy to hear from Johannes but became disheartened upon learning that Johannes's recovery from his heart attack was slower than anticipated. Johannes indicated that he wasn't sure when he would be able to resume their business dealings. Santiago wished him a speedy recovery and expressed his willingness to continue their partnership once Johannes was fully healed.

Based on these discussions, Johannes put any thoughts of an immediate return to Zimbabwe-Rhodesia on the back burner. He recognised that the chances of being arrested and court-martialled upon his return were very real, and the political situation in the country was more uncertain than ever.

By now, Johannes's nest egg from the proceeds of his illegal poaching activities between August 1977 and September 1978 was starting to dwindle, and he realised he needed to consider other ways to make a

---

[557] Pieter Willem Botha was a South African politician who was the last Prime Minister of South Africa from 1978 to 1984 and its first executive state president from 1984 to 1989.
[558] John Vorster served as the Prime Minister of South Africa from 1966 to 1978.

living. While he still believed there was money to be made from poaching, he acknowledged that the timing was not right. Therefore, in the short term, he decided to return to the kinds of criminal activities he had engaged in before enlisting in the RLI in early 1967, such as extortion, burglary, and drug dealing.

Chapter 46 – Johannes returns to Zimbabwe

Timeline - June 1981

Between July 1979 and April 1981, Johannes became deeply entrenched in Pretoria's criminal underworld.

His psychopathic tendencies, deceit, and cunning had been evident from an early age. However, his time in the RLI[559], from early 1967 until September 1978, had sharpened these unsavoury traits. He was now a seasoned killer, proficient in handling all kinds of weaponry and explosives. He had no conscience and little ability to distinguish right from wrong. Financial gain and an obsessive drive to complete any mission he undertook — or was paid to undertake — were his only motivations.

The kingpins of South Africa's criminal underworld had no shortage of shameful tasks that needed to be carried out. They had ample *dirty money* to ensure these tasks were executed, but their perpetual challenge was finding someone both willing and skilled enough to complete them successfully and swiftly.

Johannes du Toit possessed all the necessary attributes. He quickly became the *go-to man* whenever a hitman was required.

---

[559] Rhodesian Light Infantry. This was an infantry regiment and was one of the country's main counter-insurgency units during the Rhodesian Bush War.

However, in April 1981, Johannes received an unexpected phone call from Gary du Plessis[560]. Gary updated him on the dramatic events that had unfolded in Zimbabwe since their last conversation in July 1979. Bishop Muzorewa's UANC[561] government of national unity[562] had been short-lived. The British government had persuaded Muzorewa, Robert Mugabe, Joshua Nkomo, Ian Smith, and other key figures to participate in a constitutional conference, which took place at Lancaster House in London.

The conference culminated in the Lancaster House Agreement, signed by all necessary parties on 21st December 1979. Under the Agreement, a ceasefire between the warring factions was implemented, Muzorewa's government revoked Rhodesia's 1965 illegal unilateral declaration of independence[563], and the government dissolved itself. Fresh general elections, overseen by the British, were held in February 1980. In these elections, Robert Mugabe's ZANU-PF[564] party won a landslide victory[565], while Bishop Muzorewa's UANC was decimated. The country legally became independent on 18th April 1980 under Robert Mugabe's prime ministership, and was renamed Zimbabwe, regaining its place in the international community.

Although Johannes was already aware of these events, he found Gary's concise summary useful. Once Gary finished, Johannes said, "Thanks for the useful summary, Gary. But I'm not sure why you're telling me all this."

---

[560] Gary du Plessis was one of the two shooters who had participated in Johannes' illegal poaching activities in Rhodesia during the period August 1977 to September 1978.

[561] United African National Council.

[562] Bishop Muzorewa's Government of national unity had been sworn into office on 1st June 1979.

[563] Unilateral Declaration of Independence. The Government of Rhodesia declared UDI from Britain on 11th November 1965

[564] Zimbabwe African National Union – Patriotic Front. ZANU-PF is a political organisation that has been the ruling party of Zimbabwe since independence in 1980.

[565] ZANU-PF won 57 seats on the common roll; ZAPU won 20 seats and UANC won 3. The Rhodesian Front won all 20 seats on the white roll.

Gary replied, "Well, Zimbabwe has been independent for a year now. During that time, there have been some very interesting developments I'd like to share with you. First and foremost, the former Rhodesian Security Forces no longer exist. They've been replaced by the ZNA[566], which is currently totally dysfunctional.

"You may have heard that the RLI was officially disbanded on 31st October 1980. However, the unit had been ineffective for months before that, having lost most of its key personnel, with very few retained by the new ZNA. There was no transfer of administrative expertise or systems, and no attempts were made to preserve historical records from RLI's headquarters or from its three commandos. So, I'm pretty confident that any record of you going AWOL[567] would have been lost. Even if those records still exist, it's highly unlikely the new ZNA command structure would be interested in, or capable of, following up on AWOL allegations involving former white servicemen.

"Secondly, although the new government has only been in power for just under a year, corruption is already rife at every level. It seems that anyone with a bit of power, and a willingness to bend the rules, is doing so if the price is right.

"Thirdly, Zimbabwe and Mozambique are now close allies, cooperating on everything. Even the border post at Vila Salazar has re-opened."

Gary paused before continuing, "When we last spoke in July 1979, you mentioned there might be an opportunity for us to resume our earlier business dealings. Well, aside from what I've already told you, there have been some interesting developments regarding wildlife protection that Jeremy and I would like to discuss with you. I was hoping to persuade you to drive up to Fort Victoria[568] so the three of us can talk and see what might be possible."

---

[566] Zimbabwe National Army.
[567] Absence Without Leave.
[568] Fort Victoria was renamed Masvingo in 1982.

Johannes was silent for a few seconds before replying, "You've certainly shared some things I wasn't aware of. Like you, I'd love to bring our business venture out of mothballs, but I'm not sure now is the right time. Give me a week to think about it, and I'll call you. How does that sound?"

"Sounds great," replied Gary. "I look forward to hearing from you when you're ready."

With that, the men hung up.

Over the next week, Johannes conducted his own due diligence to assess whether returning to Zimbabwe would be wise and if there was any realistic prospect of resurrecting the poaching business he had established in August 1977. He quickly confirmed Gary's claims about the RLI being disbanded, noting that limited efforts had been made to preserve its historical records.

Johannes also verified that Zimbabwe was in a state of considerable disarray, with significant uncertainty about its future. A substantial number of skilled white professionals had already left or were leaving the country, creating a vacuum filled by individuals with limited experience, many of whom were unqualified or underqualified for their roles. Consequently, the government was struggling to maintain the financial, judicial, business, infrastructure, and administrative systems it had inherited. Corruption was on the rise, and law enforcement was in decline.

On a positive note, the new government was enjoying a political honeymoon. Armed conflict between the former warring parties had ceased, resulting in general peace. This tranquillity had allowed the tourism sector to recover. Zimbabwe had been accepted back into the international community and had normalised relations with all its African neighbours except South Africa. Even there, despite officially severing diplomatic ties, economic necessity kept the relationship between the two countries at some level of normalcy.

Johannes' latest assessment indicated that the country's instability, coupled with the weakening of its systems and controls, presented opportunities for shrewd and ruthless entrepreneurs to make quick profits. While the risks were significant, the potential rewards outweighed them. Compared to his work in South Africa, where the risks far exceeded the rewards, Zimbabwe seemed to offer more opportunities with less to lose. The only substantial risk was facing challenging questions at the Beitbridge border crossing. However, Johannes felt confident that such scrutiny was unlikely and that, even if it arose, his guile and cunning would enable him to navigate it and return to South Africa if necessary.

As a result, he phoned Gary and arranged to meet him and Jeremy on Sunday, 7th June 1981, at 1:00 pm in the bar at the Great Zimbabwe Hotel, just outside Fort Victoria. This was the same venue where they had met back in September 1977, after their first successful poaching sortie.

*****

The distance between Pretoria and Fort Victoria was about 780 kilometres, taking at least ten hours — potentially longer if there were delays at the Beitbridge border crossing. Johannes wanted to minimise risks at Beitbridge and had been advised that the best time to cross into Zimbabwe was on a Saturday or Sunday afternoon. Accordingly, he planned to reach Beitbridge by 3:00 pm on Saturday, 6th June. If everything went smoothly, he would be in Zimbabwe by about 4:00 pm. He intended to stay at a hotel on the Zimbabwean side of Beitbridge that night and then drive to Fort Victoria on Sunday.

He left Pretoria at 9:00 am on Saturday morning. The trip to Beitbridge was uneventful, and he arrived at the South African side of the border crossing by 2:00 pm. The immigration post was quiet, and the relevant officials appeared bored and tired, eager to get home to watch the televised broadcast of the Currie Cup rugby match between Northern Transvaal and the Orange Free State, which was being played at Loftus Versfeld stadium in Pretoria.

Johannes completed the necessary documentation and answered the pro forma questions posed by the customs official. His passport was stamped, and he was advised to return to his vehicle and proceed to enter Zimbabwe by driving across the Alfred Beit Bridge[569].

He drove the short distance to the bridge and crossed without incident. Halfway across, a sign informed him that he was now entering Zimbabwe. He knew the Zimbabwean immigration post was less than a kilometre away and hoped things on the Zimbabwean side would go as smoothly as they had on the South African side.

He needn't have worried. Once again, the immigration officials were disinterested, impolite, and officious. He particularly noted that all the officials were now black, which had not been the case when he left Rhodesia at the end of September 1978.

Johannes had been advised that to ensure a hassle-free entry into the country, it was worthwhile placing a ZAR20[570] note in one's passport before handing it over to the immigration officials for scrutiny. Accordingly, he had done so. As the immigration official opened his passport, the official discreetly slipped the ZAR20 note into his trouser pocket, then gave Johannes an imperceptible nod and advised him to proceed.

Johannes nodded and made his way to his car. While his breathing had been calm and controlled during the previous hour, he nonetheless heaved a sigh of relief once he unlocked his car and started the engine.

He drove to the small town of Beitbridge, a couple of kilometres north of the Zimbabwean immigration post. Upon arrival, he found the hotel where he had made a reservation and checked in for the night.

He awoke early on Sunday morning. It was another 310 kilometres to the Great Zimbabwe Hotel, just outside Fort Victoria, and he estimated the trip would take at least three and a half hours. Not wanting to be

---

[569] The Alfred Beit Road Bridge is named after Alfred Beit, founder of the De Beers Diamond Mining Company and business associate of Cecil Rhodes. The original bridge was constructed in 1929 at a cost of $600,000.
[570] 20 South African Rand (ZAR). At the time this was worth about US$22.50.

late for his 1:00 pm meeting with Gary and Jeremy, he showered, ate breakfast, and was on the road by 9:00 am.

The day was cool and a little overcast, making for a pleasant drive. With little traffic on the road, he made good time, reaching the hotel just before 12:30 pm. He parked his car and made his way to the bar.

Gary and Jeremy were not yet there. Knowing they would be discussing sensitive matters, he decided it would be better to find a table in the pretty garden area rather than remain in the bar. The day had warmed up nicely, and the sky was now cloudless. He was fortunate to find a table in the garden, shaded by a large umbrella and overlooking the well-maintained swimming pool.

"This will be perfect," he thought, sitting down and surveying his pleasant surroundings. As he did so, he noticed Gary and Jeremy had just entered the bar and were looking around for him. He gave a high-pitched dog whistle to attract their attention. The two men looked into the garden and beamed when they recognised him. He waved them over and stood to greet them. The three men shook hands and then sat down at the table.

Almost immediately, a waiter appeared to take their orders, handing each of them a copy of the drinks and lunch menus. All three men ordered a beer. Johannes chose steak, chips, and salad, while Gary and Jeremy both ordered curry and rice. A short time later, the waiter returned with their drinks and informed them that their meals would be ready in about ten minutes. They thanked the waiter and then got down to business.

Johannes opened the discussion. "Well, gents, as I'm here, I'm obviously interested in learning more about your thoughts. There is, however, no need to go over old ground. I've done my own due diligence and can confirm everything you told me over the phone. Fortunately, I had no issues at Beitbridge, so I'm comfortable that I'm not on any kind of wanted persons list with the Zimbabwean customs officials.

Michael Chalk

"I've also confirmed that politically and militarily, the country appears quite settled at the moment, although tribal differences between the Ndebele and Shona remain fragile and could easily flare up again. I know that corruption is on the rise — in fact, I had to pay a ZAR20 bribe at Beitbridge to ensure a hassle-free entry. I've read many reports in the South African press about the significant loss of expertise from the country and how these losses are likely to create considerable difficulties for the government in maintaining essential infrastructure and providing vital services. I also understand that the new government has been internationally recognised and that both the West and the East are trying to woo Mugabe to align with them. Additionally, the end of armed hostilities has led to a resurgence in tourism.

"But I haven't yet formed a clear view on how all these factors will impact a possible resumption of our business activities. So, I guess that's what we're here to discuss today."

At this point, the waiter arrived with their meals, and their discussions paused while he placed the meals on the table before leaving.

Over the next two hours, the three men discussed in detail the pros and cons of possibly resuming their poaching activities.

At the end of these discussions, Johannes said, "Well, gents, let me see if I can summarise what we have agreed on:

"**One**. We all agree that the poaching model we established in 1977 was excellent, and if we're going back into business, we need to replicate that model as closely as possible.

"**Two**. We all agree that international demand and prices for ivory and rhino horn are still strong. If anything, demand and prices are stronger than they were back in 1978 when we did our last cull.

"**Three**. There are still plenty of elephants ripe for poaching in the south-eastern part of the country. Their numbers and movements have not been affected by the recent political changes in Zimbabwe.

"**Four**. You blokes have identified a new potential target for poaching. This is a pilot rhino conservancy that is supposedly being established on a ranch near Chiredzi. Your[571] intel suggests that this conservancy has been created in response to a significant increase in rhino poaching in the Zambezi Valley. You've been informed that the Zimbabwean government is working to establish a rhino capture, relocation, and breeding programme, under which rhinos in the Zambezi Valley will be darted, captured, and relocated to a network of protected conservancies across Zimbabwe."

"**Five**. Now that none of us are serving with the ZNA, we can no longer use the army as a source for the recruitment of spotters. Thus, we need to find an alternative source. In this respect, you both have good networks within the Department of National Parks[572], especially in the province of Victoria. Pay and conditions in the Department of National Parks are still atrocious, meaning park rangers could be susceptible to bribery. In fact, you've already identified a few senior park rangers whom you reckon you could turn.

"**Six**. You are both willing to continue as shooters. Now that I'm no longer tied to the army, I will also become a shooter. I just need to purchase a high-calibre hunting rifle.

"**Seven**. The port of Beira[573] in Mozambique continues to be the easiest way to get ivory and rhino horn to the international markets in Asia.

"**Eight**. Because none of us have the relevant contacts in Mozambique to facilitate the transport of ivory and rhino horn from Beira to Hong Kong and China, we will, in the short term, continue to work with Santiago de Costa.

"**Nine**. As Zimbabwe and Mozambique are now friendly neighbours, this will make it much easier for Zimbabweans, which includes us, to

---

[571] Intelligence information (often military in nature).

[572] The full name is the Department of National Parks and Wildlife Management.

[573] Beira is on the east coast of Mozambique and is the capital and largest city in the Mozambican province of Sofala.

travel in and out of Mozambique and do business there, and vice versa.

"**Ten**. Government officials in Mozambique have been incompetent and as corrupt as hell for ages. The same thing is beginning to happen here in Zimbabwe. Therefore, we will set ourselves a one-year goal to establish our own network of corrupt officials in both countries to facilitate the transport of ivory and rhino horn to Hong Kong and China. As soon as these networks are in place, we will remove de Costa from the business entirely, thereby significantly reducing our expenses.

"**Eleven**. When we move to cut de Costa out of the picture, I will take steps to have him eliminated permanently. This will prevent any possible hostile reactions by him.

"**Twelve**. Assuming everything goes according to plan, we will aim to carry out our first poaching venture in the new Zimbabwe in August.

"**Thirteen**. For long-distance communications, we will use the phone, making sure we use the code words we've agreed on. This will also apply to my communications with de Costa. However, once we go operational, we will only use the VHF two-way radios that you and de Costa already have. I've acquired a similar radio for myself and will add it to the network.

"**Fourteen**. Financials. Over the next month, I will rework the existing financial model. When I return to Zimbabwe, we can go over the numbers and ensure everyone is in agreement. As a minimum, you will receive exactly what you were being paid back in 1978. However, subject to what I am able to renegotiate with de Costa, your return will increase, especially if rhinos are to be targeted.

"Between now and when I return, the major action points that I will complete are:

- I will return to South Africa and make arrangements to tidy up my affairs there. I will aim to be back in Zimbabwe by the end of July at the latest. Initially, I intend to be back in the country for at least two years.

- I will communicate with de Costa to confirm ongoing arrangements with him.
- Upon my return, I will smuggle into the country a high-calibre hunting rifle and the Banish silencer you have recommended."

He then looked at Gary and Jeremy and said, "Your tasks are:

- You will approach the spotters you have identified and get them on board. We will pay them the same retention fee that we were paying the previous spotters—i.e. Zim$200[574] per month. In addition, if any of the animals spotted are actually shot, the spotter in question will receive an additional fee of Zim$400 per animal.
- You must ensure that any spotters we take on board understand the serious consequences if they do not keep these arrangements absolutely confidential. In this respect, I will send you some photos of what happened to the last spotter who broke this confidence. Make sure you show these photos to the new spotters. Hopefully, the pictures will help them understand what will happen to them if they mess up.
- You will verify what is going on at the ranch near Chiredzi, particularly confirming when rhinos will be relocated from the Zambezi Valley to the ranch.
- We will initially continue to focus on elephants. However, if there is some low-hanging fruit at the ranch in Chiredzi in terms of rhinos, we can consider that as well.
- You will source a suitable property for me to rent in Fort Victoria, initially for six months."

Johannes concluded by saying, "I think that just about covers everything. Is there anything I have left out or got wrong?"

---

[574] From the beginning of 1981 the value of the Zimbabwean dollar started to depreciate against the US dollar. By August 1981, Zim$1.00 was worth about US$1.10. This was from its high at independence in April 1980 when Zim$1.00 was worth about US$1.50

Gary and Jeremy exchanged amazed glances, stunned that Johannes had so accurately summarised their two-hour discussion without taking any notes.

"You seem to have covered everything," Gary said. "Well done."

"Great," Johannes replied. "Let's make a toast to the resurrection of our venture."

The three men stood and raised their glasses. "To our future success," Johannes said.

"Cheers," they replied in unison, shaking hands and clapping each other on the shoulder.

Shortly after, Gary and Jeremy departed for Fort Victoria, while Johannes went to reception to book a hotel room for the night.

That night, he slept soundly, eagerly anticipating his return to the country and confident that his new partnership would be both enjoyable and profitable.

The next day, he headed back to South Africa.

Chapter 47 – The decision to resume poaching activities

Johannes returned to Pretoria on Tuesday, 9th June, after an uneventful journey from Fort Victoria[575]. Eager to resume his poaching activities with Gary, Jeremy, and Santiago, he felt more motivated than ever. With only a few loose ends to tie up in his South African underworld dealings, he could now focus fully on the tasks assigned to him to help restart their poaching venture.

One of his first priorities was to arrange for copies of the photographs showing Fritz Viljoen's injuries to be sent to Gary and Jeremy. To do this, he called in a favour from a business associate named Caleb. Caleb ran an illicit pornography film production company in Pretoria. Given the strict indecency laws in South Africa at that time, Caleb had paid hefty bribes to relevant police officers at SAP's[576] headquarters in Pretoria to ensure his business was left alone. However, a particular senior SAP officer had accepted bribes from Caleb but then ordered raids on two of his film shooting locations. As a result of the raids, two cameramen and a male and female porn star were arrested and charged under South Africa's Indecency Laws.

Caleb had enlisted Johannes' help in educating the police officer about the foolishness of his actions. Johannes executed this assignment swiftly and effectively. He brutally assaulted the police officer, leaving him permanently blind in one eye, with a severe limp in his left leg

---

[575] Fort Victoria was renamed Masvingo in 1982.
[576] South African Police.

after his kneecap was broken with an iron bar, and permanently impotent after repeated kicks to his genitalia. This incident had occurred nine months ago, and since then, the police had left Caleb's film business alone.

Within a week, Johannes received six copies of the photographs from Caleb, who did not ask any questions about their content. Johannes immediately mailed four copies to Gary, placing each set in differently sized and coloured envelopes, each of which had been hand-addressed by different individuals.

Johannes then focused on renegotiating his business arrangements with Santiago de Costa. Before he could do this, he needed to verify the current black-market prices for ivory and rhino horn. Using his underworld contacts in South Africa, he quickly discovered that the CITES[577] ban on the sale of ivory and rhino horn had proven ineffective in reducing poaching in southern Africa, which was continuing unabated. Moreover, demand and prices for African ivory remained strong. His research indicated that the black-market price for ivory had increased from US$1,500 to US$1,700 per kilogram. Based on their previous business model of selling poached African ivory for at least 50% of its estimated black-market price, Johannes decided to raise their selling price from US$750 per kilogram to US$850 per kilogram.

As for rhino horn, demand and prices had skyrocketed due to the strong belief in some Asian markets in its significant supposed medicinal powers. Additionally, possession of even a small piece of rhino horn in these markets symbolised one's personal wealth and status. On the supply side, illegal poaching had severely depleted many rhino populations, creating a reduced supply and driving prices even higher. These demand and supply factors meant that the black-market price for rhino horn had reached a staggering US$20,000 per kilogram.

---

[577] Convention on International Trade in Endangered Species of Wild Fauna and Flora. It is a multilateral treaty designed to protect endangered plants and animals. It came into force on 1st July 1975.

Accordingly, Johannes believed they could ask for around US$10,000 per kilogram if they included rhino horn in their operations.

However, the average weight of the front and rear horns of a black rhino was four and a half kilograms, considerably lower than the average weight of 50 kilograms for a pair of African elephant tusks. Therefore, in a financial sense, the economic value of a rhino to Johannes was about the same as that of an elephant. However, rhinos had an advantage, as their horns were considerably smaller and lighter than elephant tusks, making them easier to transport and conceal.

Armed with this new information, Johannes called Santiago in the Mozambican border town of Malvernia[578] on 28th June. He surprisingly reached him on the first attempt.

"*Olá*[579]," said Santiago. Johannes immediately recognised Santiago's strong Portuguese accent.

"Hello, Santiago," Johannes replied. "It's Johannes du Toit speaking."

"Hello, Johannes," Santiago responded. "It's good to hear from you again. I hope you are calling to tell me that you have fully recovered from your heart attack and are now well enough to resume our business dealings."

For a moment, Johannes thought Santiago was being facetious about his heart attack. He wondered if Santiago had somehow discovered that his claim of suffering a heart attack was a lie. But he instantly dismissed this doubt, knowing that his fabricated story had been quite plausible.

Johannes replied, "Yes, I'm pleased to say that I am fully recovered. Now that I am well again, I would like to discuss the resumption of our business venture."

"That's good news," Santiago responded.

---

[578] The town's name was changed to Chicualacuala in 1975 shortly after Mozambique's independence from Portugal.
[579] *Olá* is the Portuguese word for hello.

Johannes proceeded to explain that he aimed to resume business operations by the end of August 1981 and wanted to know if Santiago was still interested in being involved and taking responsibility for transporting the goods from the Mozambique-Zimbabwe border to the port city of Beira[580], as well as organising their shipment to Asia.

Santiago confirmed his willingness and ability to participate.

Johannes went on to explain that the business model would be similar to before, with the possible addition of rhino horn and a change in the profit share percentages to reflect the reduced risks to Santiago now that Zimbabwe and Mozambique had normalised their diplomatic relations.

At the mention of a change to the profit share percentages, Santiago became slightly hostile. "So, what are you suggesting?" he demanded.

Johannes replied cautiously, "I think the percentage split should change from 55/45 to 65/35. But before you react, you should know that our selling price for ivory will increase from US$750 to US$850 per kilogram. Additionally, if rhino horn is added, we estimate a selling price of around US$10,000 per kilogram, compared to the US$850 per kilogram for ivory."

Johannes deliberately avoided mentioning the lower average weight of rhino horns compared to elephant tusks.

There was a pause on the other end of the line. Johannes did not wish to break the silence, so he waited for Santiago to respond. Finally, Santiago spoke. "The price you're suggesting for rhino is certainly appealing. However, you haven't mentioned how easy it will be to target rhinos or the average weight of their horns. And while the risk to me in Mozambique might be a bit lower, I don't think that the small reduction justifies a 10% cut in my profit share. Remember, my risk was always more about me breaking Mozambique's laws relating to ivory and rhino horn trade rather than the dangers inherent in the

---

[580] Beira is on the east coast of Mozambique and is the capital and largest city in the Mozambican province of Sofala.

Rhodesian Bush War. As I see it, the end of the Bush War reduces your risk, not mine."

"Bugger," thought Johannes. He is no fool. He was tempted to start horse trading with Santiago but then thought better of it. Instead, he countered by saying that going forward, he would be one of the shooters but wouldn't expect to receive the shooter's fee or their monthly retention fee, in addition to his profit share. He also mentioned that spotters would now need to be recruited from the Department of National Parks[581] instead of from the Rhodesian Army, which would require a slight increase in their monthly retainers, and this would be borne solely by Johannes.

Santiago accepted these comments and, as a compromise, proposed a 60/40 percentage split.

After a few seconds of silence, Johannes agreed to Santiago's counteroffer. His acceptance was made slightly easier by his knowledge that his plan was to eliminate Santiago from the business entirely within a year.

During the phone call, the two men reached a verbal agreement on all other relevant matters. Johannes concluded the conversation by stating that he would contact Santiago sometime within the next two months once he had finalised the plans for their next poaching sortie.

*****

After their meeting with Johannes at the Great Zimbabwe Hotel on Sunday, 7th June, Gary and Jeremy were also keen to progress the tasks assigned to them. Their financial situations required that they resume poaching activities by the end of August at the latest.

They began by verifying the intelligence they'd received about a rhino conservancy being established on a ranch near Chiredzi. Their contact, Moses, was a builder who had recently worked on a project at

---

[581] The full name is the Department of National Parks and Wildlife Management.

Mhuka[582] Ranch. Gary had met him a few months earlier while visiting Bulawayo to help his parents pack up the family home before their emigration to South Africa. During his stay at the Churchill Arms Hotel in Bulawayo, Gary happened to meet Moses in the hotel bar.

During their conversation, Gary learned that Moses, a young Cape Malay man, was employed by a building company in Bulawayo. For the past four months, Moses had supervised the construction of a luxury lodge on a ranch near Chiredzi. His company was celebrating the lodge's completion with a lunch for the project team. Moses happened to mention to Gary that his company was likely to take on further work at the ranch, including building additional luxury lodges and structures related to a rhino conservancy project.

Gary took immediate interest at the mention of a rhino conservancy. He asked for details, but Moses only knew that he had overheard a conversation between the ranch owner, a man called Duncan, and the building company's owner about accommodation for anti-poaching staff and the construction of rhino enclosures. The information piqued Gary's interest, and he mentally noted the details in case they might be useful later.

Subsequently, Gary used Jeremy's contacts inside the Department of National Parks to discover that the Department, along with local environmentalists and an international organisation, was actively working to protect Zimbabwe's rhinos, which faced increasing threats from poaching. They were now implementing a programme to capture, relocate, and breed rhinos. This initiative involved darting rhinos in areas vulnerable to poaching, and relocating them to a protected network of rhino conservancies. The first pilot conservancy was indeed being established at Mhuka Ranch, near Chiredzi.

Gary and Jeremy also needed to finalise arrangements with the potential spotters they'd identified. Two were senior rangers at

---

[582] A local word meaning animals or wildlife.

Gonarezhou[583] National Park, one was at Chimanimani National Park, and another was at Rhodes Matopos National Park.

They prioritised discussions with the two rangers at Gonarezhou to ascertain their interest in becoming spotters, and re-establishing contact with Moses in Bulawayo to get a better understanding on the rhino conservancy which was being established in Chiredzi.

Once again, using their contacts at the Department of National Parks, they discovered that Gonarezhou National Park lacked a reliable telephone system. As a result, communicating with potential spotters would require establishing a radio network from scratch. This challenge left them with two options — either abandon Gonarezhou as a source for recruiting spotters or set up a mini base camp near Gonarezhou and do the spotting themselves.

Deciding to revisit the issue with Johannes later, they instead focused on contacting Moses in Bulawayo to confirm the information about the rhino conservancy. Gary called the building company where Moses worked, requesting to speak with him. The receptionist informed him that Moses was working near Chiredzi and was unavailable. Gary explained he needed to speak with Moses about an urgent family matter and asked for his contact details. After a lengthy wait, the receptionist provided a number for Moses's lodgings in Chiredzi, explaining he could be reached there after hours.

After several unsuccessful attempts, Gary finally reached Moses by phone on the evening of Monday, 22nd June. He reminded Moses of their earlier meeting at the Churchill Arms Hotel in Bulawayo, which helped Moses remember him. Gary then explained that his father, a ranch owner near Bulawayo, was interested in building luxury lodges on the property and asked if Moses's company might be interested in overseeing their construction.

Moses expressed interest but said he wouldn't be available for another fortnight, as he was still working at the ranch near Chiredzi. Gary,

---

[583] Gonarezhou is a Shona word meaning *place of elephants*.

feigning surprise, stated he would be in Chiredzi in the next few days and suggested they meet later in the week while he was there. Hoping to secure new business, Moses agreed to meet Gary on Thursday, 25th June, at 6:00 pm at the Nesbitt Arms Hotel restaurant in Chiredzi.

That Thursday, Gary and Jeremy drove to Chiredzi and checked into a shared room at the Nesbitt Arms Hotel. They met Moses in the restaurant as planned. Gary explained that he and Jeremy were the sons of a cattle ranch owner and were exploring the idea of building six high-end luxury lodges on their father's ranch outside Bulawayo. They had received preliminary approval from the Matopos District Council and planned to market the lodges to high-value tourists.

Moses believed their story and eagerly discussed how his company could assist with the design and construction. He had even brought with him design drawings for the Chiredzi lodge project and showed them to Gary and Jeremy. During the conversation, Gary casually inquired about the additional work his company was doing at the Chiredzi ranch. Keen to impress, Moses shared more details about the rhino conservancy, and stated that the first two rhinos were expected to arrive at the ranch by mid-August. Before their arrival, two bomas and a holding pen needed to be constructed, work that the ranch owner himself would undertake. However, Moses's company had now been asked to prioritise building a house for an anti-poaching manager and barracks for up to twelve rangers, and that this work needed to be completed ahead of the completion of the remaining two luxury lodges.

Moses revealed the ranch's name as Mhuka Ranch.

After dinner, Gary and Jeremy thanked Moses for his time, stating they would share his ideas with their father and contact him again before the end of September. Moses then returned to his lodgings in Chiredzi, while Gary and Jeremy retired for the night.

The next morning, they drove back to Fort Victoria, eager to share the intriguing information gathered from Moses with Johannes. Additionally, they needed to inform Johannes about the difficulties they had identified in communicating with spotters at Gonarezhou National Park.

They tried to phone Johannes on Saturday night, but the line was dead. Attempts on Sunday were also unsuccessful, and they finally reached him on Monday, 29th June.

Gary and Jeremy updated Johannes on their discussions with Moses and the communication challenges they had identified at Gonarezhou National Park. In turn, Johannes briefed them on his discussions with Santiago.

Once all the information had been shared, Johannes summarised the situation saying, "The difficulties you've identified regarding communication with spotters in the Gonarezhou area are very real. Without effective comms[584], any planned operation will fail. I will need to get technical advice on whether these communication issues can be overcome. If radio communications cannot be established, your idea of setting up a mini base inside the national park has merit. The area is too rich in elephants and rhinos for us to ignore. However, it will take time to either solve the communication issue or establish a mini base. Therefore, let's rule out the Gonarezhou area as a potential target for the next couple of months.

"For now, our focus will therefore be on Mhuka Ranch. The intel you've gained from Moses is useful, but it doesn't sound like it will be easy to get ongoing updates from him. He will become suspicious if we start focusing on the rhino conservancy instead of the construction of the lodges.

"Moses mentioned that the first two rhinos are due to arrive at the ranch by mid-August, and the conservancy is currently unprotected. It is likely to remain that way until the anti-poaching manager arrives, his house is completed, accommodation for the rangers is constructed, and they are recruited. That will all take time. I think it's fair to assume that by the time the first two rhinos arrive, only the anti-poaching

---

584 Communications.

manager will be on site. This means that the best time to strike will be shortly after the animals arrive. The longer we wait, the more likely it is that security will have been beefed up.

"I still need three or four weeks to finalise my affairs here in South Africa, after which I can travel to Fort Victoria. The least risky time for me to cross the border at Beitbridge is on a Sunday. Let's assume I will cross on Sunday, 26th July, which means I will arrive in Fort Victoria on Monday, 27th July. You'll need to secure rental accommodation for me from then. Is that achievable?"

"Yes," replied Gary.

"Good," said Johannes. "We will need at least two to three weeks to sort things out in Fort Victoria. I think we should aim to have eyes on the ranch by the middle of August. Accordingly, I'd like you to start planning the setup of a covert operation over the ranch and establish an OP[585] by Thursday, 20th August. Is that achievable?"

"Yes," replied Gary.

"Good," Johannes continued. "Let's schedule a final phone hook-up on Sunday, 19th July, which is a week before I'm due to arrive in Fort Victoria. Is that okay?"

"Yes," replied Gary and Jeremy.

"Great," said Johannes. "We have a lot to accomplish over the next three weeks. Good luck. We'll speak again on 19th July."

"Roger that," said Gary and Jeremy before hanging up.

---

[585] Observation Post.

Chapter 48 – Groundwork for Operation Chipembere

Johannes used his remaining weeks in Pretoria to purchase a vehicle to take back to Zimbabwe and to acquire a high-calibre hunting rifle.

He had ruled out returning to Zimbabwe in his S-class Mercedes Benz, which he had bought in 1978. The car was too flashy and would make him stand out — exactly what he wanted to avoid. Furthermore, he needed a vehicle suitable for rougher roads, making a 4WD[586] a more practical choice.

In early July, he sold the Mercedes Benz and bought a second-hand Toyota Land Cruiser FJ55 with only 20,000 kilometres on the clock. Having purchased the vehicle, he took it to a business associate skilled in modifying stolen cars for resale and requested the construction of a concealed compartment in the rear luggage area.

The modifications were expertly done by adding a false back to the folding section of the rear seats. This hidden compartment was large enough to store rifles, rhino horns, and smaller tusks. Crucially, it was virtually undetectable — discovery would require a very detailed and intentional inspection of the back seat and luggage areas.

Johannes' last task before leaving South Africa was to purchase a high-calibre hunting rifle. Once again, he sought advice from his criminal underworld contacts. In the end, he opted for a 0.458 Lott hunting

---

[586] Four-wheel drive.

rifle, fitted with an Aimpoint Red Dot riflescope and a Banish silencer. He also purchased 1,000 rounds of 0.458 Hornady DGS [587] ammunition.

*****

Following their phone hook-up with Johannes, Gary and Jeremy purchased two 1:500 maps of the Mhuka[588] Ranch area. Using these maps, they were able to identify the ranch's perimeter fences, airstrip, the main homestead, the Ingwe[589] Dam, cattle dips, farm roads, and tracks.

The map had been published and printed by the Rhodesian Surveyor-General in 1975. Consequently, it did not show any buildings constructed since then, meaning none of the recent improvements mentioned by Moses were included. However, based on their knowledge of topography, they made educated guesses as to where the rhino bomas, holding pen, house, and barrack-style accommodation for the rangers were likely to be located.

Assuming their guesses were correct, they identified locations that might be suitable for an OP[590].

Given the importance of this information, they decided it was best to return to Mhuka Ranch for a clandestine on-site recce. They were unsure when construction of the bomas and holding pen would begin, so they wanted to delay the recce as long as possible. However, they also wanted to complete it before their follow-up phone call with Johannes on Sunday, 19th July. Accordingly, they scheduled the recce for Thursday, 16th July.

---

[587] DGS is an acronym for Dangerous Game Series. It is a trademark which has been registered by Hornady Manufacturing Company in America. The trademark was applied to ammunition specially designed by Hornady for big game hunting.
[588] A local word meaning animals or wildlife.
[589] Ingwe is a local African word meaning leopard.
[590] Observation Post.

On that Thursday, Gary and Jeremy made the three-and-a-half-hour drive from Fort Victoria to Chiredzi. They left Fort Victoria shortly after 6:30 am and arrived at Chiredzi by 10:00 am.

Using the maps, they determined the best approach to the ranch without being seen. They bypassed the town of Chiredzi and continued on the A10 until they crossed the bridge over the Chiredzi River. About ten kilometres after the bridge, they turned right onto a dirt road marked on the map. Just after this turn, they made a left and drove towards an abandoned quarry, also shown on the map. They parked their vehicle under some shady trees and stepped out.

From the quarry, it was about a 1,500-metre walk in a westerly direction through the bush to reach the main homestead. About 600 metres before the fenced area of the homestead, there was a small kopje[591], which they believed would give them a good view of the homestead.

They climbed to the top of the kopje and found a concealed location from where they could survey the area using the high-powered binoculars they had brought with them. From this vantage point, they easily identified the main homestead, various outbuildings, sheds, and the main water storage tank. Further west, outside the fenced area of the homestead, they spotted some small buildings, which they assumed were part of the workers' compound.

Approximately one kilometre south of their position, they saw a group of workers busy erecting what appeared to be an enclosure. The site included a couple of tractors, trucks, and a road grader, leading them to assume this was the location of the bomas and holding pen.

To the east, and heading about 160° south, there was a dirt road which led to Ingwe Dam.

---

[591] The word kopje is derived from the Afrikaans word koppie, which means a small hill.

They remained at their position for about half an hour. Seeing no movement at the main homestead, they decided to move closer to the construction site to get a better idea of the activity occurring there.

As they needed to remain concealed, it took them about 40 minutes to cover the kilometre-long distance. Using the detection-avoidance techniques they had learned in the RLI[592], they then closed in to within 200 metres of the construction area. From there, they had a clear view of the two bomas under construction. The area had been cleared, and four stacks of eight-foot-high, creosoted gum poles lay on the ground. A team of workers was digging trenches into which these poles would be concreted to form the bomas' perimeter walls.

Adjacent to the bomas was a marked-off area roughly the size of a cricket oval. In this space, another team was erecting a perimeter fence using steel poles and heavy-gauge, six-foot-high wire fencing, which appeared to be designed for electrification.

Beyond this, farm workers were inspecting and repairing standard farm-grade fencing around a large grazing paddock.

"Well, there's no doubt that's where the rhinos will be offloaded," said Gary. "And it doesn't look like delivery is far off — probably about a month away. That lines up with the intel[593] we got from Moses."

"I agree," replied Jeremy. "I reckon the rhinos will be kept in the bomas for a few days, then moved into that electrified area. After that, they'll probably be released into the larger paddock before gaining access to the wider conservancy."

"That makes sense," Gary said, pausing thoughtfully. "While we're here, let's also take a closer look at the sites we thought might work as observation posts."

He pulled back the frayed and faded camouflage denim material covering his watch — a detection prevention technique commonly

---

[592] Rhodesian Light Infantry. This was an infantry regiment and was one of the country's main counter-insurgency units during the Rhodesian Bush War.
[593] Intelligence information (often military in nature).

used by the Rhodesian Security Forces during the Bush War to prevent the watch face from glistening in the sun. Out of habit, Gary still used the covering routinely.

"It's just after noon," Gary said. "We need to be off the ranch by about 3:00 pm. It's going to take us at least an hour to get back to the car, so that gives us a couple of hours to finalise our selection of a suitable site for the OP."

He pointed to a hilly, tree-covered area about 300 metres south of the bomas. "That's one of the sites we identified on the map. It looks ideal," he said. "There are no huts nearby and no footpaths either, so I think we can assume it's deserted. Once we climb the hill, we should have a good line of sight to the bomas, the electrified fence area, and the homestead beyond. We won't be able to see Ingwe Dam, but we'll have a clear view of the road leading to it. That way, we can spot any traffic moving between the homestead and the dam."

"Yep, I agree," said Jeremy. "Let's check it out. It's close by."

They moved cautiously towards the proposed OP. As expected, there was no sign of foot traffic leading to or on the chosen hill. They climbed it and found a spot ideal for the look-out point. It offered a clear field of vision for everything they needed to observe, while the trees provided excellent concealment. Close to the look-out point, there was also some shaded dead ground[594] that would serve as the perfect lay-up position.

"This looks ideal," said Gary. "Mission accomplished, I'd say. I think we can head back to the car now."

He estimated it was around 1:30 pm and reached to pull back the camouflage cover on his watch for confirmation. It was 1:40 pm but to his surprise the cover was missing. The frayed elasticated strap must have finally snapped, causing the camouflage covering to fall off and expose the watch face.

---

[594] Dead ground is ground that cannot be seen from the target that is being observed.

"Good thing," he muttered. "About time I got rid of that damn thing."

They headed back to the car. Since they knew the way, they made quicker progress than when they had arrived. They reached the abandoned quarry just after 3:15 pm and were back in Fort Victoria[595] by 6:30 pm.

Once back in Fort Victoria, Jeremy finalised the arrangements for renting a house for Johannes. Fortunately, there were quite a few properties available, as many whites had already decided to leave the country. Consequently, there was a glut of houses for sale or rent at very reasonable prices.

The favourable market conditions allowed Jeremy to secure a lease on a decent house with a swimming pool in the upmarket suburb of Rhodene at a very reasonable price. The six-month lease commenced on Monday, 27th July, with an option to extend for another six months.

*****

As planned, they had a telephone hook-up with Johannes on Sunday, 19th July. Johannes updated Gary and Jeremy on his progress and confirmed he would return to Fort Victoria on Monday, 27th July.

Gary and Jeremy reported back to Johannes about their recce of the ranch. They confirmed that the bomas and electrified fenced area were under construction, corroborating the intel they had received from Moses regarding the likely mid-August delivery date for the first two rhinos. They also described in detail the location of the OP they had chosen. Jeremy added that he had successfully leased a suitable house in Fort Victoria starting from Monday, 27th July, and provided Johannes with the relevant details.

Johannes congratulated them on their achievements and ended the call by saying, "Well, gents, I look forward to seeing you in Fort Victoria on Monday, 27th July. If something urgent comes up before then, get

---

[595] Fort Victoria was renamed Masvingo in 1982.

on the phone ASAP[596]. However, I think we can assume the raid on the rhino enclosures at Mhuka Ranch will take place towards the end of August.

"I also think we'll call this mission Operation *Chipembere*[597]. I look forward to working with you to bring it to a successful conclusion."

With that, he hung up, and the line went dead.

---

[596] ASAP is the acronym for *As Soon As Possible*.
[597] *Chipembere* is the Shona word for rhino.

Chapter 49 – Preparing for Operation Chipembere

On Sunday, 26th July, Johannes travelled from Pretoria to Beitbridge in his newly acquired Land Cruiser. The vehicle was heavily laden with items he thought might be useful for their upcoming poaching raid at Mhuka[598] Ranch. This included his 0.458 Lott hunting rifle, 1,000 rounds of 0.458 Hornady DGS[599] ammunition, and his remaining stash of US dollar bills — all safely hidden in the concealed compartment behind the rear seats.

Johannes' experience at Beitbridge was much like it had been six weeks earlier. On the South African side, the officials were bored but competent. On the Zimbabwean side, they were bored, rude, corrupt, and incompetent.

To ensure a hassle-free entry, Johannes had again slipped a ZAR20[600] note into his passport before handing it over to the Zimbabwean immigration officials for scrutiny and stamping. The official handling his paperwork deftly pocketed the note. However, this time, instead of simply being waved through, the official asked Johannes the purpose of his visit to Zimbabwe and inquired about the contents of his car.

Anticipating potential issues and, if possible, wanting to avoid a vehicle search, Johannes had prepared a sanitised list of items in his car. Attached to the list was another ZAR20 note. He handed both over to

---

[598] A local word meaning animals or wildlife.
[599] DGS is an acronym for Dangerous Game Series. It is a trademark which has been registered by Hornady Manufacturing Company in America. The trademark was applied to ammunition specially designed by Hornady for big game hunting.
[600] 20 South African Rand (ZAR). At the time this was worth about US$22.50.

the official, who swiftly pocketed the second note before nodding and advising Johannes to proceed.

Johannes mumbled his thanks and headed back to his car. "Bloody corrupt and useless officials," he muttered. "I can't stand them."

Rather than staying at the same unimpressive hotel he had chosen on his last visit to Beitbridge, he opted to overnight at the picturesque Lion and Elephant Motel, 75 kilometres from Beitbridge on the main road to Fort Victoria[601]. The motel, nestled on the banks of the Bubi River[602] amid an oasis of lush, leafy trees, promised a more pleasant stay.

That night, he enjoyed a delicious T-bone steak at the motel's restaurant before having a shower and retiring to bed.

The next morning, he drove the remaining 220 kilometres to Fort Victoria, arriving just before noon. He found his way to the estate agent's office, using the address Jeremy had given him, collected the keys to his house in the upmarket suburb of Rhodene, and made his way to what would be his home for the next six months.

The next three weeks were a hive of activity for Johannes, Gary, and Jeremy.

First, Johannes had to settle into his new house. Fortunately, it came with a fridge and stove, but apart from these, it was unfurnished. Gary and Jeremy provided him with a few camping essentials to meet his immediate needs until he could acquire the necessary furniture and kitchenware.

Johannes also needed to hire a house boy and garden boy[603]. Luckily, there were several capable domestic workers looking for work in

---

[601] Fort Victoria was renamed Masvingo in 1982.
[602] The Bubi River is also known as the Bubye River. It is a tributary of the Limpopo River.
[603] The terms house boy and garden boy were the usual terms used by white employers when referring to domestic workers. These terms continued to be used for many years after Zimbabwe became independent in 1980.

Rhodene, and Johannes quickly found and hired two suitable individuals.

His house boy, Gideon, was a hardworking and reliable fellow who could also handle basic cooking. He and Johannes quickly formed a good working relationship.

The garden boy, Esau, was quiet and reserved. However, he knew how to maintain a swimming pool and was competent enough to keep the garden tidy, clean, and watered. He stayed out of the way and focused on his work, which was exactly what Johannes needed.

Johannes also had to manage his financial needs in Zimbabwe. To meet his immediate cash requirements, he turned to the foreign exchange black market, where he exchanged US$5,000 for ZWD$25,000 without any difficulties. This rate, more than five times the official exchange rate, reflected the growing instability of Zimbabwe's financial markets and the declining value of the local currency.

After securing Zimbabwean dollars, Johannes opened a transaction account with Barclays Bank into which he deposited ZWD$20,000.

It was also important for him to conclude financial arrangements with Gary and Jeremy. He updated them on his discussions with Santiago, confirming that Santiago had agreed to reduce his profit share from 45% to 40%. Consequently, Johannes's profit share had increased from 55% to 60%, a 9% rise. To simplify accounting, Johannes proposed paying Gary and Jeremy 10% of his increased net profit, along with their current shooter's retainer fee of Zim$200 each per month, plus Zim$3,000 per animal poached, and reimbursement for expenses from their recent trips to Chiredzi and Mhuka Ranch.

Additionally, the three of them spent considerable time planning the setup of, and equipment required for, the OP[604] at the ranch.

---

[604] Observation Post.

As far as firearms were concerned, they already had their high-calibre hunting rifles. Gary and Jeremy also had their FN[605] rifles and were able to use their former contacts from the now-defunct RLI[606] to illegally obtain an FN for Johannes. In addition, Gary and Jeremy had accumulated plenty of camping gear during their time in the RLI, which they knew would suffice for their needs at the OP.

After careful consideration, they decided to drive to Mhuka Ranch on Thursday, 20th August, to establish their OP. Mindful of the need to remain concealed, they agreed to set up the OP in the secluded, hilly-treed area that Gary and Jeremy had checked out during their recent reconnaissance of the ranch.

Their plan was to depart from Fort Victoria early on 20th August, drive in convoy to the ranch, and conceal their vehicles in the same abandoned quarry they had used before.

They weren't sure how long they might need to remain at the OP, so they packed enough supplies for a week. If their stay extended beyond that, one of them would need to return to the quarry to collect a vehicle, and then drive to Chiredzi to purchase the extras supplies. That person would then drive back to the quarry, conceal the vehicle, and carry the supplies back to the OP. They believed that this plan would allow them to remain flexible, prepared, and self-sufficient for the duration of their mission.

Since the OP had to be established stealthily, all their provisions and necessities would have to be carried in on foot. The heaviest items were the water supplies for a week, the radios, FNs, hunting rifles, and ammunition. They estimated it would take at least two, possibly three, trips between the quarry and the OP site to carry everything.

Although Gary and Jeremy were experienced in removing tusks from elephants' jaws, they had never removed rhino horns from a rhino's

---

[605] This was a light automatic rifle designed in Belgium and manufactured by FN Herstal. The FN was the standard issue rifle for the Rhodesian Security Forces.
[606] Rhodesian Light Infantry. This was an infantry regiment and was one of the country's main counter-insurgency units during the Rhodesian Bush War.

skull. They debated whether it would be better to remove the horns using a chainsaw, as they had done with the elephants, or to hack them off with a machete. In the end, they opted for the former method, even though they knew this would result in a small amount of horn being left embedded in the skull.

Having decided to go operational on Thursday, 20th August, Johannes called Santiago on Monday, 17th August, to bring him up to speed. On his second attempt, he got through. Santiago was delighted with the swift progress and that the target for this sortie would be rhinos.

He wished Johannes success with the upcoming mission. Johannes informed Santiago that the operation would take place near Chiredzi, well within the 130-kilometre range of their existing VHF two-way radio network. He added that he would contact Santiago to give a sitrep[607] once the operation had been completed.

They also agreed that Johannes would use his vehicle to transport, from Chiredzi to Santiago's house in Malvernia[608], any horns they removed from the rhinos. He was confident there would be no issues crossing the border into Mozambique, as the border post was now fully operational and because the rhino horns could be safely hidden in the secret compartment of his Toyota Landcruiser.

Upon receiving the horns, Santiago would be responsible for taking them to Beira[609] for delivery to his corrupt freight agent for onward shipment to Hong Kong.

Santiago was pleased with these arrangements and said he hoped to see Johannes in Malvernia before the end of the month.

*****

---

[607] Situation Report.

[608] The town's name was changed to Chicualacuala in 1975 shortly after Mozambique's independence from Portugal.

[609] Beira is on the east coast of Mozambique and is the capital and largest city in the Mozambican province of Sofala.

On Thursday, 20th August, Johannes, Gary, and Jeremy drove in convoy from Fort Victoria to the abandoned quarry just outside Chiredzi. Gary and Jeremy led in their vehicle, with Johannes following in his Landcruiser. They had left Fort Victoria at 5:00 am, while it was still dark, and arrived at the quarry at 8:30 am.

After a quick sweep of the area to confirm it was still secure, they began the laborious task of carrying the provisions from their vehicles to the site they had selected for the OP, which was roughly 1,700 metres away in a south-south-westerly direction. It took two return trips to transport the supplies from the quarry to the selected site. To avoid detection, they needed to move slowly and carefully, but by noon they had established the concealed OP, complete with the lay-up position in the dead ground near the look-out point.

From the OP's look-out point, they had an excellent view to the north over the bomas and holding pen, and to the north-north-west onto the homestead. They also had a reasonable view of the dirt road to their east, which ran south towards Ingwe[610] Dam.

Once the OP was set up, they agreed on surveillance rosters and began the tedious task of monitoring the area using high-powered binoculars. Under their rotating schedule, one person would watch for two hours while the other two relaxed at the lay-up position. The roles would rotate every two hours.

They observed considerable activity at the two bomas and noted with satisfaction that each boma now housed a large black rhino. There was also much activity at the adjacent holding pen, which they guessed was being prepared for the rhinos' imminent transfer from the bomas.

Seeing these valuable animals confined in such confined spaces excited the men, as it meant shooting and dehorning them would be relatively simple. This confinement tempted them to consider launching their sortie the next day, Friday, 21st August, but they ultimately decided against it due to the significant human activity around the bomas.

---

[610] Ingwe is a local African word meaning leopard.

Instead, they chose to carry out the raid on Sunday, 23rd August, in the late afternoon. They reckoned that farm workers and external contractors would be less likely to be around on a Sunday, and the late afternoon timing would give them a chance to flee under cover of darkness should unexpected problems arise and force them to abort the mission.

They estimated that, given the rhinos' confinement, they could complete the shooting of both animals and removal of their horns in under 40 minutes. Even if the rhinos were moved to the larger holding pen before Sunday, they expected to be able to finish the operation in about an hour.

They also calculated that they could vacate the OP and return to the quarry in about 90 minutes. From there, Gary and Jeremy would head back to Fort Victoria under cover of darkness, while Johannes would drive to Vila Salazar. He planned to bivouac just outside Vila Salazar overnight and cross into Mozambique on Monday morning, once the border crossing opened.

The poachers' decision to postpone their raid from Friday, 21st August, to Sunday, 23rd August, initially seemed fortuitous.

On Friday, they observed a gang of workers at the holding pen for much of the day, along with considerable activity at the homestead.

At around 3:00 pm, a Toyota Land Cruiser had arrived at the homestead, driven by a young white man with a white woman as his passenger. About 30 minutes later, another vehicle, driven by a different white woman, departed the homestead and headed south along the dirt road towards Ingwe Dam. Following her vehicle and having the same driver and passenger, was the Land Cruiser that had arrived earlier.

Later that evening, the Land Cruiser returned to the homestead at around 7:00 pm, only to leave again at 11:00 pm, once more heading south towards Ingwe Dam.

On Saturday morning, at around 10:30 am, the same young man and woman returned to the homestead in their Land Cruiser. Shortly thereafter, they left in a Land Rover, accompanied by a black man who drove while they rode as passengers. The group headed to the bomas and holding pen, where they spent about an hour before returning to the homestead.

That afternoon, two white men and a woman arrived by car and stayed at the homestead.

Fate was yet to reveal what would happen on Sunday, 23rd August 1981.

Chapter 50 – Planning Operation Chipembere's counteroffensive

Timeline – 22 August

Nick and Rachel woke up late on the Saturday morning and were lying in each other's arms in the luxurious king-size bed at Ukuthula[611] Lodge. Through the large bedroom windows, they had a stunning view northwards, across the expansive decking and onto Ingwe[612] Dam. The sky was an aquamarine blue, cloudless, with just a slight breeze, which was only noticeable when the leaves on the surrounding kopje trees gently quivered as one.

"This is magical," said Rachel. "I wish we could stay here forever. I'm really looking forward to being shown around the ranch by Sipho[613]. What time did we agree to meet him?"

"We said we'd be at the homestead at about 10:00 am. If we hurry, we'll still have time for a quick swim before breakfast on the decking. But we need to leave by 9:45 am," replied Nick.

"That sounds great," Rachel said, jumping out of bed and slipping into her swimsuit. Teasingly, she added, "Last one in the pool has to make coffee!"

Nick smiled. He knew Samson would be making the coffee, but he pulled on his costume and hurried after her anyway.

---

[611] Ukuthula is the Zulu word for calmness or silence.
[612] Ingwe is a local African word meaning leopard.
[613] Sipho is a Ndebele boy's name meaning Gift.

The water in the pool, chilled by the cool night air, sent a shiver down their spines. To warm up, they swam a few lengths before coming together in a loving embrace. Climbing out, they wrapped themselves in their soft pool towels and found a sunny spot on the decking. Moments later, Samson arrived with two cups of freshly brewed coffee and took their breakfast orders. He then disappeared into the kitchen to prepare the cheese, onion, and tomato-filled omelettes they had requested.

They ate breakfast on the decking, basking in the early morning sun, its gentle warmth soothing their shoulders. Both were excited to tour the ranch, especially Rachel, who was eager to see the two black rhinos up close in the bomas.

After breakfast, they returned to their bedroom, showered, dressed, and then drove to the main homestead. After parking, they walked to the guest wing, where Sipho was already waiting. It was just after 10:00 am. He outlined their plans for the day — first, a visit to the bomas, followed by a late morning game drive, and ending with a picnic lunch overlooking Ingwe Dam.

They walked back to the parking area, climbed into Sipho's Land Rover, and drove the short distance to the bomas, arriving at 10:30 am.

The three of them climbed out and approached the bomas. Rachel had her Canon camera slung over her shoulder. The bomas were just as Hamish had described. The outer walls were made of stout, eight-foot-high creosoted gum poles, set in concrete-filled trenches. Each boma had a sturdy access gate, and the two bomas were adjacent, sharing water and feeding troughs. A thatched roof covered one corner of each boma to provide shade for the animals.

As they neared, Rachel heard snorting and the sound of scuffing feet. Between the gum poles, there was a small vertical gap, about ten centimetres wide, through which she could glimpse the distinctive outlines of the two rhinos.

The rhinos were resting in the shaded corners of their respective bomas, opposite the access gates. Sipho allowed them to climb onto the bottom slats of the gates to look over and down into the enclosures.

"If the rhinos move towards the gate, just jump back down," Sipho instructed. "I want to make sure you both stay safe!"

They followed his instructions. Observing the black rhinos up close was thrilling, especially for Rachel. She was struck by the length of their horns, estimating the front ones to be nearly four feet long, and the rear ones about two feet.

Despite their bulk[614], the rhinos moved with surprising agility and, in a curious way, seemed quite gentle. If one had long enough arms, the temptation to scratch the tops of their massive heads would have been irresistible.

Rachel busily snapped close-up shots with her camera. The animals appeared unbothered by their confined space or the proximity of their observers.

Sipho mentioned that he wanted to check the perimeter fence of the adjacent holding pen to ensure everything was in order for the rhinos' relocation on Monday, 24th August. He invited Nick and Rachel to join him, but they declined, too engrossed in watching the Two Ronnies[615]. Sipho told them he'd be gone for about half an hour and reminded them not to enter the bomas under any circumstances. Then he set off to inspect the fence.

As he moved along the perimeter, he noticed a roll of electrical cabling about 20 metres beyond the fence, left behind by the workers who were installing the electrified fencing. While retrieving it, he spotted a piece of camouflaged fabric on the ground and recognised it as the camouflaged watch covering used by Rhodesian Security Forces to help prevent detection in the field.

---

[614] Black rhinos are generally smaller than white rhinos. But a large male black rhino can still weigh over 1,400 kilograms.
[615] The two male black rhinos had been given the name, *the Two Ronnies*, by Mhuka Ranch.

That's odd, Sipho thought. I wouldn't expect to find that out here. His curiosity heightened, and he began scanning the area. His tracking skills quickly told him that several people had recently walked through the area. While the workers' footprints were to be expected, Sipho also identified the distinctive tread of soft boots typically worn by RLI[616] troops on patrol.

Adrenaline surged through him. His senses sharpened. Calmly, he moved into a shaded area to survey the surroundings more carefully.

His first concern was for the safety of Nick, Rachel, and the rhinos. But he didn't want to overreact. His military training urged him to think like the potential enemy. As he surveyed the nearby landscape, his eyes were drawn to a wooded hill to the south. Just then, he saw a flash — sunlight reflecting off something shiny.

The pieces clicked into place — the captive rhinos, the camouflaged watch covering, the RLI boot prints, and now the flash from the hill. It was clear to him that the hill was almost certainly being used as an OP[617].

Sipho was alarmed, but not wanting to alert any potential observers to their discovery, he maintained his composure as he casually walked back to Nick and Rachel at the bomas. Upon his return, he explained that he had mistakenly left his binoculars at the homestead and, since he needed them for the upcoming game drive, they would have to go back to retrieve them.

After they got into the Land Rover, Sipho shared his concerns with them. He suspected that hostile individuals had set up an OP and were watching the bomas and holding pen. He explained they would return to the homestead to plan their next steps and urged them to act normally when they arrived and got out of the vehicle.

---

[616] Rhodesian Light Infantry. This was an infantry regiment and was one of the country's main counter-insurgency units during the Rhodesian Bush War.
[617] Observation Post.

When they got back to the main homestead, they discovered that Duncan was at home, but Hamish had gone to visit Mark and Jenny. Sipho shared his findings and concerns with Duncan, acknowledging that he might be overreacting. However, in the end, it was agreed that he and Nick would conduct a covert recce[618] of the suspect OP to verify if anything suspicious was occurring there, while Duncan would remain at the homestead with Rachel.

Duncan called Mark and Jenny to confirm that Hamish was still with them. He relayed Sipho's discoveries and their plans, and suggested that they all stay at Mark and Jenny's house for the next few hours while Sipho and Nick carried out their recce of the suspicious site.

By now, it was 13:00. Sipho retrieved his 1:500 map of the area, which he and Nick closely examined. Their review confirmed that the well-treed hill would make an ideal OP from which the bomas, holding pen, and main homestead could be surveilled.

Using the map, Sipho pointed out the spot on the hill where he believed the OP had been established, as well as the best approach route to avoid detection. Once they were clear on their plan, they set out. It was now 13:30.

It took Nick and Sipho 90 minutes to stealthily navigate to the hill, followed by another 20 minutes to ascend from the steeper, more difficult route. They figured it was unlikely that the suspected trespassers would choose this more challenging approach.

They approached the site with utmost caution. It didn't take them much longer to confirm their suspicions. The area — clearly the look-out point — was occupied by a white man in bush fatigues, armed with a high-calibre hunting rifle and an FN[619] rifle. Nearby, the lay-up position was occupied by two other white men, also in bush fatigues and armed with high-calibre hunting rifles and FN rifles. They observed

---

[618] This is an informal term for reconnaissance.

[619] This was a light automatic rifle designed in Belgium and manufactured by FN Herstal. The FN was the standard issue rifle for the Rhodesian Security Forces.

that the lay-up area had been set up as a campsite and appeared to be well-equipped.

It was now 15:30. Having gathered all the information they needed, they quietly made their way back to the homestead, arriving at 17:00. When Rachel saw them safely enter the front door, she rushed to Nick and embraced him protectively.

Sipho quickly briefed Duncan on their discoveries. Duncan then called Jenny and Mark, asking them to return to the house for an urgent war council meeting, stressing the need to act normally on their return to avoid alerting any adversaries to their presence.

While waiting for Hamish, Mark, and Jenny to arrive, Nick went to his Land Cruiser in the car park and carefully retrieved the black velvet pouch containing his Bronze Cross[620] from the glovebox. He placed the pouch containing the medal into his trousers' pocket.

Hamish, Mark, and Jenny arrived shortly thereafter. The seven of them then gathered around the large dining table in the guest wing's dining room.

Duncan addressed the group in a sombre tone. "As you've all heard, a very serious situation has developed at the ranch — almost certainly one which is aimed at poaching our newly arrived rhinos. We need to decide how to respond to this emergency. Before we begin discussions, I'd like Sipho to recap on what happened today at the holding pen and what he and Nick have discovered since."

Sipho briefly recapped the events of the last six hours.

Once he finished, Duncan said, "Obviously, there are several ways we could respond to this situation. But before making any decisions, I'd like to hear your thoughts. I'd prefer to start with family members

---

[620] Nick had been awarded the Bronze Cross of Rhodesia for his exploits in June 1979 when his 3RAR platoon had been involved in a major contact with a gang of guerrillas in the Chimanimani Mountains on Rhodesia's eastern border with Mozambique.

before hearing from Sipho, Nick, and Rachel. Hamish, as the oldest son, what are your thoughts?"

"Thanks, Dad," Hamish said. "The situation is obviously very serious, and we need to take definitive steps to resolve it. The poachers are well-organised and armed, and based on what Sipho has told us, I think it's safe to assume that all three are probably former white members of the Rhodesian Security Forces. It's reasonable to conclude that they are all highly skilled marksmen. We must also remember that Zimbabwe is no longer at war, so, essentially, this is a police matter. Our safety should come first, so I think we should contact the police in Chiredzi as soon as possible and hand the matter over to them."

"Thanks, Hamish," Duncan said. "Now, over to you, Mark. What do you think?"

"I agree that our safety should be our first priority," Mark replied. "These guys are serious, and I don't want to risk getting into a firefight with them. So, on balance, I am inclined to go along with Hamish's suggestion."

"Thanks, Mark," Duncan said. "What about you, Jenny? What do you think?"

"My first priority is the family," Jenny said. "I don't think we should put ourselves at risk by confronting these men, so I agree that we should call the police."

"Thanks," said Duncan. "Sipho, your turn now. What do you think?"

"Thanks, Mr Oliver," Sipho replied. He paused for a few seconds, deep in thought, before continuing, "I agree we should avoid any unnecessary risks. However, I am not sure that handing the matter over to the police is the right call. It's Saturday evening, and the police in Chiredzi will not do anything tonight. At best, they may do something tomorrow, but even that is not assured since tomorrow is Sunday. As much as I hate to say it, we have all seen how incompetent the police seem to have become since the country became independent. I worry that if we call the police, nothing will happen until it is too late. And if it isn't too late, I am concerned that when they do finally respond, they will mess up the whole operation, allowing the poachers to escape. Therefore, I think we need to take proactive steps against the poachers first thing tomorrow morning."

"Thanks," said Duncan. "Now, Nick, even though you are a guest, I would be grateful to hear your thoughts."

Nick was quiet for ten seconds before he replied. During this time, he reached into his trousers pocket to feel for his Bronze Cross. As his fingers brushed against the smoothness of the velvet pouch and felt the reassuring weight of the medal inside, his mind became crystal clear. As had happened on previous occasions, he knew exactly what they should do.

"Thanks, Duncan," he said. "I absolutely agree that we should avoid taking any unnecessary risks. However, that does not mean we should take no risks at all. As long as we carefully consider our risks, I think we should be prepared to accept an element of danger.

"We need to remember that the poachers do not know we are aware of their location, how many of them there are, or that they are armed. So, the element of surprise is very much on our side, which gives us a huge advantage. We must also remember that, for better or worse, the country has decided to entrust the future of its rhino population to conservancies like the one you are establishing here. Rhinos are a treasure worth protecting and *fighting* for. The government recognises this - otherwise, it would not be establishing protected conservancies. So, provided we take only carefully considered risks, I agree with Sipho that we should take proactive steps to protect the rhinos, and this should be done first thing tomorrow morning.

"As you know, when I did my national service with 3RAR[621], Sipho and I worked closely together during some pretty hairy moments in the Rhodesian Bush War. Since the country's independence, Sipho has also seen significant action in and around the Bulawayo area. Sipho and I

---

[621] 3rd Battalion Rhodesian African Rifles.

think alike. If you allow Sipho and me to work together, I am confident we can devise a plan to safely eliminate the poachers."

There was silence in the room. Then Duncan hesitantly asked, "What do you mean by '*eliminate*'?"

Nick replied, "Well, the gang currently at Mhuka[622] Ranch is obviously professional and armed. They must have access to significant intelligence. It is no coincidence that they arrived at the ranch at the same time you took delivery of your first two rhinos. I believe they are likely part of a larger network and may still have strong contacts in the military. Worse still, they may be working with corrupt government ministers. If I believed the country still had the necessary expertise, resources, and willingness to apprehend and interrogate these individuals, I would advocate for that path. But if Sipho believes the police have become incompetent, then we must listen to him and *not* rely on them. That being the case, we need to take matters into our own hands and eliminate them ourselves."

There was deadly silence in the room for several minutes until Duncan said, "Thank you, Nick. That's certainly food for thought. Now, I would like to hear from Rachel. What do you think?"

Rachel was shocked that her views were being sought. She stammered before replying, "Thanks for asking, Duncan. To be frank, I do not feel qualified to speak. I know very little about Zimbabwe or poaching. While I obviously wouldn't want any harm to come to the rhinos, my primary concern is ensuring that no harm comes to anyone in this room."

"Thanks," said Duncan. He pondered for a few seconds before continuing, "While everyone has been speaking, I have been weighing the pros and cons of each of your suggestions. They all have merit, and I would like to thank you for your thoughts. However, as the owner of the ranch, I feel I must make the final decision about our course of

---

[622] A local word meaning animals or wildlife.

action. I hope we will all commit to the agreed plan and bring it to fruition.

"I agree that it is probably unwise to simply hand the matter over to the police in Chiredzi. The chances are that they will be slow to react, and that when they do, it will either be too late or they will stuff things up.

"However, I am not prepared to authorise a lethal assault on the poachers. While I have no doubt we could do that successfully, we cannot simply go around killing people who have not yet committed a crime in Zimbabwe. To do so would amount to murder or culpable homicide, and I am not prepared to sanction that.

"So, what I am suggesting is that Hamish, Mark, Sipho, and Nick — if he is willing — will carry out a swoop on the poachers' position at first light tomorrow. The purpose of the swoop will be to apprehend the poachers, not to kill them. However, since the poachers are armed, all members of the arresting party will also be armed. We have enough FN rifles here on the ranch for Sipho, Hamish, Mark, and Nick. Once the poachers are captured, we will arrange for them to be handed over to the police for prosecution. The courts will then decide what should happen to them. Personally, I hope they are found guilty and sentenced to very long prison terms in the harshest of prisons. However, that is a decision for the courts, not for us.

"Given Sipho's position at the ranch, he will be in charge of the operation. Hamish, Mark, and Nick will follow his orders. I am too old to be involved in the operation; I would only get in the way. I will remain at the homestead with Jenny and Rachel. Sipho and I will be in radio contact. As soon as the three villains have been apprehended, Sipho will let me know. I will then advise the police in Chiredzi.

"Does anyone disagree or have any questions?"

Everyone nodded in agreement.

"Great," said Duncan. "Thank you, Nick, for being prepared to be involved. I think we should now let Sipho work out how the operation will run. Let's reconvene in an hour to receive our orders from him.

Then we should all try to get some sleep. Tomorrow is going to be a big day."

After the meeting ended, everyone broke into small groups while Sipho made his way to his room to work out orders for the three other members of the arresting party. A short time later, Nick followed him into his bedroom to share some ideas.

As agreed, after one hour, they all reconvened to receive their orders from Sipho. He specified the arms each member would carry and the additional equipment they needed. He spread out a 1:500 map on the dining room table, showing the arresting party where the poachers were located. He had also highlighted the route they would follow when approaching and ascending the tree-covered hill on which the OP was located.

The four of them would leave the main homestead on foot at 03:30, under cover of darkness. They would make their way to the OP hill as a group of four. However, at its base, they would split into two groups. Nick would head to the top of the hill to the look-out point, where he expected to find one of the poachers. Sipho, Hamish, and Mark would make their way to the lay-up position, where they anticipated finding the other two poachers.

All four men needed to be in position by 06:00. The raid would commence at 06:15 sharp, just before sunrise. Sipho, Hamish, and Mark would initiate the first arrest of the two poachers at the lay-up position. Once Nick heard the noise from their arrest, he would proceed with his arrest at the look-out point. If he faced resistance, he had permission to use force if needed. Sipho, Hamish, and Mark were not allowed to open fire during their arrests unless ordered to do so by Sipho. However, if the poachers fired at any of them, they were authorised to respond with lethal force if necessary.

Once all three poachers had been captured and secured, Sipho would make radio contact with Duncan, who would then reach out to the Chiredzi Police Station. Depending on the advice he received, the poachers would be detained on the hill until the police arrived. However, if there was going to be a lengthy delay, the three poachers would be frog-marched back to the main homestead, where they would be detained until the police arrived.

While Sipho was issuing orders and answering any questions, they all ate sandwiches and sipped cups of tea prepared by Jenny and Rachel. By 21:00, everyone understood their orders, had taken possession of and thoroughly checked their FN rifles, and arranged their webbing to their liking.

Before they retired to bed, Sipho secured black card over the inside of the windows in the lounge and the largest bedroom in the guest wing, which contained two beds. He did the same in one of the bathrooms and in the kitchen, then closed all the curtains.

Once this was done, the men tried to get a few hours of sleep on the lounge carpet, while Jenny and Rachel went to the large bedroom to do the same. Everyone set their alarms for 03:00. Sipho advised that once they awoke, they should only switch on lights in areas where the windows had been blacked out and to keep the number of lights to an absolute minimum.

Chapter 51 – The unravelling of Operation Chipembere

The shrill alarm in the lounge went off at 03:00. None of the four men had slept well, and they all woke feeling sleep-deprived. However, as they thought about the task ahead, adrenaline began coursing through their veins, quickly sweeping away any fatigue or grogginess.

Duncan switched on the small light next to the TV, reminding everyone to avoid turning on any other lights in the lounge. He also switched on a light in the kitchen and another in the bathroom, then went to wake Rachel and Jenny, who were in one of the nearby bedrooms.

Hamish, Mark, Sipho[623], and Nick began preparing for the raid on the poachers' camp. They attended to their bathroom needs, changed into camouflage gear, and meticulously checked their webbing and rifles. Duncan, Nick, and Sipho also ensured that the batteries for their two-way radios were fully charged and that the radio sets were functioning properly.

Duncan went into the kitchen and made overly sweet mugs of tea for the four members of the arresting party. As the men sipped their tea and checked their gear yet again, Sipho quietly reminded them of the day's orders.

"Listen in," he said. "Remember, the poachers don't know we're aware they're on the ranch. So, we've got the element of surprise, which is a big advantage. We'll be moving from the homestead to the OP[624] on foot. I'll lead, with Hamish behind me, then Mark, and Nick bringing up

---

[623] Sipho is a Ndebele boy's name meaning Gift.
[624] Observation Post.

the rear. We'll travel in single file. The full moon from earlier tonight should provide enough light to see, but even with good visibility, we'll keep a maximum distance of just five metres between us. If visibility gets worse, we'll close that distance.

"Obviously, we need to stay silent. Make sure any buckles or straps on your webbing or clothing are taped down. Remove necklaces and bracelets, and cover your watch faces with wristbands. Apply camouflage paint to your face, neck, and the backs of your hands.

"We'll move slowly to make sure we're quiet. Keep in mind that at night, with reduced visibility, our progress will be about half the speed of daytime patrols.

"When we reach the base of the hill, we'll split into two groups— Group A and Group B. Group A will consist only of Nick. He'll make his way to the OP look-out point, where he expects to find one poacher. He's memorised the best route to reach that spot.

"The rest of us will form Group B. I'll lead us to the lay-up position, where we expect to find two more poachers. Like Nick, I've memorised the best route for us.

"We need to reach the base of the hill by 05:00. Nick will then head to the look-out point, and he must be in position by 06:00 at the latest. The rest of us will move to the lay-up position, also aiming to be in position by 06:00.

"The raid will start at 06:15 sharp, just before sunrise. Group B will engage first. Our mission is to disarm and apprehend the two men at the lay-up position. Remember, we're here to arrest them, not take them out. But if we come under fire, you have my authority to return lethal fire. However, do NOT open fire unless and until I give the order. If I'm incapacitated, Hamish will take command.

"Group A — Nick — will engage at 06:15 as well, but he'll wait until he hears activity from Group B before moving in to disarm and apprehend the remaining poacher. Nick's target will have been alerted by the noise from Group B, so Nick, if necessary, you have my authority to use lethal force.

"Mr Oliver will stay at the homestead with Jenny and Rachel. Once all three poachers have been disarmed and apprehended, I'll radio Mr Oliver, who will contact the police at Chiredzi. He'll ask whether we should remain on the hill or frog march the poachers back to the homestead.

"Nick, Mr Oliver, and I will all have two-way radios for communication."

He paused for a few seconds, then asked, "Any questions?"

There were none.

"Great," said Sipho, looking at his watch. "It's now 03:29. Time to move out. Good luck, everyone. Let's go and protect the Two Ronnies[625] and give these *skebengas*[626] a bloody nose."

Duncan gave them a thumbs-up while Rachel and Jenny hugged each of them, wishing them good luck and a safe return.

Sipho led the three men out of the guest wing and into the main homestead. They exited through the kitchen's back door, heading south towards the OP. As Sipho had advised, the moon was still high, casting enough light for them to maintain a distance of about five metres between each other. Once they were about 100 metres from the homestead, Sipho halted the patrol for ten minutes to allow their eyes to adjust. They glanced briefly at the moon before focusing on the darkness, trying to discern shapes and distances. They repeated this process several times until their eyes and brains adapted to the dim light.

The patrol then continued, moving quietly through the bush. Sipho, like many former RAR[627] *masodjas*[628], had an uncanny sense of direction and sharp eyesight, even in the dark. He had memorised their

---

[625] The two male black rhinos had been given the name, *the Two Ronnies*, by Mhuka Ranch.

[626] *Skebenga* is a local word meaning gangster or bandit.

[627] Rhodesian African Rifles.

[628] *Masodja* is the Africanised word for *soldier*.

route from the 1:500 map, and only needed to check his map and compass once. Before turning on his head torch, he was careful to cover his head, shoulders, torso, and the map with his camouflaged jacket to hide any tell-tale leaks of light.

They moved in complete silence. Even their soft boots made little noise. The night sounds of the African bush were amplified. At one point, Sipho recognised the unmistakeable husky croak of a leopard stalking prey, but his fine-honed bushcraft told him it was at least 100 metres away.

They reached the base of the hill at 04:55. Sipho halted the men for five minutes to allow them to catch their breath. No words were exchanged. They knew the enemy was close.

Sipho gestured to Nick, indicating the direction he should take. Nick patted the side pocket of his trousers to ensure his map was accessible, then touched the inner pocket of his camouflaged jacket to confirm that his woollen mittens and the black velvet pouch containing his Bronze Cross were still in place.

"*Ishe*[629], remember to wait until exactly 06:15. Good luck," Sipho whispered. Nick gave a thumbs-up and disappeared into the darkness.

A few minutes later, Sipho, followed by Hamish and Mark, headed off in a slightly different direction, leaving Nick to make his way almost due south (180°) while they veered slightly to 175°.

Despite the steep ascent, Nick made good progress. Holding his FN[630] rifle in the *patrol carry* position made the climb more challenging, but by 05:30, he was close to the look-out point. He crept into a concealed spot behind some rocks, holding his rifle in the *low-ready* position. He strained to see in the gloom, trying to pinpoint the enemy.

---

[629] *Ishe* is a term of respect used by RAR soldiers when referring to their officers.
[630] This was a light automatic rifle designed in Belgium and manufactured by FN Herstal. The FN was the standard issue rifle for the Rhodesian Security Forces.

He took long, slow breaths to calm his heartbeat. An insect landed on his nose. He ignored it until it crawled away and eventually flew off.

"Where is this bugger?" he thought, as the minutes dragged on. He checked his watch, careful to shield the watch face with his hand. It was 05:50. Not long to go.

Still unable to locate the enemy, he began to doubt himself. Don't be silly, he chided himself. This is definitely the site we laid eyes on yesterday. The enemy must be very close by!

Just before 06:00, a bird suddenly took flight about 15 metres to his right, its distinctive *'guwe guwe'* cry piercing the silence. Something had disturbed it.

The bird's sudden take-off made Nick's heart race. He slowed his breathing and focused his sight as much as he could. As he peered into the darkness with all his might, a dull ache formed behind his eyes. Suddenly, the outline of a man appeared, no more than 15 metres away. Nick heard the man unzip his trousers and take a pee against a tree. He watched him with chameleon eyes. The man zipped up his trousers, took a couple of steps, and crouched back down behind a small boulder, about two feet in height.

"Jeez, no wonder I couldn't see him," Nick thought. From his position, only the top of the man's head was visible, offering little as a target. Nick considered moving to get a better shot but realised it would take at least ten minutes to reposition without being seen. He glanced at his watch. It was 06:05 — not enough time.

Nick touched the Bronze Cross in his pocket, and an inner voice reassured him. He's less than 15 metres away. You can't miss.

Nick glanced at his watch. It was now 06:09—only six minutes to go. Thoughts of what he and Sipho had agreed upon flashed through his mind. He wasn't going to try to capture the man, who was just 15 metres away. Instead, at exactly 06:15, he would shoot to kill. The sound of his gunfire would alert the other two poachers at the lay-up site, but they would already be lined up in Sipho's sights. Sipho would open fire and order Hamish and Mark to do the same. The three poachers would be slain.

Shortly after, Nick would put on his woollen mittens, approach the man he had shot, and retrieve the dead man's rifle with his gloved hand. He would fire a burst of bullets at his previous position. When questioned, Nick's story would be that the look-out had spotted him and opened fire. Fortunately, the poacher had inexplicably missed. Nick had managed to scramble into an offensive position and returned fire, killing him.

Sipho's story would match — the poachers had grabbed their rifles upon hearing gunfire, and fearing they were about to shoot, Sipho had opened fire and ordered Hamish and Mark to follow suit.

This plan had been hatched by Nick and Sipho, with Hamish and Mark left out of the loop. If successful, it would result in the death of the three poachers. Since it would appear that Nick, Sipho, Hamish, and Mark had returned fire in self-defence, no charges could be laid against them. The new Zimbabwean Government would take credit for its new rhino conservancy initiative, claiming it had prevented the slaughter of two black rhinos. The police would state that they had foiled an international rhino poaching syndicate led by three white ex-Rhodesian Security Force members. The media would report that the operation against the white poachers had been spearheaded by a black anti-poaching manager recently employed by the rhino conservancy.

Would it work? You bet it would — he and Sipho would make sure it did.

Did it matter that the poachers were going to be killed for what they intended to do — not for what they had already done? Nick did not think so. The poachers were professional criminals who had trespassed onto the ranch with high-calibre rifles specifically to kill the two rhinos. Sipho and Nick had to stop them — and stop them permanently. If they were not stopped, who knows how many other rhinos they would end up shooting and what other collateral damage they might cause?

Nick glanced at his watch. It was now 6:14:45. He adjusted his rifle so that the middle of the poacher's head was in the crosshairs of his FN's sights. Then he counted slowly to ten. When he reached ten, he took a slight breath in and squeezed the trigger of his FN rifle. A short burst of bullets erupted from the barrel of his automatic weapon. Three bullets struck the poacher in the head with devastating and lethal consequences. The poacher died instantly.

A few seconds later, Nick heard a firefight erupt about 150 metres behind him.

The body of the slain poacher lay lifeless on the ground less than 15 metres from where Nick was still crouching. He stood up and walked quietly over to the body, felt for a pulse, and found none. He took the woollen mittens from the pocket of his camouflaged jacket and put them on. Then he retrieved the dead poacher's FN rifle with his gloved hand and fired a burst of bullets at the spot where he had been less than 60 seconds earlier.

Sipho, Hamish, and Mark arrived at their position by 05:50. It did not take them long to locate the lay-up area, and they had managed to creep within 30 metres of the poachers' camp. Both poachers were asleep on the ground in their sleeping bags. Just before 06:00, Sipho heard the distinctive sound of the grey lourie, or go-away bird, from a distance of 150 metres. He desperately hoped that neither of the sleeping men would be disturbed by it. The man closest to him rolled over in his sleep but did not awaken; the second man did not react at all.

Sipho looked at his watch. It was now 06:10. He tapped his watch and signalled to Hamish and Mark to be on high alert.

At 06:12, he moved his FN rifle to align its sights on the head and shoulders of the sleeping man closest to him, pausing for three seconds. He then shifted the rifle to the second man, pausing again for three seconds. This sequence had taken no more than ten seconds.

When Sipho's watch clicked over to 06:14, he slowly started counting to 60. At 58, the silence of the night was shattered by the clatter of automatic fire from 150 metres ahead.

The man nearest him sat bolt upright and reached for his FN, which lay next to his sleeping bag.

"Steady, steady," Sipho hissed at Hamish and Mark. An instant later, as the man got to his feet, Sipho opened fire with a short burst from his FN. He deftly moved his sights onto the man furthest from him, who was still in his sleeping bag, looking about in panic, trying to determine what was happening.

Sipho squeezed the trigger, laying a short burst of fire on him while yelling, "Fire, fire."

Hamish and Mark immediately brought fire to bear on the two poachers. Five seconds later, Sipho shouted, "Cease fire."

The two men lay lifeless on the ground. The nearest man had been shot while getting to his feet, still holding his FN. The man furthest away had been shot while still in his sleeping bag.

Before Sipho, Hamish, or Mark could move forward to examine the slain poachers, another short burst of fire ripped through the air. Hamish and Mark looked around in confusion. "Easy, easy," said Sipho. "Stay in your positions."

Sipho reached into his backpack and pulled out his radio. "Group A, this is Group B. Sitrep[631], please."

After a few seconds, Nick's voice broke through the static. "Group B, this is Group A. Mission accomplished. Is it safe for me to move back to your location?"

"Roger," replied Sipho. "All clear here. Good job."

"Over and out," said Nick.

---

[631] Situation Report.

"Over and out," replied Sipho.

Sipho looked at Hamish and Mark. "You both heard that. It looks like the mission was successful. Nick will be here in a few minutes. He's obviously a friendly. Once he arrives, we will debrief, and then I'll radio Duncan at the main homestead."

While waiting for Nick to arrive, Sipho examined the two dead bodies. Both had been hit multiple times and would have died instantly.

Nick arrived at their site just after 06:30. By now, it was quite light, allowing Hamish and Mark to identify him when he was still 40 metres away. The four men gathered in a small group.

Sipho requested a quick debrief from Nick. Nick informed the three men that he had reached the look-out position at 05:40 but had initially been unable to locate the enemy. Shortly after 06:00, something disturbed a go-away bird, but he still couldn't pinpoint the enemy's location. Remaining in his position, he desperately hoped to spot the look-out. The look-out must have seen him, because at about 06:15, the man opened fire on Nick's position. By the grace of God, the shots missed. Nick managed to scramble into an offensive position and returned fire, killing the enemy. Around the same time, he heard gunfire from a little way down the hill, which he assumed was from Group B's site.

Sipho then asked Hamish to give Nick a debrief of what had happened at their site — Group B's site. Hamish explained that all three of them had heard the sound of the go-away bird. Fortunately, it had not awakened the two poachers, although one had rolled over in his sleeping bag. The burst of fire at about 06:15 from Group A's site, however, had woken both poachers. One had jumped out of his sleeping bag and grabbed his rifle. At that point, Sipho opened fire on him and ordered Hamish and Mark to do likewise. Within seconds, both poachers were dead. A few moments later, they heard another burst of fire coming from further up the hill, which they assumed was from Group A's site.

All four men were smiling, pleased with themselves.

At 07:05, Sipho radioed Duncan, informing him that there had been a firefight in which the three poachers had been killed. Fortunately, no one from the ranch had suffered injuries, and they were all fine. He asked Duncan to contact the Chiredzi Police Station and advise them of the situation. He stated that he, Hamish, Mark, and Nick would remain on site until they received further instructions from either Duncan or the ZRP[632].

At the conclusion of his conversation with Duncan, Sipho told the others that they needed to stay on site until they received further instructions from the police. They were not to touch any of the bodies, nor were they permitted to enter the contact sites until the police arrived.

Rachel and Jenny had been listening to the radio transmission between Sipho and Duncan. When Sipho mentioned the firefight, all colour drained from their cheeks. But when he added that all three poachers had been killed and that everyone from the ranch was safe and unharmed, they burst into tears of joy, hugging and kissing Duncan.

Duncan tried to phone the police station in Chiredzi at 07:15. The phone rang but no one answered. A minute later, he tried again with the same result. He continued calling every ten minutes, without success, until 09:00, when the phone was finally picked up by a rather tired-sounding and disinterested policeman, who identified himself as Constable Makosa.

Duncan slowly and clearly explained what had occurred on the ranch. The mention of three poachers being killed in a firefight immediately heightened the Constable's interest. He told Duncan that he would need to get further instructions from the Station Commander and asked him to instruct the men who had witnessed the firefight to remain on site until a police patrol arrived.

Duncan radioed Sipho and relayed the details of his conversation with the police. He warned that it might take some time for the police

---

[632] Zimbabwe Republic Police.

patrol to arrive but added that, in the meantime, he would arrange for egg and bacon rolls to be prepared at the main homestead, which he, Jenny, and Rachel would bring to them at the OP.

He then handed the two-way radio to Jenny and Rachel, both of whom were eager to speak to Mark and Nick, respectively.

At 10:45, Duncan, Jenny, and Rachel arrived at the OP with the egg and bacon rolls and a flask of hot tea.

Joyous greetings and congratulations were shared among them, with the warmest exchanges perhaps being between Rachel and Nick, and Mark and Jenny. The four men were ravenous and quickly devoured the rolls, washing them down with the tea. Then the seven of them settled in for a long, patient wait for the police patrol, which eventually arrived at 13:30.

The patrol consisted of two constables, one being Constable Makosa. The other was the Station Commander, who introduced himself as Inspector Gwata.

Each of the four men was questioned individually, though the questioning was fairly basic. Constable Makosa took several photos of the look-out area, the lay-up camp, and the three dead bodies. He asked Sipho, Hamish, and Mark to point out exactly where they had been during the firefight at the lay-up area, marking these positions on the ground with yellow spray paint. He then asked Nick to indicate his position at the look-out site and marked that as well.

There were no inconsistencies in the accounts given by Sipho, Nick, Hamish, and Mark. More importantly, the physical evidence on the ground, including spent shell casings, corroborated their stories.

By 15:30, the police had finished taking statements. Inspector Gwata informed them they could return to the main homestead. He advised that their statements would be typed up on Monday morning and requested that they report to Chiredzi Police Station at 14:00 on Monday to review and sign them. He also mentioned they might need to answer any further questions the police might have.

Sipho, Nick, Hamish, Mark, Duncan, Jenny, and Rachel then made their way back to the homestead on foot, while the police continued collecting and bagging evidence from the two contact sites and arranged for the retrieval of the poachers' bodies.

That night, there was a celebratory dinner at the main homestead. The mood was jubilant, especially for Sipho and Nick.

Adding to the sense of victory, a large thunderstorm rolled over the ranch during dinner. As the rain poured down, Sipho and Nick toasted each other, secure in the knowledge that their secret would remain forever hidden.

Just before midnight, everyone made their way to bed. Nick and Rachel, along with Mark and Jenny, were given bedrooms in the guest wing. They all slept soundly.

Duncan was deeply grateful that no one at the ranch had been injured and that the Two Ronnies were safe. Mark and Hamish were buoyed by the excitement of the day and the parts they had played in its successful outcome. Jenny and Rachel were immensely proud of their men and eternally grateful that none of them had been hurt.

Sipho and Nick, meanwhile, could hardly believe how well their plan had worked. But more than that, their respect for one another had grown to new heights.

Chapter 52 - Farewell to Mhuka Ranch

Timeline – 25 August 1981

Nick woke early on Monday morning, 24th August. He needed to speak to his parents to let them know what had transpired the previous day and to reassure them that everyone was safe.

He waited until 6:30 am before calling his folks in Salisbury[633]. Fortunately, it was Matthew who answered the phone in his usual way. "Morning, Matthew Sinclair here. How can I help you?"

"Hi Dad. It's Nick," replied Nick.

Matthew said, "Hi, Nick. So good to hear your voice. I hope you and Rachel are enjoying your holiday. Mum and I are looking forward to meeting up with you both at Troutbeck Inn on Thursday."

"So are we," replied Nick. "It will be great for us to all be together." He paused for a second, then continued, "I'm calling because I need to bring you up to speed about a recent incident I was involved in. As you know, we're currently staying at Mhuka[634] Ranch just outside Chiredzi. Yesterday, some unexpected events took place on the ranch, and these are likely to be reported in the newspaper over the next few days, so I wanted to share what happened before you read about it."

"My goodness, this sounds serious," said Matthew. "Are you both OK?"

---

[633] The capital of Zimbabwe. Its name was changed to Harare in April 1982.
[634] A local word meaning animals or wildlife.

"Yep, we're fine, thanks," answered Nick.

Nick then told his father what had happened, using the modified version of events he and Sipho[635] had agreed upon.

At the end of the story, Matthew said, "My goodness. That's quite a tale. Thank goodness the poacher who opened fire on you was such a poor shot. Your mother will be horrified. Has Rachel told her parents yet? You know they're currently in South Africa?"

"Yes, we know they're already in South Africa," Nick replied. "Rachel will phone them later today. I'd appreciate it if you could let Mum and Russell know what's happened. We have to return to the police station in Chiredzi this afternoon to check and sign our official statements, so we'll be delayed most of the afternoon. We're hoping to head to the Vumba[636] tomorrow and will see you at Troutbeck Inn on Thursday."

With that, Nick hung up. Rachel, who had been listening, gave him an appreciative hug. "Darling, you handled that so well. You got in all the facts without underplaying or over-dramatising anything. I hope I can do as well when I speak to my folks."

Rachel knew her parents had travelled from London to Johannesburg on Thursday, 20th August. Stuart needed to attend several business meetings in Johannesburg, and he'd arranged to complete these before travelling to Zimbabwe to meet up with his old business associate, Matthew Sinclair.

When in Johannesburg, Stuart always liked to stay at the Hilton Hotel in Sandton. Rachel guessed he'd be staying there on this trip. She phoned directory enquiries to get the Hilton's number and was quickly connected. A polite receptionist answered, and Rachel asked to be put through to Mr Stuart Dixon, a guest at the hotel. After a few seconds, her mother, Lynne, answered the call.

"Hi Mum," Rachel said. "It's Rachel."

---

[635] Sipho is a Ndebele boy's name meaning Gift.
[636] The Vumba Mountains are also known as the Bvumba mountains.

Lynne was excited to hear from her daughter, even though they would be seeing each other in a few days. When Lynne asked where Rachel was calling from, she replied, "We're currently staying at a lovely place called Mhuka Ranch. It's near a small rural town called Chiredzi, in the south-east of the country. It's beautiful here, and the ranch is in the process of establishing a rhino conservancy."

"That sounds interesting," said Lynne.

"It certainly is, Mum. The conservancy is actually why I'm calling. There was an incident on the ranch yesterday. It'll probably be reported in the local papers tomorrow and may even make it into the South African press. I'd rather you hear the details from me than read about it in the news."

"Oh, my goodness," said Lynne. "That sounds ominous. Are you and Nick OK?"

"Yes, we're both fine," said Rachel.

Rachel then explained what had happened, though she downplayed some of the details — especially the firefight between the poachers and the four men from the ranch — to avoid worrying her mother unnecessarily.

Lynne was shocked — the events Rachel described felt worlds away from the kind of news she was used to hearing in England. She mentioned that Stuart was at the gym but would be back in their room soon. Lynne promised to update him on everything Rachel had shared and made Rachel promise to be careful and stay safe. She also emphasised how much she and Stuart were looking forward to seeing her, Nick, and his parents in Inyanga[637].

She ended the call by expressing her love and gratitude that both Rachel and Nick were safe.

That afternoon, Nick, Sipho, Hamish, and Mark drove to the police station in Chiredzi, where they were met by Constable Makosa. During

---

[637] Inyanga was renamed Nyanga in 1982.

their discussions, Constable Makosa advised that two of the deceased had already been identified, but the third remained unknown. He explained that the poacher whom Nick had shot and killed at the look-out point was an ex-RLI[638] troopie named Gary du Plessis. Gary had been discharged from the RLI in the mid-1970s for insubordination and had since been living and working in Fort Victoria[639].

The second deceased, one of the men found at the lay-up site, had been identified as Jeremy du Randt. He was Gary du Plessis's cousin and had also been living in Fort Victoria. Like Gary, Jeremy had served with the RLI, retiring in the mid-1970s after eight years of service.

The identity of the third deceased had yet to be established, but it was assumed that he, too, had served with the RLI.

Constable Makosa then handed each of the men their draft official statements, which he had prepared based on their verbal accounts from the previous day. He asked them to carefully read the documents and sign them once they were satisfied. Their drafts contained numerous grammatical errors, so it took some time to make the required corrections. Eventually however, the statements were accurate enough for the men to sign.

Constable Makosa then informed them that Inspector Gwata wished to speak with them and led them to his office.

Inspector Gwata greeted the four men warmly, thanking them for their heroic actions the previous day, which had led to the elimination of a dangerous gang of poachers. He then asked if any of them had previously had business or personal dealings with the two identified deceased individuals. None of the men recognised the names, and they conveyed this to Inspector Gwata.

The Inspector continued, saying that the Chief Superintendent of ZRP[640] Victoria province intended to issue a press release later that

---

[638] Rhodesian Light Infantry. This was an infantry regiment and was one of the country's main counter-insurgency units during the Rhodesian Bush War.
[639] Fort Victoria was renamed Masvingo in 1982.
[640] Zimbabwe Republic Police.

day, and to complete it, he needed some additional information. He then asked a few innocuous questions which obviously were being asked to enable the ZRP to be portrayed in the best possible light.

By 3:30 pm, the Inspector had finished and said the men were free to go. He mentioned that if the police had further questions, Constable Makosa would contact them. Nick reminded him that he and Rachel were visiting from the UK and were paying guests at Mhuka Ranch. He added that they planned to leave the following day, travelling to the Vumba and then to Inyanga before returning to Salisbury, from where they would fly back to the UK on Thursday, 3rd September.

The Inspector raised no objections but advised Nick that he would need to report to the police station in Umtali[641] on Thursday, 27th August, and then to the Borrowdale[642] station in Salisbury on Tuesday, 1st September.

Nick readily agreed but asked the Inspector why these reporting requirements were necessary. The Inspector explained that while it was clear Nick, Sipho, Hamish, and Mark had acted in self-defence, three men had nonetheless been killed. Therefore, the police needed to ensure they could contact key witnesses if any further clarifications were required.

Nick said he understood and would make sure to attend the two police stations on the specified days.

The four men then left the station and returned to the ranch, arriving just before 4:00 pm.

Once back at the ranch, Nick and Rachel had to decide if they were going to head for Leopard Rock Hotel in the Vumba the following day, Tuesday, 25th August. Alternatively, they could cancel their trip to the Vumba and stay at the ranch until Thursday, when they would travel to Troutbeck Inn in Inyanga to meet their respective parents.

---

[641] Umtali was renamed Mutare in 1982.
[642] Borrowdale is a north-eastern suburb in Salisbury.

In the end, despite the Olivers' protestations that they should remain at the ranch for another two days, they decided not to change their plans. The Eastern Highlands[643] were Nick's favourite part of the country, and he wanted to show Rachel as much of the area as he could. Additionally, the distance between Chiredzi and Inyanga was about 450 kilometres, which would be quite a long drive. By going to Leopard Rock Hotel, they would split the journey into two easy legs.

At breakfast the next day, they said their farewells to the Olivers as well as to Sipho. Leaving the ranch was going to be a bittersweet moment for Nick and Rachel — bitter because the events of the previous three days meant they had not yet had the time to explore everything the ranch had to offer — sweet because they would be travelling to perhaps the most beautiful part of the country and meeting up with their parents. As so often happens after traumatic events, they both felt they needed the love and support of family.

The farewell between Nick and Sipho was particularly difficult for both men. Nick had always respected Sipho, but the way he had led the assault on the poachers, maintaining calm professionalism throughout, had elevated Nick's admiration to new heights. If Nick was honest with himself, despite his high regard for the RAR[644] troops, he would never have expected a former black non-commissioned officer from the RAR to demonstrate such exceptional leadership qualities.

From Sipho's perspective, ever since Nick's heroic actions in the firefight against insurgent guerrillas in the Chimanimani Mountains, Sipho had ascribed almost god-like qualities to him. Nick's recent actions in the assault against the poachers had only reconfirmed Sipho's belief that Nick was truly a man among men. It was Nick who had devised the plan to ensure that the poachers would be permanently eliminated rather than merely arrested. Sipho was convinced that, had they followed Duncan's preference to treat this as

---

[643] The Eastern Highlands is a mountainous area on the border of Zimbabwe and Mozambique. It extends for about 300 kilometres from north to south and includes the Inyangani Mountains, the Vumba Mountains and the Chimanimani Mountains.
[644] Rhodesian African Rifles.

a matter for the police, even if the plan to capture and arrest the poachers had succeeded, there was every chance the poachers would have used bribes or lawyers to avoid facing any charges.

Instead, Nick had chosen to treat the poachers' actions as akin to an act of war, which is exactly how Sipho regarded them. The strategy that Nick suggested to Sipho was cunning and smart. By agreeing to play an active role in that alternative strategy, Nick willingly exposed himself to grave danger. If things had gone wrong, Nick could have been killed in any firefight or could have found himself facing charges of murder or culpable homicide.

Yes, Nick was a true InDuna[645].

At their departure from the ranch, the two men shared a heartfelt hug. "Farewell, my friend," said Nick. "You have done well. Mhuka Ranch is lucky to have you on board. I know that under your custodianship, the ranch's rhinos will be well protected and looked after. I honestly hope we meet up again one day."

"Thank you, *Ishe*[646]," said Sipho. "You are like a big brother to me. I hope that one day you will return to Zimbabwe and help it become the kind of great country it should be. But for now, you must return to England to finish your university studies and marry Rachel. When you return, please come and find me."

"Absolutely," said Nick.

The two men saluted each other and then shook hands. Nick and Rachel said their final farewells and thanks to Duncan, Hamish, Mark, and Jenny. They then climbed into their Landcruiser to commence the next leg of their trip to the Vumba Mountains.

---

[645] In Ndebele culture, an InDuna was a title meaning a great leader, headman, or commander of a group of warriors.
[646] *Ishe* is a term of respect used by RAR soldiers when referring to their officers.

Chapter 53 – Nick and Rachel visit the Vumba

They followed the dirt road from Mhuka[647] Ranch to the A10 and then turned right, heading in an easterly direction. After about 40 kilometres and just after crossing the Jack Quinto Bridge over the Sabi[648] River, the road turned sharply left and continued in a northerly direction, parallel to Zimbabwe's eastern border with Mozambique.

Just before 9:00 am, Nick switched on the radio. He wanted to find out if the incident at Mhuka Ranch had been picked up by the media yet. At 9:00 am, a solemn-sounding voice came on the air and said, "This is the Zimbabwe Broadcasting Corporation. Here is the nine o'clock national news, read by Jason Moyo."

Although the reception was a bit crackly, both Nick and Rachel listened carefully to the news bulletin.

Sure enough, the incident at Mhuka Ranch had made the news. The report stated that the far-sighted rhino protection policies of the Zimbabwean Government had resulted in a gang of white poachers being detected and eliminated in the Chiredzi area. The gang consisted of three white poachers, two of whom had been identified as former RLI[649] soldiers.

The gang had been discovered by a rhino protection unit based at the rhino protection conservancy at Mhuka Ranch, led by a former

---

[647] A local word meaning animals or wildlife.
[648] The Sabi River was renamed the Save River in 1982.
[649] Rhodesian Light Infantry. This was an infantry regiment and was one of the country's main counter-insurgency units during the Rhodesian Bush War.

member of the Zimbabwe National Army. The poachers had opened fire on the unit, and in the ensuing firefight, all three poachers were killed. There were no casualties among the members of the rhino protection unit. Chiredzi Police were investigating the incident and had already identified two of the three deceased poachers. Authorities suspected that the poachers may have had links to criminal organisations outside Zimbabwe. Investigations were ongoing.

"Well, I suppose that's not a bad summary for the media," said Nick. "Pity they didn't mention that Sipho[650] left the ZNA[651] because of its tribal bias against the Ndebele nation. The ZNA has certainly shot itself in the foot by allowing such bias in its officer selection processes. They've lost a fine soldier and are making the same mistakes the Rhodesian Security Forces made for so long by failing to commission high-calibre black soldiers."

"I understand your sentiments," said Rachel. "I really like Sipho. I can see why you have so much respect for him. I am just eternally grateful that none of you were harmed in the firefight with the poachers. This country is so beautiful, but there are so many complex problems that need to be addressed. The Zimbabwean Government will need the wisdom of Solomon if it is going to be successful. Mugabe and his senior ministers seem to be failing in many areas. I am not sure that Zimbabwe will ever be able to reach its full potential under their leadership."

"I think you may be right," said Nick. "But let's just put all that behind us for now. I want to show you the Birchenough Bridge, which is close by. Towards the end of my national service, I spent some time there."

By now, they had turned onto the A16. They travelled north for another ten minutes or so until they came to the intersection with the A9, the main road to Fort Victoria[652]. To get to the Vumba, they

---

[650] Sipho is a Ndebele boy's name meaning Gift.
[651] The Zimbabwe National Army.
[652] Fort Victoria was renamed Masvingo in 1982.

needed to turn right, but instead, they turned left, heading towards Fort Victoria.

"Birchenough Bridge is very close," said Nick. "Like the Jack Quinto Bridge, which we crossed about 140 kilometres back, the Birchenough Bridge also spans the Sabi River.

"Immediately prior to the country's general elections in February 1980, I spent three long and boring weeks guarding this bridge. During this time, I learned quite a bit about it. It was designed by someone named Ralph Freeman, who also designed the Sydney Harbour Bridge. The two bridges are similar in appearance. Apparently, when it was built, it was the third longest single-arch suspension bridge in the world. The construction of the bridge was funded by the Beit Trust[653]. At the time it was built, the Trust was chaired by someone called Sir Henry Birchenough, hence the bridge's name. I remember seeing a plaque or something saying that his ashes are buried beneath the bridge," said Nick.

They drove across the bridge. Once they had crossed it, they did a U-turn and headed back along the A9 towards the Vumba. The bridge itself was an interesting structure and quite a marvellous engineering feat, but apart from the bridge and the river beneath it, there was not much else to see or do.

"Did you say you spent three weeks here?" Rachel asked. "Gosh, that must have been boring."

"It sure was," Nick replied. "The only thing that kept me sane during that time was listening to all the military radio communications detailing what was going on at the assembly points where the ZANLA[654] and ZIPRA[655] cadres had amassed. To keep my platoon occupied, I used to get them to patrol 20 kilometres both upstream

---

[653] The Beit Trust was established by the will of the mining and gold magnate, Alfred Beit. In his will he bequeathed a large sum of money for infrastructure development in Southern Rhodesian (now Zimbabwe) and Northern Rhodesia (now Zambia). This was later expanded to also include Malawi.
[654] Zimbabwe African National Liberation Army. ZANLA was the military wing of ZANU.
[655] Zimbabwe People's Revolutionary Army. ZIPRA was the military wing of ZAPU.

and downstream from the bridge. I don't think that made me too popular with them," chuckled Nick.

The distance from the Birchenough Bridge to the Leopard Rock Hotel in the Vumba Mountains[656] was about 150 kilometres. About 20 kilometres after the bridge, the scenery started to become extremely pretty and interesting. The towering, rugged peaks of the Chimanimani Mountains along Zimbabwe's eastern border with Mozambique gradually descended into the Sabi and Odzi Valleys below, through which the A9 passed. The rugged mountain ranges in the distance created the perfect backdrop to the lush green hills and valleys in the foreground.

Once they left the Chimanimani Mountains behind and began passing the Vumba Mountains, the scenery grew increasingly spectacular. Nick told Rachel that the Vumba Mountains were known as the *Mountains of the Mist*. This was because the early mornings in the Vumba were often misty and grey. They would remain like this until mid-morning, when the bright sun would finally penetrate through the blanket of mist. The sunlight would then bring warmth and luminosity to the rich emerald and green hues of the mountain forests and rolling hills.

The Leopard Rock Hotel was nestled in the middle of this beautiful mountainous landscape. The hotel provided an extraordinary fusion of natural beauty and world-class facilities. The beauty of the mountains, the old-world English charm of the hotel, and its immaculately maintained 18-hole golf course were perfectly and harmoniously blended to create a sight that was too beautiful to behold.

In fact, the Queen Mother[657], who had visited and stayed at the hotel in 1953, is reputed to have stated, "There is nowhere more beautiful in Africa."

---

[656] The Vumba Mountains are also known as the Bvumba mountains.
[657] Elizabeth Angela Marguerite Bowes-Lyon. She was the wife of King George VI and mother of Queen Elizabeth II.

After the adrenaline-filled drama of the previous three days, the soothing calm and peace of the Leopard Rock Hotel and its surroundings were the perfect antidote for Nick and Rachel.

They walked the golf course, marvelling at the way the greens and fairways seemed to have been easily inlaid into the densely forested hills. They explored the surrounding forests and were thrilled by the sights of multi-coloured butterflies, delicate and finely spun tree ferns, and beautifully constructed cycads.

The soothing sounds of running water, bubbling streams, and brooks calmed their nerves. In the evenings, they watched spellbound as the Samango monkeys, with their cute but serious-looking hooded eyes, easily leapt the gap between the edge of the encroaching forest and the protective fencing around the tennis courts. The monkeys would nimbly land on the horizontal railings atop the three-metre-high chain mesh fencing and then scamper along the rails as they moved from one tennis court to the next.

Every now and then, a large male Samango monkey would stop to sit and survey the scene from the railings, for no particular reason. This left the rest of the troop trailing behind him, unable to pass. Before long, a *monkey traffic jam* would form, with hysterical screeching from the impatient queue of primates waiting to pass. The commotion would continue until the alpha male finally decided it was time to move along!

They overnighted at the hotel on Tuesday and Wednesday. In the evenings, they would sit in front of the log fire in the lounge, where a waiter would appear to take their drinks order. A short time later, he would arrive with two large gin and tonics in glasses filled with ice cubes and garnished with slices of lemon and cucumber. These would be accompanied by bowls of monkey nuts and thinly shaved biltong, both provided free of charge by the hotel.

From time to time, they would engage in small talk with other guests sitting in the bar. Invariably, these were white Europeans visiting from

Salisbury[658] or Umtali[659], with a fair smattering of South African tourists. Everyone had an interesting story to tell, usually about what they saw or did during the Rhodesian Bush War and whether or not they saw a long-term future for themselves in the new Zimbabwe.

After a couple of drinks and interesting interactions with fellow hotel guests, they would proceed to the beautiful Victorian-styled silver service dining room, where they would enjoy a delicious evening meal served by a cheerful waiter dressed in a crisply starched white uniform. After dinner, they would enjoy a pot of filtered coffee and hot milk, both brought to them in silver jugs.

Then, they would return to their luxurious bedroom. Unashamedly, they would slowly and deliberately undress in front of each other and climb into bed. They would turn their bedside lights down low and leave their windows wide open to enjoy the sounds from the African forest, including the occasional nocturnal calls from a prowling leopard. Then, they would make love, slowly and passionately, before finally falling asleep in each other's arms.

Their experience at Leopard Rock Hotel over the two days was enigmatic — totally delightful but so un-African.

On their second night in the dining room, Rachel remarked on this.

"This is all so bizarre," she said. "It is so terribly British but so un-African. Yet Zimbabwe is no longer a British colony. Do you think this can last?"

Nick pondered for a while, then said, "I doubt it, Rachel. These traditions have been imported from Britain. They were originally brought into the country by pioneers from England who wished to recreate the finer things from their homeland. The traditions have continued, not because the local Africans wanted to perpetuate them, but because the white pioneers and their offspring did. When you really think about it, they do not really feel as though they belong here

---

[658] The capital of Zimbabwe. Its name was changed to Harare in April 1982.
[659] Umtali was renamed Mutare in 1982.

in Africa. Somehow, they feel out of place. I really doubt whether the local Africans feel at ease with them.

"Now that the country is independent, I think these things will begin to disappear. Just as the dinosaurs were unable to survive the climatic changes that occurred when that meteor hit the Earth millions of years ago, I doubt these British traditions will survive the new political order in Zimbabwe that has just come into being."

Michael Chalk

Chapter 54 - Nick and Rachel visit Inyanga in the Eastern Highlands

On Thursday morning, Nick and Rachel checked out of the Leopard Rock Hotel and headed off to Troutbeck Inn in Inyanga[660]. This was about 150 kilometres away.

To get to Inyanga they had to pass through the pretty provincial town of Umtali[661]. This was fortuitous as Inspector Gwata, from the Chiredzi Police Station, had told Nick that he was required to report to the Umtali Police Station on Thursday, 27th August.

When they arrived in Umtali, Nick drove to the Police Station and parked in the car park. He said to Rachel that he had no idea how long he would be, so suggested she come with him.

They walked into the police station. The reception area was being staffed by a black policewoman. Nick went up to her and explained why he was there. He said that Inspector Gwata from Chiredzi Police Station would have sent all relevant details to the Umtali Police Station on either Monday, 24th or Tuesday, 25th August.

Not surprisingly, the policewoman was unaware of what he was talking about. She asked him to take a seat while she went to make some enquiries.

After what seemed like an eternity, she eventually came back to the reception area and said that an Inspector Dube was expecting him. She

---

[660] Inyanga was renamed Nyanga in 1982.
[661] Umtali was renamed Mutare in 1982.

showed them both into his office, which was located down a passageway to the right of reception. The office was small, grubby, dimly lit, and furnished with old and drab furniture, which looked as though it had been kept in some forgotten storage area for many years.

Inspector Dube himself was a smallish man with black-rimmed glasses. He welcomed them both and asked them to take a seat. Nick and Rachel sat down in the chairs which Inspector Dube had indicated to them. The brown vinyl on Nick's upholstered seat was cracked, and its wooden arms were inscribed with inked scribblings and etchings from decades ago.

"Thank you for coming," said the Inspector.

"Our pleasure," replied Nick.

"Would you mind confirming for me where you have come from and where you are going to?"

"Not at all," replied Nick. "We have come from Leopard Rock Hotel in the Vumba, and we are on the way to Troutbeck Inn in Inyanga. We are meeting our respective parents there."

"And how long will you be staying at Troutbeck Inn?"

Nick answered, "We will be staying there from tonight until Saturday night. We will be checking out on Sunday, 30th August, and returning to Salisbury[662]."

"Very good, very good," said the Inspector. "You are now free to proceed. But please remember to make sure you report to the Borrowdale Police Station on Tuesday, 1st September."

"Sure thing," said Nick.

With that, Inspector Dube showed them out of his office and escorted them back to their car.

---

[662] The capital of Zimbabwe. Its name was changed to Harare in April 1982.

Nick and Rachel climbed back into their Landcruiser and pulled out of the car park.

"How bizarre," said Nick. "What a pointless exercise."

They drove through Umtali and made their way to the A3, which was the main road to Salisbury. They drove past the Wise Owl Motel on the outskirts of Umtali and then travelled up and over the Christmas Pass[663]. After driving over the pass, instead of continuing on the A3 to Salisbury, they turned right onto the A15, which was the main road to Inyanga. Just before Inyanga, they turned right onto the A14, which took them to Troutbeck Inn. They travelled along that road for about 20 kilometres, arriving at the hotel just before 2:00 pm.

They drove through the pillared gateway and up the long winding bitumen driveway to the car park. Lined up outside the entrance to the hotel was a row of golf buggies. Nick hoped that while they were at Troutbeck Inn, they might be able to squeeze in a game of golf, as he knew that both their fathers would enjoy playing on the hotel's beautiful golf course.

They climbed out of the Landcruiser, removed their suitcases from the back, and walked to the hotel's reception area. They asked the receptionist if Mr and Mrs Matthew Sinclair and Mr & Mrs Stuart Dixon had checked in yet. The receptionist checked the register and told them that they had not yet arrived.

Nick knew that Rachel's parents had arrived from Johannesburg the day before and had spent the night at his parent's house. He also knew that all four would be travelling to Troutbeck Inn together, but he was unsure of what time they might be arriving. So, he suggested to Rachel that they should check in and drop their suitcases off at their bedroom. They would then go and enjoy a light lunch on the outside veranda

---

[663] Christmas Pass is a mountain pass that leads into Mutare from the west. The pass was so named by some of the colonial pioneers who camped at the foot of the pass on Christmas Day 1890.

overlooking the lake. After lunch, and assuming that their parents had not yet arrived, they could take a stroll around the lake.

Rachel thought that was a good plan.

After checking in, a porter led them to their bedroom, which was in the hotel's western garden wing. From their bedroom, they had direct access to an expansive lawned area, which sloped down to a very pretty lake. Across the lake, Rachel could make out some golf fairways and greens, while on this side of the lake, she saw a swimming pool, tennis courts and squash courts. The bedroom itself was tastefully decorated and had a large en-suite bathroom, which looked as though it had recently been upgraded.

"This looks lovely," said Rachel. "I guess it is going to be too cold to swim, but I am certainly going to enjoy lying by the pool and finish reading *Jock of the Bushveld*[664]. It really is a good book."

After unpacking, they made their way to the outside veranda area, which was near the main restaurant. Nick ordered a steak sandwich and a beer, while Rachel ordered lasagne with salad, and a glass of chardonnay wine.

They sat on the veranda enjoying the afternoon sun and the pleasing view down to the lake. After they had finished their lunch, there was still no sign of their parents, so they decided to take a stroll around the lake.

The walk around the lake was about three kilometres in length. They followed a well-worn path through a pine forest on the lake's north-eastern shore. There were three small wooden jetties leading from the water's edge out over the lake's glistening water for a distance of four or five metres. On these jetties, there were a number of fishermen who were trying to land an elusive trout.

---

[664] Jock of the Bushveld was written by Sir James Percy Fitzpatrick and first published in 1907. It is a true story about Fitzpatrick's travels with his dog, Jock, a Staffordshire Bull Terrier cross.

On the northern shore of the lake, they passed a group of four horse riders following a trail through the pine forest. On the lake's north-western side, Nick and Rachel's path wound between the shoreline and the fairway of one of the golf holes. The path completed its circular route by leading them down to the dam wall at the southern end of the lake. They walked across the dam wall and headed back up the lawn towards the hotel.

It was now 4:00 pm. As they walked towards the hotel, Rachel saw their parents who were waving madly at them. They were sitting on the outside veranda, enjoying the late afternoon sunshine, and a pot of tea with jam and scones. Rachel skipped up the slope to where they were sitting. She gave both sets of parents the warmest of hugs. These were duly returned.

Nick followed a short distance behind. He gave both his mother, Brenda, and Rachel's mother, Lynne, a big hug and kissed them on the cheek. Then he gave his father, Matthew, and Rachel's father, Stuart, a manly handshake.

Questions and answers abounded. Brenda and Lynne were forever grateful that neither of their children had been hurt during the Mhuka[665] Ranch incident. Matthew and Stuart wanted more details about how they had managed to locate the poachers and the events leading up to the firefight.

Nick answered all their questions as truthfully as possible but without revealing anything about how he and Sipho[666] had actually initiated the firefight. His fudging of the truth at certain junctures of the story, left him feeling slightly guilty.

Matthew had brought with him, from Salisbury, a copy of *The Herald*[667] newspaper dated Wednesday, 26th August. The headlines read,

---

[665] A local word meaning animals or wildlife.
[666] Sipho is a Ndebele boy's name meaning Gift.
[667] *The Herald* is the country's foremost national paper. Its origins date back to 1891.

'Former RLI[668] servicemen shot and killed on rhino conservancy in Chiredzi.'

Matthew said that the story had dominated the news for the last few days. Nick read the lead article in the newspaper and was interested to learn that the third poacher had now been identified. His name was Johannes du Toit. According to the paper, he had been a sergeant in the RLI but had gone AWOL[669] in September 1978, after which he had disappeared.

By now, it was beginning to get quite cool. Matthew suggested that they should move inside to the cosy bar, which they did. They were lucky enough to find some seats in front of the log fire. They sat there enjoying one another's company for a couple of hours. Matthew and Stuart reminisced about their last meeting in the mid-1970s at the Grande Hotel in Beira[670], while Lynne quizzed Brenda about what it was like living in Zimbabwe now that the country was independent.

Inevitably, the conversation reverted to the difficulties and challenges facing Zimbabwe and what the future might hold. Stuart implied that on his recent trip to South Africa, he had met with senior South African businesspeople and politicians who had disclosed some worrying developments, but he did not go into details.

Nick and Rachel only had eyes for each other but were happy and contented to see their parents getting on so well and obviously enjoying each other's company.

Just before 7:00 pm, they entered the hotel's comfortable dining room, where they enjoyed a delicious meal together. The banter flowed back and forth among them all. By this time, Brenda and Lynne had each drunk three or four glasses of wine. Neither of them was a heavy drinker, so they both felt a little tipsy. This lifted their spirits

---

[668] Rhodesian Light Infantry. This was an infantry regiment and was one of the country's main counter-insurgency units during the Rhodesian Bush War.
[669] Absence Without Leave.
[670] Beira is on the east coast of Mozambique and is the capital and largest city in the Mozambican province of Sofala.

even higher, and they entertained the group with amusing anecdotes from Nick and Rachel's childhood and school years.

At one point in the evening, their conversation returned to the wonderful conservancy work that the Olivers were doing at Mhuka Ranch. Rachel turned to her father and said, "I really admire what they are doing at the ranch, Dad. They really are making such a difference, both to the wildlife and to the local community. They have financed the upgrading of classrooms and sports fields and have provided funds to enable trained nurses to be employed at the local community clinic. They have sunk wells, have built cattle dips, and made paddocks available to the local farmers for them to graze their cows upon. And the new rhino conservancy will help protect the country's threatened rhino population and will also provide employment for about a dozen rangers. I wish you could see it, Dad. I am sure it is a venture that you might be tempted to support financially."

Stuart scratched his chin thoughtfully, then said, "Well, you know I am passionate about wildlife conservation, and if this can be done in conjunction with improving the lot of the local tribespeople, then that is something I would definitely look at seriously. When we get back to the UK, you can give me Duncan Oliver's contact details, and I will get someone from my office to get in touch with him."

Rachel jumped up from her chair and went to give her father a big hug and kiss. She hugged him, and said, "Thanks so much Dad. It really is a worthwhile project and the Olivers are the most wonderful people you could ever hope to meet, as is Sipho."

At about 10:00 pm everyone was starting to feel tired. They all left the dining room and made their way to their respective bedrooms, where they all enjoyed a deep and restful sleep.

*****

Following breakfast on Friday morning, they all drove to World's View, located on the opposite side of the lake. Access was via a dirt road called Joan MacIlwaine Drive, a circular route that encompassed World's View along with several small lakes.

On the way to World's View, they passed a place called the Tsanga Lodge Convalescent Centre. Nick told Rachel that the lodge had opened in 1976 as a rehabilitation centre for injured servicemen. He told her about one of his school friends who, after school, had joined the Selous Scouts[671]. During a particular frenzied firefight with a gang of terrorists, his friend had been shot in the head, as a result of which he had suffered significant physical and mental injuries that were to have lifelong effects. After various major surgical procedures, he had been sent to Tsanga Lodge for six months for convalescence. Nick said that the care, love and fellowship his friend had received at Tsanga Lodge had helped him to come to terms with, and accept, his changed life.

World's View itself was a scenic viewing spot situated on the western edge of the Inyanga Downs plateau at a height of 2,000 metres above sea level. From the viewing point, they enjoyed spectacular panoramic views over the Eastern Highlands, including the small village of Inyanga, which was some 1,400 metres below them. The air was beautifully clean, fresh, and pure. They were exhilarated by the whistling wind which blew through their hair, and flushed and reddened their cheeks.

Rachel took some stunning landscape shots using the panoramic settings on her Canon F1 camera.

From World's View, they visited the Inyangombe Falls. The staff at Troutbeck Inn had told them that the Falls were a wonderful place to enjoy a picnic lunch. So, they had asked the kitchen staff to prepare a picnic lunch for them, which Nick had packed into his Landcruiser.

It took them about 40 minutes to drive to the Inyangombe Falls from World's View. When they arrived, they parked in the car park and retrieved their packed lunch from Nick's Landcruiser. Then they

---

[671] The Selous Scouts were a special forces unit of the Rhodesian Army. It was mainly responsible for infiltrating the black majority population of Rhodesia and collecting intelligence on insurgents so that they could be attacked by regular elements of the Rhodesian Security Forces.

carefully navigated their way down a steep and slippery slope to the Falls.

The Falls were on the Inyangombe River and were very pretty. The access path took them to a point about halfway up the Falls. Here, there was a flat rocky ledge with a shallow, natural rock pool. They decided this would be the perfect spot to relax and enjoy their picnic lunch.

Nick and Rachel, feeling a bit more adventurous than their parents, carefully clambered up to the top of the Falls. From the summit, they were able to enjoy a spectacular view down the length of the Falls and into the steep ravine through which the Inyangombe River flowed.

"It may not have the same grandeur and power of the Victoria Falls," said Rachel. "But it is still very pretty. I just love how everything is so natural and unspoilt. If this was in England, there would be railings and manmade steps everywhere."

"Yep, I know," said Nick. "I think that is one of the things that I still find so attractive about Zimbabwe. It has a rawness and sense of impending peril that is kind of intoxicating, especially if you are still young and able."

"You are right," said Rachel. "It is difficult to explain and understand, but I definitely feel that, as well."

After about half an hour, the two young lovers clambered back down to where their parents had made themselves comfortable. The picnic lunch, which comprised sandwiches, fruit, and bottles of spring water, had been unpacked but not yet eaten. Once Nick and Rachel arrived back at the rocky ledge, they all dug into the food.

After lunch, they sat together, chatting and enjoying the scenery and each other's company. Rachel took off her sneakers, rolled up her jeans, and dipped her feet into the shallow rock pool. However, the water was so cold that she quickly pulled her feet out and put her shoes back on.

"My goodness," she exclaimed. "The water is freezing. It must have come from quite some height."

Later in the afternoon, they drove back to Troutbeck Inn and enjoyed a late afternoon snooze.

They had decided to reconvene at the bar for pre-dinner drinks at 6:30 pm. The evening's drinks and dinner followed a similar pattern to the night before, other than far less alcohol was consumed. Given the long and eventful day they had, everyone felt quite tired, and they all retired to their respective bedrooms before 9:30 pm.

Nick and Rachel had decided to climb Mount Inyangani on Saturday — the highest peak in the country at 2,600 metres. Since it would be a day trip, they excused themselves from their parents' plans, who intended to stay at Troutbeck Inn to enjoy its many facilities.

*****

Nick and Rachel woke early on Saturday morning. It had been years since Nick last climbed Mount Inyangani, and he was looking forward to experiencing the wonderful views and enjoyable climb once more. Although the ascent was quite strenuous, it wasn't dangerous and didn't require any climbing gear. However, Nick was aware that weather conditions on the mountain could change rapidly, and that there had been several instances of people getting lost or even killed due to sudden shifts in the weather.

Nick went to reception to check the weather forecast. He was informed that the weather would be fine and sunny all day, with a maximum temperature of 20°C. While there, he ordered a packed lunch, which the receptionist said he could collect after breakfast.

After breakfast, Nick collected their lunch and packed it, along with a couple of bottles of water, into his small backpack. Despite the favourable weather forecast, Nick cautioned Rachel that it was wise to be careful about the weather. As a precaution, they both crammed warm, rainproof jackets into the backpack. They then drove the 15 kilometres to Mount Inyangani's access car park, which was in the

Rhodes Inyanga National Park[672]. The car park was empty, which surprised Nick given the good weather.

They prepared for the 5-kilometre hike to the summit, estimating it would take about three hours on the way up and an hour and a half on the return.

The early part of the hike was gentle, along a well-worn, signposted path that took them across green-grassy heathlands. They passed many small streams and brooks. Though they weren't thirsty, the sound of the glistening water was irresistible, and they were delighted to find it beautifully cold, soft, and pure. It became almost mandatory to scoop up handfuls of water to splash on their faces and drink whenever they encountered one of these brooks.

As they ascended higher, the gradient increased, and at times the landscape changed from grassy heathlands to rocky ledges, though it was never difficult to navigate. Occasionally, however, they had to scramble up steeper gradients on all fours.

About halfway up, the weather unexpectedly changed. The sun disappeared, and heavy clouds of mist and fog rolled in. Visibility remained reasonable, but the temperature dropped by several degrees, prompting them to put on their jackets. Nick was glad they had brought them.

Just before they reached the summit, the fog and mist lifted, and by the time they arrived at the summit beacon, the sun had reappeared. The exertion of the climb and the returning sun made them feel warm again, and they gladly removed their jackets.

At the summit, they found a spot to sit and take in the magnificent views. The expansive vista stretched before them. The silence was strangely comforting, broken only by the soft rustling of the plains as a gentle breeze swept over the grasslands.

---

[672] This was renamed the Nyanga National Park in the 1980s.

The warmth of the sun on their faces was soporific. They lay back, closed their eyes to savour the moment, and soon both drifted into a short snooze.

After their nap, they unpacked their lunch. Their long walk meant that they were both hungry. This made their simple lunch of sandwiches and fruit taste a lot better than it really was.

After finishing their meal, they packed up and began the gentle walk back to the car for the drive back to Troutbeck Inn. Altogether, they had been away nearly the entire day — about seven hours.

Upon returning to Troutbeck Inn, Nick and Rachel found a note under their bedroom door from their parents. It stated that their parents had driven to the Pungwe Falls and didn't expect to be back until around 6:00 pm. The note ended by saying their parents would meet Nick and Rachel in the dining room at 6:45 pm.

"I'm glad they're being so proactive," said Nick. "I think Mum and Dad are enjoying showing your folks around. They used to come to Inyanga often, but that all stopped after 1976 because of the war. This part of the country had become quite dangerous, and I think it was easier for them to stay around Salisbury."

"Well, I'm glad they're showing Mum and Dad around," said Rachel. "I've loved seeing the mountains here and in the Vumba, and I know Mum and Dad will love it too."

After showering, Nick and Rachel headed to the bar, where they ordered two pre-dinner soft drinks.

At dinner, they all enjoyed recounting the events of the day. Rachel's parents had loved the visit to the Pungwe Falls. Lynne roared with laughter as she recounted how they had surprised a group of international tourists skinny-dipping in a natural pool at the top of the Falls. "Judging by the size of the two men's private parts, the water must have been freezing!" she joked.

*****

The next day, Sunday, 30th August, they were set to return to Salisbury. Nick, Matthew, and Stuart still wanted to play a round of golf, while Rachel, Lynne, and Brenda were content to enjoy a late breakfast and relax by the pool.

Matthew had arranged a late check-out and an 8:00 am tee-off time. Though the morning was chilly, walking the course soon warmed them up. All three men were decent golfers, though Nick, with the advantage of youth, could easily outdrive both older men. However, they had stronger short games than Nick. Nick played off a handicap of 10, Matthew 12, and Stuart 14. Since the course was relatively short, Nick's longer drives didn't provide as much of an edge as they might have on a longer course.

Their caddies, meanwhile, had placed bets on which of the three would win. With a par score of 71, the game remained tight until the end. After the 17th hole, they were all tied. But on the final hole, a par 5 and stroke 13, they all scored a 5, meaning Stuart won the match, much to the delight of his caddy — who at the start of the game, had introduced himself as Gary Player!

After golf, they enjoyed a beer and steak pie on the veranda. They then showered, rejoined their partners, packed their bags, and set off for Salisbury, feeling satisfied after a memorable stay at Troutbeck Inn.

The morning had been one of bonding and camaraderie among the men. However, one troubling topic had emerged during the round of golf. Stuart shared some information he had learned while in Johannesburg, where he met with several senior South African intelligence agents. These agents worked for BOSS[673], South Africa's intelligence agency.

---

[673] South African Bureau for State Security. This was the main South African intelligence agency from 1969 to 1980. In 1978, the Bureau was renamed the Department of National Security (DONS). In the early 1980s, BOSS/DONS was significantly restructured and transformed to become the National Intelligence Service (NIS). However, NIS is now defunct.

Stuart explained that since Zimbabwe's independence in April 1980, BOSS had been trying to sow discord between ZANU-PF and ZAPU[674]. They had recruited former members of Rhodesia's CIO[675], both black and white, who now worked as double agents within Zimbabwe's CIO. Their mission was to provoke racial tensions between Zimbabwe's two major political parties in an effort to weaken the country, thus reducing its potential threat to the white apartheid South African Government.

These double agents had succeeded in distributing misinformation and planting evidence that suggested ZAPU was planning a military coup against Mugabe's newly elected government. The accusations centred on those loyal to Joshua Nkomo, leader of ZAPU, who allegedly opposed Robert Mugabe, ZANU-PF leader and Prime Minister of Zimbabwe.

According to Stuart, the misinformation was having its desired effect. Mugabe had grown increasingly paranoid, unsure of whom he could trust within ZAPU. BOSS double agents were now urging him to deploy an elite force to neutralise the perceived military threat from ZIPRA[676], ZAPU's former armed wing.

Nick couldn't help but recall what Sipho had said over dinner on Friday, 21st August, at Mhuka Ranch. If external forces were indeed attempting to incite tension between the government and the Ndebele people, then perhaps the rumours Sipho had heard weren't merely whispers but part of a broader strategy.

Nick resolved to call Sipho once they returned to Salisbury.

---

[674] Zimbabwe African People's Union.
[675] Central Intelligence Organisation.
[676] Zimbabwe People's Revolutionary Army. ZIPRA was the military wing of ZAPU.

Chapter 55 – Nick and Rachel prepare to leave Zimbabwe

Timeline – 31 August to 2 September 1981

Nick and Rachel's last few days back in Salisbury[677] were busy.

Early on Monday morning, Nick phoned Mhuka[678] Ranch to let them know that he and Rachel had returned safely to Salisbury. He also wanted to inform Sipho[679] about what Stuart Dixon had learned from the South African intelligence agents he had met during his recent business trip to Johannesburg.

The phone was answered by Duncan. "Hello, this is Mhuka Ranch. Duncan speaking."

Nick replied, "Hi Duncan, it's Nick here. I'm sorry to disturb you so early."

"That's absolutely fine, Nick," said Duncan. "I've already been up for an hour anyway. This is a working ranch, after all! We have a big day today — we're expecting the delivery of the two black rhino cows later. They will stay in the bomas for a few days before we introduce them to the Two Ronnies[680]. No doubt the two bulls will be mighty pleased."

---

[677] The capital of Zimbabwe. Its name was changed to Harare in April 1982.
[678] A local word meaning animals or wildlife.
[679] Sipho is a Ndebele boy's name meaning Gift.
[680] The two male black rhinos had been given the name, *the Two Ronnies*, by Mhuka Ranch.

"That's wonderful," said Nick. "How exciting! I guess Sipho must be trying to fast-track the recruitment of his rangers."

Duncan replied, "Yes, that is progressing well. The advert for those positions has been finalised and will appear in the press next week. Sipho is expecting a strong response, especially after all the media reports about the shooting of the three poachers. How are you and Rachel?"

"We're both fine," said Nick. "We got back to Salisbury yesterday after six lovely days in the Vumba and Inyanga[681]. As you know, we had to report to the police at Umtali[682], which we did last Thursday. A complete farce and waste of time, but no problems, thank goodness."

"That's good to hear," said Duncan. "The Chiredzi Police haven't created any issues here either, so that's good. As I mentioned, there has been a lot of media interest about Mhuka Ranch following the news articles in both *The Herald*[683] and *The Chronicle*[684]. A number of potential donor organisations are interested in learning more about what we're doing here, so something good might still emerge from that vile gang of poachers. What scumbags! Unfortunately, their actions may have somewhat tarnished the RLI's[685] fine name."

Nick replied, "Any blemish to the RLI's name would be unfortunate. But I do hope that some of those potential donor organisations come through with financial support. Rachel has also spoken to her father about a potential donation, and he seems keen to make a contribution. Fingers crossed. But, changing subjects, I need to chat to Sipho. Is he around?"

"Yes, I think he is. Just hold on while I check," said Duncan.

---

[681] Inyanga was renamed Nyanga in 1982.
[682] Umtali was renamed Mutare in 1982.
[683] *The Herald* is the country's foremost national paper. Its origins date back to 1891.
[684] *The Chronicle* was published in Bulawayo and mostly reported on news affecting the Matabeleland area in the south of the country. It was first published in 1894.
[685] Rhodesian Light Infantry. This was an infantry regiment and was one of the country's main counter-insurgency units during the Rhodesian Bush War.

After a short wait, Sipho picked up the handset and said, "Hi Nick. Good to hear from you. I hope you and Rachel are doing well. Duncan tells me you're now back in Salisbury."

"We're both well, thanks," said Nick. "We got back yesterday. I know you have a busy day today with the two rhino cows arriving. That will be exciting. But I wanted to bring you up to speed on some worrying intel[686] I received from Stuart Dixon yesterday. As you know, he is Rachel's father. He lives and works in the UK but has very good political, business, and military connections with senior people in both South Africa and England. He's just been in South Africa and is now spending a few days in Zimbabwe before flying back to England."

"Yep, I remember you telling me about him. So, what have you heard?" asked Sipho.

Nick then proceeded to tell Sipho what Stuart had relayed. In particular, that the South African intelligence agency had recruited current members of Zimbabwe's CIO[687], who were now working as double agents for South Africa.

Nick explained that Stuart's intel suggested that these South African double agents were stirring tensions between ZANU-PF[688] and ZAPU[689] by spreading misinformation. This included planting evidence implying that ZAPU's political hierarchy was planning a military coup against the newly elected government. As a result, Robert Mugabe had grown paranoid, unsure of whom he could trust within ZAPU. The double agents were now encouraging him to deploy an elite force to eliminate any perceived military threats from former ZIPRA cadres in Matabeleland.

When Nick finished, Sipho said, "Geez, that's worrying. It matches with what I've been hearing about the disillusionment and anger among

---

[686] Intelligence information (often military in nature).
[687] Central Intelligence Organisation.
[688] Zimbabwe African National Union – Patriotic Front. ZANU-PF is a political organisation that has been the ruling party of Zimbabwe since independence in 1980.
[689] Zimbabwe African People's Union.

former Ndebele members of both the Rhodesian Security Forces and ZIPRA towards ZANU-PF, and Mugabe in particular. If Mugabe truly plans to take military action against these dissidents, there could be significant collateral damage to innocent Ndebele civilians. I need to warn my parents — they are still living and working at the Inyathi Mission. I appreciate you sharing this information with me."

"That's fine," said Nick. "I hope nothing more comes of it, but you never can tell. As you know, Rachel and I are flying back to the UK this Thursday, but I will definitely keep in touch. Go well, my friend."

After he hung up, Nick phoned Russell to say goodbye. Russell had already returned to UCT[690], and Nick managed to catch him at Driekoppen House of Residence, where he was living. Russell wanted to know more about what had occurred at Mhuka Ranch. He had read the lead article in *The Herald* but wanted more detailed information, which Nick gladly provided, but carefully omitting the fact that he and Sipho had initiated the firefight with the poachers, not the other way around.

Nick thanked Russell again for the loan of his car and for organising the camping trip to Lake McIlwaine. The two brothers promised to keep in touch. Russell mentioned that he and his girlfriend, Yvonne, hoped to visit England and Scotland sometime in 1982. Nick was delighted and said he would ensure that he and Rachel could spend time with them while they were in the UK.

On Tuesday, 1st September, Nick had to report to Borrowdale[691] Police Station as required by the police in Chiredzi. To avoid a repeat of the long wait he had experienced at Umtali Police Station, he had phoned on Monday to give the Borrowdale police a heads-up about his upcoming visit. After a long wait on the phone, he was told he would be interviewed by Inspector Chaora at 9:30 am on Tuesday.

Nick arrived at Borrowdale Police Station at 9:20 am and was eventually seen by Inspector Chaora at 9:40 am. The meeting was

---

[690] University of Cape Town.
[691] Borrowdale is a north-eastern suburb in Salisbury.

largely a repeat of what had occurred a few days earlier at Umtali. However, Inspector Chaora was better briefed on the events at Mhuka Ranch and congratulated Nick and the other men involved in eliminating the poaching gang.

Inspector Chaora asked Nick to report again the following week. Nick explained that this would not be possible, as he was returning to the UK on Thursday, 3rd September, to resume his university studies. He suggested that if the police needed him again, they should contact his parents in Ballantyne Park, who would pass on the relevant information.

Inspector Chaora agreed, and Nick was allowed to leave.

That afternoon, Brenda, Nick, and Rachel took Rachel's parents to the airport. Matthew had returned to work and was unable to join them. Stuart and Lynne were catching an SAA[692] flight to Johannesburg at 2:30 pm, connecting with a BA[693] flight to London Heathrow departing at 7:00 pm.

Stuart and Lynne thanked Brenda for all her and Matthew's kindness and hospitality over the past week. Lynne said she hoped it would not be too long before Brenda and Matthew visited the UK again so that they could reciprocate the hospitality.

Rachel and Nick also said farewell to Stuart and Lynne. However, this parting was easier, as they would be seeing Stuart and Lynne again on Friday, 4th September, when they were due to return to London.

---

[692] South African Airways.
[693] British Airways.

Chapter 56 – Nick and Rachel's farewell dinner

Nick and Rachel spent much of Wednesday, 2nd September, packing for their return trip to London. They were catching an SAA[694] flight from Salisbury to Johannesburg, departing on Thursday, 3rd September, at 2:30 pm, then connecting with a BA[695] flight to London, leaving Johannesburg at 7:00 pm and arriving at Heathrow early on Friday morning.

Having recently said goodbye to Russell, Brenda dreaded parting with Nick and Rachel. To soften her heartache, she organised a farewell dinner for them that evening at 7:00 pm by when Matthew would be home from work.

As expected, the dinner was fabulous. Brenda, with her maid Dorothy's help, had gone all out. During the meal, lively discussions unfolded.

Brenda turned to Rachel, asking, "So Rachel, what have been your impressions of Zimbabwe?"

Rachel replied enthusiastically, "I've absolutely loved it! The kindness of everyone has been incredible, and the places we've explored are breathtaking. Victoria Falls, for instance, is unlike anything else in the world — no wonder it's considered one of the Seven Wonders! I also expect Zimbabwean safaris are as good as they come, not to mention how stunning the Eastern Highlands are."

---

[694] South African Airways.
[695] British Airways.

"That's wonderful to hear," Brenda said. "I often worry about how Zimbabwe is portrayed in the British media."

Rachel replied, "You are right to be concerned. The media generally paints a negative picture of your country. I must admit, the negative reports made me a little apprehensive about holidaying here. However, despite some significant issues, there are also many positive stories. Just look at what Mhuka Ranch is doing to protect rhinos!"

Matthew leaned in and looked at Nick. "And what about you, Nick? After being away for over a year, do you think things have changed, and if so, has that change been for the better or worse?"

"That's tough, Dad," Nick replied. "But it's important, especially as Rachel and I think about our futures, either here or elsewhere. Are you sure you want to hear my thoughts?"

"Absolutely! Don't keep us in suspense," Brenda encouraged.

"Alright," Nick said, gathering his views. "In the last 18 months, I've come to better appreciate just how much our country has accomplished in a relatively short period of time. Just a century ago, it was mainly bush! Now, our cities are modern, and the infrastructure is impressive — in fact, in many respects it's even first world. Additionally, the agriculture and mining sectors are strong, and the manufacturing sector is surprisingly robust, thanks to sanctions."

"Sounds like a good start," Matthew commented.

Nick nodded. "Yes, it certainly is. However, as always, there's a catch." He paused for a moment, and then continued, "When I reflect on the country's political history as a whole over the last 50 years, I believe that the previous white minority governments have totally dropped the ball on some critical issues."

"What sort of issues?" Matthew asked.

Nick thought for a few seconds before answering. "Well, for starters, they didn't invest in properly educating black leaders or the black population about democracy. The Rhodesian governments' treatment of the blacks was hardly exemplary. Black Zimbabweans have never had meaningful political representation, and the governments of the day actually deliberately discriminated against them. It's no wonder their understanding of democracy is so poor and often viewed with scepticism."

Matthew frowned. "I suppose that's true. In the short term, it was probably easier for the government to keep the blacks well away from politics, but that has only created significant problems for the future."

Nick replied. "Indeed. While some black Zimbabweans may have enjoyed better living conditions than exist in other African nations, systemic inequality has been entrenched here for decades. Basic services like health and education were, and still are, woefully underfunded for blacks compared to whites. Similarly, employment prospects and housing opportunities have also been bleak in comparison to what has been available for whites. And with no social security systems in place, many blacks have had to endure pretty tough lives."

"So, what do you think needs to happen?" Matthew asked, intrigued.

"Well, like it or not, the status quo under the RF[696] had to change. Sure, the RF might have eventually addressed some of the issues. But it had little incentive to do so, especially since the electorate was nearly all white. The world was watching, and the world demanded change. How could the white community expect to hold onto power when they were outnumbered twenty to one?"

"I can see that," Brenda interjected. "But do you think there were moments when change might have been possible?"

Nick continued, delving deeper into the past. "I suppose before 1965, there was a chance for change from within. The black nationalist parties had hoped Britain would ensure that the Rhodesian government moved relatively quickly to a system of *one man, one*

---

[696] Rhodesian Front

vote. But once the RF declared UDI[697], it sealed the country's fate. The white government no longer saw itself as answerable to their colonial benefactor, which of course was Britain. Political change had been slow while the Rhodesian Government had been ultimately answerable to Britain. But once the RF was only answerable to itself and a predominantly white electorate, any political change was going to be glacially slow, if it occurred at all. So, from 1965, the black nationalists realised that real change would only come through the barrel of a gun."

"So, the black nationalist parties felt abandoned by Britain?" Brenda asked.

"Exactly," replied Nick. "Moreover, the RF then naively thought they could sideline the more radical black nationalist leaders by imprisoning them and banning their political parties. But that was a huge miscalculation. They grossly underestimated the aspirations and resolve of the black majority, especially when this resolve was being actively encouraged by foreign powers like Russia, China, and North Korea."

Brenda asked, "What about the elections that brought Muzorewa to power?"

"Good question!" said Nick. "Like most Zimbabweans, I originally felt that the results of those elections ought to have been recognised by the rest of the world, thereby allowing the country to be brought back into the international community. However, I now understand that those elections were seen as illegitimate by both the nationalist parties and the world because the true representatives of the black population were absent — and by that, I mean people like Mugabe and Nkomo. By focusing on black leaders whom the RF deemed more moderate, the RF mistakenly thought they could suppress black nationalistic aspirations. Moreover, that misjudgement undermined their negotiating power later. If Ian Smith had engaged with Mugabe

---

[697] Unilateral Declaration of Independence. The Government of Rhodesia declared UDI from Britain on 11th November 1965.

and Nkomo earlier, he might have secured a better deal for everyone than the one achieved by Muzorewa at the Lancaster House Conference[698]."

"That's a lot to unpack," Brenda remarked. "Do you think the new government under Mugabe will be better for the country?"

"I wish I could say yes, but I don't think it will be," Nick replied. "While independence could serve as a catalyst for progress, I worry that Zimbabwe might instead face the unravelling of both the positive and negative legacies of colonial rule. Many African countries that gained independence after WW2[699] saw not only the harmful aspects of their colonial past swept away but also the beneficial ones. Zimbabwe faces numerous challenges ahead — political inexperience, democratic vacuums, loss of technical knowledge, economic struggles, corruption, tribal tensions, unrealistic public expectations, and interference by global powers. With so many potential obstacles, it's hard to predict how things will turn out."

"Is it hopeless, then?" Rachel asked, her brow furrowing.

"No, not necessarily so!" Nick reassured her. "But it's essential for Zimbabweans to shape their own future, free from the over-bearing influence of a privileged white minority. I genuinely love this country; it has incredible potential. But I'm also realistic. If the country moves in a direction I'm not comfortable with, that's OK — it is all part of the democratic process. What matters is that it reflects the will of the Zimbabwean people. The risk is that, without a deep-rooted democratic tradition, Zimbabwe could quickly become a one-party

---

[698]. In August 1979, the British Government invited Bishop Abel Muzorewa, the Prime Minister of Zimbabwe-Rhodesia, Ian Smith, the leader of the Rhodesian Front and former Prime Minister of Rhodesia, the leaders of the Patriotic Front, Robert Mugabe and Joshua Nkomo, and other relevant political persons to participate in a Constitutional Conference at Lancaster House in London. The purpose of the Conference was to discuss and reach agreement on the terms of an Independence Constitution, to agree on the holding of elections under British authority, and to enable Zimbabwe-Rhodesia to proceed to lawful and internationally recognised independence, with the parties settling their differences by political means.
[699] The Second World War.

dictatorship. If that happens, the future will depend on the nature of the dictator and his or her supporters, and that's always a dangerous situation."

He paused, then added with a smile, "But enough of my rambling. Whose glass needs a top-up?"

The rest of the evening passed without further political talk, which was just as well, as Nick's thoughts provided plenty for Matthew, Brenda, and Rachel to ponder. Rachel, in particular, found herself struck by Nick's reflections. Though she knew little about Zimbabwe's history, she felt her instincts aligned closely with his.

Chapter 57 – Nick and Rachel's farewell to Zimbabwe

Timeline – 3 September 1981

The next day, Thursday, 3rd September, was grey and wet, quite different to the glorious weather they had experienced during the rest of their trip.

"Maybe the country is telling us it is time to leave," mused Nick.

"Don't talk such nonsense," said Rachel. "The country loves you as much as you love it."

The rest of the morning dragged slowly by.

At 12:15 pm, Brenda took them both to the airport. She was teary-eyed and did not want to linger around the terminal. She wished them both safe travels and gave them a hug and kiss. She then turned away and headed out of the terminal building. Her shoulders were slumped, and they saw her raise a hand to wipe away a tear from her cheek.

"The African diaspora is hard for us all, but especially for mothers," Nick reflected, his voice tinged with empathy. He knew that Brenda had always taken pride in keeping her family close, and with Nick and Russell now beginning to distance themselves from Zimbabwe, it would be especially hard for her. It was made even more difficult by the fact that their decision wasn't driven by personal ambition or family concerns, but by genuine worry for the long-term political and economic future of the country.

Their plane took off on time, and by 1:00 pm, they were enjoying a cold glass of wine, served by one of the SAA[700] air hostesses.

Nick slid his right hand into his trouser pocket and felt the comforting shape of the black velvet pouch holding his Bronze Cross of Rhodesia. He placed his other hand on Rachel's denim-clad thigh. "I love you, darling," he said. "This last month with you has been the best month of my life, and I have absolutely loved showing you around my country."

"I couldn't have said that better myself," said Rachel. She reached over and gave him a generous kiss on the lips.

Nick continued, "I don't know when we'll next return, but I'm certain we will. The universe has a plan, and it will be revealed to us in its own good time. When we are ready, Zimbabwe will still be here waiting for us. Those things in the country that need to pass will fade, those which need to remain will grow, and those which need to change will adapt.

"The government and its institutions will change and evolve. But the matchless splendour of Victoria Falls will be unchanged, as will the grandeur of the Eastern Highlands[701]. And the country's temperate climate will continue to be one of the best in the world.

"I am sure Zimbabwe will be fine. For a while, she may unravel, but in time, she will rediscover herself and find her rightful place in this crazy, complex world.

"I pray that Zimbabwe may become a shining light to the rest of Africa and perhaps even to the rest of the world. I believe her people's kindness and friendliness will endure, even through turmoil, struggle, and persecution. Hopefully, in the fullness of time, the nation will find love, purpose, success, and contentment in all that it does.

"Finally, I trust that the fate of the country's wildlife treasures will be determined solely by Mother Nature, not human greed or ineptitude. I

---

[700] South African Airways.

[701] The Eastern Highlands is a mountainous area on the border of Zimbabwe and Mozambique. It extends for about 300 kilometres from north to south and includes the Inyangani Mountains, the Vumba Mountains and the Chimanimani Mountains.

want our children to be able to experience the thrill of an African safari, seeing elephants, lions, leopards, rhinos, and buffalo roaming free in the wild — not confined to zoos or performing in circuses."

They both closed their eyes and dreamt of their next visit to this amazing, enigmatic land.

They hoped that day would not be too far off.

Epilogue

Timeline - 1982 to 2022

During this 40-year period, and despite its enormous potential, the country sunk to never-before-seen lows. The lows were however interspersed with occasional moments of significant achievements.

The details below summarise some of the more significant moments during this period.

Significant events

1982 to 2010	The economic policies of the government, led by Robert Mugabe, led to hyperinflation and economic collapse in the 2000s. At its peak in 2008, hyperinflation reached an all-time high of approximately 200 million %.
1982 to 1987	The *Gukurahundi* massacres were a series of political killings that took place in Zimbabwe in the early 1980s. The killings were carried out by a North Korean-trained unit of the ZNA[702] known as the Fifth Brigade, and targeted ethnic Ndebele civilians and former Ndebele soldiers from ZIPRA[703] and RAR[704], who were perceived to be supportive of the opposition ZAPU[705] party.
	The term *Gukurahundi* means *'the early rain which washes away the chaff before the spring rains'* in the Shona language. This term was used by the government of the then Prime Minister, Robert Mugabe, to describe the military operation.

---

[702] Zimbabwe National Army.
[703] Zimbabwe People's Revolutionary Army. ZIPRA was the military wing of ZAPU.
[704] Rhodesian African Rifles.
[705] Zimbabwe African People's Union.

The massacres were the result of political and ethnic tensions, perceived threats to national security, and the desire of the ruling ZANU-PF[706] party to consolidate power and eliminate political opposition, especially from the ZAPU party.

The massacres resulted in the deaths of an estimated 20,000 people and have been widely condemned as a serious human rights violation and possibly as a campaign of ethnic cleansing. The events remain a sensitive and controversial topic in Zimbabwe, and many families of the victims have yet to receive justice or compensation for their losses.

1990 to 2010   The land reform program was a policy implemented by the Government of Zimbabwe to redistribute land from white commercial farmers to black Zimbabweans. The program was controversial and led to a significant decrease in agricultural production, as well as allegations of human rights violations. The program was implemented through a combination of legal reform, illegal seizures of land, intimidation, and violence, sometimes lethal, against white farmers.

1999   The formation of an opposition party known as the Movement for Democratic Change (MDC).

2002   Presidential elections, which were marred by allegations of voter fraud and intimidation.

2008   Presidential elections, in which Robert Mugabe and the ZANU-PF party were defeated by Morgan Tsvangirai, the leader of the MDC[707]. The results of the elections were however later annulled.

---

[706] Zimbabwe African National Union – Patriotic Front. ZANU-PF is a political organisation that has been the ruling party of Zimbabwe since independence in 1980.
[707] The Movement for Democratic Change.

2009	After three significant re-denominations of the Zimbabwean dollar, it was eventually abandoned in early 2009 as being valueless.
2009	The formation of the Government of National Unity.
2013	Presidential elections, in which Robert Mugabe was re-elected as President in an election that was widely criticised as not being free and fair.
2017	The impeachment of Robert Mugabe.
2018	Presidential elections, in which Emmerson Mnangagwa from the ruling ZANU-PF party, was elected as President.
2019	The re-introduction of the Zimbabwean dollar.
2019	The death of Robert Mugabe on 6th September 2019, aged 95. He served as Prime Minister of Zimbabwe from 1980 to 1987, and then as its President from 1987 to 2017.
2020	The COVID-19 pandemic in 2020 which led to significant adverse economic impacts.

Economic collapse

In the late 1990s and early 2000s Zimbabwe experienced a severe economic crisis, characterised by hyperinflation and a shortage of basic goods. This was caused by a combination of factors, including the government's land reform program, which led to a decline in agricultural production, and the government's economic policies, which included price controls and the printing of money to finance government spending.

In an attempt to address the hyperinflation, the RBZ[708] began issuing new currency denominations in 2006, but this did not have the desired effect of stabilising the economy.

In 2008, the RBZ announced that it would demonetise the Zimbabwean dollar, and that all bank accounts would be converted to US dollars at a rate of Z$1,000,000,000,000 to US$1. This effectively made the Zimbabwean dollar worthless, as the hyperinflation had reached such high levels that the largest denomination of the currency, the Z$100 trillion note, was not even enough to buy a small bag of groceries.

The demonetisation of the Zimbabwean dollar was a significant event, as it effectively ended the use of the local currency and marked the adoption of the US dollar as the main currency in Zimbabwe.

The Zimbabwean dollar was re-introduced in June 2019.

The country has subsequently adopted a multi-currency system and, as at the end of 2022, the Zimbabwean Dollar, the US dollar and South African Rand were the main currencies that were used in the country. However, significant inflation remains a major problem for the country.

Major infrastructure projects

Hwange Thermal Power Station	Commissioned in the 1980s, this is Zimbabwe's largest thermal power station and provides a significant portion of the country's electricity.
National Sports Stadium	Completed in the early 1980s, this is one of the largest stadiums in Africa, and has hosted a number of international events and matches.

---

[708] The Reserve Bank of Zimbabwe.

Harare International Airport	Completed in the 1980s, this airport serves as the main international gateway to Zimbabwe.
Victoria Falls Airport	Completed in the 1990s, this airport was built to cater for the increasing number of tourists visiting Victoria Falls.
Robert Mugabe International Airport	Completed in 2017, this airport serves as the main international gateway to Harare, the capital of Zimbabwe.
Beitbridge-Harare-Chirundu Highway	Completed in 2018, this project aimed at upgrading the road network to cater for the increasing truck traffic between Zimbabwe and South Africa.
Expansion of the Victoria Falls bridge	Completed in 2019, this project aimed at expanding the capacity of the bridge to cater for the increasing number of tourists visiting the Victoria Falls.

Major achievements of ZANU-PF

Independence and majority rule:

ZANU played a key role in the liberation struggle against white minority rule and the attainment of independence for Zimbabwe in 1980.

Land reform program:

The ZANU-PF Government implemented a land reform program that aimed to redistribute land from white farmers to black farmers. This was seen as a step towards addressing the historical injustices of colonial land ownership in the country. However, the manner in which the program was implemented resulted in significant long-lasting damage to the agriculture sector.

Education and health care:

The ZANU-PF Government has implemented policies that have expanded access to education and health care for many citizens, particularly in rural areas.

Regional & international relations

The ZANU-PF Government has worked to strengthen relations with other African countries and has played a key role in regional organisations such as the African Union[709] and the Southern African Development Community.

Securing Kariba Dam

The Zimbabwean Government has taken several steps to secure the Kariba Dam wall and ensure the safety of communities living downstream. Some of these steps include:

Rehabilitation and maintenance

The Zimbabwean Government has invested in the rehabilitation and maintenance of Kariba Dam, including upgrading its infrastructure and strengthening the dam's walls.

Monitoring & early warning systems

Zimbabwe has set up a system for monitoring the dam's water levels, as well as early warning systems that can alert communities in the event of a potential breach.

Emergency response plans

The government has developed emergency response plans in the event of a breach of the dam walls, including evacuation plans for communities living downstream.

---

[709] The African Union superseded the OAU in 2002

Community awareness

Zimbabwe has launched awareness campaigns to educate communities about the dangers posed by the dam and the importance of taking precautions in the event of an emergency.

International collaboration

Zimbabwe has sought the help of international organisations and experts to ensure the safety and stability of the dam walls. For example, the government has sought assistance from the International Commission on Large Dams to develop and implement a risk management plan for the dam.

Rhino protection

Zimbabwe has been taking various measures to provide greater protection to its rhino population in recent years.

These include:

Anti-poaching efforts

The country has increased patrols and surveillance in rhino habitats to deter poaching and arrests poachers.

Rhino translocation

The government has been relocating rhinos from high-risk areas to safer, more secure locations.

Community involvement

Zimbabwe has been working with local communities to raise awareness about the importance of rhino conservation and to encourage them to report any suspicious activity.

Legal measures

The government has increased penalties for poaching and introduced stricter laws to regulate the trade in rhino horn.

International cooperation

Zimbabwe has been working with other countries, including South Africa and China, to combat the illegal trade in rhino horn.

Rhino breeding program

Zimbabwe also has a breeding program to increase the rhino population in the country.

These efforts are making a positive impact on the rhino population in the country, but the population still remains fragile due to ongoing poaching and the lack of resources for anti-poaching.

Current challenges

Zimbabwe continues to face a number of significant challenges, including:

Political challenges

Zimbabwe has been criticised for its lack of political freedoms and its human rights abuses. The government has been accused of electoral fraud and intimidation of political opponents. The government has also been accused of violating the rights of the press, civil society organisations and the opposition.

Humanitarian challenges

Zimbabwe is facing a humanitarian crisis, with a large number of its citizens suffering from food insecurity and malnutrition.

Environmental challenges

Zimbabwe has been facing environmental issues such as deforestation, soil erosion, and pollution. Climate change has also been affecting the country in terms of droughts and flooding which are affecting the agricultural sector.

Health challenges

Zimbabwe is facing a number of health challenges, including a shortage of medicines and medical equipment, and a lack of access to basic health care services. The COVID-19 pandemic also had a significant adverse impact on the country's health system.

Energy challenges

Zimbabwe has been facing intermittent power shortages and an energy crisis for several years. The country has struggled with electricity generation capacity, leading to frequent power cuts that have affected businesses, industries, and households. The power shortages are due to various factors, including aging power infrastructure, limited investment in the energy sector, and challenges in securing fuel for thermal power plants.

Glossary of Terms

1RAR	1st Battalion of Rhodesian African Rifles.
2IC	Second in Charge.
2RAR	2nd Battalion of Rhodesian African Rifles.
3RAR	3rd Battalion of Rhodesian African Rifles.
4WD	Four-wheel drive.
African Frontline States	These were a loose coalition of African countries from the 1960s to the 1980s committed to ending white minority rule in Rhodesia. They included Angola, Botswana, Mozambique, Tanzania, and Zambia.
AK-47	This was a light automatic rifle developed in the Soviet Union by small-arms designer Mikhail Kalashnikov. The AK-47 was the preferred rifle of the ZANLA and ZIPRA forces.
A-Level	A-Levels were the Advanced Level of school examinations. It was conferred as a school leaving qualification to senior school pupils as part of the Cambridge International General Certificate of Education.
Alfred Beit Road Bridge	The Alfred Beit Road Bridge is named after Alfred Beit, founder of the De Beers diamond mining company and business associate of Cecil Rhodes. The original bridge was constructed in 1929 at a cost of $600,000.
ANC	This is the acronym for the African National Congress. The ANC is one of the oldest and most well-known liberation movements in South Africa. It was founded in 1921 and played a central role in the fight against apartheid.
Apartheid	Apartheid is the Afrikaans word for apartness. It was a system of institutionalised racial segregation that existed in South Africa and South West Africa (now Namibia) from 1948 to the early 1990s.
Assembly points	During the lead up to the general elections in February 1980 the British Governor of the country, Lord Soames, granted a general amnesty to all guerrillas. Those guerrillas who chose to take advantage of the

general amnesty were required to disarm and assemble in 16 assembly points which had been established across the country. By the deadline of 6th January 1980, just over 18,000 guerrillas had done so.

AWOL	Absence Without Leave.
BA	British Airways.
Baas	*Baas* is a word derived from Afrikaans and means boss or master.
BBC	British Broadcasting Corporation.
Beira	Beira is on the east coast of Mozambique and is the capital and largest city in the Mozambican province of Sofala.
Bilharzia	Bilharzia is also known as snail fever. It is a disease caused by parasites (known as schistosomes) carried by freshwater snails. In parts of Africa, it is endemic.
BMATT	BMATT is the acronym for the British Military Advisory and Training Team.
Boerewors	Boerewors is a type of spicy sausage which originated in South Africa.
Bonsella	Bonsella is an Afrikaans word meaning showing thanks with a gift. The word was in common use by both whites and blacks in Zimbabwe.
BOSS	South African Bureau for State Security. This was the main South African intelligence agency from 1969 to 1980. In 1978, the Bureau was renamed the Department of National Security (DONS). In the early 1980s, BOSS/DONS was significantly restructured and transformed to become the National Intelligence Service (NIS). NIS is now however defunct.
Braai	Braai is the Afrikaans word for a BBQ.
BSAP	British South Africa Police.
CBD	Central Business District.
Chief Chirau	Chief Chirau was a notable figure amongst Rhodesia's traditional black chiefs.

Chilojo cliffs	The Chilojo cliffs are a spectacular 30 km stretch of red and white-banded sandstone columns that stretch along the shoreline of the Lundi River.
Chipembere	*Chipembere* is the Shona word for rhino.
CIO	Central Intelligence Organisation.
CITES	Convention on International Trade in Endangered Species of Wild Fauna and Flora. It is a multilateral treaty designed to protect endangered plants and animals. It came into force on 1st July 1975.
CHOGM	Commonwealth Heads of Government Meeting.
Civvy street	The expression *civvy street* refers to life and activities which were not connected with the Rhodesian Security Forces.
DAs	District Assistants were junior staff members in the Ministry of Internal Affairs ('INTAF'). INTAF was responsible for the welfare of rural black Africans living on Tribal Trust Lands.
Dassies	These are also known as the rock hyrax or rock rabbit. They are a medium-sized terrestrial mammal native to Africa.
Dead ground	Dead ground is ground that cannot be seen from the target that is being observed.
Department of National Parks	The full name is the Department of National Parks and Wildlife Management.
DGS	DGS is an acronym for Dangerous Game Series. It is a trademark which has been registered by Hornady Manufacturing Company in America. The trademark was applied to ammunition specially designed by Hornady for big game hunting.
Eastern Highlands	The Eastern Highlands is a mountainous area on the border of Zimbabwe and Mozambique. It extends for about 300 kilometres from north to south and includes the Inyangani Mountains, the Vumba Mountains and the Chimanimani Mountains.
Entumbane uprisings	The Entumbane uprisings took place in January and February 1981 around Bulawayo when ZIPRA and ZANLA troops clashed over political differences. The

uprising was crushed by the ZNA who heavily relied on forces from the former Rhodesian Security Forces.

Essexvale	Essexvale is a small town in the Matabeleland province of Zimbabwe located approximately 45 kilometres south-east of Bulawayo. It is now named Esigodini.
Fort Victoria	Fort Victoria was renamed Masvingo in 1982.
FN	This was a light automatic rifle designed in Belgium and manufactured by FN Herstal. The FN was the standard issue rifle for the Rhodesian Security Forces.
Frelimo	The Front for the Liberation of Mozambique.
Goffel	Goffel was a Rhodesian derogatory term used to describe persons who were of mixed-race.
Gonakudzingwa	This is a Shona word meaning *where the banished ones sleep.*
Gonarezhou	Gonarezhou is a Shona word meaning *place of elephants.*
Gook	A defamatory word for a terrorist.
Greystone Park	An upmarket suburb of Salisbury, about 15 kilometres north-east of Salisbury CBD.
Gukuranhundi	*Gukurahundi* is Shona expression which loosely translates to *the early rain which washes away the chaff before the spring rains.* It is estimated that during the *Gukurahundi* massacres, more than 20,000 people were killed, the vast majority of whom were of Ndebele ethnicity. The massacres commenced in January 1983 and ended in December 1987, when a unity accord was signed between Mugabe and Nkomo.
HQ	Headquarters.
Imire	Imire is the Shona word for meeting place.
Indaba	An indaba was the name given by the local tribespeople to collective meetings of chiefs and headmen.
Induna	In Ndebele culture, an InDuna was a title meaning a great leader, headman, or commander of a group of warriors.

Ingwe	Ingwe is a local African word meaning leopard.
Inyati Mission	The Mission had been established by the Reverend Robert Moffat in 1859. It is situated some 75 kilometres north-north-east of Bulawayo. Moffat was a member of the London Missionary Society, which had been established in England with the aim of spreading the knowledge of Christ among heathen and unenlightened nations.
Inyoka	Inyoka is the Ndebele word for snake or serpent.
Intel	Intelligence information (often military in nature).
Inyanga	Inyanga was renamed Nyanga in 1982.
Ishe	*Ishe* is a term of respect used by RAR soldiers when referring to their officers.
IUCN	International Union for the Conservation of Nature. This is an international organisation working in the field of nature conservation and sustainable use of natural resources.
JOC	Joint Operations Centre.
Jock of the Bushveld	Jock of the Bushveld was written by Sir James Percy Fitzpatrick and first published in 1907. It is a true story about Fitzpatrick's travels with his dog, Jock, a Staffordshire Bull Terrier cross.
John Vorster	John Vorster served as the Prime Minister of South Africa from 1966 to 1978.
Knobkerrie	A knobkerrie is a wooden club with a large knob at one of its ends. Traditionally, they were used by South African tribespeople for throwing at animals or for clubbing an enemy's head.
Kopje	The word kopje is derived from the Afrikaans word *koppie,* which means a small hill.
Lake McIlwaine	The lake was named after Sir Robert McIlwaine, a former judge of the High Court of Rhodesia and founder of Southern Rhodesia's soil and water conservation movement. It was renamed Lake Chivero in 1982.

Michael Chalk

Lancaster House Conference	In August 1979, the British Government invited Bishop Abel Muzorewa, the Prime Minister of Zimbabwe-Rhodesia, Ian Smith, the leader of the Rhodesian Front and former Prime Minister of Rhodesia, the leaders of the Patriotic Front, Robert Mugabe and Joshua Nkomo, and other relevant political persons to participate in a Constitutional Conference at Lancaster House in London. The purpose of the Conference was to discuss and reach agreement on the terms of an Independence Constitution, to agree on the holding of elections under British authority, and to enable Zimbabwe-Rhodesia to proceed to lawful and internationally recognised independence, with the parties settling their differences by political means.

Lancaster House Agreement

The Lancaster Agreement was negotiated between relevant parties during the period from 10th September 1979 to 15th December 1979. Its signing on 21st December 1979 included and provided for: -

- The terms of the ceasefire agreed to by the warring parties.
- The return of the country to direct British rule for a few months whilst elections based on a universal franchise were held. The return of the country to direct British rule nullified the illegal UDI of Rhodesia from the United Kingdom, which had been declared on 11th November 1965.
- The dissolution of the unrecognised state of Zimbabwe-Rhodesia, which had come into existence in June 1979 following an Internal Settlement between Ian Smith and the moderate African nationalist leaders comprising Bishop Abel Muzorewa, Ndabaningi Sithole and Senator Chief Jeremiah Chirau.
- The terms of a new constitution for the country, the provisions of which could not be altered for a period of 10 years.

Lion lager — Lion lager is one of Zimbabwe's top selling beers.

Lobengula Khumalo — King Lobengula Khumalo (1845 to circa 1894) was the second and last official King of the northern Ndebele people.

498 | P a g e

Locstat	Ordnance survey map reference.
Long drop	A pit latrine.
Lookout Masuku	Lookout Masuku was the leader of the Zimbabwe People's Revolutionary Army (the military wing of ZAPU).
Lowveld	The term lowveld refers to low-lying, generally semi-arid region characterised by savanna or bushveld vegetation.
Lozikeyi Dlodlo	Queen Lozikeyi Dlodlo (c 1855 to 1919) was one of the favourite wives of King Lobengula and a senior queen until 1893.
Lundi River	The Lundi River was renamed the Runde River in 1985.
MAG	The Belgian designed Fabrique Nationale (FN) 7.62mm general-purpose machine gun which was standard issue for the Rhodesian Security Forces. MAG is the acronym for the French phrase "mitrailleuse à gaz" (which means gas operated machine gun).
Malvernia	The town's name was changed to Chicualacuala in 1975 shortly after Mozambique's independence from Portugal.
Mandla	Mandla is a Ndebele boy's name meaning Power and Strength.
Maputo	The capital and largest city in Mozambique. Prior to July 1975, Maputo's name had been Lourenço Marques.
Masodja	*Masodja* is the Africanised word for soldier.
MDC	The Movement for Democratic Change.
Merde	This is the Portuguese word for *shit*.
Mess	A shared house.
Methuen Barracks	These were previously named the Heany Barracks.
Mhuka	A local word meaning animals or wildlife.
Military call-ups	By 1978, all white men up to the age of 60 were subject to periodic call-up to the army. Younger men up to 35 years in age were required to spend

alternating blocks of six weeks in the army and at home. These mandatory call-ups had posed a considerable burden on the country's workforce.

Modus operandi	This is a Latin phrase meaning method of operating.
Mombies	This is the Shona work meaning cows or cattle.
Mosi-oa-Tunya	*Mosi-oa-Tunya* is the local Lozi name for the Victoria Falls. It means *The Smoke that Thunders*. The Lozi people live primarily in south-west Zambia and surrounding countries.
Murungu	This is the Shona word for a white person.
Nandi	Nandi is a Ndebele girl's name meaning Sweetness.
NCO	Non-commissioned officer.
NDP	National Democratic Party.
Ndabaningi Sithole	Ndabaningi Sithole was the leader of a more moderate faction of ZANU.
NGO	Non-government organisations.
Nookies	Slang term for sexual intercourse.
Nzou	*Nzou* is a Shona word for elephant.
OAU	The Organisation of African Unity (1963 to 2002). It was superseded by the African Union in 2002.
O level	O Levels were the Ordinary level of school examinations. It was conferred as a school leaving qualification to senior school pupils as part of the Cambridge International General Certificate of Education. The qualification is at a lower level to the Moderate and Advanced levels of qualification.
One Flew over the Cuckoos Nest	This was a 1975 drama film based on the novel by Ken Kesey. The movie is set in a mental institution and follows the story of Randle McMurphy, a rebellious inmate who feigns insanity to avoid prison time. While in the institution, he clashes with the strict and oppressive Nurse Ratched, who runs the ward with an iron fist. McMurphy attempts to disrupt the status quo and bring hope to his fellow patients.

OP	Observation Post.
Operation Noah	Operation Noah was a wildlife rescue operation on the Zambezi River which lasted from 1958 to 1964. The operation was necessitated by the flooding of the Kariba Gorge following the construction of Kariba Dam. The operation to rescue wildlife was led by Rupert Fothergill. It is estimated that approximately 6,000 animals, birds and snakes were rescued and relocated.
Porks	Colloquial Rhodesian term for the Portuguese people living in Mozambique.
PW Botha	Pieter Willem Botha was a South African politician who was the last Prime Minister of South Africa from 1978 to 1984 and its first executive state president from 1984 to 1989.
PWO	Platoon Warrant Officer.
R&R	Rest and Recuperation.
Rain tree	The Rain Tree or Apple-Leaf Tree. The botanical name is *Philenoptera Violacea*. The name Rain Tree is derived from the fact that the tree can become infested with a spittlebug, which causes apparent rain to fall from the tree.
RAR	Rhodesian African Rifles.
RAT-packs	Army ration packs.
RBZ	The Reserve Bank of Zimbabwe.
Recce	This is an informal term for reconnaissance.
RENAMO	The Mozambican National Resistance Movement. It was opposed to FRELIMO. The name RENAMO is from the Portuguese phrase - *Resistência Nacional Moçambicana*.
Rex Nhongo	Rex Nhongo was the leader of the Zimbabwe African National Liberation Army (the military wing of ZANU).
Rinderpest disease	Rinderpest, also known as cattle plague, is a disease which can be fatal. It is caused by the rinderpest virus, which primarily affects cattle and buffalo.

RF	Rhodesian Front.
RLI	This is the acronym for the Rhodesian Light Infantry. This was an infantry regiment of the Rhodesian Army which was formed in 1961 at the Brady Barracks in Bulawayo. It was relocated a year later to the Cranborne Barracks in Salisbury, where its headquarters remained for the rest of its existence. The RLI became one of the country's main counter-insurgency units during the country's bush war.
Royal Harare Golf Club	The Club changed its name to Royal Harare Golf Club at independence in 1980. Prior to that, it was called the Royal Salisbury Golf Club.
RPD	The RPD was a 7.62 x 39 mm light machine gun developed in the Soviet Union.
RPG	Rocket-Propelled Grenades.
RSM	Regimental Sergeant Major.
SAA	South African Airways.
Sabi River	The Sabi River was renamed Save River in Zimbabwe in 1985. But it was still called the Sabi River in Mozambique.
Sadza	Sadza is a thickened porridge made with white maize meal. It is one of the staple foods in Zimbabwe.
Salisbury	The capital of Rhodesia (now Zimbabwe). Its name was changed to Harare in April 1982.
SAP	South African Police.
SB	Special Branch. This was the unit within the BSAP which was responsible for matters of national security and intelligence. During the Rhodesian Bush War, most of their work related to counter-insurgency activities.
Selous Scouts	The Selous Scouts were a special forces unit of the Rhodesian Army. It was mainly responsible for infiltrating the black majority population of Rhodesia and collecting intelligence on insurgents so that they could be attacked by regular elements of the Rhodesian Security Forces.

Servants	The terms servants, house boy and garden boy were the usual terms used by white employers when referring to domestic workers. These terms continued to be used for many years after Zimbabwe became independent in 1980.
Internal Settlement	Black signatories to the Internal Settlement, signed on 3rd March 1978, included Bishop Abel Muzorewa, leader of the UANC, Ndabaningi Sithole, leader of a more moderate faction of ZANU, and Chief Jeremiah Chirau, a notable figure amongst Rhodesia's traditional black chiefs.
Sipho	Sipho is a Ndebele boy's name meaning Gift.
Sitrep	Situation Report.
Skebenga	*Skebenga* is a local word meaning gangster or bandit.
Skellum	Skellum is a local word meaning rogue or troublemaker.
Sweet Banana	This was a song that was created in 1942 and which was used by the Rhodesian African Rifles as its regimental marching song.
SRANC	The Southern Rhodesia African National Congress.
Terrs	*Terrs* was the colloquial term for terrorists.
The Chronicle	*The Chronicle* was published in Bulawayo and mostly reported on news affecting the Matabeleland area in the south of the country. It was first published in 1894.
The Great Zimbabwe Ruins	The Great Zimbabwe Ruins is the name of the stone ruins of an ancient city known as Great Zimbabwe. The ruins are located just outside Fort Victoria (now called Masvingo). People lived in Great Zimbabwe from around 1100 but abandoned it in the 15th century. The city was the capital of the Kingdom of Zimbabwe, which was a Shona trading empire. Zimbabwe means "stone houses" in Shona.
The Federation	The Federation of Rhodesia and Nyasaland was a colonial federation that consisted of three southern African territories, namely the self-governing British colony of Southern Rhodesia and the British

	protectorates of Northern Rhodesia and Nyasaland. It existed between 1953 and 1963.
The Herald	*The Herald* is the country's foremost national paper. Its origins date back to 1891.
The Tube	This is London's underground railway system that services the London metropolitan area.
The Two Ronnies	The two male black rhinos had been given the name, *the Two Ronnies*, by Mhuka Ranch.
TMB	Tobacco Marketing Board.
Troopie	Colloquial term meaning a regular member or national serviceman of the Rhodesian Army.
Tsetse flies	Tsetse flies are a species of a blood sucking fly which are found in Africa. They can transmit sleeping sickness in humans and a similar disease called nagana in animals. If left untreated these diseases can be fatal.
TTL	Tribal Trust Lands. These were large tracts of land, usually sub-optimal, which were set aside for settlement by black Africans.
UANC	United African National Council.
Ubaba	Ubaba is the Ndebele word for father.
UCT	The University of Cape Town.
UDI	Unilateral Declaration of Independence. The Government of Rhodesia declared UDI from Britain on 11th November 1965.
UFP	The United Federal Party.
Ukuthula	Ukuthula is the Zulu word for calmness or silence.
Umfana	Umfana is the Ndebele word for son.
Umama	Umama is the Ndebele word for mother.
Umtali	Umtali was renamed Mutare in 1982.
Umyeni	Umyeni is the Ndebele word for my husband.
VHF	Very high frequency.

Victoria Falls	Victorian Falls, or *Mosi-oa-Tunya* (which means *The Smoke That Thunders*) is one of the seven natural wonders of the world.
Vila Salazar	The town is now named Sango.
Vlei	A vlei is an Afrikaans word meaning *low-lying marshy ground covered with water during the rainy season*.
Vumba Mountains	The Vumba Mountains are also known as the Bvumba Mountains.
WW2	The Second World War.
ZANU	Zimbabwe African National Union.
ZANU-PF	Zimbabwe African National Union – Patriotic Front. ZANU-PF is a political organisation that has been the ruling party of Zimbabwe since independence in 1980.
ZANU PF	ZANU PF was a political alliance between ZANU and ZAPU, which was formed during the lead up to Zimbabwe-Rhodesia's first *one-man-one-vote* general elections, which were held in February 1980, and which were won by ZANU.
ZANLA	Zimbabwe African National Liberation Army. ZANLA was the military wing of ZANU.
ZAPU	Zimbabwe African People's Union.
ZIPRA	Zimbabwe People's Revolutionary Army. ZIPRA was the military wing of ZAPU.
ZNA	Zimbabwe National Army.
ZRP	Zimbabwe Republic Police.

Appendix 1

Information	
Weight of product purchased	135.5 kgs
Price per kg	$750 US
Purchase price before deductions	**$101,625** US
Deductions	
Agents commission at 3.5%	$3,557 US
Freight (Beira to Hong Kong)	$980 US
Incidentals - customs	$480 US
Incidentals - shipping	$920 US
Incidentals - port	$220 US
Total deductions	**$6,157** US
Net purchase price after deductions	**$95,468** US
Rounded to nearest $100	**$95,500**

Appendix 2

Information	Rh$	US$
Weight of product sold to purchaser in Hong Kong		135.5 kgs
Sale price - per kg		$750 US
Sale revenue before deductions		**$101,625 US**
Deductions		
Agents commission at 3.5%		$3,557 US
Freight (Beira to Hong Kong)		$980 US
Incidentals - customs		$480 US
Incidentals - shipping		$920 US
Incidentals - port		$220 US
Total deductions		**$6,157 US**
Net sale price after commission, freight and incidentals		**$95,468 US**
Rounded to nearest $100		**$95,500**
Expenses		
Fees to shooters - 2 elephants @ $3,000 per elephant	$6,000 Rh	$9,000.0 US
Fees to spotter - 2 elephants @ $400 per elephant	$800 Rh	$1,200.0 US
Incidentals - reimbursing shooters for trip from Fort Victoria to Hlaro to RV point and return 690 kms @ US$0.50 per kms	$345 Rh	$517.5 US
Incidentals - reimbursing shooters for cost of setting up bush camp	$50 Rh	$75.0 US
Total expenses	**$7,195 Rh**	**$10,793 US**
NET PROFIT		**$84,708**
Agreed profit share - Johannes 55%; Santiago 45%		
So Johannes profit share		**$46,589**
So Santiago profit share		**$38,118**
FIXED COSTS PAYABLE BY JOHANNES		
Shooters retention fees - 2 shooters for 2 months @ Rh$200 per month	$800 Rh	$1,200.0 US
Spotters retention fees - 4 spotters for 2 months @ Rh$200 per month	$1,600 Rh	$2,400.0 US

NOTES

1. The fixed monthly costs of Rh$1,200 relating to retention fees will continue to be met by Johannes after August 1977

2. Santiago responsible for meeting his own costs in relation to round trip from Malvernia to RV point to Beira and return to Malvernia

3. Johannes responsible for meeting his own costs in relation to round trip from Buffalo Range to Malvernia to Great Zimbabwe Hotel to Buffalo Range

4. Rh$ converted to US$ at the exchange rate of Rh$1.00 equals US$1.50.

About the Author

www.authormichaelchalk.com

Michael's novels invite readers to witness the seismic shifts in southern Africa's recent history, through characters whose lives are marked by love, war, and political upheaval.

Born in Durban, South Africa, in October 1955, and raised in Rhodesia (now Zimbabwe), Michael experienced firsthand the complex dynamics that fuel his storytelling.

After completing his education in Rhodesia and earning a Bachelor of Laws in Scotland, he returned to Rhodesia, where he worked as a public prosecutor and later as the operations manager of Zimbabwe's leading medical aid society. During his 12 months of national service, he served as a 2nd Lieutenant in the Rhodesian African Rifles. His experiences gave him a deep understanding of the era's conflicts and camaraderie — insights he brings to his books.

In *The Unravelling*, Michael captures the tensions of the 1970s and 1980s as Rhodesia's colonial rule collapses. Following two comrades-in-arms, Nick and Sipho, through war and its challenging aftermath, the novel reveals the scars left on both individuals and nations alike.

The story continues in *A Moment of Madness*, set amid Robert Mugabe's brutal consolidation of power after his victory in the country's first universal franchise elections in 1980. As Nick and Rachel navigate life in the UK and grapple with Zimbabwe's ruthless Gukurahundi campaign, they are drawn into dangerous political currents that put love, loyalty, and integrity to the test. With vivid portrayals of Cold War geopolitics and Zimbabwe's internal strife, Michael offers readers a gripping narrative of a country in turmoil.

Michael has also compiled and published a compendium of memories and other material relating to his time at Prince Edward Senior School in Salisbury (now Harare). This compendium is entitled *Prince Edward Class of 1968 to 1973 – Like Feathers in the Wind.*

In March 1990, Michael emigrated to Australia with his wife and two sons. Settling in Adelaide, South Australia, he worked in various senior roles in the private health sector for over 30 years.

Now retired and living in Adelaide, Michael remains deeply connected to Zimbabwe. Through his writing, he explores the powerful intersections of history and personal destiny, inviting readers to uncover the untold stories behind Zimbabwe's transformation.

www.ingramcontent.com/pod-product-compliance
Lightning Source LLC
Chambersburg PA
CBHW070150120726
47909CB00001B/48